"OH, MY GOD . . ."

Even as he saw the face and heard that *voice* say "Crow . . ." he was throwing himself backward out of the shaft. Then the top of the elevator car blew out and the air was filled with shrapnel, everybody hit the deck, and Crow grabbed his crossbow, yelling,

"Get back! It's him, the vampire!"

But it was too late. The vampire rose with the grip of a single beautiful hand, almost levitating toward them, his power and eyes and smile and terrible beauty so alien but so familiar, so pale but so solid, so horrible but so magnetic. And he came closer and closer.

"Get back," ordered Crow, and the Team started to obey.

"Too late," the vampire said, halting them with the voice. "You've let me get too close."

Crow raised his crossbow all the way then and said: "Hold it there."

The thing laughed and said, "Are you joking?"

"Stop!" said Crow.

And the vampire smiled and showed his big teeth and said: "Stop me. . . ."

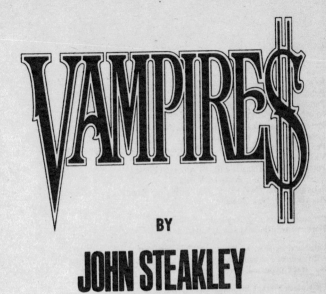

VAMPIRE$

BY

JOHN STEAKLEY

A ROC BOOK

ROC
Published by the Penguin Group
Penguin Books USA Inc., 375 Hudson Street,
New York, New York 10014, U.S.A.
Penguin Books Ltd, 27 Wrights Lane,
London W8 5TZ, England
Penguin Books Australia Ltd, Ringwood,
Victoria, Australia
Penguin Books Canada Ltd, 10 Alcorn Avenue,
Toronto, Ontario, Canada M4V 3B2
Penguin Books (N.Z.) Ltd, 182–190 Wairau Road,
Auckland 10, New Zealand

Penguin Books Ltd, Registered Offices:
Harmondsworth, Middlesex, England

Published by Roc, an imprint of Dutton Signet,
a division of Penguin Books USA Inc. Previously published in a
Roc trade paper edition.

First Mass Market Printing, May, 1992
10 9

REGISTERED TRADEMARK—MARCA REGISTRADA

Printed in the United States of America
Ornament designed by Jim Thiesen.

AUTHOR'S NOTE
This Felix is no other Felix
This Jack Crow is no other Jack Crow

the true Lady
is more than woman
and far beyond mortal man

to the very finest of these
this book is gratefully dedicated

she is Marjorie Larrance
Marge to her friends
Mrs. Larrance to you
Mom to me

Thank you, God

I know fucking well there's a God because I kill vampires for a living. Are you listening? I kill vampires for money. A lot of it. So don't tell me there ain't no God. I know fucking well there's a God.

I just don't understand Him.

—Jack Crow

PART ONE

Team Crow

Chapter 1

They were all there when Crow and his Team came rolling in for that last job. All the policemen and local officials. The mayor. The school board. It was that kind of small Indiana town.

It was that kind of hot summer day, too. The crowd faded quickly back from the billowing dust raised by the semis on the milk-white gravel driveway, holding hankies to their faces and coughing. Then they stood on the brown grass and watched the procession circle deafeningly around them and pull up in front of the great house.

The engines on all five vehicles stopped at once. Jack Crow stepped from the lead Jeep and stood there, all six-feet-two of muscle and resolve and mean. He stood for a moment, glancing up at the target. When he turned back the local officials stood about him in a semicircle, as if for warmth.

In fact for warmth.

Crow smiled easily at them. He shook hands with the round nervous-faced mayor. He glanced at his watch. It was high noon and 105 degrees.

Time to start killing.

They dynamited the south wing ten minutes later. The charge went off on a second-story balcony and drove the entire section flat to the ground like an angry fist. There was a lot more smoke, a lot more dust. They waited. Soon it was sunny again. The grapples began snagging at the wreckage and dragging it away.

The townsmen watched it all, wincing at the first screech of steel members on the masonry. They watched the machinery lumbering into position. They watched the crew of five appear from the van with their eight-foot-long pikes and stand ready. Mostly, they watched Crow.

They probably didn't jump more than a foot the first time the rubble moved on its own.

"Boss!" called a young blond man named Cat from his lawn chair crow's nest atop one of the semis. "I think we have one." He stood up, shading his eyes against the bright sunlight and pointing. "Right there on the end."

"Okay," replied Crow calmly. "Rock and roll."

The crew moved into position encircling the area as best as the broken shard footing allowed. From their back pockets they took what looked like women's long opera gloves and put them on. The steel mesh fabric glinted brightly. The townsmen, probably without realizing it, stepped closer together.

Then Crow, dragging cable from the broad grapple clenched in his huge right fist, stepped through the circle of his men and stabbed a prong deep into the cornice lodged heavily over the target area. He stepped back and held out his left hand. Somebody handed him a crossbow the size of a swingset and then everybody just stood there for a moment.

It started almost the instant Jack's signal to the crane pulled the cable taut. The masonry had barely tilted to one side when the first fiend came whistling and smoking into the agony of the sun's rays, shrieking like a harpy and stabbing out with black claws and dead gray fangs and then spouting a vile black glob as Crow's first shot drove a bolt the size of a baseball bat through its chest and spine and eight inches into the cornice behind it.

It writhed and howled and burned and cried and dragged with maniacal frenzy at the wooden stake, but the umbrella barbs kept it lodged tight, killing it, killing it, rubbing it away from the world of earth and man and bright summer Indiana afternoons.

"Now that," offered Cat after several seconds of heavy silence, "was weird."

The mayor turned to the elder town councilman and chuckled. The latter responded in kind. Soon all the townsmen were laughing and laughing with the break of the tension and with the relief that maybe after all the horror of the past few months and—

And nobody else was laughing. Not Cat, peering disgustedly down from his perch above them, none of the other members of the crew, and not Jack Crow, whose look of withering disdain turned them pale to a man.

When they had gotten very quiet for a very long five seconds Jack said, "The leader shouldn't have popped first. He usually sends everyone else ahead."

"How . . ." began the mayor before his voice cracked. He cleared his dry throat and tried again. "How do you know it *was* the leader?"

Jack lit a cigarette and stared at the ground. "After a while," he replied softly, "you can tell."

He stood there quietly like that for several seconds. Then he looked at them, actually looked at the individual townsmen for the first time.

It had wilted them. The horror, the losses, the sense of total naked impotence.

Wilted.

And it was only going to get worse.

So what, he thought next, are you gonna do when it's over, gents? When your town has seen you as worthless and craven and you feel your manhood has been stomped?

Are you gonna do what others have tried?

Are you gonna take it out on us?

When it's over, are you going to cheat us to show you're still men?

Because it really is gonna get worse. That was just the first one.

"All right," he barked abruptly, clapping his hands sharply together.

"Let's get on with it. Rock and roll."

And they did. And it did get worse. The second eruption was a howler and a screecher, again vile and terrifyingly fast, and the black bloody flecks fountained when the bolt struck it and slammed it back down and still it would not die until long seconds after one of the crew had punctured its skull with his pike.

It was horribly gruesome.

It was a broad-daylight nightmare.

It was a woman each townsman had known for over forty years.

After the schoolteacher came the local postmaster, the prom queen and her fullback fiancé, some hapless young college girl with the irreversible misfortune to blow a tire on a country lane that actually was dark and long but only appeared empty.

The usual. But there was something wrong with the proportions.

"Nine in all, counting the leader," said Anthony reading from Cat's clipboard an hour and a half after the last appearance. "But only three goons." He looked up from the page at his boss. "They weren't very busy, were they?"

Crow took the clipboard from his hand and glanced at it. "Nope," was his only response.

Both men looked up at the sound of the Jeep returning up the driveway bearing Cat and the graveyard team. One of the townsmen approached them while they unloaded empty cans of soil coagulant and tossed them into the back of the semi.

"Do you think there's another pit somewhere?" asked Anthony after a few seconds.

Crow looked at his questioner, whose bull neck and massive shoulders remained taut from the pressure of the day. Crow decided he looked awful after five hours of slaughter, decided that was probably good.

"No," he answered. "This is it. I never heard of them keeping goons somewhere else. New ones need to be around the leader anyway."

"Then how come—"

"Dammit, Anthony! I don't know why they didn't turn more recently. Maybe they had something else to do."

"Like what?" Anthony wanted to know.

Crow sighed. They always came to him with questions like this. He was the elder veteran, three years at it now, and probably had, in fact, the longest career of this type in the world. But that didn't mean he knew shit about vampires. Nobody knew shit about vampires. Nobody lived long enough to learn, and it pissed him off the way they all looked at him to know all the answers. What right did they—

He caught himself, took a deep breath. He looked again at Anthony, who had been an all-pro outside linebacker with the Seattle Seahawks when Crow had hired him. A man who was deeply loyal, sharply intelligent, and one of the bravest human beings he had ever seen, and who goddamn well deserved an answer from the man who claimed to be his boss and leader.

"I'm sorry, buddy. I just don't know."

Crow told the pikemen to stand at ease, brought the demo bunch in to punch the last of the charges deep into the rubble and went over to talk to Cat who still stood chattering away with the townsmen. On the way he passed the local priest, Father Hernandez, stepping dully forward to turn his trick over the nine piles of ashes. Crow swallowed the resentment the old man's sighing gait brought up in him. Priests!

". . . call it Joplin juice on account of Carl Joplin, the guy who put it together for us," Cat was saying to the mayor and another man whose name Crow didn't recall. "It just makes it hard to climb up out of. Even without it, y'know, it's too hard for most of 'em. Getting the damn coffin open at all is most of it. Remember—"

"Cherry Cat!" Crow called abruptly, not being able to stand it any longer. The townsmen, who just hours before had been too frightened to speak, were now full of patronizing pretend-interest questions about procedure. It was the kind of transition Crow had expected since noon, of course, but that didn't make it any better.

Cat excused himself and stepped through their disapproving looks. Crow put an arm about Cat's shoulders and turned away with him, speaking in an obvious but inaudible whisper sure to be taken as the insult it was.

"Don't you see what's happening, goddammit?"

Cat sighed. "Yeah." He looked hurt. And was, Crow reminded himself with more than a little amazement. "Damn," continued Cat, "I liked these people. Y'know that banker guy, Foster? He's planning to build—"

"Planning to cheat your ass blind and mine both."

Cat frowned. He glanced in the direction of the townsmen without seeing them.

"Yeah," said Cat at last.

They lit cigarettes and started walking toward the trucks.

"But, y'know, Jack? Not really," cried Cat in an abrupt plaintive whisper. "They're just trying to pull themselves up outta the hole they're in." He stopped. "You're the one who told me all this yourself."

Crow was adamant. "Then they shouldn't have got themselves in the hole in the first place."

"The vampires did that, Jack."

"Like hell they did. No sympathy, Cat. If they'd had the damn guts to face it . . . And now they're trying to take it out on us for doing it for them."

"Right in front of them, *and* the whole town. *Their* town."

Crow stopped and looked back the way they came. "No sympathy," he repeated.

"Look, just because they're feeling a little . . . I don't know—ashamed, I guess . . ."

"Did it ever occur to you that they have something to be ashamed about?"

They were silent for several seconds.

"All right," said Cat at last with a sigh. "I'll get it ready."

Crow shook his head. "No need. Not this time. I'm not gonna put up with this shit this time."

Cat eyed him briefly. "Just the same I think I oughta— "

"No, dammit!" Crow all but shouted. "Look! I'm so tired of these bastards crawling over and begging us on bended knees because they aren't man enough to stand up to the creatures turning their wives and daughters into blood-whores. And then they try to pretend they aren't groveling little cretins by haggling over the price, like this is just another business deal, this had nothing to do with the fact that we just cratered when it counted."

Crow stopped and panted with the anger, slamming his cigarette to the ground and lighting another.

Cat waited him out until he was calm. "Well, just in case," he began as casually as so guileless a man could, "I'll set up the—"

"Do what you want," Crow interrupted fiercely. "But I'm telling you I've fucking had it with these twerps and all the others like 'em. I'm putting my foot down." He jabbed his trembling index finger under Cat's nose. "Do you hear me?"

Cat nodded meekly. "I hear you."

Crow nodded with satisfaction. He tossed his new cigarette to the ground, hitched up his pants, and stalked toward the circle of men still at the Jeep. He paused and jerked a ferocious glance back at his friend. "I'm putting my foot *down*!" he snarled.

Then he stalked ahead even faster. Halfway to the townsmen, Cat overheard his harsh whisper to himself: "Putting it fucking *down*!"

Chapter 2

It was a nice jail—if you liked old westerns.

Crow's cell reminded him of every *Rifleman* he'd ever seen. It had a cot, a stool, a chamber pot without a lid, and a door that required the keys to the city to open it.

But the deputy was something so special it was almost worth it.

The deputy was a miracle.

To begin with, he had a gut Crow considered an anatomical triumph. But it was in the region of nose-picking where the man achieved greatness. Never in his lifetime (and, he suspected, anyone else's) had Crow seen anybody pick his nose with such fervor—not to mention tangible results—for so many hours at a stretch.

He had other virtues. Besides being a social slug he was also the town bully. During his first hour in the slammer Crow saw him grovel obscenely to his mayor's son-in-law, thump a large red-stoned ring off the crown of some high-schooler for being late to pay a parking ticket, and smash Jack's fingers with a reinforced flashlight to keep them off the bars.

The idea of killing him made Crow feel all warm and tingly. It made the hours bearable. Or rather, setting him up did. "Bullies don't like to fight," Crow's grandaddy had long ago told him. "Bullies are scared of fighting. Bullies like to beat people up." Keeping this in mind, Crow worked on a plan for the first hours. He decided at last on whining.

He whined about being shut up in the jail, about being

cheated by all "those rich guys who think they're such a big deal 'cause they got money." He whined about the food—or lack of it—claiming he was starving. He whined about the taste of the water and the smell of the chamber pot and suggested a connection.

He said his fingers hurt, sucked them loudly and often, held them up to show how swollen they were, and demanded to see a doctor.

The third time the deputy told him to shut up it was a snarl.

Crow's reply was equally ferocious. "Make me, fatso!" he snapped back but dropped his eyes when he did.

The deputy smiled, and stood with the flashlight in hand. He stepped around the desk smacking the weapon rhythmically into his fat palm.

"Maybe I will," he purred menacingly.

Crow took a half-step back from the bars, appeared to catch himself, stepped back up, and declared, "I ain't scared of you!" in the least convincing tone he could muster.

It was bully heaven. The deputy's little pig eyes gleamed as he reached for the keys. His yellow front teeth—all three of them—were bared with delight as he saw the prisoner backing to the far wall of the cell. But when he opened the door of the cell his raspy fat-punk voice changed from a smug chortle to a clear-bell high-pitched scream.

Crow bounced him across the desktop.

The deputy pulled himself up off the splintered remains of the desk chair and peeked over the desk in shock. He couldn't believe this was happening to him.

It was.

Crow didn't hurt him. He just dribbled him about the office floor long enough to make him start to cry. Then he put him in the cell.

From the middle desk drawer he took an army Colt and an extra clip. He looked longingly at the telephone, wanting desperately to talk to Cat. But there was no way of telling who would answer the phone at the motel. Hell, he hadn't heard from the rest of his team the whole time he'd been in the slammer. There should have been the usual effort to get him. . . . Then he remembered his braying at Cat about not needing help. But *surely* Cat hadn't listened. On the other hand, Cherry Cat had the most infuriating habit of obeying him at the worst conceivable times. Damn.

He forgot the idea of calling. Best just get the hell away from the damn police station. He stuck the automatic down deep in his belt and headed to the door. He gave the deputy a little salute.

"See ya, Homer. It's been real."

"How," whimpered the deputy like the blob he was, "did you know my name was Homer?"

Crow laughed and eyed the heavens. "There is a God," he whispered to himself. "And He's got a sense of humor."

Then he dropped all other thoughts. He keyed off the lights in the room, took a deep breath, and put his hand on the door.

"All right," he hissed, "rock and roll, dammit!" and jerked it open.

On the sidewalk outside the jail stood every cop in the world.

It was not Jack's best moment.

"Stop him, please!" cried a man Crow recognized as Banker Foster, and the cops surged forward en masse. Crow thought about the automatic in his belt, thought about the odds of winning, about the idea of shooting any policeman under any circumstances, muttered "Shit," and lifted his arms over his head.

"No! No!' shouted the mayor, elbowing his way through the eager constables, "not *him*!" He grabbed Crow by the upper arm and tugged on it like a child. "Mr. Crow, stop *him*!" he pleaded and turned and pointed across the street to the town square.

The crowd parted with the gesture and Crow could see, at last, his team. They had the crane set up on its highest elevation clamped onto their longest pike, which ran straight down from the starry sky into the chest of a vampire writhing and hissing on the base of the statue of the town's founder.

Anthony, standing on the hood of the Jeep, had his arm poised meaningfully in the air ready to signal the crane operator, who was even now taking out the slack in the cable.

"Let him go!" roared Anthony, "or we'll start your troubles all over again!"

Crow eyed the "vampire" as it spat and arched and wondered idly why they never recognized Cat in gray makeup. Then he turned to the mayor and said, "Well, what's it gonna be? Do we get paid or not?"

"Really, Mr. Crow!" spouted Banker Foster, "there was never a question about paying your *fee*, as such. It was just that the expenses seemed somewhat—"

"Foster, you are such a goddamn bore," Crow drawled. He turned to the mayor. "Yes or no?"

"Yes" was decided upon. The procession made its way across the square to the bank. Anthony walked side by side with Crow, but every other member of the team—especially the crane operator and the still-writhing (and now silently giggling) Cat—stayed firmly in place. Crow noticed that there really weren't as many cops as he had at first thought. Perhaps a half-dozen or so counting state troopers and the sheriff's *real* deputies. The rest were the same crowd present at the mansion all afternoon.

There was some trouble at the bank door, it being ten o'clock at night. Banker Foster claimed he had no keys on his person and suggested they all wait until the next morning and while he chattered away about the door Sheriff Ortega kicked it in with a size-thirteen Tony Lama. It wasn't so much the kick that won Crow's heart but the mischievous grin on Ortega's face while he was doing it.

The vault itself, time lock and all, was a different problem but one Crow & Co. had met before. "You got a cashier's check machine, don't you?" Anthony asked bluntly. So the check was made out and Crow endorsed it and gave it to gray-faced Cat amidst a surprising amount of good-natured laughter—especially from the cops—and Cat drove away to mail it from any other nearby township.

Though Jack Crow was something less than a PR wizard,

neither was he a complete fool. "Party time," he announced gaily, being sure to invite each and every one of the city fathers and cops present. Most accepted. The liquor store owner was persuaded by Ortega's dead-eyed smile to give Jack credit. The "store," as befitted a dry county in a God-fearing state, had no sign but was amply stocked. By now everyone was getting into the spirit of the thing. It took only twenty minutes to overload the Jeep with everybody helping.

"To the motelll—hoa!" cried wagonmaster Ortega, waving a bottle of bourbon from the window of his patrol car–Chevy pickup.

"Rock and roll!" chirped the little mayor who then blushed while everyone else laughed and cheered.

And the party began.

Chapter 3

The crossbow bolt through the Dr Pepper machine aroused the motel manager from his bed to find Crow and Sheriff Ortega—arms around shoulders, swaying gently in unison—outside his office.

"We wuz outta change," said Ortega. The sheriff was being helpful.

"I can vouch for him on tha' one," added Crow, and they grinned at each other and pounded backs.

The manager simply stared. This (to be kind) bizarre sight of two giants grinning down at him—and worse, nodding so fiercely at him out of synch it looked like a pair of paddling heads—it was all too much. The manager went back to his bed and pulled his pillow down over his ears.

There were equally valid excuses for most of the other destruction. High spirits could be blamed for some of it, true enough. And carelessness. But most of the sheer carnage was entirely unavoidable due to the very nature of competitive sports at this, the Championship level. The list of events included Spin the Coffee Table, Pike Vaulting and the ever-popular Ash Tray Rug Hockey. All of this being merely ancillary to the main event: Drinking Yourself Blind While Waiting for The Goddamn Whores to Show Up, which, as everyone knows, is strenuous enough by definition and only becomes uglier the longer it takes.

All in all they did $5,000 worth of damage to the motel. It was a lot of fun.

The party started out with about two dozen members, counting Team Crow, the locals, and the cops. It later swelled to about fifty or so. But by 3 A.M. it was back down to the twenty or so serious-minded. Father Hernandez turned out to be hilariously funny. He sang dirty limericks in Spanish and English. Most thought that a little weird. But it turned out that Hernandez had once been a real father, as in husband, with two little girls and a red-haired wife—all of whom had died of bubonic plague, of all things, twenty years before in northwestern Mexico.

Everybody got real misty about that and drank to their passing, and each man present agreed privately to stop calling him "Nutless."

They got a lot more depressed when a towheaded kid named, no shit, Bambi, who had wandered into the party some hours earlier from who knows where, started to cry about Hernandez's lost family. This pissed Crow off. He was already in a bad mood on account of the sheriff's badge and gun. Actually he liked wearing the badge pretty much. It was shiny and made him feel official and all and reminded him of which pocket his cigarettes were in. But the gun was one of these forty-four magnum artillery types two inches longer than his waist and every time he sat down the barrel would dig him in the balls causing him to yelp and leap to his feet to rub 'em and *that* only reminded him that the whores still weren't there and on and on and on.

So this crying Bambi was too much on top of everything else. He cleared everybody off of the suite's main sofa with one swipe of the back of his hand and unzipped the cover off the largest cushion. Then he stepped over and picked up the sobbing Bambi by both ears and tried to zip him up inside.

Anthony simply wouldn't have this. "Show a little goddamn consideration, Jack!" he snorted and unfolded the kid from the cushion. Bambi rewarded Anthony by throwing his arms around the other's neck, gurgling, "Thank ya, brother," and vomiting onto his chest.

Anthony didn't even get mad. He just took 'em both into what was left of the bathroom, cleaned them off, held

Bambi's head while he got sick in the tub. Then he carried him, still sobbing, in his arms back to the middle of the room and sat down and began to lecture everybody present about kindness, ending with two exquisitely pertinent statements: "Showing a certain measure of respect and tenderness to your fellow human souls is the way a real man exhibits class" and "By the way, are the fucking bimbos gonna show up or not?"

The combination of statements sent Cat—long since returned and almost as long dead drunk—into a cackling frenzy. He held onto his sides and rolled back and forth kicking his feet.

The rest of the party stared at him in abject bewilderment. All, that is, except the sheriff. Ortega had been both stung and humiliated by the bimbo remark. Being sheriff, procurement was clearly his responsibility and them not showing up by now, almost 4:30, infuriated him.

But the telephone—that really enraged him. He'd been trying to call for two hours to see what the hold-up was but for the life of him he couldn't get the sonuvabitch to work. He couldn't even get a goddamned dial tone.

This in turn made David Deyo awfully guilty. Deyo, a member of the pike crew, had been responsible for tearing the phone out of the wall the first time hours earlier. A veteran of three years' duty on the destroyer *Hepburn*, and therefore a man of breeding and culture, he had spent hours reconnecting the wires using his very best navy knot. But for some reason the phone still wouldn't work.

A half-dozen of them got down on all fours to examine the situation. All agreed the knot was a thing of beauty and that the phone should by God phone. The real problem, of course, was that each of them had drunk enough to kill a steer. But this did not occur to anyone. Except maybe Cat, whose suddenly renewed cackling was a continuing mystery.

Somebody suggested using the phone in the next room. This was Cat's turn to be helpful. "I'll get it," he screeched. He rose, reeling with laughter, and ricocheted into the adjoining bedroom, ripped out that phone and brought it in to be retied.

This one didn't work either.

It was the phone company, everybody agreed. The phone company was fucked. And everybody had a drink to that.

It was starting to get really late. Only the hard core remained. Team Crow, three cops, including the sheriff, Father Hernandez, and Bambi. Somebody suggested going and getting the women, a Quest. That was cheered until somebody else pointed out that they were almost out of liquor.

One of the deputies reminded everybody of the time. The liquor store owner had long since locked up and gone home to bed. Then Ortega, desperate for redemption, allowed as how they had already robbed a bank, more or less, so knocking over a liquor store was no big deal.

"Whores first!" piped Bambi.

"I'm too drunk to fuck," snarled Anthony, spilling Bambi onto his head and standing up.

Ortega stared at Anthony. "You're kidding."

"No kidding," Anthony assured him. "I'm too drunk to do anything but drink." He held up his index finger like a lecturer's pointer. "And I gotta get sick first to do that. 'Scuse me."

The spirit of comradeship rapidly degenerated into a squabble that sounded like two competing college cheering sections.

"Booze first!"

"No! Sex first!"

"Booze!"

"Sex!"

"Booze!"

"Sex!"

"Booze!"

Somebody yelled, "Less filling!" and got slapped around a great deal.

Then Bambi rose to the occasion. "I've got a van outside," he piped gleefully. "We can go fill it full of both!"

"Yea!" shouted the crowd as Bambi took his bow, high-stepped carefully over to the door, opened it, and—

And the vampire was on him and ripping his claws deep

into his ribs and spreading them and then . . . it . . . pulled . . . his . . . chest . . . apart. Bambi died, screeching horror and spraying organs and blood and then clumped to the floor in a little pile and the vampire was on *them*, on the rest of them, coming at them too fast, too damn fast, too damn fast to be believed, and the first guy, some member of the pike team, just had enough time to raise his forearm in front of his face before the fiend snapped it through and ripped him open from throat to shoulder and *he* screamed— Jesus *God*, how he screamed!

The bolts! Where's the fucking crossbow? was all Crow could think and he spun around looking for it, taking his eyes off the fiend for a second because this was a vampire and that was the only way to stop it, the only way in the world and this was night! Nighttime and maybe that wouldn't do it either but there it was, propped up against the end table under the lamp and Crow dove for it across the sofa full of horrified mortals, some of them just now rising to their feet because this was all so fast for them, this was just too . . . this couldn't be happening, could it? I mean, we were just having a *party* and everything was just—

Crow crashed across the back of the sofa over the tops of somebody's rising head and they flipped him sideways in the air in mid-dive and he came down right shoulder first onto the point of the bolt.

"*God*!" he gasped, as it sank into his tissue. He twisted to the side off of it and it tore loose raggedly from his skin and shirt. "God, God, *God*!" He was bleeding like crazy, agonizing pain, and the lamp teetered and fell to the carpet right beside his head and started shorting out and then Crow rose to his knees blank-faced and beaten to watch the rest of the strobe-lit nightmare continue.

Darkness . . .

Light: David Deyo in mid-black-belt leap driving the side of his right foot picture-perfectly up under the vampire's chin where the throat was soft and making the sound that would have popped the skull off any normal man—

Darkness . . .

Light: The fiend using David's . . . oh, God! using his *spine* like a handle as he slammed him back and forth from the floor to the ceiling. David long dead already, all his bones crushed, flopping gruesomely and Anthony! Sweet Anthony with his huge shoulders slamming forward into the fiend, tackling him for chrissake like this was Astroturf and—

Darkness . . . And then *crash* in the blackness just a couple of feet away . . .

Light: Anthony's body hanging on the sill of the shattered picture window and then sliding horribly, slowly, on through, his legs dragging the curtains *pop-pop-pop*— off the curtain rod to billow gently to the ground covering him and—

Cat beside him, lifting him up, hissing, "Yes! Yes! Yes! The window!" as if that had been Anthony's plan for escape all along.

"What . . ." stuttered Crow but he knew what Cat meant. They had to run. The fiend roared and slaughtered invincible in the night air. There was no chance, and he stumbled toward the window, Cat shoving him, grabbing him by the shoulder that already bled, and "Ohh!" spouted forth from Crow's mouth with the pain and Cat said "Jack, you're hurt!" in surprise and Crow mumbled back, "We're *all* dead!"

And then more darkness and he was tumbling forward through the last of the glass and landing on something soft and dead like an old and trusted friend but not to think about it. He rose to his feet and turned for Cat, Cherry Cat, without whom there was no point anyway and—

And it was light again for the last time and Cat was out and beside him and lifting him up and there—back there through the window was the priest, Father Hernandez, not nutless at all, stabbing the edge of his huge silver cross right *into* the fiend's forehead before dying, decapitated, from a backhanded, almost casual, blow. . . .

All blood and horror everywhere back there, on the walls and the ceiling and—

And the sheriff, stunned into immobility, stood like a lump in the middle of the parking lot staring at the old battered Cadillac convertible alongside his patrol car pickup.

"Jack, *please*!" Cat moaned, shoving him along and Crow looked down at him and saw the tears in his eyes and realized that it was fear for his own safety that so terrified his friend.

So he hurried, because he couldn't stand to see Cherry Cat crying.

Crow opened the side door to the pickup Cat shoved him at and climbed in beside the sheriff that somehow Cat had collected from the driver's side. And then Cat was inside too behind the wheel and Omigod! The *keys*! Where are the . . . but they were there, the sheriff had just left 'em there in the ignition, why not? Who would steal it?

And Crow found himself laughing at this as they screeched out of the parking lot onto the highway. Because it was better, it was fun, to have something to laugh at besides crying at the continuing thumps of horror from inside the motel or allow himself to actually focus on the slaughtered occupants of the convertible, the whores who had been too late, but not late enough and—

"CROWWW!" sounded out in the darkness, piercing through the roar of the engine and the distance and twisting each man in the cab of the truck into a little ball. "CROWWW!" shouted the vampire, as Cat gunned the engine even harder and the truck vaulted forward to sixty, seventy, eight miles an hour down the two-lane state highway.

"CROWWW!" blasted them as the vampire caught them and leapt onto the back of the truck bed and slammed his hands through the rear window and Crow found that he had the sheriff's huge cannon pistol in his hand and he jabbed it in the monster's face and—why not?—pulled the trigger.

The fiend, all shiny blood-red teeth of his ghastly smile and soul-ripping gleam of intelligence, disappeared backward rolling from the concussion of the cannon-pistol, cracking through the tailgate and slamming it open like it wasn't there and then skidding all asprawl on the sandpaper asphalt.

"Oh! Yes, yes! Ha! Hey!" the sheriff whined delightedly at the sight, the thought that the monster could be killed. But even knowing better, the other two in the cab still crumpled a little more as the sheriff's cry of gasping pleasure changed to a shrill baby-boy whimper at the sight of the monster back on his feet almost immediately, almost before he had stopped kicking, and coming back at them again.

It got close enough for them to see the hole from the cannon pistol already closing up, trapping the trickling black blood left from the priest's stabbing cross and—

"Jesus Christ!" screamed Crow as they topped over a hill at over a hundred miles an hour up behind a farm truck doing maybe twenty in the center of the highway.

Cat wrenched the truck to the left and missed the farmer but got onto the shoulder and got sideways and careened back across the center line starting to spin around and around and topping up over another hill so they could see the city square in the distance and Crow thought, Well, at least we almost made it into town. And he mourned the unattainable sight of redemption of that little town square with the morning sun just starting to peek out over . . .

The sun! The fucking sun! was his last thought before the truck began to tumble, rolling over and over on its sides and then end over end and then sliding forever and ever down the main street of the little Indiana town.

He awoke first and got himself up. And then he got the other two up. And then he got the three of them through the gathering crowd down the three blocks toward the hospital before the ambulance met them halfway. He got them inside and got their blood types, and when they were all set and going to make it, he lay down and collapsed, his last thought:

I thought *sure* it was the leader.

First Interlude

The Man sat calmly, in regal white, waiting for his aide to compose himself. When at last he seemed in control, the Man smiled and nodded.

"Holiness," began the aide, his voice rich with frustration and almost childlike pique, "this man Crow is a catastrophe."

"Tell us," said the Man.

"Holiness, the man arrived drunk. He was loud. He was obnoxious and profane. He insulted everyone in sight. He referred to the priests as eunuchs. He called the sisters penguins. He attempted to engage one of the guards in a fistfight on the steps outside the private entrance."

"Was there a fight?"

"No, Holiness. I intervened." The aide sighed. "Forgive me, Holiness, but I almost wish I had not. It would have done that buffoon good to have been thrashed by the Swiss . . ."

"Our orders were very clear, we hope?"

"Yes, Holiness. And it was for this reason that I intervened. I received scant appreciation for my concern. Mr. Crow called me . . . *me* . . ."

"Called you what?"

"Nutless."

The Man sighed. "It is very difficult for you, my old friend. We are sorry."

"Oh, please, Holiness. I am not complaining. I only . . ." The aide stopped and smiled with some embarrassment. "I suppose I am complaining at that. Forgive me, Holiness."

"There is nothing to forgive."

"Thank you, Holiness."

"We hear the man is injured."

"Yes, Holiness. His entire right shoulder is wrapped in bandages. But he will not let any of our doctors examine him." The aide paused, looked at the window at the far end of the ancient room. "He claims he is fine, Holiness. But he lies. I believe him to be in great pain when he moves."

"He is indeed, my friend," said the Man softly. "Even when he does not." The Man smiled sadly. "Great pain."

The aide was silent for several moments. Then: "Holiness, I know this Mr. Crow is of great importance to . . . But it would help greatly if—Holiness, can we not know who he is?"

"You cannot."

"But Holiness, if we could just . . ."

"You cannot."

The aide sighed once more. "Yes, Holiness." He took a slow deep breath, seemed to rid himself of the concern, said, "All is in readiness. The dining room is prepared. American food, as your Holiness ordered, will be served."

"Thank you. You have been very thorough."

"Thank you, Holiness. The man Crow is already in the dining room, has been for"—he checked his watch—"almost fifteen minutes. He is already intoxicated, Holiness. Perhaps there would be a better time."

"There will be no better time," replied the Man in a voice of such infinite sadness and despair that the aide found he could not speak for a bit.

He made ready to go, kissing the ring. But at the door the aide paused. The Man could see how clearly the other felt driven to utter this last.

"Holiness, be very careful with Mr. Crow. He has much anger in his soul. And . . . I believe he hates you."

The Man waited until he was alone before rising. Then he padded softly across the room to the side entrance. He paused before opening the door to his private dining room.

"So he does," the Man muttered softly to himself. "And why should he not?"

Then he opened the door and went in.

Tapestries. A broad arched ceiling. A carpet over three hundred years old. A long, thin table with a single heavy wooden chair at each end. In the far one sat Jack Crow, one leg over an arm, a glass of wine in one hand and a cigarette in the other.

The Man nodded to the bows of the four servants—two on each wall and recessed like the paneling—and stepped easily to the center of the room. He waited.

"Well, there he is at last," barked Crow. He stood ponderously, still carrying his glass and cigarette, and walked over.

The Man waited until the other had come within a few feet. "It is good to see you again, Jack," he said easily. Then he offered his ring.

Crow stared at the ring with apparent bewilderment. Then he smiled. He put his cigarette in his mouth, transferred the wineglass from his right hand to his left, shook the hand holding the ring, and said, through cigarette smoke, "How the fuck are you?"

Despite repeated and insistent orders, it was all the servants could do to restrain themselves.

The Man did not stir. He met Crow's piercing gaze without rancor. He smiled. "We are quite well, Jack. But I see you are injured." He indicated the bulky bandaging underneath Crow's corduroy jacket.

Crow felt his arm absently. "Oh, it ain't much, priest, considering. Everybody else is dead. Except for Cat and me. Everybody else, though. The Team is dead. All of 'em."

"Yes, Jack. We know."

The two locked eyes for several seconds. Then Crow turned abruptly away, flicking an ash onto the carpet and reaching for the decanter of wine. "All dead. Everyone of 'em slaughtered." He poured some more wine into his glass. Then he plopped back down into his chair and spoke with a voice blood-rich with bitterness. "So, tell me about *your* week."

Crow became increasingly more profane, more insulting. He referred to the man as "Your Assholiness." He put his cigarettes out on whatever was nearby, the plate, the glass, the tabletop. He was loud. He was vicious. He was disgusting.

The Man said little, his mournful sadness filling his end of the small chamber. He was becoming more and more concerned about the servants, who seemed frozen into a comalike state certain to erupt in violence.

"All of you," whispered the Man, his gaze taking in the four servants on both sides of the room. "Leave us now."

It took them several moments to react. But they did, moving stone-faced and dry-hinged to the exits. Luigi stopped briefly before the door and looked back.

The Man smiled reassuringly. "We will call you if we need you."

Luigi still stared.

"It will be all right, my friend," added the Man gently.

And then they were alone.

"Now that's more like it," cackled Crow. "Now we can get down to the serious drinkin'."

He reached over to grab a chair from the wall and slide it over next to the Man. But he had trouble, first with his balance, then with the weight of the massive chair on his right arm. It seemed to bring out something even darker than the bitterness and fury. Something deeper. Something worse.

He finally got the chair alongside the Man and banged down into it. Then he realized he was almost out of wine. He stared forlornly into the near-empty decanter in his lap.

The Man, still calm, still cool, said, "We have some, Jack," and reached for the carafe by his plate.

"Fuck, *no*!" roared Crow suddenly, inexplicably. He half-rose to his feet. He shot out one hand to intercept the wine and with the other, his right one, his injured one, slammed the pontiff back into his chair.

Dead silence. Each man stared, wide-eyed in shock at what had just happened. Crow dropped the decanter onto the table. It shattered. Red wine began to flow around the plate and toward the edge of the table.

Crow tried. He really tried. He lurched crazily forward to stem the flow. He cracked his forearm down on the edge to dam it up. But nothing could stop the scarlet stream from spattering across the Man's milk-white, snow-pure robes.

And for a moment each simply stared, not at each other but at this.

And then Crow exploded. He leapt to his feet and roared and screeched, splashing the wine from the table onto the robes over and over again, roaring and roaring louder and louder as he sprayed it, yelling at the top of his lungs: "Take it, goddammit! Take it, you papist motherfucker! It's about time *you* got some of the goddamned blood!" and the Man just sat there, frozen in his chair, his eyes closed to the spattering drops covering his robes, his head, his face, and above him Crow still raged and roared and then . . .

Then was utterly silent.

The Man opened his eyes to the vision of the giant trembling above him, his hands and face and clothes covered with wine and fury and . . .

And agony.

"My son," he whispered and his compassion was a thing alive. "Oh, my son."

Jack Crow's face, rock-taut with ferocity, cracked in two. Then it began to melt. Tears welled up in his eyes and began to rush down his cheeks. His cry of pain was irretrievable and lost.

Then he was falling to his knees and sobbing, his massive arms snaking out to wrap around the other man's waist as a child's for safety and comfort and the old man held him and rocked him as the great shoulders shook with the great sobs that simply would not stop but went on and on and on.

"Oh, Father! It was so horrible!" whimpered the giant. "I'm sorry! I'm so sorry!' he cried later and both men knew it was for nothing that had happened there this night. And later, when the giant was almost asleep and his voice was a dry cracking hiss pleading, "God, forgive me, forgive me, forgive me . . ." over and over the old man forgave him again and again and again.

And later, hours later, when they could not get their master to rise rather than disturb the sleeping giant curled into his lap, they thought it was his infinite compassion, his infinite love that kept him praying all this night for the soul of this great weeping beast.

But it was fear.

For the Man was certain that Jack Crow would be forgiven for his sins.

But who would forgive *him* for sending this poor soul out still again to face the monsters once more?

Chapter 4

Jack Crow awoke with a start from some nameless horrible on the flight from Rome and beheld the angelic face of his newest team member, Father Adam, sleeping across from him.

He's a sweet kid, thought Jack. I'll probably get him killed, too.

Then he went back to sleep because any other thoughts were better than these.

"I need a vampire," said Carl Joplin for the hundredth time. Cat burped and ignored him. Annabelle placed a soft white hand on Carl's great fat shoulder and said, "I know, dear."

The rest of Team Crow had been at the bar at the Monterey Airport for four hours. One hour to get primed for the homecoming and the three more the plane turned out to be late. It was not a pretty sight.

Except, thought Cat, for Annabelle. She was always a pretty sight. Even when she wasn't. He propped his elbow very carefully against the edge of the bar, made a fist with his hand, put his cheek on it, and examined her.

He had known her his whole life and . . . Waitaminute. That wasn't true. He had known her six years. No. Seven years. Almost seven years, since before her late husband, Basil O'Bannon, had founded Vampire$ Inc. And anyway, she was still the same. Still pretty and still plump and still

29

mostly blond and still forty-something or sixty-something years old—it didn't seem to apply—and still able to outdrink God.

Time to take a piss, he decided. He lifted himself off the barstool, careful not to get the toe of his boot caught on the railing like last time, and ambled off on his mission.

Carl Joplin looked up from rubbing his wondrous belly and said, "I need a vampire."

"I know, dear," said Annabelle.

"It's gotta be tested!" he insisted.

"I know, dear. We'll ask Jack when the plane gets in."

Carl snarled and sipped his drink. "Jack! Shit!" He was still mad at Jack and likely to stay that way. "Jack!" he repeated disgustedly.

Carl Joplin was the weapons man and the tool man for the team. He made the crossbows for Jack and Cat's wooden knives and everything else they took with them into battle, but did he ever get to go into battle? Hell, no! "Too valuable," Jack would always say. Somebody had to be free and clear of the fight at all times to make sure the fight could go on. Carl could buy that. It made sense. But how come it had to be him every goddamn time?

But it was. Sure, he was a little overweight and maybe pushing sixty but that was no reason not to let him duke it out just once. Just one time, baby!

The detector was his best chance. Joplin had actually come up with a vampire detector based on the presumed electromagnetic energy of any object and/or critter able to totally absorb all sunlight. It was an ingenious gadget but it required a vampire to test it. Carl knew damn well they could never hope—or, for that matter, be so stupid as to try—to capture a fiend and bring it to him. Ergo, he would have to be there on sight to run the buttons and knobs the rest of the peckerwoods were too damned ignorant to follow in the first place. He'd get into it one way or the other, by God!

And in the meantime he went back to rubbing his great belly and snarling and refusing to see Annabelle's smile when he did it. Which reminded him: how come he was sloppy drunk and she wasn't? How come she never was? Huh? Explain me that!

Cat, weaving his way back through the tables from the rest room, was wondering the very same thing. He had never in all of his whole entire life seen Annabelle drunk. And she drank as much as anybody, didn't she? Well, didn't she?

Did she? He thought back. Yup. She did. In fact, she was the one who had really gotten the serious stuff going with that schnapps shit. Waitaminute! Schnapps! She always drank schnapps! Maybe if *I* drank schna . . . Waitaminuteagain! I am drinking schnapps. I've *been* drinking it. That's how I got so polluted.

He plopped back down on his stool thinking: Mystery of the Universe!

"I need a vampire," said Carl once again at Cat's reappearance.

"In a minute," Cat finally retorted.

And they hissed at each other.

Annabelle smiled again. But not too much or she was certain she'd lose her balance, keel backward off the stool, skirts flying, and crack her head on the side of the bar like a ripe grapefruit.

And then, she giggled silently to herself, little purple butterflies would sparkle out.

She had never been so thoroughly plastered in her life. She doubted if anyone had. And the thought of actually being able to sit down and pee was her notion of heaven. But do women pee? Sure they do. No. They dew. Horses sweat, men perspire, and women dew. Right? No, that was something else.

But urinate sounded so dreadful. So unladylike.

And if she didn't risk weaving to the rest room in front of the men she was about to do something a lot more unladylike. Being a lady—setting the standard—was paramount. She bore the entire responsibility, she was quite certain, for Team Crow.

In a very real sense, more than she would ever fully comprehend, this was quite true. Annabelle O'Bannon was more than a simple regal beauty who kept her raucous men in line. She was their symbol for the rest of the world they were surely going to die trying to protect. She was why they kept going out to fight knowing damn well they would eventually lose. It had happened to everyone else. It would happen to them. But this way it wouldn't happen to Annabelle.

They didn't know this, her men. That is, they had never consciously voiced it, even inside their own heads. But it was so. It was so because she, Annabelle, was so. Just so.

She had that way with men only certain ladies and other magical creatures possessed. A way of making them sit down and eat their porridge or drink their drink. Of making them shut up and listen to someone else talk.

She could make them wear ties.

She also possessed the unique ability to actually stop violence, like the time she made Jack put that Harley down—and *not* on that poor moaning biker like he wanted.

None of this was getting her off the barstool and into the ladies' room. And she simply *had* to go. Then a thought occurred.

"Young man," she called to the middle-aged bartender, "I'll have another." Then she slid off the stool and landed, thank God, on both high-heeled feet and had weaved her way several steps toward sweet release before Carl and Cat could get over the shock.

The two men looked at one another. Another drink? A-nother-goddamned-drink? She was going to have another round and here they were, the two of them big tough guy Fighters of Evil trying desperately to focus on their cocktail napkins for *balance*, for chrissakes, and she's having another . . .

But what could they do? What choice did they have? It was awful and grisly to do it but the alternative was worse, giving in was worse.

Carl gulped, said, "Me too."

The bartender, bright, sober, and sadistic, asked Cat, "Another all the way around?"

And Cat, his face gray and his life passing before his eyes, nodded dully.

Annabelle's timing was, as always, exquisite. She had made it almost out of sight while the men were occupied with machismo. She paused at the entrance to the bar and, with apparent unconcern, spoke back over her shoulder, "Young man," she called sweetly to the bartender, "I guess not after all."

All three men turned toward her, the bartender with hands full of fixings. "You don't want another, lady?"

Annabelle smiled. "I guess not."

The bartender's annoyance barely showed. "You're sure?" he pursued.

She paused, seemed to take the question of chemical suicide seriously, then shook her pretty head again. "I guess not," she repeated and then she was gone.

Her men all but leapt at the opening she had provided. "I guess not, too." "Me either, now that I think about it." Both burst out in the rapid staccato of machine-gun fire.

The bartender stared at them, glanced at the rest of the lounge, which was completely empty, and sighed. Too good to be true, he thought. He'd *known* that just three people making his overhead for the day was too good to be true. But still, they'd almost made it.

Annabelle neither heard nor cared about any of this. She was too busy stamping her awkward path to the ladies room door, bashing it open with both hands and part of her hairdo, jerking herself awkwardly into a stall, unsheathing herself, and then reveling in one of those mini-orgasms reserved for those lucky creatures made in God's image.

Later she thought: I'm so tired.

It had been a busy two weeks for her. With Jack in Rome it was left to Cat and Carl and herself (meaning her) to handle all the arrangements. Contacting the next of kin had been easier than it might have been. Crusader types, she had long ago discovered, had a tendency to be loners.

Except for Anthony. She had gone to San Antonio to tell Mrs. Beverley in person. When that sainted woman had opened the door and seen her she had known. The two of them had held each other and rocked and cried and rocked and cried for two straight hours, their minds filled with the

rich memories of the sweet, handsome, brave huge black
Anthony they had loved so much. No loss, except of her
husband Basil, had ever touched her so much. And she had
known right then that when Jack's and Cat's time came—as
it certainly would—that would be all for her.

She knew it was up to her to keep going. She knew that
Carl Joplin, as amazingly competent as he truly was, would
need her desperately. Would fail, probably, without her help.

She knew this and she didn't care. When Jack and Cat
went, that would be it. Even the hinted image of that loss,
so wickedly brutal, so thoroughly devastating, was inter-
twined with one of herself sitting quietly in her room lining
up the pills to swallow. Interesting enough, it had never occurred to her that she might die another way. Vampires? She
had never seen one, never wished to, and could think of no
reason in the world why she ever should. That was the men's
job. They were hers.

Later, of course, when the horror was roaring in on them,
it would be different. But she couldn't have known that now.

Her thoughts turned to the move. They were leaving
Pebble Beach and moving back home to Texas. To Dallas.
They were going to miss their mansion with its view of the
bay and the sculptured golf courses and the ocean fog rolling
across the tops of the pine trees and, most of all, the miniature
deer eating her flowers every morning.

She had claimed, loudly and often, that she hated the
creatures and believed them to be a scourge of nature. The
world, she insisted, would be better off if every single deer
was burned at the stake.

"Bambi, too?" someone would invariably ask.

"Especially Bambi," she would sharply retort. "That vile
little mutt has only encouraged them."

This fooled absolutely no one, of course. But still every
morning she would put on her sneakers and her one pair of
blue jeans and her late husband's lumberjack shirt, tie her
hair back in a scarf, grab her weapon (the back porch broom),
and rush out to do battle. Everyone would race to the windows, even braving some truly monumental hangovers, to
laugh and applaud and tap on the glass and just generally

cheer on the deer. Especially that one awful creature who she was certain was the leader. So smug and cocky and sure of itself, it would actually stop eating and stand there, just stand there and stare at her as she ran at it waving the broom, showing not one ounce of fear until *just* before she could whack it, and then vault effortlessly over the ten-foot fence she had had especially constructed. The boys loved him and named him Rambi after that silly movie and—

And . . .

And *the boys* . . .

The boys were all gone. The boys, her boys were all dead, all destroyed horribly and forever and . . .

And for a long time the only sound in the room came from the muffled sobs filling the tiny stall.

It was why they were moving. The Zoo, the nickname for the wing now holding seven unoccupied bedrooms, was empty. Empty and hollow and dark and sad. It had been the only postmassacre order Jack had been able to manage. Near-incoherent with pain and rage and shame, his last comment before boarding the plane to Europe was to take everything home to Texas where they belonged.

Annabelle had thus been left with the project of packing everything up, flying to Dallas, selecting and buying another house (with room for Carl's workshop), and most difficult of all, sorting out the boys' belongings.

So *many* belongings. And such, such . . . boyish things. She smiled at that thought and wiped away another tear.

Because they *were* such boys. They were grown men, too. All of them. The youngest almost twenty-five, the oldest just over forty, older even than Cat, the second in command.

But they were such boys, too. Oh, she knew why. She did. She understood why. It was their job, the nature of it, the fear of it, the . . .

The certainty of it.

They weren't going to get married and raise children and grow old and pass away retired in some resort community. They were going to die. They were going to be killed by some desperate lunge of talon or teeth, too fast for anyone to do anything to stop it. And then they were going to have to be staked and beheaded by the survivors who couldn't even use the funeral as a time to mourn because of it.

They were going to die. And soon. And they knew it. Every single one of them knew it. They were going to die.

And so they were kids. Her boys. She packed up so many *toys*. Video games and stereo sets and model airplanes and pinball games (everybody had to have his own machine) and hookah pipes and science fiction books and comic books, some of which were, inexplicably to Annabelle, in Japanese. (She could never understand that. None of the boys spoke Japanese, much less read it.) And then there were the stacks of porno books and magazines and she found it was apparently legal to actually *entitle* a magazine *Fuck Me*.

So much stuff and plenty of money for it—the Man saw to that knowing they would never live to accumulate their own fortunes. And they spent it.

But what was appalling and, she admitted it, endearing to Annabelle was what they did with it all. All that healthy maleness and alcohol and fear pent up in even so large a place as the mansion made for an extremeley vibrant household to say the least.

The alcohol. So much alcohol. Team Crow got dead drunk the way normal people had a single cocktail. The monthly bill for liquor consumed on the *premises* was over a thousand dollars. And that didn't even count the bar tabs Annabelle was forever driving around to pay off. The huge garage area was filled with Corvettes and four-wheel drives and motorcycles everyone was too drunk to drive home. After eight DWIs in two weeks, Jack had installed a taxi-home policy for everyone not going out with Cat (who drunk, could talk any cop out of his gun).

But it wasn't just the booze. They were none of them alcoholics. It was just all that overgrown energy. They terrorized the maid service, inevitably springing themselves on the poor women stark naked and dripping from the shower and offering to help. It was so hard to keep cooks they were finally forbidden to even enter the kitchen while the cook was on the property. If they wanted something they had to phone in and ask for it. The amount of food pleased and frightened the cooks at the same time. They were able to consume astonishing amounts of food. Any kind of food. Junk food. Gourmet buffets. Munchies. Anything. Everything.

They never got fat. None of them—except for Carl, of course—even got beer bellies. Every morning they would get up and work out rigorously, the sweat running salty past their grins. It was not that they were especially disciplined. They most certainly were not. They were . . . committed. They were faithful. And they were alone together. It wasn't just each one of them who worried about himself. If one couldn't spin his body around quick enough with that brutish wooden stake in his grip, then it might not be just him slashed from throat to thighs. It might be one of his mates. No. It *would* be one of his mates. Because there was, quite literally, no one else in the world to save them but them.

It was why, recalled Annabelle, Jack had forbidden wrestling matches. Which were always happening in the stairwells, for some reason. She supposed it was because those broad shoulders were always clipping past one another in a hurry and then one thing led to another and . . .

Jack wouldn't have it. They were already wrapped far too tightly to be adrenaline-bruising their only kin.

So instead they tore up the house. That time they decided to play indoor golf because of the rain.

She busied herself in front of the lounge mirror, thinking back and trying without success to keep the smile from her face. To be fair, Jack had not even been in town. He and Cat had gone up to San Francisco with Anthony to watch his old team beat the 49'ers. But that didn't mean she believed for one single instant Jack would have stopped them. Probably would have just sat there in that big chair of his and laughed and bet on the winner.

Indoor golf. She sighed. They had broken six windows. Three of them cut glass.

She paused and inspected her appearance before returning to the bar. She supposed she looked fine.

For what she was.

For what was left.

For what there was to look forward to.

I'm so tired, she thought again. And then she thought: No. That's a lie: I'm frightened.

And then she thought: No. I'm both.

Both.

Jack! Hurry back. Hurry back to us and still be you!

Father Adam looked to his left, at the seventy-ish man sleeping across the aisle from him and said in his silent TV commentator's voice, There are, for your information, sir, over six hundred exorcisms officially performed in America each year. And to you, it's just something that made a great movie that may or may not have been true once but isn't now.

Adam's gaze slid across the aisle to Jack, dozing in front of him.

And this man, he continued, kills vampires for a living. How about that?

Adam sighed, resting his eyes on Crow a bit longer before turning and viewing the mountains of the western United States sweeping below.

I'm in a dream. But maybe not. This is real and this has been happening, bile flowing from the Beast, since the dawn of man and before. This isn't a dream.

He turned again to look at Jack Crow.

It's simply that this man is a movie. A walking, talking, bleeding, cussing, bigger-than-life bear of a man. He's a movie, just being alive.

But movies aren't real, are they? he asked himself.

Neither is the priesthood. Isn't that why you're here?

He started to ignore himself. But then he decided he no longer had to. He was here now and into it. He was no longer some lanky, dark-curled kid too pretty for his own good hiding out from girls in seminary and from the meat-eaters' man's world in his black-and-white king's X uniform.

He looked again around the cabin. It wasn't the real world of this plane, perhaps. Of men striving to earn first-class seats or pilot's stripes. It wasn't the real world of men at all.

But it was the real world of man.

Of man and God.

And he, Adam the schoolyard trembler, had grown up and come here to fight for them both. At last.

To the last.

He slept.

I don't know who else to get, thought Jack Crow. And I'm tired of getting them. We need the best kind of person around. No one less will do.

But they will die. And that means I have to find the best men I know and condemn them to a certain violent end just *because* they're the best.

Shit.

And they always said yes. That was the worst part of it. The good ones, once they knew it was being done, had to be doing it.

So they did it and they died.

Doubleshit.

Oh, God! Please don't call us now! There's only four of us left and this kid-priest and one of 'em's a middle-aged woman and another is pushing sixty and fat and damn well not scared enough for me and another is the finest man I've ever known.

And, tripleshit, the last one is me.

Please, phone, don't ring!

The plane landed and Jack Crow shook himself hard and reminded himself that he was supposed to be a leader of some kind so: Rock and roll, goddammit! Off your butt and off this plane and here we go again! Come *on*!

Don't think about the phone.

They knew the priest was coming but they didn't know anything about him. Jack strode through the gate to Annabelle with Adam close behind. He leaned down and kissed her and said, "Folks, this is Adam."

"*Father* Adam," Adam amended firmly.

Team Crow exchanged rolled eyes.

"I'm her Royal Highness Annabelle."

"Lord High-Muck-a-muck Carl Joplin."

Adam blinked, stared at them. Cat, grinning, stepped forward and shook his hand.

"Pay no attention to that man behind the curtain," said Cat. "I am the Great and Powerful Oz."

And then they were all walking rapidly toward baggage claim without further explanation. Adam found himself offered Annabelle's arm. He took it and shut up and walked.

"I need a vampire," began Carl.

Jack barely glanced at him. "Is it working?"

"It was working last night."

Jack stopped. They all stopped and stared at Carl.

"Well, to tell the truth, I don't know what made it beep then." They resumed walking. "But it should work," Carl persisted. "And it's gotta be tested."

"How does it work?" Jack wanted to know.

"You wouldn't understand it, Jack, and you know it."

"Hmm. Possibly. Then how are we supposed to test it?"

"*We* ain't. I am."

Jack sighed, shook his head. "Oh, great. Here we go again with your . . ."

"Goddammit, Jack! There ain't anybody else!"

"How do you figure that?"

They had reached the baggage claim area. They stopped. Carl took a deep breath and hitched up his pants. He began counting off fingers.

"Well, Annabelle can't do it 'cause she watches the soaps during the day. You're supposed to be guarding my ass while I'm doing it. Cat . . ."

"I could do it," Cat offered with a sly grin.

Carl gave him a dirty look. "What do you know about the electromagnetic spectrum?"

"I'm for it."

"What do you know about EEGs? Brain waves?"

Cat frowned. "Is this a surfing question?"

Carl snarled. "As I was saying: Annabelle is out, you and Cat have your own little trick to do. That leaves me." He paused, stepped up to Jack. His face was dead serious. "Look, Jack. You'll be able to operate it after I get it right. But I must be there to twitch it until it's on."

Jack stared at him but did not speak.

Carl grimaced. "I'm telling you straight."

But Jack had never doubted that. All he could think of was: Here I go again. I'm going to have to risk you, too. Dammit, am I going to lose everyone?

He stepped closer to Annabelle and hugged her without realizing why.

"I'll think about it" was all he said, but it was already done and everyone but Adam knew it.

There was an awkward pause while they stood about. No bags appeared from the chute, though they heard the usual destructive noises from somewhere beneath them.

Cat's voice sparkled into the silence. He slapped Adam on the shoulder. "Don't know about you guys, but it's great to have a father, huh, folks?"

Adam smiled uncertainly in reply. Annabelle grinned widely.

"Now," continued Cat. "If we only had a mother . . ."

Annabelle looked offended. "What's wrong with me? Besides being far too young?"

"Well," he replied, rubbing his jaw and eyeing her immaculately tasteful dove-gray pants suit, "now that we've got a priest and all for a father . . . For a mother we need someone a little less . . . slutty."

Adam stared wide-eyed. But Annabelle only nodded soberly.

"I suppose you're right," she replied thoughtfully.

Only then did Adam notice the grins around him.

But Cat was still talking. ". . . nominate Davette for the job," he said with a gentle leer.

"Who's that?" Jack asked.

Carl growled, "Investigative journalism come to save the world from the scam of Vampires$ Inc. What else?"

"*Or* . . ." retorted Cat with a finger in the air. "Come

to tell the world of our plight so we can get a little decent cooperation for a change. And I think that's it. She likes us, Carl."

"They all like us. So what."

"You mean a reporter?" Adam asked.

"That's what they mean," Annabelle told them.

"You didn't talk to them, did you?" cried the priest.

"All day yesterday," Annabelle replied sweetly. "And some of last night. Interviewed everybody but Jack." She paused. "And now you, dear."

Adam looked flabbergasted. Frozen.

Again Team Crow exchanged rolled eyes.

Adam finally spoke. "You didn't tell them anything . . . ? Did you?"

Cat smiled. "Not much really. Just what we do for a living, how we do it, who we've done it for, their names and how to get in touch with them to confirm it . . . that sort of thing."

Adam looked even worse than before. He looked like he was about to explode. Finally, he did:

"*How* could you be so indiscreet? How could you . . . To actually *tell* her! What got into you? What possessed you to *do* such a thing?"

Cat regarded him calmly. "Well, I'll tell you, padre. It's what I always do with the press. Of course, she's gonna be back at the house this afternoon to talk to Jack. And then you can tell her I was only fooling."

The luggage carousel grumbled, began to turn, spouted out a single suitcase. It was Adam's. He stared at it for a moment, then grabbed it up with a single jerk and began stalking away.

"Where are you going?" Carl wanted to know.

"To take off his collar," replied Jack dryly.

Adam stopped, looked at Jack with surprise, then anger. "That's right!" he snapped and continued on to the men's room.

Cat lit a cigarette. "It's just a guess, of course. But offhand, I'd say the Church policy on publicity hasn't changed much."

Everybody laughed.

Jack lit his own cigarette and spoke: "Oh, he's not so bad. Poor kid's had that stuff drilled into him by the Man. Afraid we'll start some sort of panic and that'll start a witch hunt and on and on . . ."

"And on and on and on," Carl finished for him. "Stupid fools. This deal could use a little panic. The vampires are *there*, goddammit!"

Jack looked at him. "Are you trying to convince *me*?"

Carl grinned about halfway. "Well . . . yeah. But that kid's a stupid punk if he thinks we're gonna do anything Rome says."

The rest of the bags began to appear. Cat stepped forward to get Jack's.

"Maybe so," said Cat. "But unless that bag of his was empty, he's strong as an ox. See the way he grabbed it up?"

Jack smiled. "Oh, he's fit all right. I suspect he's actually been working out. Training to join the Vampire Quest."

Annabelle beamed. "I like him."

Jack smiled at her. "I do, too."

Carl frowned. "He still made an ass of himself."

Cat smiled brightly. "So who'd notice that around here?"

Carl snarled at him.

"So what about this reporter?" Jack asked. "Any good?"

"Well, she's gorgeous," offered Cat.

"She's young," added Annabelle. "Couldn't be over twenty-two."

"Who does she work for?" asked Jack.

"Nobody," said Carl.

"Oh, Carl," sighed Annabelle. "She's freelance. She thinks she can sell us to *Texas Monthly*."

"What's she doing in California?"

Cat shrugged. "She came to see us. Heard about us back home. She knows Jim Atkinson on the magazine."

"Does she know he couldn't get his story about us printed?"

Cat smiled. "I told her. I don't think she believed me."

Jack sighed. "Oh, great."

"Did I mention she's beautiful?" asked Cat.

Jack looked at him seriously. "Gorgeous, I believe you said."

"Oh, she's that, too. And weird-looking."

Annabelle frowned. "Cherry Cat, how could you say that?" She turned to Jack. "She's a very nice-looking girl. Very polite. Very hard-working. I like her."

"You like everybody," growled Carl.

"I don't like you," she pointed out.

"That's true."

"What do you mean, weird-looking?" asked Jack.

Cat took a puff and thought a moment. "I don't know. Strange. I mean, she doesn't have a mohawk or anything. She just . . . Well, sometimes she looks like a princess, you know, all regal and pure."

"And other times?"

"Other times she makes me think of a gang-bang victim waiting for the motorcycles to start."

The men laughed. Annabelle said, "Oh, Cherry!" and gave him a playful slap on the shoulder.

Cat was feigning grievous injury when Father Adam returned wearing civvies and a grim look.

"Are we ready?" he asked.

"We are," replied Jack with equal seriousness.

They found their way outside and climbed into the truck. Cat insisted Jack drive, saying he was so drunk Jack looked handsome to him. Jack drove without replying. On the way he tried talking to the still stiff young priest.

"Father Adam," he began.

"Aha!" chirped Cat from the back seat. "Tact!"

"Shaddup, Cat!"

"Yes, bwana."

Jack tried again. He was fairly gentle, the others thought, for him. He explained that the priest needn't worry too much about this—or, for that matter, any other—reporter. Jack told him about all the reporters they had met and been interviewed by in the past. About all the stories that had been written. About all the editors who had killed the stories. Or their careers trying to push the stories on through.

Because nobody believed in vampires.

Or wanted to believe in vampires.

Or wanted to admit they believed.

Or wanted it known that they believed.

Or anything else.

Jack told him some more about it in their brief drive through Carmel and into the Del Monte Forest. He told about the big stack of apologetic letters from a long string of publications. Told about the one story they did get printed, for the "Inquiring Minds" people. About how that story, despite all the fuss and silliness it caused, actually led to their getting a legitimate call from a sheriff in Tennessee.

Jack ended with: "So I wouldn't worry too much about this girl—what's her name? Yvette?"

"*Davette*," corrected Annabelle.

"Whatever. I wouldn't worry about her. Her tale won't get printed either. Even if it slams us. They don't even publish those for some reason. But . . ." And he pulled up at a stop sign and turned in his seat and faced the younger man. "But I wish they would. This ain't Rome, kid. This is the battleground. And if I could get on *Good Morning, America* tomorrow morning, I would. One of the biggest troubles we got is belief. Most people don't or won't believe until it's too late. But if they knew about somebody to call without going through all the rigmarole of the feds or the Church or whatever—Well, most times their local priests don't even buy their fears. But if they knew about somebody who did—and just one or two goddamned days quicker—we could save lots of lives. You get it?"

Adam coughed, cleared his throat. "Yes, well, it's just that . . ."

Jack's voice was iron. "Nope. Yes or no, son. There is no third way. Are you here with *us* or someone else? Yes or no."

The young priest stared out the front window of the truck for a few moments. Then he glanced at Annabelle, who smiled at him warmly. Finally he looked at Jack.

"Yes, sir."

"Good."

Behind them another car at the stop sign honked for them to move. They did.

A few minutes later Jack pulled off the famous 17-Mile-Drive and onto a side road that climbed and curved up the side of a hill overlooking the Pebble Beach Golf Course and beyond, the glittering blue of Carmel Bay. Down below had been mostly cottages, but up here astride the ridge were the great estates, walled and spread-out and beautiful, with their towering pines and tennis courts and postcard courtyards and flower-eating deer. The home of Team Crow was one of the grandest atop the ridge, a huge multiwinged tudor mansion set back far from the road, with a five-car two-story garage, a Japanese garden in the rear surrounding a steamy heated pool, and eight acres left to play in.

A true palace, thought Jack as he negotiated around a parked car and started up the drive. And incredibly, it had felt too small.

But that was before.

Don't think about the phone.

Cat and Annabelle were craning their heads to look behind them.

"Is that her?" she asked.

Cat nodded. "I think so. Looks like her car."

"What are you talking about?" Jack asked.

"It's Davette," Annabelle replied. "I think she fell asleep out front waiting for us to pick you up from that late plane of yours."

"Oh."

"Want me to run down and get her?" Cat asked.

"No!" blurted Annabelle firmly.

Jack glanced at her, surprised, as he pulled the truck to a stop in the empty carport. "I thought you liked her."

"I do. But we leave in six hours and I want to put you under first. After that you can talk to her."

"Put you under." Jack sat cringing behind the wheel as a wave of misery flushed through his system. Put me under, hypnotize me, make me remember back, remember everything that just happened—two weeks ago? Yesterday? Go back there and remember everything and make a tape of that same everything because any one detail might mean the difference later on. Nobody knew shit about vampires and they had to learn, had to, had to . . . Anthony! Oh, God! I don't want to go back there again!

Adam spoke up from beside him. "Haven't you made that last tape yet?"

And Jack's memory scrambled desperately to help him.

"Sure I have," he insisted, looking pale into their faces and feeling sweaty and lost. "Haven't I?"

"No" was all Annabelle said in reply and it was gentle but it was also firm and that meant she loved him and understood even, but he was going to have to do it anyway.

Jack closed his eyes and let the wave pass.

He hadn't thought back once. Not specifically, not in detail. Not once.

Not awake.

"How come you know about the tapes?" Carl asked Adam, and his voice sounded suspicious.

And that woke Jack up. Leader again. Depend on me. Rock and roll.

Jack turned in his seat and faced Carl. "This is the kid who keeps track of the tapes for the Man. Been doing it for three years."

He noticed Cat was also leaning forward with interest, eyeing the man who, he had suddenly learned, knew all his secrets under fire and fear.

But all Cat said was "Oh," and leaned back.

"Okay," said Jack, yanking the door open. "Okay," he said again, more quietly, to Annabelle.

And then they were all clambering out and reaching for bags and starting up the walkway to the front door.

"Six hours, huh?" Jack asked no one in particular. "You've moved everything already?"

Annabelle was cheery. "You actually could have flown

straight to Dallas, if we could have gotten hold of you to tell you. Carl just has the one load left."

"Weapons," Carl offered, walking along beside him. "Crossbows and the like. Gonna have to truck 'em to Dallas tomorrow. Stupid F.A.A. feds! Scared to death a closed crate of medieval weapons is gonna take Pan Am to Cuba." He laughed. They both paused on the front step. Jack thought he could already hear it ringing. He tried smiling along with Carl as the others gathered in a bottleneck before the door. Somebody was jingling keys.

"Funny thing," Carl was saying. "If it was guns, something they're already scared enough to know something about, they wouldn't mind so much." He paused, laughed again. "We oughta be using guns."

Jack Crow, stepping numbly along with the others into the empty grand foyer, thought: Guns.

And then he thought: guns? Guns! *Guns!*

"Guns?" he all but shouted.

All turned toward him, surprised, alarmed, worried.

"What?" Carl asked him.

"Guns!"

"Guns?"

Jack hugged him and yelled: "Yes, goddammit! Guns! Hot Damn! *Guns!* Don't you see?"

"Guns?"

"Rock and roll!"

Chapter 5

Surrounding the bar, surrounding the last of the booze, surrounded *by* Jack Crow's obvious glee, they played his little guessing game.

Carl evinced irritation. Annabelle tried to look bored. Cat was amused. Adam was just as bewildered as he had been since Rome. But Jack . . . !

Jack was having so goddamn much fun that nobody really cared.

He's back, thought Cat to himself.

And when he spotted the misty affection in his comrades' eyes, he knew they were feeling the same.

"Look," Jack began again, propping his boot on the railing behind the bar with a thump that echoed in the now-empty room. "It's just a matter of putting the pieces together."

He stared at their blank faces. He somehow managed to smile while still grinning.

"All right, class. We shall begin again," he said and they did.

And this time they began to see.

". . . and the bullet hole from the sheriff's gun—in his forehead, remember? It was already closing, right? And it was trapping the blood from Hernandez's silver cross gash, right?"

No one spoke.

"Right?" repeated Jack.

"Right," Cat responded slowly.

"Well?"

"Well, what, goddammit?" growled Carl.

Cat suddenly sat forward. "The gash hadn't healed . . ."

"From the cross . . ." continued Adam.

"From the *holy silver* cross," Jack corrected.

"But the bullet wound was already closing!" Carl jumped in, seeing it all now. He stood up from his stool and slapped the flat of his hand loudly on the top of the bar.

Jack was grinning mischievously. "You see it, don't you?"

Carl looked disgusted. "I see it, all right. I just don't believe it."

And then Cat saw it. He moaned. "I don't believe it either," he said. But now he, too, was starting to grin.

Annabelle looked lost. "If somebody doesn't tell me what's happening pretty soon . . ."

Cat leaned close to her against the bar. "A cloud of dust and a hearty Hi-yo fucking Silver!"

And everybody, save Annabelle, laughed. She looked downright angry. "Would someone *please* tell me what's going on?"

"Silver bullets," said Father Adam. Then he paused and, with a nod toward Jack, amended, "Holy silver bullets, blessed by the Church."

"But I thought silver bullets were for werewolves," Annabelle asked.

"They are," replied Adam calmly.

Too calmly, thought Jack. He held up a hand to cut off the questions all had turned to ask the young priest. "No!" he barked firmly. "No! I don't even want to know, Adam."

Adam smiled, eyed his glass.

"You hear me?" Jack insisted.

"I hear you."

Jack turned to Carl. "Can you pour the bullets?"

Carl grinned smugly. He sat back down. "Sure, I can pour them. But can anybody here shoot except me?"

Jack frowned. "You're not going, Joplin. You're the base man. How many times do I have to—"

"This is different," Carl insisted. "I'm a marksman. Somebody else could . . ."

Jack leaned his elbows on the bar and stared him into silence. His voice was gentle but absolutely final. "It's not going to happen, my friend."

Carl hated this. "Well, dammit!" he retorted. "Can *you* shoot?"

"Qualified whenever Uncle Sam asked."

Carl snorted. "Qualified! Shit! Any fool don't shoot himself in the foot can qualify!"

"Then good news, everyone," popped Cat brightly. "I can probably qualify."

Jack sighed, looked at him. "That bad?"

Cat smiled back. "Pretty bad. I *can* hit the broadside of a barn, but . . ."

"But what?"

"It would help some if I was *inside* the barn at the time."

Jack put his face in his hands. "Oh, great."

"Jack," Carl began. "I . . ."

"Shut up, Carl. You'll do no shooting."

Carl laughed. "Like hell I won't, big boy. I'll have to just to teach you bums." He turned to Adam. "Unless you're a fast draw or something."

Adam smiled thinly. "They didn't teach that in seminary."

Cat nodded. "It's why *I* didn't go."

"Quiet, Cherry Cat," snapped Jack. "Carl's right. We need the training. Tell me, Crack Shot, how long till we get as good as you."

Carl took a sip from his glass. "Forever." He held up his hand before Jack could say anything. "I'm serious. Jack, this is a very different, very special tool. You've gotta have a knack for it. A certain touch. I was just thinking that it's small enough that you could both carry it as a backup. That damn crossbow of yours is too unwieldy and too tough to load in a hurry, and Cat needs something besides those stakes and wooden knives he carries. Always has."

He sat back, drained his glass. "But neither one of you is good enough to depend on your shooting. If you were that good, you'd already know it. I can teach you to be better than you are. But if you're serious about this you're gonna need something else.

"You're gonna need a gunman."

Annabelle spoke up. "You've already said you need at least two more men."

Jack looked at her. "At least two."

"Then one of 'em had better be a shooter," added Carl.

"Or both," said Adam.

"Or both," Jack agreed.

Carl rattled the ice cubes in his empty glass. Jack took it and started to refill.

"The thing is," Carl mused, almost to himself, "that the kind of man we need, the kind that fits in around here, well, he's not likely to be good at this sort of thing."

Annabelle frowned. "It's nothing to be ashamed of."

"Well, no . . ." Carl admitted.

"You're good at it."

Carl nodded, took a sip from his new drink. "I am. An expert pistol shot. But the real gunmen I've known . . . and for our work it's what we need . . . real gunmen. That's just a different kind of a dude."

Jack stood up suddenly. "Well, I'll be damned." He grinned and looked at the others. Then straight at Carl. "Carlos! Everything you say tonight reminds me of something. Silver bullets, and now . . ."

"A gunman?" Annabelle asked quietly.

Jack ignored the question. "Adam, call the Man and have some silver shipped to Dallas in a hurry. Annabelle, give him the address."

"I can get us silver," protested Carl. "Can't the kid here bless it?"

"Kid." Adam frowned. "It should at least be a bishop."

"Okay," said Jack. "Call the Man. Have him send an ingot or three. . . . Hey! How about a shotgun? Anybody could with *that!* Or an M-16 or . . ."

Adam shook his head. "It must be a single bullet. It must be a small one. And it must have been part of a cross at one time."

"How do you know this?" Carl wanted to know.

Jack did not. "Never mind. How small a bullet?"

"Any pistol will do."

Jack looked at him. At his confident face. The kid knew his facts, it seemed.

"Okay," he said. "Have 'em send us enough for a thousand rounds."

Adam smiled. "How much is that?"

"We'll know when it gets here. Carl, you sure you can melt the crosses? Pour the silver?"

Carl snorted. "Fuck off."

Cat, grinning, leaned close to Adam. "Allow me to interpret. 'Fuck off,' in *this* case means: 'Why, of course, Mr. Crow! I'm surprised you asked!' "

Adam smiled readily, but distantly. Cat noticed it. "You still with us?" he asked smiling.

Adam shook his head, embarrassed. "I'm sorry. I was just thinking." He looked at Jack. "For over four hundred years . . . longer, really. But for four hundred well-recorded years man has been fighting vampires. And nobody has ever thought of using silver bullets before." He paused. "His Holiness was right. You do have good instincts." And then he blushed and sipped.

And when Cat saw that Jack was almost doing the same thing, he about laughed out loud. But he didn't, thank God.

"Yeah . . . well . . ." mumbled Jack and then, abruptly, shook all that away and raised his glass in a toast. Everyone else did the same.

"Here's to the great ones . . ." he began.

"There's damn few of us left," finished Cat and Carl and Annabelle and for a single instant, as Adam watched, a look of infinite sadness and . . . and what? Something else, passed between them. What is that look they share? wondered Adam. And then he recognized it.

Fatigue.

Bone-aching, soul-grinding tiredness. Because this job would never, ever, ever be over.

"So!" began Jack, suddenly almost cheerful again. "Tell me about the house in Big D." The goddamn toast had been just a little too pertinent in this great empty house. "How many bedrooms?"

Annabelle offered him her empty glass. "Seven," she replied. "And quite lovely."

"There's even room for Carl's hobby," Cat added, grinning wickedly.

Carl growled, drained his glass. "Hobby, my ass!"

"I'll try," replied Cat with an absolutely straight face. "But you have such a big ass. And I have such a small hobby."

"Children!" snapped Annabelle, pretending offense.

"Right," agreed Jack. "Enough of this shit." He stopped mixing more drinks and came around from behind the bar. "C'mon, Annabelle. Let's go get it over with."

"You want to do the tape now?"

"Yeah. Let's get it done."

"But you can't go under drunk!"

He gave her a hug and lifted her off the stool to the floor. "Young lady, you'd be damn surprised at the stuff I've done drunk."

"Humph," she said, rearranging her skirt. "No, I wouldn't."

"Hell," Jack cackled, "I've even fought vampires drunk."

She stopped, looked serious and school-teacher-like. "You have never gone to battle drunk."

Jack nodded. "True. But if things keep on like this, I'm gonna start."

And together, arm in arm, they marched in step from the room.

So Cat and Carl sat and talked to the young Father Adam to see what he was about. The first thing they discovered, with more than a little embarrassment, was that he considered them both to be heroes—make that Heroes. Heroes for Mankind, Heroes for the Church, Heroes for God.

It was awful.

Cat not only hated it but found it a complete mystery. This kid has heard my tapes and *still* thinks I'm a hero? Has heard all the times I was scared and all the times I screamed?

Hell, he's *heard me scream,* by God, 'cause Annabelle said I did that once making a tape under hypnosis. And he thinks I'm a hero?

Cat fixed himself another drink and eyed the young man suspiciously.

I wonder if he's on something, he thought to himself.

Carl was pretty much miserable, too. Not as much as Cat. Being base man got him a little less (but damn well not enough less) hero worship from the priest.

They learned a lot more about him. He was, for one thing, a good one. Adam was true Boy Scout blue, secure in his faith and in what it all meant and eager to do the right thing.

Maybe a little too eager, actually, but who knew if that was bad in this stupid job?

Born Adam Larrance, originally, in Berkeley, California, and infused with the "in" thinking of both that place and the new lefist leanings of so many priests concerning Liberation Theology for the masses in Central and South America, gun control, the death penalty, women's lib, the two superpowers as synonymous and, of course, more welfare. But even with all of that, and the driving antiviolence that pervaded it, the lad knew just why he was there—to kill vampires. Just kill them. He didn't want to "communicate" with them or get them government benefits or free mental health care or even try to bring them back to God.

He wanted them slain, purged, wiped out, wiped away.

He wanted them *gone.*

The punk had even learned to shoot a goddamned crossbow.

And yes, he did believe the silver bullets would work. And better still, he didn't tell them why he thought so. It was close, but they managed to stay out of the werewolf business, too.

Then the kid did something else that surprised and confused and pleased them. He got up to go to the bathroom, paused, looked back at them and spoke: "I just want to say that I know I acted like an ass at the airport about the press thing. It was wrong of me. I humbly apologize."

And then he was gone to pee.

Carl and Cat looked at each other and frowned. They didn't speak. Then Carl leaned away from the bar and fixed them both another drink. They went back to sipping and staring. Still, they said nothing.

Adam came back in shortly and resumed his place in the triangle. He looked a bit nervous and stayed quiet. At last, Carl met Cat's eyes and turned to Adam.

"If you're gonna apologize that easy," he said, "you're not gonna be much fun to pick on."

Annabelle returned to tell them that she and Jack were up to date and Cat thought she looked damn good, considering. A little pale, a little shook up, but overall just fine.

Maybe it *was* better to do it drunk.

And then again, he reminded himself, she's already cried for all of them once.

Jack was sleeping comfortably, she informed them, and would continue to do so for another forty-three minutes on the nose.

Aha! thought Cat. So it took you seventeen minutes to get yourself together before coming back in to see us. Still damned good, Annie.

And he gave her a little mental pat.

But he was still worried about Jack.

"Is he all right?" Cat asked gently.

She looked at him, surprised. Then she smiled reassuringly. "You heard him, Cherry."

He considered, thought back. "So I did," he replied and smiled himself.

"Who's that?" asked Adam, gazing past them out the leaded-glass window.

They all turned to look. A young lady with light blond hair and rumpled clothing was walking rather stiffly up the walkway to the front door. She was trying, all at the same time, to smooth out her dress, check her makeup in a hand mirror, and feel her teeth with her tongue to see if they were clean enough.

"Aha," announced Carl, lifting his glass. "The press has arrived."

"The reporter?" Adam asked nervously.

"Yep," Cat told him. "Looks like she spent the night in her car waiting for us. Or part of the afternoon anyway."

"Bless her heart," mused Annabelle. "She must want this awfully bad." She looked at Adam. "Relax, dear. We just won't tell her you're a priest."

"Naw," offered Carl. "She'll find out if she's any good at all. Better just make her keep that part tied down. Off the record or whatever it is they call it."

"And if she doesn't?" Adam wanted to know.

Cat grinned. "Our father's met the press before, sounds like."

"Oh, I think she will," said Annabelle.

"But what if she doesn't?" insisted Adam.

"Then," snarled Carl, "we'll knit her tits together." He drained his glass. "Behind her back. Somebody wanna answer the door?"

Somebody did. Cat fetched her to the bar and offered her a drink. She declined, looking nervous and flustered and . . .

And incredibly beautiful, Adam realized. Incredibly beautiful and incredibly vulnerable and something else, too, as Cat had said. Imperial. Regal. As though touching her was possible but a horrible sin.

It was very strange. Adam saw her no more sexually than any other priest but her aura was still unmistakable.

My Lord, he thought to himself, what a reporter she's going to make! People would tell her anything.

He rose from his stool to be introduced. Annabelle called him simply Adam Larrance. Her hand was cool and her eyes warm and friendly but also penetrating and assertive. Adam wondered how she learned so much so young.

There was an awkward pause after they met until Annabelle patted the stool next to her and she took it. Adam, feeling unreasonably at sea, nudged Carl Joplin beside him.

Carl glanced at him, read his unease, felt it necessary

to provide a little in-character show of tedium, and then
proceeded to explain to the girl what Adam was and what
it meant and what she could write about it—which was
zero.

He did not mention her tits.

He didn't need to. One glance around her and Davette
saw they meant it. They were polite and friendly and they
liked her (she felt sure of that) but they were also quite firm.
Don't write about the priest. She tried comforting herself
with the thought that she had never meant to. But there was
no way around the fact that it changed things that these people
had their very own priest with them.

These people! she thought and sighed. She had never
seen any group like them. They had a glow of health about
them that seemed to radiate for ten yards in every direction.
Not physical health particularly, though all save round Carl
seemed fit enough. And not really mental health or so much
emotional . . .

Soulful health. Is there such a term? she wondered idly.
For that's what they seem to have. Soulful health.

She rather supposed thinking yourself a crusader for
Right versus Wrong would do that to you.

"Is Mr. Crow in?" she asked Cat.

Cat was caught napping.

"Huh?"

"Is Mr. Crow in?" she repeated, smiling.

"He'll be down soon."

They talked about Dallas. They were moving there, and
Davette lived there. She had come all this way across the
country just to see them.

"It's not, " she reminded them, "the kind of story you
run into every day."

They talked about restaurants in Dallas and people they
knew there and famous Texans in general. It turned out Davette was Davette Shands of the once-notorious Oilfield
Shands family.

"But that's all gone now," she assured them with a self-
deprecating smile.

I doubt it, thought Annabelle. This child has been rich all her life and always will be.

And then she thought, I *can* be a little bitchy, can't I?

Adam smiled in reply to the banter but offered not one word himself.

"Offhand," offered Carl, mixing himself another drink, "I'd say the kid's met a reporter before."

"Do you believe all reporters are dishonest, Mr. Joplin?" she asked.

Carl grinned, sipped. "That depends on whether it's a reporter or a journalist."

She sort of smiled back. "What's the difference?"

"Well, a reporter lies to get himself a better story and a raise."

"And a journalist doesn't lie?"

"Well, yes. But only out of a deep sense of compassion and concern."

She laughed gamely enough along with the rest of them.

Not bad, thought Cat.

Annabelle checked her watch. Jack was due in a few minutes. So they all chatted some more before he showed and heard an odd story from Davette. Seems she had been the editor-in-chief of her college newspaper but had quit last spring, in the final semester of her senior year. Quit school entirely, as a matter of fact, and gone home to get to work.

"I needed to get off my . . . rear," she offered with a patronizing smile. "I needed to get out in the real world."

God! groaned Cat to himself. I hate to be conned.

The great oaken door burst open and Jack Crow strode in, looking fresh and invigorated and thirsty. While Carl played bartender he met Davette, shaking her hand firmly and telling her outright what a beauty she was. She seemed a little taken aback after all the beating around the bush she was apparently used to.

"You wanna talk to me, do you, young lady?"

"Why, yes. If it's convenient."

"It is for the next coupla hours. Then we hit the road. C'mon."

And just like that they left the room.

"What do you think?" Cat asked after they had gone.

"I'd like to know what she was kicked out of school for," offered Carl.

"So would I," said Annabelle.

"Please, God," sighed Cat, "let it be prostitution."

Chapter 6

"It's not the kind of job you can turn down," replied Jack Crow with more than a little exasperation.

They were in the Zoo's main corridor, leaning against opposite walls facing each other. Jack sipped from his drink.

"Why not?" Davette asked.

He thought about a reply, said, "To understand that, you'd first have to buy it."

The young girl glanced briefly away then back to him.

"Well, you have to admit it's pretty hard to believe."

By God, I think she *does* believe! Jack thought suddenly. Or at least she's trying.

"What put you onto us, anyway?" he asked.

She smiled. "An old friend of my family owns the weekly newspaper that covered your last . . . uh, mission. I got into that little town, what's it called?"

"Bradshaw, Indiana."

"Yes, Bradshaw. Anyway, I got there two days after you'd left." She frowned. "Nobody would talk about it by then. But I got your address."

"Lucky you weren't on time."

"I heard you'd had some trouble."

He took a sip. "Some."

"Anyone hurt?"

"Seven."

"Was it serious?"

"Dead. Seven dead."

She went pale. "You're joking! You can't be serious!"

He just looked at her. "Okay," he said.

They were quiet for several seconds. She could tell he meant it. And he could tell it had gotten to her.

Finally, he said, "Let me give you a little advice."

"What's that?"

"This is real."

And they were quiet again for a while."

At last she said, "I don't know what to say. Or do."

He stepped away from the wall, shrugging off the somber mood.

"I'll tell you what you can do. If you ever get this story printed anywhere—which I frankly doubt—you can put this in it." He drained his glass and set it down on the carpet. "Got your pad with you?"

"Tape recorder," she answered. She dug quickly in her purse, produced it, and held it up.

"Okey doke." He stuck a cigarette in his grinning teeth, lit it. "I'll give you the grand tour."

She smiled back, gestured about her. "It's certainly a big house. How many bedrooms?"

"Seven too many."

"Oh," she said quietly, gazing down the row of empty rooms. Four on one side. Three on the other.

"Don't despair," he said. "It's just eulogy time."

And then he did something she knew she would never, for all the rest of her life, forget. Grinning all the while, chain-smoking like mad, he strode from room to room and in each one told one outrageous, impossible, hopelessly funny and (invariably) obscene story about each of its martyred occupants. Smiling, but unable to really laugh along with him, she padded along behind gazing, transfixed, by his every word and gesture.

Jack Crow cried easily, readily, as he spoke. But without choking or moaning or even allowing it to interfere with his own laughter. His tone went up and down, was pretend-serious or pretend-drunk or pretend–little boy.

She was utterly hypnotized throughout by his blazing

pride in his lost team. No. She would never ever forget this.

Jack seemed to enjoy it as well. And he seemed to understand her reaction for the compliment it was. He spent an hour and a half being animated and dramatic and hilarious and when he had finished they were both exhausted.

Cat appeared in the hallway and reminded him their plane was ready to fly and then was gone.

He turned to her and told her where they were going.

She said she knew. She said she was from there. From Dallas.

He said he missed Texas.

So did she, she said.

There was a long pause. Downstairs, rock and roll began thumping from somewhere.

Then why don't you come along? was his next question.

She looked up at him, her head tilted to hear the muffled sounds.

"I will," she replied.

And she did.

Chapter 7

They were having a drink or three in the bar at LAX waiting for their connecting flight to Dallas when two young coed types waltzed in wearing aquamarine shorts and deep equatorial tans followed by two boys just as dark wearing sombreros on which was stitched "Acapulco."

Jack Crow, about to climb aboard his fifth jet in less than twenty-four hours, zonked by in-flight sleep and in-flight food and three or four drinks ahead of the Planet Earth, found this an inspiration.

"That's what we oughta do," he announced. "Go to Acapulco! Or better, Cancún or Isla de Mujeres! It'll take a coupla weeks to get settled into the new shack anyway."

"We've already checked our bags on through to Dallas," Cat pointed out.

Jack frowned at Cat's lack of enthusiasm. "So we leave from Dallas."

"Naw," said Carl, burping softly. "I gotta get all our bullet stuff ready."

Jack looked at him. "Yeah. Well . . . But the rest of us can go. Annabelle?"

Annabelle barely smiled. "Who's going to do all that 'settling in'?

"But the rest of you can go ahead," offered Annabelle in her very best martyred tone.

Jack stared at his drink. "Naw."

Annabelle smiled. "You may as well, Jack. You never do any unpacking anyway."

Jack grinned back at her. "Doesn't mean I don't want to be near you while *you* do it."

"How near?"

"I thought I'd stay at the Adolphus Hotel downtown." He looked at the others. "I thought we all would the first couple of days."

Annabelle sipped and smiled. "If you like."

Carl had his hands clasped across his great belly and was mumbling to himself. Adam, seated beside him, leaned closer.

"What's the matter?" he asked, concerned.

Carl looked at him. "I don't unnerstand it, padre!"

"What, Mr. Joplin?"

"Call me Carl."

"Okay, Carl. What is it?"

"My drink." He pointed to the glass before him.

"It's empty," Adam noticed.

"That's what I don't unnerstand! It was full only minutes ago."

Adam stared, comprehended, grinned.

"Oh my God!" Cat all but shrieked, shoving his empty glass away from him across the table in mock terror. "It's happened to mine, too!"

And then Carl and Cat looked at one another and began humming the theme from *The Twilight Zone*.

While the others laughed, Jack held his face in his hands and shook it mournfully. "My Team," he muttered. "Nurse!" he called to the young waitress scurrying by. "An Emergency Round."

On the plane they gathered together in the first-class lounge to hide from the food. One more airline meal, Jack felt certain, would make him left-handed. So they sat and drank and played cards and chatted. Jack brought up the subject of Mexico again but in an odd way and with an odd look on his face.

"I used to work in Mexico," he dropped briefly and then

blatantly waited for someone else to urge him to continue.
Davette complied and Team Crow wondered if she could
possibly have known him well enough this soon to feel the
oddness his eyes could shed.

Cat curled up in his seat like his namesake and prepared
not to miss a single word.

What's going on? he wondered, but said nothing out
loud.

He didn't have to, for all who knew Jack Crow were
thinking the same.

And as for Jack himself . . .

They are going to have to know this. They won't understand him otherwise. They might not understand him even
then. Or me, for bringing him along.

But they're going to have to know.

And maybe if I tell them the good part first . . .

He smiled and turned to the others. "It was during the
initial phase of my government career."

Cat frowned, said nothing. Annabelle spoke up. "You
mean before you joined the army."

"Nope. Afterward."

"But you said the first part of . . ."

"No," he corrected with a smile. "I said during the *initial*
part of my government career."

"Which means?" asked Carl sounding as bored as he
knew how.

"Which means I was under deep cover for the NSA on
assignment to the CIA working as an agent for the DEA."

"What the hell is all this supposed to mean?" Carl wanted
to know.

"Well, my job was to check out the Cuban connection
into raw brown Mexican heroin, so I was along the Texas
border trying to find out if all the rumors about a big-time
purging of the hippie smugglers was true."

"Was it?" somebody asked.

"It was. They were wiping out all the amateurs to get
ready for the big money they were monopolizing."

"So what did you do?" somebody else asked.

Jack shrugged, grinned. "Got in the way mostly. It was a dumb assignment and a dumb idea to send me along. I liked the NSA but they didn't trust me. I liked the CIA but they didn't even trust each other. I was scared of the DEA and they hated me but had to take me because of orders from upstairs.

"It was a mess."

He paused, looked around, and grinned easily. "But I did have an interesting couple of weeks."

And Cat thought, Here it comes. He glanced around at the others in the lounge and wondered how they were gonna take whatever it was that Jack was trying to sneak up on them.

And then he thought, He's trying to sneak it up on me, too. First time ever. Of course, there's a first time for everything, so . . .

So why am I so scared?

And once more Jack Crow began to speak.

Second Interlude: Felix

Raw brown heroin changed everything. Those little doper camps used to be so cute, like a piece of the Wild Frontier. They'd camp out in the weeds somewhere in their motorhomes and the Mexicans would spring up a village out of tarpaper shacks to be close to the loose change spilling off. And there was quite a bit of that to be had. Life was pretty good.

I remember they used to string Coleman lanterns on poles for streetlights.

Playing undercover G-man, I left my weapons in the motel and parked my truck off the road before walking into a camp that night. It was one of the last really big ones and I could hear lots of shouting as I got close. But when I stepped through into the clearing there were only two guys there, both Mexicans, both drunk. I walked up beside one of them and said: "Qué pasa, hombre?"

He hit me.

Smacked me good right across the chops, my lip bleeding, then swings at me again and misses and the guy beside him starts yelling out, "Another one! Here's another one!" And then he jumps at me, too.

They were both too drunk to do any more damage but that yelling brought reinforcements amazingly fast. More Mexicans started spilling out of the darkness from all directions, all drunk and all angry and all coming at me.

I ran like hell.

The wrong way, of course, that being the kind of night it was. Toward the river, away from my truck. I was lost in about two seconds, stumbling through the brush with Spanish obscenities echoing from behind. I had no idea what was going on except the basics: I was in deep shit.

But I was old enough. Old enough means I was too smart to try to stop and moralize with a meat-eating mob. There really are people out there who, while you're trying to explain it's not your fault, will pound you into putty.

I found the river when I fell into it. Well, stepped into it. The Rio Grande isn't much but thirty feet across around those parts. So anyway, I step back and start shaking my boots dry and I hear this smartass voice pop through the night with "Hey, gringo! Where're ya goin'?"

I probably didn't jump over a mile or two. And I had already started to run when I realized the voice had sounded out in English, not Spanish. I spun around and first laid eyes on William Charles Felix, lounging in the door of an abandoned boxcar with a cigarette in his mouth, a bottle of tequilla in his hand, and the biggest shit-eating grin you ever saw in your whole life. Had a World War II leather flying jacket, a faded blue navy work shirt, jeans, cowboy boots, and a Humphrey Bogart hat.

I found myself grinning back. Couldn't help it.

I walked over and took the bottle from his hand and had a swig and asked him who the hell he was and he told me and invited me inside. So I propped a squishing boot on a strut and climbed up into the boxcar. It was even darker in there than outside.

"What are you doing in this thing?"

I could barely see his grin. "Same as you, Yankee pig. Hiding."

"How'd it get down here by the river?" I asked him. I hadn't seen any tracks.

"Got me," he said, taking back his bottle. "Ask her."

He struck a match and held the flame high. The boxcar had everything it needed to go from being a moving crate to a first-rate hovel, from rug scraps and cardboard furniture to a bleeding Jesus on the wall. Sitting in the midst of it all was a woman.

Just about the most aggressively ugly woman I'd ever seen.

Felix had lit a candle with the match after carefully pulling a battered blanket-something across the opening to shield the outside from the glow.

"Who is this?" I asked him.

He grinned again. "I'm not sure." He sat down on another box, sent the grin at her, and patted a spot on the floor beside him. "I think this is her place."

He made a gesture for me to sit down on another box across from him. I did. He offered me another sip. I took it. The woman came over and sat down on the spot Felix had indicated.

"What's your name?" I asked her, unthinking, in English.

She said: "Twenty-five dollars American," and wiggled her chest.

Lord.

Felix took the bottle back and sipped through his grin. "Interesting name, don't you think?"

And we both laughed. So did the woman.

I lit a cigarette and leaned forward with my elbows on my knees.

"What the hell is going on?"

Felix was enjoying this. "What do you mean?" he asked innocently.

"Why are we hiding?"

He lit a cigarette of his own. "Well, *I'm* hiding to keep from having the living shit beat outta me by the locals." He took a puff. "And you?"

"C'mon, dammit! What's going on? Why are they so pissed?"

He eyed me strangely. "You mean you haven't heard about the García sisters?"

I sighed. "Who the fuck are the García sisters?"

He laughed. "Well, let's have another little drink and I'll tell you."

He gave me another sip, took one himself. As an after-thought, he offered one to the woman.

She damn near took his arm off grabbing for it. Then she started chugging.

"Don't worry," said Felix, watching along with me. "I've got two more bottles." He stopped, looked uncertain. The woman was still chugging. "It's probably enough."

At last he took the bottle after about a fourth of it was gone and told me all about the García sisters.

Sixteen and seventeen, respectively, beautiful, sweet-tempered, and, most important, virgins, which means a hell of a lot more in Mexico than it does in Texas. They were the pride of the area. A ray of hope in a place where the future looked too much like the past. Everyone loved and bragged on them.

And then they ran off to Houston with two gringo drug dealers.

"But don't worry too much," Felix assured me. "To-morrow morning nobody will be after us or even remember why they were mad tonight."

I wasn't convinced. "What makes you so sure?"

He shrugged. "It's happened before."

There was a sound from outside. Felix had the candle blown out, his cigarette coal hidden, and the blanket-thing shoved out of the way in one motion. He peered out into the darkness, listening intently.

They were out there. You could hear their unmistakable mob clamor. They sounded pretty close. I began to feel a little claustrophobic in that boxcar. I got down next to Felix by the door.

"I've got an idea," I whispered.

"Love to hear it," he whispered back over his shoulder.

"Let's run away."

He leaned back in, smiling. "Normally, I would consider that a brilliant move. My first reaction, come to think of it. But where do we run?"

"How about across the river? We could hide out in Big Bend until morning."

He sat back on his heels, picked up the bottle. "I can think of at least six reasons why that's a bad plan," he replied taking a sip. He wiped his mouth. "And all of them are snakes."

I laughed. "Then what do you suggest."

"Well," he replied, closing the blanket-thing back across the gap, "if we stay here I figure we got a fifty-fifty chance."

I frowned. "You mean they'll either find us or they won't."

"Yup."

We had another drink. The woman had two more. We talked. The woman said nothing at all until, some five or twelve drinks later, she decided to change her name to "Fifteen dollar American."

We drank and talked some more, about another half hour, before she decided to change it to "Five dollar American."

Fickle.

Somewhere into the second bottle, after the third and closest wave of mob rustling occurred just outside, we, Felix and me, decided to make ourselves a pact.

We were clearly doomed, we decided. So the thing to do was to tell each other, in these the last moments of existence, the Major Truths About Our Lives, like passengers on a falling airliner.

Which is how I found out he was a drug smuggler and he found out I was a narc.

It's funny now but at the time I was pissed as hell. Well, grumpy, anyway. Felix laughed, knowing, as per the pact, that I couldn't do anything about what he told me. Until I pointed out to him that neither could he tell anyone else about me and then we were both quiet. And then we both had another drink.

And then we both said, "Fuck it!" in unison, and laughed.

It was fun.

What was strange about it was me being so surprised in the first place. I mean, what the hell else did I expect Felix to be, way out there like that? It's just that he wasn't at all the type or something.

Something.

Anyway, about then two bad things happened in a hurry. The first was that horrible woman deciding to change her name to "Free" and leaning back and pulling up her dress and spreading her legs so wide you could see her liver.

I swear to God it gave me vertigo.

The second bad thing was her husband showing up through the other door.

I'd figured the other door was rusted shut or something. The rest of the place looked like it should be, anyhow. And maybe it was, but Ol' Hubby just slid it open with a flick of his wrist and there he stood, all six and a half feet and two hundred plus pounds with a headless chicken in one hand and a bloody machete in the other.

Next to his wife he was the ugliest human I'd ever seen.

"I think I know how the boxcar got down here by the river," whispered Felix from beside me.

I whispered back without taking my eyes off Hubby. "He carried it down here on his back."

And then the woman, the wife, screamed and Hubby roared and Felix and I were scrambling around and that machete was slashing through the air flinging drops of bright red chicken blood and the candle got turned over onto the cardboard furniture and flames rose up and the woman jumped between us and the giant to protect her furnishings and Felix and I used that moment to basically run screaming into the night.

Except Felix stopped long enough to grab the tequila and I got my metal wristwatch stuck in the blanket-curtain over the doorway and ripped it off when I jumped through into the weeds.

Outside, the mob was waiting.

Not close enough to see us. Not yet. But close enough that they were about to and close enough that there was no way to get around them and close enough for them to see the flickering light from the boxcar almost immediately and start toward it.

Too damn close, in other words.

"C'mon, Felix!" I hissed. "The river!"

"Hell, no!" he hissed back. "The snakes!"

We were running out of time. I grabbed him. "Fuck the snakes!"

And then he grabbed me back, all calm for a moment, looked me right in the eye, and said, "That's really sick!"

I just had to laugh. He was just too weird.

But in the meantime we were in a bad spot, stuck between two groups anxious to pound on us, and we needed a plan.

To this day I still don't know how we got up that tree, as drunk as we were, and as scared, and the whole time giggling insanely. It was pure Looney Tunes, but we did it. It cost me a lot of skin on the bark, but Felix shinnied right up using only one hand.

He carried the tequila in the other. Incredible.

So we sat up there and watched as the mob and the monster came together. Reminded me a lot of *Frankenstein*, with all those lanterns bobbing and that huge Hubby roaring. I don't think he was much smarter than he looked because he thought they were us for a while, hammering on a half-dozen or so before they calmed him down. Then they got about halfway organized and all of them started searching for us.

Never looked up, though, and never came near us, though I think they may have heard us giggling once.

They were very persistent. Kept us up there all night long. Felix and I spent the time swapping sips from the bottle and gabbing more about ourselves like we had before. It was dumb as hell, I guess. But it was also our tree.

I told him a lot more about Viet Nam than I'd ever told anyone else and was frankly amazed at his considerable knowledge and understanding of that war, coming as he did from the sixties generation. He told me a lot about what he did and I listened to all of it and couldn't make sense of any of it. Felix only smuggled marijuana, though he had been offered fortunes to run heavier dope. He didn't seem to make very much money at all, in fact.

He didn't even smoke the stuff. Hated it.

I was about to ask him what the hell he was doing there when we got onto the subject of brown heroin and the Cuban connection and the rest of it. He confirmed everything we'd heard, including the danger for his brand of amateur along the border. His own supplier, he said, regularly used Cuban ports and Cuban radar assistance to cross the Caribbean. Or had, until Fidel had started going into business for himself.

At first I thought he was just being upfront and straight about our pact when he went into such elaborate detail concerning his trade. But then I realized that he was also taking advantage of it. Every time I would later run across this info I would have to toss it out and he damn well knew I would stick to it.

How? How does anybody know about anybody? Sometimes you just do. I told him about me. He told me about him. Nobody else's business.

Our tree.

He was getting out that month. He wanted to live. He didn't want to join and he didn't want to fight. He was worried about his partners, though.

"They're young and greedy and stupid and they think that kind of craving makes them tough," he said once, cupping his cigarette coal against a sighting from the now-scattered posse. He sighed. "And they know all the excuses."

I asked him what he was going to do and he said, "Nothing," and I knew he meant it. As long as they didn't involve him, it was their choice and their life.

It got very quiet there for a long time. Dawn was coming and the searchers had given up and it was a bit chilly until the wind died down. The last thing I remember was our finishing the bottle at last telling elephant jokes. Felix knew a thousand elephant jokes.

And then I woke up in the Rio Grande.

It was the sound, more than the water, that scared me

at first. Splashing in from several stories up makes quite a racket. And then the water was in my scream and my ears and cold and moving but the sun was there somewhere and then I was awake enough to realize where I was and pretty soon after that awake enough to remember what swimming was and that I could do it. I lived.

But barely, dragging myself back into Mexico about thirty feet downstream, gasping and whimpering and shivering from the cold. I got on my knees on the bank and searched around for the tree and when I found it I started laughing again immediately.

Felix, dead asleep and drooping from the branches sunk deep into his leather jacket, was still holding the empty tequila bottle. And then I saw something else that made me stare. And think.

Underneath that jacket, my smuggler had a very professional-looking shoulder holster and inside it a nine-millimeter Browning. A couple of times during the raucous night before I had thought longingly of the arsenal back in my motel room and knew damn well I might have used it if I had had it—if only to warn them off.

But Felix had been armed all along and had never, I knew instinctively, thought to use it.

Not once.

Chapter 8

Jack Crow stood at the baggage claim in Dallas–Fort Worth International Airport gazing longingly at the bank of pay phones and rattling the change in his pocket.

It was probably too late to call the people he had in mind. Too late at night, too late in his career. And he didn't much want to get involved with them again. What was that old joke? One of the three Big Lies? "Hi! I'm from the Government. I'm here to *help* you!"

But still, nobody could find someone like the old crowd. And God knows they were fair to me. Just let me walk away from it all.

He stood where he was, undecided, idly watching the others gather the bags. Annabelle and Davette stood chatting amiably on the edge of the activity, picking up all sorts of looks from the other passengers. Crow didn't blame them. Damn few women looked like Annabelle at her age. And come to think of it, fewer looked like Davette at any age. She was really something to see.

Then he noticed something odd.

"Davette? Where are your bags?" he asked, innocently enough but absolutely everyone turned and looked at him and Davette blushed to her dress line and Annabelle trotted over to him wearing her "Hush!" look.

Oh, God, he thought. What have I done now?

Well! If he'd just be quiet for a minute, she'd *tell* him. It seems this dear sweet little girl has had a falling-out with her family. She, Annabelle, hadn't gotten all the details yet but it was some sort of major blowup and the poor girl is just desperate and she needs this story and I *know* she probably won't get it printed, Jack! But that's not the point! The point is: she's lost and alone and away from her family and she's going to stay with us for a while, doing her job as a reporter— I'm sure she's a dandy little reporter, she's *so* smart—and then we'll worry about the rest of it later.

Please? Please, Jack?

For me?

Jack absolutely hated it. He hated the whole bit—the girl, the sob story, the responsibility, Annabelle's tone. But what the hell was he going to do? Annabelle had yet to be wrong about someone, and besides, what could he do anyway? He hated it. He just hated it.

He looked down at her pleading eyes. He was a foot taller and one hundred pounds heavier and one day, when he grew up, he was going to stand up to her.

He just nodded and slunk his ass away toward the taxis.

Shit.

Davette, visibly tense, watched him pass by. She turned to Annabelle.

"Is it all right?" she asked.

"Of course it is, dear."

Davette relaxed somewhat. "He agreed?"

Annabelle stopped and looked at the younger woman. She laughed. "You sweet thing," she said, patting Davette's cheek. "Did you get the impression I was *asking* him?"

The young night clerk at the Adolphus Hotel, Dallas's rejuvenated downtown palace, had no better luck than Crow. Annabelle was *terribly* sorry they hadn't made reservations but it's just that they *always* stayed at the Adolphus—it was like their second home and one hardly makes reservations at one's home, does one? Ha ha ha.

And the next thing the poor young man knew, Team Crow had its pair of connecting suites and Davette had her single on the same floor.

Everyone was starving to death so they ordered down

for . . . How many of us are there? Six? . . . for eight steaks and big baked potatoes with everything on them and tossed salad and asparagus and a round of drinks, make that two rounds, and a half dozen bottles of Mondavi red . . . No. That's *eight* steaks and *six* bottles of wine. Whaddya think we are? Alcoholics? Right. Thank you.

Davette further endeared herself to everyone by falling asleep twice. Once after her first drink and again at the table during the meal. Annabelle clucked and had the men carry her, still sleeping, into her room. The poor girl had been both exhausted and starving and, No thank you very much, Cherry Cat. I can undress her myself.

The next morning Jack Crow declared a holiday. It didn't apply to Carl Joplin, who was going to be busy setting up his workshop and getting ready to make silver bullets and it didn't apply to Annabelle, who was going to be busy screaming at movers and temporary servants, at least during the day, but everyone else could play.

And they did. Jack and Cat and Adam and Davette did Dallas in a big way for the next couple of weeks. The others joined them at night for dinner, but during the day they got silly on their own. They went to movies and amusement parks and go-cart tracks. They bowled. They golfed. They played tennis, hard, every day to stay in shape. They lunched, huge lunches lasting three hours and costing as many hundreds of dollars. They ran up an enormous tab at the hotel (everyone still slept there), paid it, ran up another, paid that.

In the meantime the house was getting ready; the vehicles arrived from California in time for Jack to get a DWI. He stood there, furious, while a twenty-year-old policeman dressed him down, quite rightly, for driving across a cemetery at three o'clock in the morning scouting picnic spots for the next afternoon. Jack was forced to renew his old acquaintances downtown before he really wanted to think about such things. The lieutenant he spoke to knew (unofficially) who he was and what he did and got him off but lectured him some more.

Jack shut up and took it and leased a limo the next morning.

In the meantime, all had their own little chores. Davette went shopping with Annabelle once it was discovered she had only what she had been wearing. Cat chased and caught several women, at least two of whom had a sense of humor. Adam went to mass every morning.

And Jack made his phone call to the nation's capital.

They were surprised to hear from him but not entirely distant. They said they would see what they could do. Two weeks later they called him back and gave him an address. He thanked them, hung up, checked the address in the yellow pages, nodded to himself.

During the whole two weeks they never once mentioned their jobs. Nobody said the word: vampire. Jack even stopped jumping whenever the phone rang.

He shouldn't have.

The silver had arrived from Rome through the local see. The bishop was a new man who knew nothing about Team Crow or, for that matter, his parishioners. Persuaded by his aide that anyone with enough clout to receive a package from the Vatican through diplomatic channels was worth knowing, he grudgingly consented to share his sumptuous evening feast with Crow & Co.

It took less than fifteen minutes in his presence for Team Crow to know all the important facts about this man. He was cold. He was haughty. He was better than his flock, more cultured, more intelligently pious, more . . . how shall one put it? More aristocratic.

The bishop was an idiot.

He was also Carl Joplin's meat. Carl's and Cat's. The two of them took rich delight in infuriating the man, pretending all the while to be unaware at how offended he was by their every gesture and semicrude remark. They had descended to triple entendres when the bishop had absolutely had enough.

He rose curtly and left the room, gesturing for the uniformed Father Adam to follow.

Adam loved the Church. He loved it deeply and fully, without reservation, both as an institution and as a vehicle for Almighty God. He loved priests also, knowing them to be as fine a collection of human beings as existed on the planet. Many times in even a career as short as his he had felt . . . no, he had *known* he had seen, in the shining eyes of some simple servant of Rome, the hand of Christ.

But this bishop was an ass and he ignored the man's clipped demands for explanation and instead laid before him on his desk the pouch he had brought with him from the Vatican.

With a snort and a sneer, the older man reluctantly began to read. When he was finished, his face was pale.

It was worth seeing.

Suddenly (almost miraculously, thought Adam wryly), all was well. Anything the bishop or his office could do for them would be done without question. Why, he'd be *glad* to.

Right. Great. They all shook hands and left.

As much fun as Cat had been having, he hadn't been neglecting his job, which was to fret over Jack Crow. Everybody had his own relationship with their leader and each relationship was close but none as close as Cat's and everyone knew it. Cat found it strange that he received such attention, that his feelings of . . . well, approval, he guessed, should be so important. But they were.

For now.

Because one day, Cherry Cat was very sure, someone would stop by from the Home Office, some field man in charge of Karma, and inform him that there had been a dreadful mistake. We're very sorry, Mr. Catlin, the man would say, but you're not supposed to be here. By some clerical error, your soul was classified under Hero when it should have been under Intelligentsia. Let's face it, Mr. Catlin, you are hardly the crusader type, now are you? You should have been a film critic.

It was bound to happen, thought Cat. But until that time, until they caught him, he was going to stick. Because he couldn't imagine any other way that a fellow like him, a smartass and a determined coward, could hope to hang around these giants. So he would stay until they dragged him away. Just to be there. Just to see it.

He only hoped the Home Office wouldn't prosecute.

But in the meantime he watched Jack Crow and he'd noticed an odd look on his leader's face all night. He hadn't joined in with their game of Piss Off the Bishop, hadn't even seemed to notice it much. Something was going on, Cat knew. And it was something that he ought to be able to . . .

Of course! Mexico! That story he told about that funny smuggler guy. What was his name? Fre . . . No. Felix. Like Felix the Cat. Hmm. So. *That* was that look.

Hmm, again. When do you suppose he's going to get around to telling us? Maybe he could use a feed.

At the moment there was no decent opportunity. Jack had directed the limo to Greenville Avenue, the American model, from New York to Chicago to L.A.'s Marina del Rey, of the Singles' Strip. For six straight miles, ninety percent of the real estate was devoted to night life. Everyplace was a bar or a restaurant with a bar and all served steak and lobster and silly drinks with sillier names designed to sound obscene when drunkenly pronounced and all were filled with nubile young ladies, a terrifying percentage of which had received herpes from dirty toilet seats.

Cat moved through this place like International Harvester in the fall. Women loved his blond looks, his sly smile, his five-foot-eight build. Even the tall ones and that was okay because some of them were worth the climb.

But the bar Jack was taking them to was a lot different. For one thing, the name (the Antwar Saloon). For another, the clientele. This was a bar bar. No foo-foo drinks with little umbrellas for them. This was a place for men, mostly, where they could come and talk and do serious drinking without showering after the office. They didn't seem particularly anxious to get new customers, or even happy about the arrival of six cash-carrying strangers. The waitress who took their order after they had filled up a corner booth seemed friendly enough, and she did her job quickly and well, but Cat could tell she didn't care if they returned or not or lived or died.

It was a nice place anyway. Somehow.

Cat glanced again at Jack, saw him surveying the room with that look strong on his features, and decided it was time for the feed.

"So," he began cheerily, "whatever happened to that Felix guy?"

"Yes," echoed Davette, who seemed genuinely interested. "I'd like to hear."

"So would I," said Adam, now without his collar once more. "Did you ever see him again?"

Jack eyed Cat briefly, surprise and dawning gratitude on his face. He smiled and nodded to the question. "Yep. Twice more."

Annabelle's smile was a knowing one. "What happened?"

"Well, to answer that, I've first got to talk about Mr. Peanut."

Carl frowned. "What's Carter got to do with it? He wasn't president then."

"No," Jack agreed slowly. "But the damage was done. Who else told the world a bunch of unshaven purportedly religious punks could mob-storm an American embassy and capture and torture the diplomatic personnel for four hundred and forty-four days and get away with it?"

Carl frowned again. "So what's the point?"

Jack sipped and grinned. "That is the point. The whole world knew we lacked the one thing absolutely required to stop outlaws: the resolve to get the dirty job done. Without that, they knew if they pushed us hard enough and long enough, we'd back off.

"So they decided to murder DEA agents. One, anyway, so there would be a chance for Congress to whoop and holler and then do nothing and the agents themselves would see they had no backup after the second killing and quit. Not quit their jobs. Just quit doing them. And why shouldn't they? Why be targets for people who didn't care anymore about them than to say they did?"

"So what stopped it?" Adam wanted to know.

Jack's face was hard. "It wasn't stopped."

Adam stared at him. "You're kidding."

"Read the papers much, kid?"

"No."

Jack snorted, smiled. "Don't blame you. Anyway, they've killed five DEA men since 1983."

"And they tried to kill you?" prompted Davette.

"Kidnapped me first." Jack drained his glass and signaled the waitress for another round. "Which was stupid. Felix tried to warn me. He got word to me two days before but I had John Wayne fever or something and wouldn't get out like I should."

"How," asked Cat slowly, "did Felix know?"

"They were his gang. Those partners he was so worried about, trying to prove they could make it in the raw-brown-heroin business."

Third Interlude: Audition

They trussed me up good. Four of 'em. They took me right out of my motel room in the early morning during my shower.

Stupid, stupid, stupid on my part. Just stupid!

But not bad on theirs. They were fast and rough and scared and they had me down and wrapped up tight and then they pounded on me to show they meant it and then we left. At least they gave me my trousers.

Two hours later we're out in some abandoned mobile home way out in the sticks and I'm tied to a chair at the legs and armrests and shoved up against this rickety old kitchen table like they're going to feed me and then they sit down and shoot some more speed into their arms.

It was plenty scary. All four were Americans, all four young. All four wired to the gills. The dope didn't even seem to affect them, so God knows how long they'd been awake and psyching up to do this. Two or three days at least. Maybe a week.

I was dead meat.

There was a fifth guy there. Hispanic, but I knew damn well he wasn't a Mexican. He was cold sober and cold-eyed and dressed the way he thought American gangsters were supposed to dress. He chewed a toothpick and played with the gold on his wrists and fingers and around his neck. He was the one they were trying to impress. They kept offering him speed. He shook his head and smiled. Then he looked at me with a sly sneer of personal triumph. He suggested they keep the gag in my mouth. They did.

The moment came. They all exchanged nervous looks and then looked at the Hispanic and he looked at them as if to say, "Well?"

The leader looked a bit like Cat, thin and blond, and he licked his lips and nodded to the others and they all stood up. The leader reached for his gun. Two of the others did the same.

Felix appeared without warning in the doorway behind them.

"Knock, knock," he said quietly.

They jumped like they'd been zapped by a laser beam. They spun around, cocking their pistols, or trying to get them out with jerking slippery hands—

And I thought they were going to shoot him. Or at least shoot *at* him. But they didn't. They recognized him at the last split second, and didn't shoot. The air was filled with the sound of their roaring breath.

Felix, feigning concern, took a step back and raised his hands. He smiled. "Don't shoot, Yankee!"

There was about a three-beat pause while everyone's heart was restarted. Felix, still smiling, lowered his hands and strolled casually into the room. He stopped in front of my table and lit a cigarette. He regarded the blond.

"Cliff, you look like shit," He looked around at the rest of them. "The rest of you look worse." He paused when he came to the Hispanic. His smile remained but his eyes looked hard. "I see the company rep is here."

Then he did a scary thing. He took one of the chairs abandoned by the others, the one next to me, and plopped down in it. He looked at me, said, "Hi, Jack," and tapped his cigarette in the ashtray.

Cliff's eyes went wide. He stared, took a step toward us without thinking. "You *know* this guy?"

Felix remained calm. "Sure. Got drunk with him a month ago."

One of the others, a dark-haired scruffy one with tattoos, all but lunged forward.

"Did you know he was a narc?" he demanded.

"Not at the time." Felix took a puff. "I found out later."

"Then why didn't you tell us?" the guy wanted to know.

"What for, Randy?" Felix replied calmly, looking him dead in the eye. "You told me you were getting out of the business."

Randy looked like he was about to explode—embarrassed, ashamed, and worse, angered by it.

"You knew we were lying!" he spat.

Felix continued to eye him coldly. "Did I?" he replied with a faint touch of hurt in his voice.

It got quiet for a second, then Felix said, "Sit down, Cliff. Or shoot me."

Cliff looked down at the gun still in his hands—a big monster .357—glanced at the others, then stuck it into his holster and sat down. Randy sat down, too. But he put his Colt automatic on the table in front of him. The third and fourth Americans—one was fat and one had a beard—put guns away and drew up chairs on the edge of the circle.

They all kept glancing over at the Hispanic, who hadn't moved but clearly didn't like what was going on.

"What the hell are you doing here, Felix?" asked Cliff abruptly.

"I came," he replied with a jerk of his head at me, "to rescue Jack, here."

Then he smiled again.

There was a pause . . . and then everyone, save the Hispanic and me, started to laugh.

But it didn't last very long. It couldn't. The scene was just too hot.

"C'mon, Felix," continued Cliff. "Be serious. What are you doing here?"

Felix smiled. "I am serious."

And it all got very tense again. Cliff lit a cigarette with shaky fingers, leaned toward Felix, and spoke the way he probably thought real men do.

"Felix, look. I know you want to get out and I know you never liked this part of it, the smack. And we all understood that, didn't we?"

And the other three nodded soberly.

"But," he continued, "we're moving up. We understand

 now you feel—really—but we're going ahead. There's just too much at stake here."

Felix leaned back. "Let's see if I can get this straight, here. You're about to murder an American policeman for the privilege of going on the Cuban payroll to smuggle raw heroin onto the streets of the United States?" He dropped his cigarette on the floor and stomped on it. "And you call it moving up?"

Randy exploded. More rage and shame and hatred for Felix for making him see it. "Goddamn you, Felix! You always put things like that! You love putting things in the worst possible way!"

And Felix just stared at him like he was from another planet.

It was getting hotter in a hurry.

"However you wanna put it, Felix. Fine. That's what we're going to do," said Cliff, trying to stay calm. "Now the best thing for you to do is just leave and . . . just leave us alone."

Felix's voice was ice-crystal clear. "You know I can't do that, Cliff."

And then he did a spooky thing. The whole time we'd been drinking that night I'd never noticed his shoulder holster and I'm used to looking for them. But he turned in his chair a certain way and suddenly it was exposed to the room.

"Let me put this so you can understand it," he said in a gentle, dead voice. "I'm not going to let this happen. I love you all. Even when I don't like you. But I won't let you kill him. Look, I disagree with those bullshit drug laws as much as anyone alive but I *will not* let you murder an American cop just for doing his fucking job. Do you understand that? Am I being *very* clear?"

He sat back in his chair and looked right at Cliff. "Let him go," said Felix.

Cliff exchanged half-glances with the others. Then decided to sit tough. "No," he said simply.

Felix sighed. "Then we fight."

Long pause. Cliff spoke: "Felix, you can't really mean this. You're not gonna do it—track us down to avenge some pig narc? C'mon!"

"I'm not going to do that. I'm going to stop you from killing him."

Randy, wired up and all but hopping in his chair, said, "How?"

Felix eyed him. "I'm going to shoot you if you don't let him go."

Randy tried a sneer. "When?"

And Felix said, "Now," and I thought he was the craziest sonuvabitch I'd ever seen in my life. There were *five* of them and he just sat there for a second and so did everyone else except Cliff, who stared hard at him and saw he meant it, saw he was serious, saw he was going to start it right there and then against all of them, all of them and more—it didn't mean a shit to Felix. It was really going to happen. Felix was really gonna—

And Cliff reached for Randy's automatic on the table in front of him.

Felix shot him through the cheek, rose, shot Randy through his open gaping mouth already covered in his friend's blood, shot the fat one square in the chest and blew him back, shot the one with the beard, who had managed to get his gun out and cock it, through the throat. And the Hispanic, the Cuban, who had risen frozen at the far side of the room, he shot right between the eyes.

It took three seconds.

Felix's face was beet red. Tears streamed down his cheeks. He took his nine-millimeter in his left hand and turned to me, roaring, "I told you to leave, you dirty stupid motherfucker!"

Then with his free right hand he slapped me so hard my chair flew over backward and shattered beneath me. I lay there stunned and gasping for breath. When I looked over, Felix was vomiting onto the floor, still bawling like a baby, sobbing so hard it looked like it hurt.

After a while he stopped. He stood up, gun still in his hand. He gave me this kinda vacant look, then walked out the door and out of sight. He didn't even bother to untie me.

I didn't see him again for years. Until . . .

Chapter 9

"Until when?" Annabelle asked.

Cat saw her face. It looked pale.

"Until . . . " began Jack, suddenly looking past them across the room to the bar, "a few minutes ago."

Everyone turned to follow his gaze. Davette recognized the young man standing up from his stool at the corner of the bar, had noticed that old WWII leather flying jacket when they had come in.

But I never would have guessed just by looking at him.

And then she thought, still watching the man approach them; But now that I've been told . . .

Yes. Yes, it's him. He's the one who did that.

Felix stopped beside their booth and stared down at Jack Crow. His voice was a harsh bitter crackle.

"Come to bust me at last, Crow?"

Jack's smile was grim. "It's worse than that."

Felix barely nodded. "It would be."

PART TWO

Gunman

Chapter 10

Felix led the way up some back stairs to a small one-bedroom apartment and office with a huge picture window of one-way glass overlooking the bar. Felix sat down at his desk with his back to that window, chain-smoking and listening with stony silence as Jack spoke the tale of Vampire$ Inc.

His only discernible reactions came from his face, already thin, which seemed to stretch into a death mask's gauntness, and from his eyes, already piercing, which became uncomfortable to meet.

Watching him all the while—for no one could take eyes from his steaming intensity—Annabelle could not pin down her feelings. She recognized Felix easily from Jack's story. The laugh lines were there from the happy drunk who climbed Mexican trees.

And so was the helpless acuity of a man vised so tight he'd had to gun down four friends and a stranger at a kitchen table for a principle.

Eerie, she thought. I don't know whether to run screaming into the night or pull him into my lap and cuddle him until he can sleep.

Something else bothered her. His few looks away from Jack were at Davette. Everyone else he had dismissed with his first glance. But his face, that rock face, kept coming back to the young journalist. His face did soften, Annabelle thought, when he did this. But damn well not enough for Annabelle.

Not nearly enough.

When Jack had finished, all were quiet for several seconds. Then Felix reached forward and stubbed out his last cigarette. He spoke in a harsh, rasping, bitter voice:

"Get out.

"Take your band of merry men and your fairy tales and your"—he glanced briefly, painfully, at Davette—"your . . . *siren* . . . and any other reasons you've got to get me to do more killing and get the fuck out!"

Team Crow, save for Jack, sat in collective stunned silence. It was absolutely the very last reaction they had expected.

No one had *ever* turned them down before.

Carl Joplin opened his mouth to speak, to protest, but Felix stood up quickly, cutting him off.

"*Now!*" he thundered.

They left. Without anyone saying a word, they left, Felix by then standing in the center of the room glaring ferociously at them as they went.

Save for their limo, the street was all but deserted. Jack tapped lightly on the glass and the dozing driver scrambled out to open doors. But for a moment no one moved to get in. They just stood there looking at the night.

"Well," offered Carl at last, "he was pretty weird for us anyway."

Jack looked at him and laughed. "Are you kidding, Joplin?" He laughed again. "The man is *ours!*"

All eyed him warily.

"Correct me if I'm wrong, O Great Leader," said Carl. "But wasn't that a 'no' he gave us?"

"I'll correct you," added Cat. He turned to Jack. "It was, in fact, about the firmest goddamn 'no' I've ever heard."

The other three, Annabelle, Davette, Adam, nodded without speaking.

Jack laughed again.

"He's ours, I tell you. You know what he'll do? Next time I see him—"

"You're going to see him again?" asked Annabelle.

"You think that's wise?" added Davette.

Jack grinned. "Got to. He doesn't know how to reach *us*. Anyway, next time I put it to him he'll demand something outrageous. Money, probably. A hundred grand or the like." He nodded to the driver who walked around and got behind the wheel. He waved the others into the car. "I'll agree, we'll shake hands, and then he's in. C'mon."

They obeyed. Reluctantly, suspiciously. When they had all gotten situated, Cat finally spoke up for the rest.

"Bwana? Are you sure we're all talking about the same dude?"

Everyone smiled.

"How," Annabelle wanted to know, "can you be so sure, dear? I mean about the money and the rest. Why didn't he just ask for it tonight?"

He smiled warmly at her. "He was bluffing tonight. Hoping we'd all go away. When it doesn't work—which he knows damn well it won't—he'll just make it tougher on me out of spite. He needs the money as an excuse to give in to himself."

Everybody thought about that for a second.

Finally, Cat asked, "Are you *sure* we're talking about the same dude?"

"Let me tell you something, old buddy," replied Jack before anyone else could speak. "More than you, more than me, that man was made to do this job."

He paused, sighed. "Poor bastard." He looked at the driver. "Hit it."

If anyone noticed Davette's furious blushing or triphammer heartbeat they didn't say anything. Thank God! she thought. Because she couldn't explain it either. But Lord, what a tug . . .

Thirty minutes later Felix still stood as he had when they had gone, stiff and silent in the middle of the room.

Why can't I cry? he thought. And then he thought: I should be allowed to cry.

It isn't fair.

He had doubted not one word Jack Crow had told him.

That a world existed where vampires really lived was no surprise at all. A world of evil incarnate gnawing men only made sense.

What surprised him was how long it had taken for that world to finally find him and drag him inside.

It's not fair, he thought. I wanted to do something real.

Lord; but she was beautiful.

Jack Crow, lying sleepy-drunk in the huge bed of the suite's master bedroom, felt oddly content.

He felt for Felix. He really did. But no more than he did for himself or for Cat. And besides, he'd really meant it when he'd said Felix was made for the job.

Funny, he'd thought of Felix a lot in the years since Mexico but almost never in terms of the killing. It was as if that part of Felix, that killing part, had been kept under the surface. Or in his dreams. Or something.

He rolled over on his side and scrunched his pillow better. He loved these pillows. Not the usual hard-as-a-rock hotel pillows. Made to last a lifetime and probably float until help came. "Ladies and gentlemen, should we experience turbulence and the hotel begin to sink, your flotation device is found under your bedspread . . ."

Ha. Yep, Felix was the right move. Silver bullets was the right move. And for the first time he was able to think back to the night of the massacre with something less than bone-grinding anguish, something more than impotent horror. Now it was something like: Gotcha, bastards. Gotcha! Right where I—

And then he remembered for the first time . . . No, not the first time. He'd *always* remembered that. But he'd never *thought* of it, never really *seen* it, but it *had* happened, not once but three times. God! Three times it had done it Three times! *Three times!*

The fiend roaring out of the motel and them jammed in the sheriff's truck—

Three times . . .

And hauling ass down the highway leaving David and

Anthony and the priest and the slaughtered whores and it had come down the highway after them—

Three times . . .

And it had caught them, actually caught them, and leapt onto the goddamned truck and then had done it again before it smashed through the back windshield and he'd blown that hole in its face.

Three times.

The vampire had called his name three times.

Jack Crow sat up in bed and his face was pale in the dark and he trembled and sweated and was as scared as he'd ever been in his life.

The vampire had known his name.

It had known him.

It knew me. Hell! It . . . It . . .

It *knows* me. It's still *alive*!

His eyes darted to the curtained window.

Does it know where I am?

And he sat there, for hours, trying to think how such a thing could be and what it meant and . . . and . . .

And I don't even have my crossbow. It's at the house. But even if I did, what difference would it make? It's night. It's night and dark and you can't kill them at night anyway. At least, no one ever has.

But what if it comes for me right now? What if it comes for all of us? Cat! And *Annabelle*! Oh, God! Annabelle.

He started to get up and race into the other rooms and gather everyone up and they could run, get out of the hotel and—

And what? And go where? With what plan?

He lay back down in the bed and did an amazing thing, something only one of his breed could have done. He thought:

I'm tired and drunk and I *will not think about this now*. Fuck it.

Then he rolled back over on his side and went to sleep.

And the next morning, right on cue, the phone finally rang.

Chapter 11

Cat was having a very weird day.

He sat there in the bishop's office between Father Adam and Jack and decided their new client, who was a Mrs. Tammy Hughes and who was also the mayor of Cleburne, Texas, was just a little too cheerful for this tale she had to tell.

And that was pretty weird.

Then there was the tale itself, all about half-formed goons (they couldn't be full vampires yet from her peeling-cheek description) stomping around the downtown Cleburne square chewing on people. The local police had tried to help, emptying magnum after magnum into those decomposing husks, and the goons had noticed it—roaring and spinning in pain—but had not stopped feeding. The only injuries were to the victims, who were dragged brutally away into an abandoned department store warehouse across from the county courthouse. The cops had cordoned the area off.

And that was pretty weird, too. Cat had never heard of 'em being that obvious before. And besides, where was the master vampire during all of this? It was almost as if they were trying to advertise.

Naw. That was *too* weird.

And then of course there was Jack, who looked like hell and acted worse. Cat thought he hadn't slept the night before, and knew damn well something was bothering him, but when he tried to get to it, Jack told him to leave him alone.

And that was weirdest of all.

Cat glanced casually to his side and eyed Jack once more. He really looks awful sitting there with his neck crammed down in his shoulders and his throat pulsing hard. He looks like . . . I dunno. Like he's . . .

Scared.

Holy shit! What's going down here?

All Adam felt was admiration at Jack's full and complete concentration. He didn't read Jack's fear, couldn't have through the haze of his own.

Here I go at last, he thought.

Jack listened to the rest and then got them out of there and back to the suite at the Adolphus. He didn't speak during the drive and didn't answer questions. He glanced occasionally at the rest of the team while Cat relayed what had happened in the bishop's office but he looked away when they looked back.

It was a trap. And he didn't know how to tell them. He didn't know *what* to do. He didn't . . .

He didn't know.

He excused himself about the time they got down to making plans for the job in Cleburne the next morning. He couldn't think, couldn't focus, couldn't face them. He went to the bathroom and closed the door and lit a cigarette and just sat there and feared.

Three years at this. Three years and eighteen straight pits wiped clean. All of it dangerous. All of it bloody. All of it awful. And certain death hanging around all along.

But now it's not a matter of blowing up buildings in broad daylight. Now it's a matter of staying alive through the next night anywhere in the world.

Because if they know me, they can find me.

Shit.

And if they know me and find me they can set me up in Cleburne, Texas, and that's exactly what they've done and there's not one thing in the world I can do about it.

Because we still have to go. It's what we do. It's where the vampires are.

I wonder if—

There was a *tap-tap-tap* on the bathroom door and he heard Cat's voice saying it was the mayor on the phone and did Jack want to take the call? Jack frowned. Hell, he didn't even know the mayor. What was his name? Goldblatt, or something? And then he realized the mayor Cat meant. Her, that Cleburne mayor. Calling him. Knowing where to call.

He got up and dropped his cigarette in the bowl and flushed it because he didn't want the rest of them to know he was only in there to be a chickenshit and then he strolled into the main living room of the suite with all eyes on him and picked up the receiver.

"Yes?"

"Mr. Crow?" asked that same too-country voice.

"Yes."

"Mr. Crow, I hate to disturb you at home. Or at your hotel, I mean. Or do you live there?"

So. You wanna know where I live do you?

"I live here."

"Oh. Well, I should think you'd want to live with the rest of your employees. Your team, is it?"

"We all live here."

"I see."

"Miz Hughes, did you call for a reason?"

"Oh, yes. It's about your check for $50,000 . . ."

"What about it? I told you we don't work without half up front."

"Oh, I know, I know. I understand. I wasn't complaining. You'll get your check tonight as we agreed."

"Then what's the point?"

"Well, I just thought that I could bring it over instead of using a messenger."

"Okay. Come on over."

"Oh. Well, I couldn't do it right now. I've got some . . . well, some shopping to do in town first. I so rarely get to come to Dallas. But being a man I don't think you'd understand. Anyway, I just wondered if you were going to be there when I finished so I could give you the check personally."

"When would that be?"

"Oh, I don't know. About nine o'clock?"

"Hmm."

"Would that be all right?"

What Jack *wanted* to say was:

Let's get this straight, bitch. First you wanna know where we're gonna be after sundown because, while there are ghouls slaughtering your citizens in your courthouse square every night, you're gonna take the time to pick up some pantyhose?

Right.

But what he *said* was: "We'll be here," and the both of them hung up with the mayor adding how anxious she was to meet the rest of the team.

There was a mirror on the wall over the table holding the phone and Jack Crow stared at his reflection in it, stared at it good and hard until some things fell away and some others came clear to him again.

"Asshole," he whispered angrily at the face.

It was time to be a leader. So do some leader-type shit for a change, you whining bastard!

Rock and roll!

He spun around and there they all were, his team, watching and waiting and wondering what was going on.

He didn't tell them—this was his burden, godammit!

He gave them orders instead.

Get out. Get all the stuff you can carry easily and walk out of the hotel. *Don't* check out or in any way hint that you're not coming back soon. Women, take the limo.

Gents, I want you all to . . .

"Carl? What's the range on that detector? Can you put the sensor in one spot and have it ring or whatever someplace else?"

Carl shrugged. "If it's not too far."

"How about from this room to a truck parked down on the street?"

"Sure. I . . . Hey! What's going on?"

"Shaddup. Annabelle, take Davette and go to the Seven-Eleven on, I dunno, Mockingbird and Central, and get the

number of the last pay phone in the row and start calling it
after sundown every half hour. Don't stop moving except to
do that. Adam? You go with them. Make sure they call from
a different spot each time. In fact, you do the calling. Don't
let them outta the car and don't let the driver stop the motor.
You hear?''

Adam nodded. "Yessir."

"All right. Let's go, folks. Now. The rest of us have got
weapons to collect."

No one moved. Then Annabelle stood up and faced him.

"Jack, I want to know what's going on!" Her voice
sounded frightened.

Jack regarded her calmly. "I don't blame you. Get moving."

"But I . . ."

"Woman! This is not a debate! *Move!"*

They moved.

At a quarter to nine their Chevy Suburban slid silently
to the downtown curb. Cat was at the wheel. Jack sat beside
him in the front seat, the crossbow between them. In the back
seat Carl sat fiddling with his gadget.

Jack rolled his window down and began to chain-smoke
and told the others to shut the fuck up until he said otherwise.
They shut up.

At 8:54, on the dot, the detector went off like a fire bell.

Carl and Cat jumped about a foot apiece. Jack just nodded to himself, a grim smile on his face.

"What," asked Cat, staring up at the hotel, "does all
this mean?"

Jack Crow took his eyes from the building and faced him.

"Rock and roll. Same as always. Only more so. Hit it."

They made their connection at the phone outside the
Seven-Eleven. Crow told Adam where to meet them, hung
up, got back into the Suburban, and ordered Cat to drive to
the Antwar Saloon.

Cat did so. But nervously, with difficulty. For he found
it hard to take his eyes from Jack Crow, whose silently roaring
presence filled the cab.

Jack stomped through the saloon doors with Cat and Carl trailing him. He hushed the waitress who tried to bar their ascent to Felix's apartment. They found him at his desk beside the widow overlooking the bar. He had seen them coming.

Now he rose, frowning. "Look, Crow. I—"

"Cut the shit, Felix!" snapped Crow, striding toward him.

"But I—"

Jack's fist slamming onto the desktop sounded like a thunderclap. It made the lamp jump.

"I said cut the shit! There's no *time*!"

And it was suddenly very quiet. Slowly, Crow sat down in the visitor's chair. Just as slowly, Felix sat down in his own. They both lit cigarettes.

Then Jack leaned forward and told Felix what was what. In a calm, deliberate tone he explained about having to go to Cleburne, Texas, in the morning to fight vampires who not only knew they were coming but had arranged the trap just for them. Cat and Carl, standing by the door, exchanged pale glances.

"What do you mean it's a trap?" Cat interrupted.

Jack didn't bother to turn around. "Think back, Cherry. He called my name when he chased the truck."

Cat blinked, thought back, went suddenly more pale.

"My God," he whispered, almost to himself.

Felix listened without a sound, looking tight and grim and dark through the smoke, as Jack finished his monologue.

Jack was quiet for several seconds after he'd finished. Then he leaned backward in his chair and held out his hand. After a second Carl reached into a pocket and brought out a slim wooden box. Jack took the box without looking at Carl. He flipped the lid open and slid the box across the smooth desktop.

The silver bullets gleamed brightly in the light from the lamp.

"You still use a Browning nine-millimeter?" he asked gently.

Felix was staring at the bullets. He nodded. Then he

looked up at Crow. "But I don't own one," he added hopefully.

Jack smiled. He snapped his fingers above his head. Cat stepped forward carrying a canvas bag. From inside he took and unwrapped from cloth three automatics and laid them heavily on the wood-grained desktop.

Then he stepped back.

Felix stared at the guns. He rose slowly, put his hands in his pockets, and stepped over to the window and gazed blankly down. No one spoke, watching him.

"I want fifty thousand," he said after a while.

"Done."

Felix nodded, looking miserable. Then he stepped to his phone and picked up the receiver. He pushed a button. Faintly, they heard the buzz of the phone at the bar below.

"Zuhere? Felix. You'll have to take over for a couple of days. Yes. Yes . . . No, I'm fine. Fine."

Felix hung up. He stared through the window a few seconds longer. Then he lit a cigarette and put his free hand back in his pocket. When he turned back to them he said, "I meant it about the fifty grand."

Jack Crow's laugh was strong and loud and pure. He jumped to his feet and clapped his hands.

"I oughta charge you!" He stepped to the center of the room and raised his fist into the air. "Don't you feel it? You're about to go fight evil. Real live goddamned evil. The real stuff. You get to fight for the good side. How many people ever get a chance to do that?" He laughed again, strode to Felix, and shook his fist under his face. "Don't you *feel* it?"

Felix stared at him in amazement. He laughed shortly, shook his head.

Damned if I don't, he thought with astonishment. A little.

"Well, *I* do!" cried Cat from behind them. And he found himself grinning wildly. The Return of Jack Crow, he thought to himself, starring Jack Crow.

He turned to Carl.

"Rock and roll!"

Carl smiled crazily back. "Rock and roll," he echoed.

Felix peered incredulously at the other three. "I must be crazy!"

Jack laughed again. "You really think that?"

Felix didn't answer. But he really did think that. He shook his head again. This time they didn't even need that girl, he thought.

And then he thought: I wonder what her name is?

He looked at Crow & Co., still bright and vibrant and ready.

I wonder if I'll live long enough to find out?

Chapter 12

When he saw Jack Crow striding across the courthouse square—coming to get him—Felix turned and bent his head to light a cigarette and hide his screaming fear.

Crow was wearing full-length chain mail that covered everything from the soles of his boots to the top of his head with just the oval for his face left exposed. Around his waist was a thick black utility belt. Across his chest was a great white cross.

He does look like a crusader, thought Felix. Even if the chain mail was some high-tech plastic instead of steel and even if the cross was an electric halogen spotlight.

A crusader . . . I've got to get away from this man.

He had actually started to turn and walk away, when he remembered. He had taken the money. He had signed up. He was in.

They had him.

And all those periodic nightmares throughout his young life, thirty years of them, wrapped tight around his brain.

There had been no pattern to their details. Always a different setting and always a different enemy. But the endings were identical. Too many of them coming at him too fast, overwhelming him, besieging him in some claustrophobic no-exit room or with his back to some crumbling cliff or steaming quicksand or . . .

Or whatever. No way out. Too much evil. Coming too fast.

He would awake screaming with the feel of evil still ripping at his throat. And he would stay up all night drinking and trembling and trying to convince himself it was only a dream.

But he had always known better somehow. Always.

And now he looked down at his own little crusader outfit and he knew the dream had come to him at last and he knew he was going to die and he had never known such utter paralyzing terror.

He had thought he could handle it. It was his time, so what? Everybody dies, right? Right? Be cool. Stoic. That's a good word.

Stoic for shit.

He turned back to face Crow, who stopped a step away and stood and eyed him carefully.

"All set?" he asked.

Felix just stared. What the hell does he expect me to say?

Crow read the look, nodded, dropped his eyes. Then he turned and looked across the street at the shuttered building that was their target.

"Okay," said Crow, still eyeing the building, "we'll be going in in a few minutes."

He paused a moment, then looked Felix in the eye. "Right?"

Felix wanted to spit. Instead he sighed and nodded.

Crow strode over to where Joplin and Cat stood talking to the chief of police and some others on the courthouse steps.

The courthouse steps . . .

Not even a hundred yards, thought Felix. More like seventy. Or fifty.

And he turned around and around, sweeping over the empty setting where only a handful of people, most of them uniformed, remained inside the police cordon. The shops were all closed up. There was no traffic on the streets. And it was quiet.

And none of that mattered. This place still looked just like what it had always been: the safest place in the world.

Felix had spent most of his life in cities. But he had been brought up in a place just like this one and he knew what it was. It was the place the small-town world came together to buy and sell and laugh and joke and record deeds and vote and pay fines and see each other again today just like the days before and the days to come and it was *safe*, dammit! *Safe!* Maybe boring and maybe (certainly) provincial and maybe a lot of other things. But *safe* is what it was first.

Felix stared at the flagpole atop the courthouse building. As a boy he had been taught to walk toward that if he got lost from his parents while shopping. Taught to go there and go to the front steps and sit down and wait and not cry—don't worry—Mother and Daddy would soon come to find him and "you'll be safe there, son."

During the last three nights at least six people had been slaughtered there in full view of the police, dragged screaming and *pleading* into the only abandoned building by hulking drooling ghouls. Usually the monsters howled when the worthless bullets and shotgun pellets slammed into them. Sometimes they didn't. But they never stopped, except to turn and hiss, their new yellow-gray fangs glistening red in the squad cars' whirling lights.

The only policemen to go in there after them were still in there.

Felix finished his cigarette and dropped the butt onto the sidewalk and flattened it with a chain-mailed boot and then stood there bent over and staring until the last mote of glowing coal went out.

He sat in the motorhome, at the little table in the motorhome, a cigarette burning in the ashtray next to his chain-mailed elbow, an untouched plastic glass of ice tea next to that, while Cat, also in chain mail, paced clinking back and forth amid the weapons, speaking with his hands and trying to . . .

Trying to what? Felix wondered idly, as if from a great distance, suddenly realizing that he had been so preoccupied with his own sense of dread and impending doom that he had not really been listening at all. He had nodded a few times when that felt polite, but he could not imagine, quite frankly, what Cat could possibly have to say that mattered. Except . . .

Except to say they had decided to call it off.

Felix drew out of his horror just far enough to find out if that was it.

It wasn't. It was . . . Well, now, Felix wasn't absolutely sure what it was. But it seemed that Cat was trying to convince him that vampires were real so he wouldn't be shocked or something when he saw them. Something about the difference between knowing something was so in your mind and really feeling it was so in your gut.

Or something. It sounded to Felix like the standard lecture to new recruits and that was okay by him. As long as he was sitting in this motorhome getting a lecture he wasn't stepping into that building across the street. He wasn't in danger. He wasn't fighting monsters or being ripped apart by their fangs, which Felix had no trouble whatsoever believing in from his brain to his gut to his trembling fingers raising the cigarette to his lips.

So he just watched Cat pacing and talking and he looked about the trailer at the simple little meaningless items he might never see again after an hour, a bottle of scotch with the label torn, a fast-food carry-out sack, a cheap ballpoint pen with its cap all chewed up poking out of a rent in the carpet under the driver's seat, and he stared at these things, reveled in these things, rather than think about what was about to happen.

Anything but that.

I-don't-want-to-die-here he mouthed silently without realizing it.

About then Cat wrapped up his agitated presentation with a rousing clap of his hands.

"Okay?" he asked Felix excitedly.

Felix, who had no notion what the question was about, looked the other man in the eye.

"Okay," he replied dully.

Carl Joplin opened the outer door of the motorhome and stuck his head inside.

"Father Adam's ready," he said.

Cat nodded to him. "Okay," he said.

Carl nodded in return and disappeared again, closing the door behind him.

Felix looked questioningly at Cat.

"Mass," Cat explained.

Felix nodded. "Oh."

Felix believed.

He knelt in the courthouse parking lot with the others while Adam, high-mass robes covering his own chain mail, conducted the service and he believed.

In God. In Jesus. In the vampires waiting across the road. In 'most everything around him. He believed the police standing over there in that little group were not going to help them. He believed the crew standing beside their ambulance were not going to save him. He believed this was all a trap, as Jack Crow had told him.

He believed he was going to die.

He even believed in their gear. He figured the chain mail would slow 'em down. A little. And he believed Holy Blessed silver bullets might slow 'em down. A little. And when Carl had ringed the buildings with his little detectors and turned them on, Felix believed the instant clanging alarm was, in fact, caused by the presence of vampires within the building. He believed his radio headset would enable Carl Joplin to hear his death shrieks.

He even believed in the Plan. At least, that it was a good Plan. And he turned his unseeing eyes away from the young priest and focused once more on the electric winch with its huge spool of cable and decided once again that Jack had had an inspired idea here.

Forbidden by the city powers to destroy a downtown building with explosives, which is what he would have preferred, Jack Crow had given up on the idea of trying to kill the goons while they were in the building itself. Too dark in there. Too many teeth. Too much to go wrong too fast.

No. Jack's plan was to get them outside, where the sunlight would do the work, and that's where the winch came in. Jack was going to fire that massive crossbow through a ghoul's chest, wait a second for the barbs to get lodged tight, then holler on the radio for Carl Joplin to start the winch pulling that long cable attached to the crossbow bolt, and with it the ghoul, right through the front doors of the building into the sunlight to burn.

Then Adam was to grab the cable and bring it back inside to attach it to another one of Jack's bolts. It was Cat's job to keep the monsters off Jack in the meantime. Felix was supposed to back up Cat.

Felix believed it was a good Plan.

He didn't believe it was going to work.

And he caught himself mouthing those words again.

Then the mass was over. They stood. It was time.

"Rock and roll!" barked Jack fiercely.

Felix stared at him. Then he took his position beside the others. He took several deep breaths, heard the others do the same. There was a brief distraction when some new cop type, a young redheaded man wearing a different kind of uniform, appeared beside the other cops and began arguing loudly with them.

Too late, thought Felix. Nothing that could be said or argued or written out or screamed was going to stop this thing.

Jack gave the signal and the four men stepped through the doorway into the dark.

Cooler in here, he thought before the stench hit him and he thought God—my God, what *is* that awful . . . Oh my God is that them? Is that the vampires? And he started to reach down and turn on the halogen cross so he could *see*, see what was making that awful smell, but then he remembered they weren't supposed to turn on their crosses because that would drive the monsters back and they wanted them coming, coming *at them*, for chrissakes, and Felix thought of that idea and wondered if Jack Crow was completely and totally insane— Let's get the hell *out* of here!

And then the lanterns came on beside him, one in Jack's

hand and one in Adam's. Jack moved off to the right to place his and Felix heard his hard voice calmly instructing the priest to place his lantern farther to the left to give a wider range of view and everything seemed to be whizzing around Felix, his ears thumping and throbbing with his pulse and the slightest sound amplified in that cavernous dusty cement floor with the walls all torn out before remodeling and only the fifty-year-old support posts left spaced every dozen paces like a checkerboard and . . . Oh, yes! There in the dust in front of him he saw the sliding footprints going this way and that and crossing back over one another.

Oh, yeah. Somebody's been walking around in here. A lot of somebodies. A lot of somethings . . .

Damn-damn-damn, he couldn't seem to get set, couldn't seem to get placed, like he was always leaning backward ready to run but he wasn't going to run, was he? So why not just get set and placed or at least reach down and get your weapon in your hand . . .?

But he couldn't even do that. He knew he was wearing guns but he couldn't remember exactly where they were on his body and the notion of taking his eyes off the shadows for even a split second to find them, and having some fiend bolt at him slavering from out of the dark while he was looking down . . .

No. He couldn't move.

He was frozen, staring wildly into the darkness, gasping dry-mouthed and waiting to die.

Then BEEP . . . and Felix jumped a foot in the air before he remembered it was the vampire detector Joplin had given them to take inside. The others had bells on them but Joplin had converted this one to have one of those smug little electronic BEEPS . . .

"Cat!" growled Crow harshly in Felix's headset. "Turn that down."

"Right, bwana" was the calm reply and in the corner of one eye Felix saw the blond silhouette in the right-side lantern bend to work the controls.

BEEP!

"More, dammit!" snarled Crow.

" 'More' it is," replied Cat in the same tone.

Beep . . . Beep . . . Beep . . .

"How's that?" asked Cat.

"It's okay," said Crow.

Beep . . . Beep . . . Beep . . .

Felix hated it.

Beep . . . Beep . . . Beep . . .

Felix hated it because he knew what it meant.

Beep. Beep. Beep.

The faster it beeped the closer came those . . .

Beep Beep Beep Beep Beep Beep

"Okay, sports fans," whispered Cat, peering into the darkness directly in front of him, "here we go."

She was fresh from the grave and slivers of skin peeled and curled at the corners of eyes glowing a red so bloody and deep they seemed almost black. Not yet a full vampire, but no longer a corpse—and totally unaware of self. She was no longer a she either, Felix knew. She was just a thirst-thing and he could by God *feel* her smelling the blood pulsing in their veins. And she *came* at them, came at them and it seemed she moved so damned *fast* though he knew it was just a lurching, dragging, walk.

Beep. Beep. Beep. Beep.

"Cat," ordered Jack calmly, stepping in front of her and raising his crossbow, "shut that damned thing off."

"Yes, bwana," replied Cat serenely and in a moment all was quiet.

Except for the sound of the creature dragging itself on grave-rotted feet toward Jack.

And then the deep THONG of the crossbow and the awful punching crunch as the massive arrow split the woman's chest cavity and cracked out her back.

The impact drove her backward several feet, arms flung outstretched, but somehow she remained upright.

Felix stared in horror. My God! The damn thing splitting her is as big as she is and it didn't even knock her down!

And for just an instant some deep adult in him was outraged, offended at such defiance. And he saw himself drawing and firing and plunging silver bullets into her throat—

But he couldn't move. He was gone. He couldn't handle this.

He just stood and stared and trembled as the woman thirst-thing reacted to the agony of impalement with maniacal frenzy, her eyes bugging, her mouth barking shrieks and howls, her vile matted hair whipping thin cuts into her moldering cheeks. Something oozed thickly from the wound. But even in the uncertain light Felix could tell it wasn't blood. The only blood came from the red flecks that spat forth from the howling, crumpled mouth.

"Hit it, Carl," ordered Jack into his radio headset.

The cable attached to the arrow went instantly taut. The woman, still howling and warping in pain, fell forward onto the dusty cement as the cable began to drag her writhing toward the exit. She didn't want to go. She fought the shaft of the huge arrow, she scratched sparks on the concrete floor. She howled and spat some more. But she went.

"Adam," chided Crow gently, "you want to get the door now?"

The young priest unfroze himself from the sight, nodded, and all but tripped over himself in his hurry to obey.

She went to something beyond hideous when the sunlight struck her. Felix had never heard anything like those screams, had never seen anything like that blurred, vibrating frenzy.

And that fire, those bursting flames that erupted from deep inside her skin as if they were being blown outward by some fierce vindicatory pressure. The flames didn't look real. They looked like dozens of tiny acetylene torches rocketing out of her.

The cable was relentless as it dragged her through the double doors of the building, across the sidewalk, and into the street. Felix hadn't realized he was following her until he saw the others closing in to stare.

They were all there. The cops. The local powers. That mayor, Tammy Something, was there. They had left their police barricades and their whispering cliques and everything else and rushed forward to stare.

The screams abruptly ceased, so suddenly it made everyone jump. And then the flame itself began to shrink, as if curling its fuel into a little circle. The thing in the flame was no longer recognizable as anything but a roaring blue-and-white fire. There came a loud hissing sound, as though gas was escaping.

Then sparks. Then a loud POP.

Then the flame was gone. Everything was gone save for a foot-wide circle of ashes.

And still nobody moved. They just stared.

"Supernatural," said Jack Crow gently from just behind Felix.

Felix turned and looked at him.

Crow was smiling grimly. "Supernatural," he said again in the same gentle tone. "Super natural. Not of this earth." He stepped over to the circle of ashes and looked down. "Evil. Satanic." He looked at Felix, then kicked the ashes with his boot. "Damned, Felix. Big Time Evil." He kicked at the ashes again. They were extremely fine and they scattered easily in the soft breeze. Crow lit a cigarette and stared some more at Felix before speaking in that same easy tone:

"But we can kill 'em, Felix. We *can* kill 'em. We just killed this one and we're about to go back in there and kill the rest." Crow looked past Felix. "Right, people?" he called.

"Right, bwana!" "Yes, *sir*!" "Hell, yes!" sang out from behind Felix, from Cat, Adam, and Carl Joplin respectively.

Felix turned around to see them all watching him just as: "Go get 'em!" sounded out from an unknown source.

It was the redhead Felix had noticed earlier arguing with the other policemen, the one wearing a different type of uniform. He stood there holding his fist in the air like a cheerleader.

Team Crow stared blankly at him. They were used to being alone. The last thing in the world they expected was local support. The redhead took their stares as hostility—or worse, scorn. His face turned as red as his hair.

Jack saved him. "Who the hell are you?"

The redhead pulled himself up straight. "Deputy Kirk Thompson, sir."

Crow smiled. The kid—he couldn't have been over

twenty-five—had managed to give the impression he had saluted without actually doing it.

"Who called the sheriff's department?" asked Crow.

The deputy seemed confused. "No one had to, sir. This courthouse is our headquarters. Nobody called the sheriff," he added meaningfully, looking around at the locals who were watching. "And I think he's going to want to know why when he comes back."

Jack grinned. "Could be. Hang around, deputy. We'll talk later."

"Yes, sir. Is there anything I can do now?"

Jack frowned. Where was this kid yesterday so he would at least have had a chance to train him? Or get him some chain mail anyway. No. He might need him after all, short-handed as they were. But stupid, criminal, to risk him now.

He shook his head. "Not right now," he told the deputy. "Though I'd appreciate it if you'd stick close to Carl there." And he gestured toward Joplin, who still stood beside his winch.

"Yeah, come over here, deputy," said Joplin with a knowing look to Crow. "We'll talk a bit."

Crow started back to his team but stopped. The spectators, the policemen, and the mayor's people were still standing there watching. Some still hadn't taken their eyes off the pile of ashes at Jack's feet. Some looked a little stunned. The mayor's party looked scared.

Scared we'll lose or scared we'll win? he wondered to himself.

But he had no time for them.

"Something I can do for you?" he asked harshly.

No one replied or even met his eyes. Instead they faded back to the sidewalk across the street under the courthouse. The policemen went back to their barricades, looking uncertain and uneasy.

Crow felt the urge to go talk to those cops, to find out what the mayor had told them, to get them on his side, to . . .

But his team was waiting. This was no time to take a time out and have them lose their edge. He picked up another arrow for the crossbow and joined Cat, Adam, and Felix, who stood by the curb in front of the target.

"Okay, people," he said, kneeling down to arm his weapon, "huddle up."

And so he set about firing them up to go in again. He made his voice strong and confident and, as always, sounding that way to others made it seem that way to himself. He made a change in the Plan. They were originally supposed to wait inside while Adam fetched out another cable and loaded crossbow, but Felix had led them all outside, staring at the dying monster. Crow made a joke about Felix changing the schedule, but while the others smiled, Felix didn't even seem to get it.

Felix didn't seem to be getting much of anything, come to think of it. And while Crow sounded strong and confident for the others and himself, a gnawing fear tried to grow in him that Felix wasn't going to cut it. He was just going to stand there in a petrified daze and if something went wrong and they needed his gun . . . Or worse, somebody would have to save him and while they were worrying about Felix they wouldn't be worrying about themselves and . . .

No, dammit! No! Felix will come out of it. Felix will come through. He will. He will. After a couple of kills, after he sees the fiends aren't invincible, he'll be all right. He will. He *will!*

He must.

And with that Jack Crow stopped worrying about it and concentrated instead on psyching everyone else up. He did a good job. By the time they re-entered the building and got set up between their lanterns and had the detector going Beep-Beep-Beep again, they were ready. And by the time the second goon appeared, a spindly middle-aged man with his throat still jaggedly gashed from his murder, Crow just knew they could pull this off.

And at first it was just the little things that started to go wrong.

Chapter 13

First the cable to the crossbow fouled. Jack had just lifted the weapon and prepared to fire when he realized he had no slack. He called Joplin on the radio to find the trouble and then stood there with the others, waiting for a reply, as the second fiend lumbered slowly toward them.

It had almost reached the left lantern when Joplin called back that he knew where the trouble was, that the cable had snagged in the doorjamb, that he would have to open the door to fix it. Jack sighed and cursed, then ordered the others back to the doorway.

He had to call Felix's name twice. The man seemed to be mesmerized by the sight of the ragged tissue on the goon's neck.

So they all faded back to the door and stood there, intermittently blinded by periodic bursts of harsh Texas sunlight, as Joplin fiddled with the door.

The repair took five minutes.

It made sense to keep the detector on, standing there blind as they were. But it was unlikely anything would attack them in that glare of sunlight either. And by the time the detector had gone from BEEP-BEEP-BEEP to beep . . . beep . . . beep, showing the second monster had retreated, Jack couldn't stand that sound anymore. He reached over to the machine in Cat's hands and snapped it off with an angry flourish.

"All set," announced Joplin, sticking his head inside.

"Good news," replied Cat wryly. "Now maybe you can fix this."

And he held up the detector to show where Jack had broken the switch off.

So they had to stand there blind some more while Joplin, wearing a miner's light on his head, replaced the toggle switch with a paper clip and wire.

That took another five minutes.

Jack was not in a good mood by the time they had resumed their stations behind the two lanterns. The delays had lost them their stride. His team looked jumpy—except for Felix, who looked paralyzed—and he wasn't feeling so hot either.

And he couldn't *stand* that goddamned beeping.

But the detector was doing its job. The beeps got closer and closer just as before, and when they reached the previous interval, the goon reappeared, this time from the right side. Cat's side.

"Okay, people," ordered Jack, lifting the crossbow, "get set."

It was about then that the right-side lantern began to flicker.

"Shit!" hissed Jack and he lowered the crossbow and stared with the rest of the team as the light blinked on and off. The only movement was from the goon. It was now only twenty feet away. And coming steadily.

Jack didn't know what to do. He didn't want to fight in the dark. But he didn't want to have to start everything up again. And besides, dammit, this was just a little short one!

"Cat!" he barked angrily. "Fix that light!"

Cat, whose mechanical ineptitude was legendary, just stared back and said, "How?"

"I don't know, dammit! Fiddle with it."

Cat hesitated. The goon was now only fifteen feet away.

"And hurry!" snarled Jack.

Cat nodded. "Right!" And he rushed forward and bent down over the flickering lantern.

"Well?" demanded Crow a few seconds later. The goon

was now only a dozen feet—six shuffling steps—away. And whenever the lamp would flicker, it would seem to disappear completely. It was unnerving.

"Well?" repeated Jack, louder than before.

"I don't believe it," replied Cat excitedly.

"What?" cried Jack, concerned.

"I think I can fix it!"

"Huh?" replied Jack dully, still staring at the shuffling monster coming closer.

"I really think I can. It's just the bulb, I think."

The goon was now less than ten feet away. Only it didn't really seem to be moving toward Cat. More toward Jack, who stood in the center of the formation.

But no. Too tight. Too close.

"Cat! Bring the light over here and fix it."

"No. Just a sec. I've got it."

"Cat! Get over here!"

"Would you shut up a minute? I know I can . . . Yeah. Here. I've got it!"

And the lantern went completely dark.

"Cat!"

No answer.

"Cat! What are you doing?" yelled Adam, who had managed to be quiet until now.

But still, no answer.

"Adam! Hit your chest lamp. That'll . . ."

"That'll drive 'em away, bwana!" snapped Cat, sounding irritated.

"Cat!" yelled Crow, relieved. "Come on . . ."

"Quiet, dammit! I've got it fixed. Here!"

And the light came on and the monster's gnarled hand closed on Cat's throat and the gray teeth came flashing down and Cat yelled, "Jesus!" and tried to pull away but the monster had him and Jack jerked the crossbow into aim and fired from the hip and the great arrow cracked into its chest and it shrieked and vibrated and jolted into the air but *it still held Cat*, who flopped and jounced about in its grip like a rag doll and Jack called out for Adam and Felix to come and help because he knew Cat would never survive that pounding.

Adam was already on his way, rushing forward with his pike in his hand, calling out, "Cat! Cat!" But he never made it. He was only a few strides away when the monster leapt and howled once more and the long cable warped through the air like a jump rope and cracked Adam full force on his left temple, spinning him upside down through the air and smashing him hard onto the dusty cement.

Jack saw Adam move out of the corner of his eye and knew he was all right, just stunned, but that didn't matter now. Adam couldn't help them.

"Felix!" cried Jack. "Felix!"

But Felix just stood there unmoving, staring at the sight, not even acknowledging Jack's voice.

When Jack reached them, Cat was barely conscious. He doubted the vampire was even aware of its prey as it lurched and cried in the agony of impalement. But it still held Cat, tossing him this way and that in its pain. Jack had no idea how to get Cat loose.

He took a deep breath and threw himself forward, tackling them both to the floor.

It made it worse. The vampire might have forgotten it held Cat, but it sure as hell noticed Jack. It hissed and spat and struck fangs at him like a snake. Only Cat's grip on its jagged throat kept the gray teeth from Jack's face. And when one of the gnarled hands loosed itself from Cat to grab at him, Jack had about half a second of triumph before he felt that awesome vise-grip on his arm. And he punched and kicked at the monster to free himself but he was as helpless as Cat, who, crazily, still held on to the light.

"Felix!" hollered Jack desperately. "FELIX!" as the three of them bounced and crashed and hissed and punched, with the lantern throwing shadows through the dust.

There was a sharp tug as the winch came on and began to drag them toward the doorway. At first Jack was delighted—the sunlight would kill it—and then he remembered *how* it would die and how hot those flames would be.

"No!" he cried into his headset. "Carl! Turn it off! You'll burn us alive!"

The cable went immediately slack.

"Felix!" cried Jack desperately. "FELIX!"

The monster began twisting and spitting at them again.

"Cat!" yelled Crow. "Drop that damn light!"

"Huh?" muttered Cat. Then: "Oh . . . yeah!"

And he finally released the lantern so he could use both hands and the light bounced and clanked loudly on the cement and began to roll away from them, over and over, spilling light into the dust, before it was kicked back toward them by the shoe of a six-foot-four-inch black man who had been killed while working the graveyard shift at the Texaco station.

The man still wore his uniform. It still bore his name, "Roy," on the little patch above his left breast pocket.

But he didn't care. He didn't care what he wore. He didn't care that he was "Roy." He cared only for the smell of living, pumping blood.

The half dozen others looming behind him out of the darkness felt the same way.

The first man to see the horde appear was Adam, sprawled stunned and bleeding on the edge of the light from the other lantern. Still unable to do much more than stumble, he could only moan, "Sweet blessed Jesus! Jack! Look out!"

Jack saw them. He saw—what was it?—six, seven, eight of them? Coming for them, shuffling at them and he couldn't get loose from this little squirt he had already *shot*, much less save Cat, much less do anything about the others.

"FELIX!!" he screamed and then, in his panic, went into a frenzy of his own.

He grabbed one end of the huge arrow already piercing the monster and began to work it fiercely back and forth in the wound. The monster howled and spat and writhed some more and its gnarled hands began clutching and opening spasmodically and during one of the openings Cat came loose for just a second and Jack kicked his friend brutally to safety with a chain-mailed boot to the chest.

But it still had him, the little spitting fiend still had him and he could see the others shuffling closer, could hear the sound of their dry dead feet in the dust, could almost *feel* their gnarled hands and gray fangs . . .

"FELIXGODDAMMIT!" he wailed and grabbed the little monster and rolled over and over and flung it, with every ounce of fear he had, away from him.

There was the sound of chain mail popping, fabric and flesh ripping, and Jack Crow was free.

When he lurched triumphantly to his feet, Roy was there, face to rotting face. Roy hissed. His great black hands closed on Jack's throat.

Jack was helpless and knew it and he hit the switch for his chest cross and the halogen light was blinding to both of them and painful to the vampire. It arched and shrieked from the agony of the cross of light, steam already rising from the surface of its dead skin.

It saved Jack's life when it threw the light, and Jack, away from its body.

Jack smacked the concrete floor chest first and the halogen bulbs exploded into dusty darkness beneath him and suddenly all was as it had been only he had no light and no hope and Felix *would not move* and that's when Deputy Kirk Thompson, terrified by the sounds he had heard on Joplin's radio, burst into the cavernous darkness with his .44 magnum in hand.

He took one incredulous look then, pure hero type, braced his feet wide, supported his right, shooting, hand with his left, and began to fire. He was a sharpshooter. His first two hollowpoints struck Roy full in the chest. The next one struck the little impaled one, the thrashing one, in the left side of the head. The third shot blew a hole in the shoulder of an old woman, already lame, who had managed to drag herself within one more step of Adam without the young priest having yet seen her.

It was excellent shooting. The shots were dead-on accurate, spaced no more than a half second apart, and worthless against the undead.

They did have some effect. The vampires roared and

jerked, the old woman after Adam was flung back briefly out of range, all eyes were turned to the deputy . . .

All eyes . . . Felix's eyes . .

My God, thought Jack, staring at his gunman, he made a move!

And then Team Crow saw him start to draw.

Chapter 14

Felix's first two shots, like the deputy's, struck Roy. But while Kirk's hit Roy's chest, Felix's slammed into his forehead. And while Kirk's were .44 magnum hollowpoints, they were only lead. Felix's were nine-millimeter silver blessed by the Vicar of Christ on Earth and they tore half-inch-wide holes through the skull. Roy shrieked and smacked his hands over the wounds and fell writhing to the cement.

But Felix didn't see this. By the time Roy had fallen, Felix had already shot the old woman behind Adam twice, in the throat and the chest, had shot the small one on the crossbow once, in the stomach, and had put one shot each in the next three ghouls to emerge from the shadows: a high school teacher still wearing his shattered glasses, a middle-aged mother of three reported missing for two weeks, and a young drug dealer who waited too late one night to make a buy.

They were goons, still. All of them. Too recently dead to have thoughts or ideas or notions or sense of self. But they had always known hunger.

And now they remembered pain.

Searing, irredeemable agony shot through their wounds, wounds that would never heal. For a moment, the monsters forgot their prey, forgot the smell of blood, forgot their thirst. They thought only of the pain.

Felix strode forward during that instant, ejecting the clip with his right hand and snapping in a second with his left.

125

Then he worked a cartridge into the chamber, making all three actions appear, somehow, to be a single motion.

Like a robot, thought Cat at the time. Like a machine.

Felix paused in the center of the area lit by the two lanterns and briefly surveyed the tormented creatures surrounding him. Then he shot them some more. When the second clip was emptied and the third had replaced it, he stepped over to Cat.

"Are you all right?" he asked, his voice calm and unhurried.

And oddly kind, thought Cat, staring into those dead eyes.

Cat nodded.

"Can you get up and move?" asked Felix in the same tone.

Cat nodded again.

"Then let's do it," suggested the gunman, holding out a hand to help. "Let's get out of here."

Cat took the hand and pulled himself up. He still felt wobbly after the pounding he had taken. But he was all right. Beside them Adam, who had been following it all, was also rising. The wound at his temple had stopped bleeding.

"C'mon, everybody," called Felix in Jack's direction. "Let's move."

Then he started firing again and for the next few seconds there were only the explosive sounds from his weapon and the raucous misery of his victims. The goons who had managed to drag themselves upright after the first two volleys were sent back to the floor, screaming and writhing and pounding at their wounds.

None approached the Team and only one other appeared from the shadows, a middle-aged man wearing farmer's overalls and a jagged gash from his left ear to left shoulder.

Felix shot him three times, twice in the chest, once in the head. He fell shrieking to the floor like the rest.

Jack, staring as transfixed as the others at this incredible display of cool destruction, managed to gather himself and everyone else up and get them toward the door while Felix guarded their rear, emptying clip after clip into the monsters.

"Okay, Felix!" he called as the door came open and the sunlight flooded the chamber. "Come along."

Felix was in the middle of reloading. He paused, looked at his boss, nodded, and trotted toward the sunlight.

A few seconds later all of them, Jack, Cat, Adam, Felix, and the young deputy were standing in the sunlight beside Carl's winch. And amazingly, none were seriously hurt.

Incredible, thought Jack. Five minutes ago I thought we were *all* dead. And then, like everyone else, he just stood and stared at the gunman for a while.

Felix didn't seem to notice. He sat down on a curb and lit a cigarette and stared at a spot on the street between his feet.

Carl watched them watching Felix awhile.

"What happened?" he asked at last.

Jack looked at him, thought a minute. "Silver bullets," he replied.

Carl smiled. "They worked?"

Cat nodded toward Felix. "They worked for him."

"Did they kill 'em?" asked Carl excitedly.

The gunman surprised them all by answering.

"No," he replied firmly, looking at Carl. "They didn't kill them."

"Well, no," conceded Jack after a moment. "But they sure as shit got their attention."

And everyone who had been there laughed.

Except Felix.

"It *hurts* them, Carl," added Adam excitedly. "It really *hurts* them!"

"It sure did that," added the deputy, shaking his head and putting his own pistol back in its holster.

"That reminds me," said Jack Crow, "thanks, deputy. What's your name again?"

"Kirk Thompson. Only I didn't do much."

Cat smiled. "We'll get you some silver bullets."

Kirk looked at the others. "Are they silver? Really silver?"

"Blessed by Holy Mother Church," replied Adam.

"Reckon I could use some at that," smiled the deputy.

"We could all use 'em," Jack Crow said brusquely, "and we all will." He lit a cigarette and announced a decision. "Carl, get everybody that goes inside a gun with silver bullets. And you, Adam, are gonna tote the extra crossbow if you're still sure you can handle one."

"I'd be happy to demonstrate," offered the priest confidently.

Jack gave him a wry smile. "I'll take your word for it, padre." Then he turned to the others. "This is the new deal: Cat, you're on the far right to do the detecting. Adam, you stand inside Cat next to me with the other crossbow. Then it'll be me and then Felix on my left. Cat, you tell us when they're coming, Felix'll hold 'em off until I can shoot one, with Adam backing me up. Then we go straight out the door, with Felix holding the rest of 'em off until we can get to the sunlight. Nobody else shoots unless Felix or I tells them to."

He looked at the gunman, still sitting on the curb staring between his boots.

"That okay with you, Felix?"

Felix looked at him, nodded dully. "I'd like some more light," he said calmly.

"We got more light, Carl?"

"I think there's one or two in the motorhome. I'll have to look."

Jack shook his head. "We'll look. C'mon, Felix, let's . . . Hey! Hit the winch."

All turned and followed Jack's gaze to the cable running from the winch to the warehouse door.

"It's stopped moving!" noticed Carl.

Jack tossed his cigarette angrily to the street. "Hell, yes, it's stopped moving. Did you expect the damn thing to stay caught forever while we stood around yappin'?"

But it hadn't gotten loose. Carl's winch dragged out the crossbow bolt still tangled in the monster's clothing. But the monster was dust.

"We killed it!" cried Cat, amazed. "Indoors! Without sunlight!"

"Yeah," muttered Jack.

"I don't understand," said the deputy. "You've never done this before? In the movies, they always . . ."

"Forget the movies," growled Jack. "They don't change into bats or wolves, either."

"But stakes *do* kill them," offered Adam.

"Yeah," replied Jack, lighting another cigarette. He walked over and shifted the dusty clothes with a chain-mailed boot. "You know, we *knew* the stakes hurt 'em. I guess we just never managed to keep one on one long enough. Before, they always tore loose if we didn't get 'em out and burning pretty quick."

"That," suggested Cat with a smile toward Felix, "was before the Lone Ranger, here."

Felix eyed him blankly. "Could be," he said at last.

Jack laughed. "Damn well 'could be,' gunman. Those bullets keep 'em too miserable to get loose until it's too late." He walked a fast circle around the dusty clothes, surveying them from all sides. Then he stopped and stared at the locals, still too scared to approach.

"Ha!" he said at last, clapping his hands together and smiling. "C'mon, Felix! Let's see about your light."

"Hey, Cat," snarled Carl suddenly, reaching down for the first-aid kit at his feet, "did you know you and the padre are bleeding?"

Cat grinned. "We *assumed* so. We were so popular."

"All right, dammit!" snarled Carl after he had tended their minor wounds, "what the hell happened in there?"

Cat and Adam exchanged a look. "Well," began Cat, "first Felix froze."

And then they told Carl about Cat fixing the light and about the little fiend wrapping him up and about Adam getting whipped by the cable and then about Jack getting Cat loose just in time for the wave of ghouls and then Kirk came in and . . .

"And then Felix saved us," he added with a smile. "And here we are."

Carl snarled. "I thought you said Felix froze."

Cat shrugged. "He unfroze."

"And that's all it took?"

"You should have seen him."

"Pretty good?"

Cat looked at him. "More than 'pretty good.' You ever see a spaghetti western?"

"That good?"

Cat and Adam exchanged another look. "Better," they replied in unison.

Carl lit a cigarette and looked at them thoughtfully. "Fast draw?"

Adam shook his head. "More like a fast *shot*."

Cat nodded. "Like a goddamn machine gun."

"Hmm," muttered Carl to himself. "Did he aim?"

Cat stared at him. "Did he what?"

Adam spoke up. "I know what Carl means. No. He didn't. He just sort of . . . pointed?"

Carl grinned and nodded. "I knew it! Only uses one hand, too, right?"

Adam nodded.

Carl laughed. "I knew it," he repeated. "It's why he uses that tiny gun. It's the heaviest thing he can use with one hand." He stood and carried the first-aid kit back to his chair by the winch controls. "We got ourselves a gunman."

Jack Crow hadn't given a damn about the light. He had just wanted to get Felix alone. Oh, he went through the motions, finding two lanterns in their storage chest in the motorhome's bedroom. And he made sure they both worked, replacing the battery in one.

And then he got ready to talk.

Only, sitting there at the table with Felix blankly across from him, he didn't really know what to say. Or ask.

Finally, "You all right?" he blurted, too loudly.

Felix didn't startle. He just raised his eyes and looked at him.

"I mean," Jack amended, "are you ready to go back in?"

Felix's voice was soft. "Sure."

Jack still wasn't satisfied. "What woke you up in there?"

Felix thought a moment. "I'm not sure. The deputy's gun, I think."

And they were quiet for a while.

"Think it'll happen to you again?" asked Crow gently.

Felix's smile was so sad it hurt Jack to look at it as he said, "No. That part's over."

"Okay," replied Jack gruffly. Because he didn't know what else to say.

Chapter 15

At the last minute they decided to go with flares instead of more lanterns. Lanterns were a more steady light, but they couldn't figure out a safe way to carry them as far into the darkness as Felix wanted.

Only they didn't have any flares and they weren't at all sure the local cops would give them any.

Deputy Kirk Thompson was sure.

"*I'll* get your flares," he said ominously and walked over to a patrol car.

They couldn't hear what he said to them. But they got the tone.

And they got their flares. The deputy had three dozen delivered to them within five minutes.

"So," said Jack Crow as they assembled before the warehouse once more. "We're all set. Rock and roll!"

And as he led the Team inside he thought: Please, Felix! Don't fold on us again!

He didn't. Felix was, if anything, more impressive the second time. He was cool and calm and deadly accurate, and the closest monster to them was the one Jack picked to crossbow, Roy.

Roy was as big and strong as he looked. But not as strong as the winch. Not with Felix continually, mercilessly, shooting him. By the time he'd been dragged to the sunlight, Roy had forgotten all about the stake through his chest. And then it was too late.

They waited five minutes and went in again and got another, as easily as the last. Then they did it again. And again and again and again. The crowd watching them began to grow as their success continued, some of the policemen going so far as to actually stand just behind Carl's winch to watch.

Carl ignored them. So did the others.

They always followed the same procedure. Jack led them in, then they fanned out on either side of him into position. Felix would light a flare, toss it way into the shadows at the edge of their lanterns, and begin to shoot everything that moved but the one Jack had picked to stake. After Jack made his shot, the others would fade back toward the door while Felix kept the rest at bay. They would all exit with the burning vampire. Then a sip of something cool, a quick puff on a cigarette, and back they'd go.

And then the vampires began to change.

There were only a handful left, most of them shot several times, and they weren't moving much. Some weren't even on their feet. Not dead, not nearly dead, but hurting.

And waking up.

It was the pain, decided Adam. The pain was shocking them back into consciousness after the zombie-limbo of death. Whatever, they were no longer the same. And their eyes were no longer just the blank thirst-stare. They were alert. And angry.

They found this out on their sixth trip inside the building. It started off just like the other times, Crow in first, followed by the others fanning to either side of him. There were no goons in sight, which wasn't especially unusual. But Cat's detector showed nothing approaching and that was strange.

Felix tossed a flare anyway, flinging it with a long side arm to avoid the low ceiling.

It landed on a vampire.

It was a young woman in her early thirties. She was wearing boots, blue jeans, and a black sweatshirt advertising "Z Z Top's North American Tour." Felix remembered that sweatshirt. He had put at least three silver bullets through it that day.

The woman had been lying there in the dust, unmoving, when the flare landed on her chest. She sprang to her feet, yelping and brushing wildly at the flame flickering from her sweatshirt. Then, once she was free of the fire, she stopped.

And looked at them.

And then she felt the bullet holes in her chest.

And then she looked right at Felix. Right *at* the gunman.

And then she let out an awful screaking cry, like a satanic infant's tantrum, and ran straight at Felix, the source of her anguish.

Felix shot her twice more, without thinking. Both bullets struck her high in the chest, flipping her over backward. After she hit, she lay still.

"Good Lord," whispered Cat harshly, "I think you killed her!"

"Does anybody remember how many shots it took?" asked Adam. "Felix?"

"Hold it, goddammit! Cat! Anything else coming?"

Cat bent over his detector. "Not yet," he replied.

"Okay, then," Jack announced. "We can afford to wait a bit to see if she's really . . ."

She wasn't. The second wailing was even worse than the first. And her scrambling headlong charge for the gunman was even quicker. Felix's startled third shot was from the hip. It struck her in the left thigh and she cartwheeled forward onto her shoulder . . .

Then leapt back to her feet and came at him again, right at him, shrieking that shriek, and bounding on that shattered left thigh.

Their eyes had met before Felix managed to shoot her again, this time in the exact center of her pulsing throat.

She slammed backward into the dust, writhing and flinging that mad baby's cry all around her.

Jack made a quick decision. He stepped over in front of Felix and raised the crossbow.

"That tears it," he barked gruffly. "We're taking this one."

And they did. When next she rose, Jack's crossbow almost folded her in half.

But it held and the cable held and a few seconds later they were watching her burn just as all the rest had.

No one moved after the fire was out. They just stood there.

"She knew you," Cat said at last, looking at Felix. "She knew you were the one who'd hurt her."

Felix took a long puff on his cigarette, nodded.

"Yes," added Adam. "They are definitely waking up."

"Let 'em," snarled Jack Crow. He fixed the Team with a frosty stare. "It's too late for 'em. We just stay a little tighter, work a little faster, be a little more careful. We still got 'em."

They were right. From then on, every ghoul Felix had previously shot would scream that insane wail and rush him as soon as they saw him. There was no doubt they recognized him. No doubt they hated him.

But Jack Crow was also right. It was too late. The system worked. It worked on zombies or vampires or any combination of the two. Felix's shooting was too quick. Jack's crossbow was too accurate.

The only trouble spot came toward the end. They were getting tired, with some four hours at it by then, and due for a mistake. The mistake was Felix's, and it was a beaut: he dropped his gun during a charge.

First he slipped, in that awfully gooey stuff the monsters used for blood. It was a clear, viscous, odorless mucus that had been pouring from the wounds onto the cement and Felix made the mistake of stepping in it as he spun to shoot the third of the trio, which had rushed screaming out of the flare's light toward them. When he went down, Felix's right hand went out instinctively to catch himself and it went into another puddle of the junk and the pistol squirted out of his grip like a bar of soap.

Jack had already made his shot, the vampire already wriggling on the huge arrow, when it happened. He frantically fished for the pistol on his belt. Cat did the same and had actually managed to draw his pistol before Adam, calm and cool, stepped forward and fired his crossbow through the last monster's chest. It dropped like meat on a spit.

Seconds later they were out watching another fire while Carl toweled the clinging mess from Felix's hand and gun and everyone else exchanged proud grins with the young priest. It had been his only chance for action in hours and he had been flawless.

They felt good.

Nothing else even slowed them down. And only one thing actually frightened them again: going down into the basement.

The detectors said there were no more inside. Jack Crow believed them. They had already killed twenty-four and that was something like the third highest number Jack had ever seen in one place.

But they were still going to have to go down there and see for themselves.

And while they were sitting there trying to figure out the best way of going about it an old man wearing a faded pastor's collar started across the street toward them. They had noticed him before and ignored him. Just another one of the local biggies come to oversee.

But as he got closer, they could tell this was no bigshot. The knees to his slacks were worn through. The lining of his jacket was hanging loose on one side. And he looked like he hadn't shaved that white beard in a week.

He began to walk faster and faster as he approached them. He was carrying a piece of pipe in one hand, holding it in front of him like an offering. Jack had stood up to introduce himself, had even stuck out his hand to be shaken, in fact, when the old man swung the pipe at his head.

Jack half ducked but the pipe still banged him good on his left shoulder before glancing hard against his ear. Blood splattered from his ear and he reeled from the stunning ringing in his head and if he'd been alone the old man might have finished him off.

But he wasn't alone. The old man was down hard on the street with the deputy handcuffing him within three seconds. The next minutes were spent bandaging up Jack's ear and screaming at the local cops for an explanation as to just who in the hell let this crazy old fart *in* here, anyway?

That's just Old Vic, they were told.

Who?

Old Vic Jennings. He's just a crazy old coot lives down there by the railroad tracks. He's an Englishman. Uh, ya'll don't wanna press charges or nothing, do you?

Jack stood up and pointed to the bandage covering the left side of his head. "I sure as Hell *do*!"

The cops looked back and forth between each other, shrugged, and tried to explain that "there's kinda somewhat of a problem with that."

Oh, really? Team Crow asked.

Jack looked down at Old Vic, who seemed delighted with all the attention. He was grinning a satisfied death's-head grin at Jack. The two men exchanged silent looks while the Team heard the song and dance about being able to *arrest* him, okay! We can *arrest* him easy. Only they couldn't put 'im in the jail on account of the jail being closed because of two prisoners we got down there got AIDS and we don't wanna risk no epidemic thing.

Jack was listening as he stared at the old man's grin and tried to keep from grinning back. He asked one question:

By whose order was the jail closed?

The mayor, he was told.

Jack nodded, told them to take the old man away anywhere they wanted—to the Hood County Jail, if necessary—but keep him away from Team Crow.

"Because," he added, "we'll be finished here in another hour and I don't want anything to screw it up. Dig?"

They dug. They hauled Old Vic, still grinning, to a squad car. He had never, Jack suddenly realized, said a single word.

Didn't have to, thought Jack, finally letting himself smile. He got what he wanted, attention, without it.

Thirty minutes later, Jack and his gunman were ready to hit the warehouse basement. Just the two of them.

Jack had fussed and fretted over the choice but he couldn't think of another way to do it. He had to go; he was in charge. Felix had to go; he was too good. But what about backup?

Well, what about it? They were going after master vampires, the ones in charge, the ones who'd created the goons in the first place, and if they came across them in that narrow stairwell anything that was going to happen would crack too fast for anyone to stop it. Jack didn't believe the masters were down there—they were in that goddamned jail—but if they were they might very well wipe out the entire Team. This way there'd at least be somebody left to do it the old-fashioned way, with plastique.

And besides, he wasn't sure he wanted a lot of trigger-happy well-meaners shooting off pistols and crossbows past *his* head.

No. Just him and Felix would go down, with both halogen crosses blazing from their chests. Felix first.

Crow felt the last part deserved an explanation but Felix didn't need one. Felix didn't even raise an eyebrow. Gunman first made sense to him too. Then Jack tried to explain about master vampires, the real live movie types that could throw cars and move so fast they literally blurred, but he didn't think he had the gunman's attention.

"You're saying they're worse, right?" Felix interrupted at last, sounding irritated and bored.

Jack just nodded.

Felix nodded in turn. "I *figured* that," he whispered harshly. "Now let's get *on* with it!"

They did.

The rich, rotten-sweet smell of death and decay rose up to them from the dark basement stairs through the harsh smoky halogen beams. Jack nodded one last time to Cat and Adam, who would wait there on the first-floor battleground for them. Then he touched Felix on the shoulder and the gunman started down the steps. There was no trouble on the way down, save for their occasional starts and jumps at some imagined movement at the edges of the shadows. The detector never beeped, their radios retained clear and crisp reception.

But it scared the hell out of both of them.

The stairwell was too goddamned narrow and the shadows too goddamned dark and the smell grew so strong they felt they could lean against it and their boots sounded harsh and rasping on the dusty steps and they couldn't help but notice the scores of other footprints besides their own.

The basement was worse.

It was a crypt. Nine bodies in all—six townspeople and the three policemen who had gone inside to save them. Their bodies were rank and swollen, unevenly, grotesquely bloated. And there were maggots. Thousands of maggots swarming in the chests.

"How could they rise up after that?" gasped Felix, staring at the maggots.

Jack shook his head. "I don't know. But they do. Every time. Unless we do this right." He put down his crossbow and reached back for the ax strapped across his shoulders. "Or unless I do, rather. You don't have to do anything. But pay attention to what I do. Okay?"

Felix nodded, moving over against a bare wall.

Jack steeled himself. Get hard, dammit! he screamed inwardly. But it didn't work. It didn't help. Not even the hatred of the vampires made it any easier. It never did.

But he did it. He chopped the heads off and put them in one pile and then he dragged the torsos into another heap and then he poured gasoline on both piles and set them alight.

They burned like dry, dead leaves.

Jack and Felix hunkered down in one corner underneath the cloud of smoke to breathe.

"Sometimes the fires go out," offered Jack by way of explanation.

After that they didn't talk for several minutes. They just sat there and watched the flames that burned so brightly and so angrily, flames that never would have appeared over normal corpses.

Only here, thought Jack, and he sneaked a look at his companion. He couldn't see much in the uncertain light but . . . there! There was the glimmer of tears! And only after he had seen Felix's could Jack bear to lift a hand and wipe away his own.

How can this sicken me so much, he thought as he always thought, and still break my heart at the same time?

And then he stood up to retrieve a blazing skull that had rolled away from the flames. He eased it gently back into the fire with the head of his ax.

Eventually the flames did their work and Jack was able to get up and spread the ashes and then the two of them walked back up the stairwell that seemed not frightening at all now, only sad and lonely and forever and ever empty.

Outside in the sunshine, Madame Mayor had already begun the celebration. She had a table set up on the sidewalk in front of the courthouse. On it was a white tablecloth and a large silver ice bucket holding a magnum of champagne. All the city father types stood around her as she began some little speech about the gallantry and bravery of Team Crow.

Jack's inclination was to insert that bottle of champagne, cork and all, into a certain place in her body. But he was smart enough to control his anger. Even smart enough to signal to his troops to play along. And so they all stood there on that sidewalk while somebody began to pour and they all drank and they all smiled and they all pretended not to notice that too-strident cheery tone the mayor was pumping out.

That's a terrified woman, Jack thought behind his grin. What if we win? Or, hell, what if we *lose*? Either way she's had it.

But he just kept smiling until he had a chance to interrupt graciously and inform the audience of Team Crow's desire to rest and get cleaned up and change clothes and all that before the dinner in their honor.

Fine! they all said. That's just fine! Good idea! 'Cause ya'll are gonna need your rest for the shebang we're hitting ya with tonight! And we got just the place for ya!

And with that they escorted Team Crow the two blocks through the early afternoon sun to the William Willis Inn, the finest hotel in town. Through the lobby door and past the desk to an ancient elevator that required three trips to accommodate all the hangers-on to the top floor and the presidential suite, where food and drink and a cashier's check were waiting.

It took another fifteen minutes before Cat could usher out the last of the instantly drunk partyers, and then only by promising they'd be down soon.

Then he locked the door behind them.

Then he went to the window and joined the rest of the Team.

And then they went out the window and down the fire escape and into Deputy Thompson's patrol car waiting in the alley. They hunkered down in the back seat until they were outside the city limits. Twenty minutes later they made their rendezvous with Annabelle and Davette at a trailer court thirty miles away.

Then they sat down and ate the food the women had ready while Jack Crow curled their hair with his plan to enter the police station, subdue whatever cops were on duty there, go downstairs into the basement where the cells were, and, without a trace of sunlight to aid them, slay however many master vampires were down there waiting for the night to come.

"It's three thirty," he announced. "Five more hours of daylight. We gotta do it right. And we gotta do it now. Questions?"

There were one or two.

But Jack didn't seem to care. He leaned back in the room's faded and moth-eaten easy chair and smoked cigarettes and let them rant for some time.

Then he grinned, leaned forward, and said, "Relax. I've got a Plan."

Cat eyed him sourly, disgusted. "Think you can give us a hint, O Great Leader?"

Jack laughed. "Sure. Remember the flare Felix bounced on that woman?"

Cat was still suspicious. "Yeah . . ." he replied cautiously. "It didn't hurt her a bit."

"Didn't *harm* her maybe. But it *did* hurt her."

"So?"

"So," replied Jack easily, turning to the deputy, "you know where we can get some thermite?"

Chapter 16

Somehow, in all the comings and goings through the three rooms the team had rented in the trailer court, Davette ended up alone in the same room with Felix.

And she didn't think she was up to it.

It was only the third time she'd seen the man. The first she remembered quite well. He had called her a "siren," while boring shivering holes in her with his angry eyes. The second time was again at his saloon office. By the time she had arrived accompanying Annabelle and Adam, Felix was sitting behind his desk examining Jack's check for $50,000 and studiously ignoring her. And *that* had been as bad, somehow, as being stared at.

But this time was the worst of all. Because this time she knew what he'd just done. She had sat there beside Annabelle while Cat patiently related the events of the day. There was no time to do a hypnotic total recall—the Team was on again in two more hours—but Cat was a natural storyteller, wise in his use of detail. Besides listening raptly, Davette noticed, Annabelle kept a small tape recorder going as he spoke.

And *that* had gotten to her, reminding her of just how incredibly dangerous their line of work was. They had to make records *now* because it was entirely possible that every single man on the Team could be dead by sunset and someone had to be able to pass on what they had learned so far.

But what had really gotten to her was the story itself. The Felix part of the story. The lightning-fast, deadly accurate, cold-calm-killer part of the story.

142

"He saved our lives, Annie," Cat had said with quiet sincerity, carefully looking her in the eye. "We'd all be dead without him, sure as hell."

And Annabelle had smiled that knowing smile she had and asked him gently, "Then you're happy with him, Cherry?"

He had smiled back and softly replied, "Got to be."

Davette hadn't been at all sure what that had meant. But she was sure of one thing: Felix was *not* happy.

He hadn't actually said so. He hadn't actually said much of anything, now that she thought about it. But she could read it. And so could everyone else. He moved slowly about the edges of their chaotic planning. He did answer when asked a specific question or even when asked for an opinion on some aspect of Jack's Plan. And his answers were concise and to the point. But he wasn't really with them.

"Are you all right?" people kept asking him and he kept saying he was. But he didn't look it. He looked stunned. Almost dazed.

But no one pursued this, because Jack Crow did not.

And now he sat there in the dusty easy chair in the corner of that musty room cleaning his weapons. He had newspaper spread out on a lumpy ottoman and the parts of his pistols spread out on that and the only sounds were the rustle of the newsprint and the precision snicks and clicks of well-oiled firearms.

At the far corner of the room, Davette stood in the little kitchenette where they'd cooked the Team's lunch. She had offered to tidy up but that had been awhile back when the room was filled with people and now she didn't know if she was still there because she wanted to stay or was just frightened to walk past Felix to get out.

So she stayed there in the corner, cleaning and recleaning like some rabid housewife on speed, sneaking constant glances at him and feeling like a complete idiot until she couldn't stand it anymore and just made herself stop, just stop and stand there with her hands on the edge of the sink and stare out that grimy window and catch her breath.

She said things like: What's the matter with me? and

Get yourself together, and it worked a bit. She was almost calm when she felt the silence and turned around and he was just sitting there staring into space.

Then he looked up, caught her watching him, and smiled.

It made her fumble a bit. But she managed a: "Can I get you something?"

He glanced at his empty glass, reached for it. "Some more ice water?" he asked.

"No!" she almost shrieked. And then, more calmly, "I'll get it."

And as she walked toward him she cursed herself for the way she was acting and wondered if anything in the world could make her stop behaving like such a fool and then she reached for his glass and saw his face and it all went away.

My God! she thought, seeing those tired, tired eyes, he looks terrible!

He did. He looked beaten, blasted, worn down, worn out. He looked like a man who had just decided to commit suicide.

It wasn't until she had taken his glass and walked back to refill it that she realized that that was exactly what had happened when he had decided to join Team Crow and she knew suddenly what he was thinking about and why he looked the way he did and her butterflies went away and something else, warmer, more solid, replaced them.

But she didn't speak. She just gave him his full glass and sat down at the tiny little built-in breakfast table and sipped her cold coffee and for several moments that's all that happened in the room—the two of them sitting and sipping in silence.

And there's nothing I can say to change it, she kept thinking.

Adam, wearing full priestly regalia, appeared at the connecting door to the next room.

He always looks ten years older dressed like that, she thought.

"Felix?" he called quietly. "Would you like to take confession?"

The gunman looked up, a quizzical expression on his face, and replied, to the others' total surprise, "Yeah. I would."

Felix put his cigarette out in the ashtray and stood up. "How does it work?"

Adam smiled, held out a beckoning, robed arm. "It's easy."

Less than five minutes later, Felix came strolling briskly back into the room alone. He stopped, looked around the room, at Davette, at his chair, at his guns. Then he walked over and picked up his glass of ice water and drained it down.

Adam appeared behind him in the doorway looking mournful.

"I'm sorry, Adam," said Felix when he saw him.

But Adam just shook his head to say it was all right. And when Felix turned away from him to light a cigarette, the young priest made the sign of the cross to his back. Then, with a sad smile for Davette, Adam left.

Felix surprised her by sitting across from her at the tiny breakfast table. He seemed to feel the need to explain to her and she could see him start to speak several times before he finally shrugged, laughed a rueful silent laugh, and said, "I wasn't having any fun."

She smiled at him and blushed to the roots of her light-blond hair. And so they sat there for several more moments, she feeling foolish and excited and infinitely sad and he feeling . . . what? Numb, she supposed. He certainly *looked* numb the few times she braved a glance.

After the dozenth dry sip, she realized she must look pretty odd drinking from an empty cup. She got up and went over to the kitchenette for another refill. When she turned back around, he was gone.

Two hours and forty minutes later, they hit the Johnson County Jail.

Jack's Plan was based on Felix's flares. Or rather, what they had done to that woman wearing the ZZ Top sweatshirt.

"Of *course* it didn't kill her," he explained patiently to a doubtful Cat. "But it sure as hell got her attention. And remember, while she was frantically brushing those sparks off, she wasn't attacking anyone."

Carl had frowned. "So?"

Jack smiled slyly. "So what *else*—for just a few seconds, mind you—takes their minds off feeding?"

Of course, no one knew. Not for sure. But everyone—even Felix—had an idea or three. But it was Carl Joplin who really brought it home.

"I read somewhere," he offered calmly, "that a pig's blood is a lot like a man's."

Thirty minutes later, they had a serious list of goodies.

But Jack wanted something else; he wanted some form of official sanction. He was willing to go without it—the job had to be done and done right now—but he wanted the effort made.

He and the deputy went to the telephone and started tracing down the sheriff. It took several minutes, several calls, and some patching through by radio before the deputy put his hand over the mouthpiece to whisper, "I've got him."

Jack reached for the phone. Deputy Thompson pulled it out of his reach.

"Mr. Crow, I don't wanna insult you. But I think you'd better let me handle this."

Jack thought a moment, nodded. "I'll be right outside when he wants to talk to me."

The deputy barely smiled. "I'll keep that in mind."

Fifteen anxious minutes later the deputy came out of the room smiling. He'd gotten everything the Team needed for the job—except the sheriff.

"Sorry, Mr. Crow," offered Deputy Thompson. "But there's just no way he can get there before four P.M."

Crow lit a cigarette. "It'll have to do." He turned to the rest of the Team, gathered in chairs around the crowded sitting room. "Okay, sports fans, we're on. Rock and roll."

"Rock and roll!" echoed back at him.

And then everybody went shopping.

Cat, ever bold, directed the driver of the limo to downtown Cleburne, only four blocks off the main square, to Prather's Feed & Seed. He escorted Annabelle and Davette inside and commenced to buy poison for rats, mice, fleas, ticks, fire ants, and coyotes—all together some five pounds of the stuff. Then he chose, from an impressive display of pet supplies, a thirty-gallon aquarium. He declined the offers of gravel, plants, starter guppies, and angelfish. He did buy, for reasons only another Cat would understand, an aerator in the form of a happy-faced salvage diver with bright red boots.

"I always wanted one," was his only response to the women's puzzled looks.

Kirk drove Jack and Felix to Wal-mart. There they bought two five-gallon gasoline cans and two funnels, three of the largest fire extinguishers available, and two packets of ballons in various colors.

They filled up both gas cans at the next-door Exxon station.

Carl and Adam drove the Blazer to a local slaughterhouse that specialized in preparing game meats but agreed to the killing and draining of the six pigs in the back pen. When the owner found out they weren't interested in the carcasses—just the blood—he assumed they were Satan worshippers. A devout baptist, he then doubled the price as a matter of principle. The technician and the Catholic priest exchanged tired looks between them. Then they paid up without a word and drove away with the blood.

The three groups met, an hour and a half later, in the empty driveway of the sheriff's empty home, where Jack lost no time cutting the women loose.

"Get out of here, Annie," Jack told her firmly. "Get out of this county. You still have your gun?"

Annabelle nodded nervously and clutched her purse more tightly.

"Okay," said Crow. He looked over at the uniformed limo driver, looking out-of-place and worried.

"Fire that guy," Jack ordered her. "Have him take you to a car-rental place . . . Or better, have him take you to the airport. Then take a taxi to the car-rental place. Make him think you're leaving town.''

Annabelle frowned. "I don't think he knows anything that's going on. Or cares, for that matter.''

Jack smiled grimly. "I don't either. But do it, anyway. Right?''

She nodded. "Right.''

"Okay. Move.''

She started to go, stopped. She put a hand to his cheek.

"Be careful, dear," she said softly.

Jack stared a second. Annabelle had never done that before.

But then he shook it off and the smile he chose was wry and he replied, "First chance I get.''

And Annabelle smiled back and herded in the silent Davette with a look and then, without another word, the ladies and the limo drove away.

There was a moment—not a long one—when the men simply stood there and watched the car drive off.

"Okay, people," said Jack quietly, "let's saddle up.''

And he walked over to the Blazer and pulled out his own chain mail and started putting it on. The other inside warriors—Cat, Adam, and Felix—did the same. Carl and Deputy Thompson stood and watched them. No one spoke.

Jack did a quick check to see that the four were buttoned up tight, then nodded to Deputy Thompson, who produced a key from a hiding place deep in his holster. Then he went over to what looked to the others like a garden storage shed beside the sheriff's garage.

Except that it took two dead bolts and a combination to open its four-inch-thick fire door. From inside, the deputy produced one case, twenty-count, CS (Military) Type tear-gas grenades and seven gas masks. Carl, Jack, and the deputy showed Cat and Felix how to adjust the masks and how to pull the pins on the grenades. When everybody seemed to have a mask strapped to fit, they got in the vehicles, with the patrol car in the lead, and headed back for downtown Cleburne, Texas.

When they got to the Johnson County Jail, there were three police cars and six uniformed officers, complete with shotguns, flak jackets, and riot gear, waiting for them.

"Dammit!" hissed Jack Crow when he saw them. "How the hell did they know?"

"They didn't," offered the deputy from beside him. "I had to tell them."

At first Crow couldn't speak. When at last he tried, the deputy wouldn't let him.

"Hold it, Mr. Crow!" Kirk snapped. And then, more calmly: "Before you say anything, let *me* talk. There's nothing wrong with the Cleburne Police. They aren't corrupt. They aren't cowards. And they aren't stupid. People being killed by monsters in their town square and they can't do anything to stop it—and then the mayor hires somebody who can and then their chief tells them not to help out. Don't you think they *know* there's something strange going on?"

He paused a moment, took a breath. Crow sat silent. Waiting.

"Now," the deputy continued, "I know these six men well. And they know me and . . ."

"Are you saying they're on our side?" piped Cat from the back seat.

"Nossir!" hissed the deputy, eyeing Jack Crow. "They don't *know* you. As far as they could tell, you might be the *cause* of all this!"

"Then whose side," asked Jack quietly, "are they on?"

The deputy smiled. "Mine."

Jack grinned. "Good enough. They'll watch our backs while we go inside?"

"They will."

"Do they know what we're about to try?"

"Yes."

"Do they know what has to be done if we can't cut it?"

"They know."

"Okay, deputy. Let's do it."

The Team piled warily out of the three vehicles at Jack's signal and stood on the sidewalk in front of the jail assembling their equipment. The police said nothing to anyone except the deputy and that was so low no one else heard what was said.

But they didn't try to arrest anyone. Or even slow them down. And they *did* appear to be on guard.

"Looks like we got a break," whispered Cat to Crow.

Crow nodded. "Looks like," he whispered back. "Quite a kid, that deputy."

"You're not thinking about recruiting him, are you bwana?" Cat asked wickedly.

Jack's face was blank. "Don't need to. He'll volunteer. If . . . you know."

"Yeah," growled Cat sourly. "I know. If we live long enough to be volunteered to."

"Right. Now, Kirk and I will go inside and get the rest of the stuff we need."

"You want us to start pouring the blood?"

"Wait till we get back. Deputy?"

The deputy stepped away from the two policemen he had spoken to.

"Ready?" asked Jack.

"Ready," said the deputy. And with a nod to the policemen, went inside and arrested everyone in sight.

There were only four. Two at the booking counter, one in the back sitting behind a desk staring dully at a typewriter, and the last drinking thirstily from the water fountain.

All were pale, dead eyed, weak . . .

And owned.

It was there in their faces, in their posture, in the resigned, almost relieved, manner in which they stood there and allowed themselves to be handcuffed. The only thing that could be thought of as some form of resistance came from one of the two standing at the booking desk, a pale fair-haired man of about thirty named Dan, who made a frantic lunge for a jury-rigged red button stuck to the wall with masking tape.

Jack snatched the other man's wrist away from the alarm in midair and felt the bones in Dan's arm bend under the pressure of his grip. Dan yelped and groaned so sharply, Jack instinctively let loose of him and saw a deep purple bruise in the shape of his gloved fingers already forming on the wrist.

"Good Lord!" whispered Kirk.

Jack looked at him over Dan, who had crumpled to the floor holding his arm. "You see it, too?"

"Hell, yeah, I see it!" cried Kirk. "What the hell's the matter with him?"

"Offhand, I'd say it was loss of blood."

It was about then that Dan began to sob.

Soon the other two were also crying, deep tortured heaves that shook their shoulders painfully.

It hurt to watch it. Jack had been planning to get whoever was inside outdoors and into the squad car and out of the way as soon as possible, but this was just too good a chance to let by.

The fact was that Jack had never, in all his battles, actually met someone he knew to be under the influence of vampires. He knew there were always two or three suicides in the places where the Team had done its job. And he figured those were the ones who couldn't bear to live with the shame of what they'd been made to do.

But he'd never actually seen it. He looked down at the four, now huddled together and weeping. He could feel their shame. They reeked of it. And how they wept! It was the totally unleashed, uninhibited weeping of children, red-eyed, runny-nosed, and moaning.

No. It was too good a chance to pass up. He hated to do it. But he had to question them.

He paused, took a deep breath, and knelt down beside the one he'd grabbed away from the alarm button, Dan. The bruise on his wrist was now multicolored and swelling. He cradled it tenderly on his other forearm.

"I'm sorry about that," he said tenderly.

But Dan just sobbed some more and shook his head as if to say he deserved it.

Part of Jack wanted to grab this man and shake him, this grown man crying like a baby. But the rest of him knew better. These four really *couldn't* help it.

Supernatural.

"How many are down there?" he asked Dan.

Dan looked at him, uncomprehending. "How many?"

"Yeah. Downstairs. In the jail. How many?"

"How many . . . masters?"

Jack gritted his teeth but managed to keep his tone gentle. "Yeah. How many masters?"

The oldest of the bunch, the guy who had been sitting in front of the typewriter when Jack and the deputy had come through, shook himself and leaned forward. He held up three fingers.

Like a child.

"Three!" he whined.

Damn! thought Jack. He had been prepared for more than one. But goddammit, *three*?

Damn!

The other slaves began nodding. One of them, the kid who had been drinking from the fountain, held up three of his fingers and nodded fiercely.

And when he did his collar was pulled away from his throat and Jack saw the bite.

The deputy saw it, too, and gasped. Jack reached over to Dan, the closest one to him, and pulled his collar out and there it was.

"Jesus!" whispered Kirk.

It looked like the bit of a spider. But one impossibly large, impossibly vicious. Impossibly thirsty.

The two puncture marks were just over an inch apart, with overlapping black and yellow rings swollen out from their centers. The bites were recent, deep, and horribly infected.

Loss of blood, Jack had said.

Now he thought: loss of soul . . .

"They're . . ." gushed Dan and his gaze was plaintive, with a terrible yearning. "They're . . . They're so *beautiful*!"

And all four of them began to weep again. Weep and nod and huddle together and Jack couldn't stand it anymore. He stood up and grabbed two of them by the upper arms and led them outside. The deputy brought out the other two.

Jack said nothing to the wary stares of the six flak-jacketed patrolmen on the sidewalk except: "These men aren't to be harmed. Just keep 'em out of the way."

The patrolman who seemed to be their leader glanced first at Deputy Thompson for his nod of confirmation before taking the prisoners in tow and depositing them in the backs of two police cars.

Carl appeared beside Jack. "You were right?" he asked, though it wasn't really a question.

Jack sighed. "Yeah. They're in there. Three of 'em, looks like."

Cat whistled. "Three? Holy shit!"

Felix was there, too. "Is that a lot?" the gunman wanted to know.

"That's the most so far," offered Adam from off to one side.

Cat looked sharply at him, then relaxed. "Yeah. I keep forgetting you're our historian."

Adam smiled. "Not anymore."

Cat smiled back. "Guess not."

"We'll be back in a second," Jack informed them, and then he and the deputy went back inside, past the front desk, down a corridor, into another corridor, and down to the end of it to a vault door with a sign on it that said: "Johnson County Sheriff Property Room." While Kirk went to work on the combination, Jack started to light a cigarette.

"I wouldn't," advised the deputy as he swung the vault open.

The chemical stench from inside the property room all but staggered Crow. He looked at the deputy.

"Ether," Kirk explained. "We get a lot of speed labs in this part of Texas."

"Oh."

Kirk was waving the air with his hat. "It usually airs out in a couple of secs," he explained.

It seemed to, anyway. Though Jack wasn't sure it wasn't just his sense of smell numbing out.

In any case, they went inside and got to work.

The evidence was found in thick, tightly sealed manila

envelopes with names and case numbers on the outside.
Kirk only read them long enough to see what was inside
before tearing them open. Jack emptied one of the envelopes
onto the floor and filled it with the stuff the deputy handed
him.

They took one hundred and sixty tablets of "purple mi-
crodot" and thirty more hits of "Blotter" LSD. They took
two and one half ounces of pure, uncut cocaine, three
ounces, eighty-four grams, of PCP. They took three grams
of raw brown Mexican heroin. They took six ounces, one
hundred sixty-eight grams, of milk-white methamphetamine
crystal. They took it all outside to where Cat and Carl had
the jugs of pig's blood and the aquarium set up on a little
wheeled table. On the grass alongside slumped the various
sacks of poison from Prather's Feed & Seed. The balloons of
various colors looked like water balloons now except for the
rich smell of gasoline that wafted from them. Next to the
balloons were the tear-gas grenades and the gas masks all
ready to go.

Jack looked at his watch. Three hours and fifteen minutes
to sundown.

"Okay," he said to Carl, "can you rig the elevator now?"

"Yep," Carl nodded and picked up his tool box. The
two went back inside.

When Carl saw the elevator doors facing the front entrance he stopped and smiled. "My God, that deputy was
right. I never would have believed it."

Jack nodded. "Lucky."

It was, in fact, incredibly lucky. Team Crow had known
the cells were in the basement and they had known the only
way to reach them was by a single elevator. But it wasn't
until Deputy Thompson had drawn his little sketch of the jail
that they had known the route to the elevator was so short
and clear. Crow had cringed at the thought of trying to winch
a full-fledged master vampire around corners and up stairs
into the sunlight with the damn thing trying to rip the crossbow free every step of the way.

But this was a straight shot. It was less than thirty feet

from the elevator door to the sunshine, and the passageway was wide and free of obstacle.

Now all they had to do was get the fiends to get in the elevator.

He joined Carl, who stood fussing over an antique electrical box on the wall beside the elevator doors. He had wires running from the maze to a black metal box with a half dozen toggle switches on top.

Carl looked up from his work. "Okay, I think I've got you all set."

Jack frowned. "You 'think' you do?"

Carl shrugged. "Jack, this elevator's older than I am. I wouldn't count on it being too responsive."

"What *can* I count on?"

"Well, this switch starts it up. This one down. This one stops it. Anywhere. Between floors. Whatever you want. This one opens the doors. This one closes them. Again, anywhere you want."

Jack nodded. "Okay. Label 'em."

Carl groaned. "You can't remember that much?"

Jack looked at him. "I don't want to have to remember. I want to be able to *know*."

Carl sighed. "Yes, bwana," he said and set about doing it.

Crow went back outside and spoke to Cat, who stood on the jailhouse sidewalk talking to the deputy. A few feet away Felix sat quietly on the curb, smoking.

"I'm off to do my bit," Jack told Cat. "Wait a few minutes, then start pouring the blood."

"Right," said Cat.

Crow looked at the deputy's patrol car, parked a few steps away.

"Mind if I borrow that a sec?" he asked.

The deputy looked surprised, then shrugged. "Okay," he offered uncertainly.

Crow nodded, climbed into the car, and pulled away without another word.

"What does he mean by doing 'his bit'?" Kirk wanted to know.

Cat smiled. "He always goes off just before we move to be alone."

"To focus his concentration," finished Kirk, nodding.

Cat's grin was wry. "Or swallow his fear," he suggested and then smiled even wider when he saw the deputy's pale look.

Felix, sitting on the curb smoking his sixty-third cigarette of the day, made no comment. Between his feet he had arranged his last five smokes in a ragged line. He had just stomped out the sixth on the asphalt and added it to the row when Jack Crow suddenly reappeared in the patrol car.

"Something wrong?" asked Cat.

Jack shook his head. He made no attempt to get out of the car, just sat there behind the wheel and stared at Felix.

Eventually, the gunman looked up and met his eyes.

"Get in," ordered Crow, gesturing toward the front passenger door.

Felix eyed him a beat, then stood up. He started toward the car, stopped, went back, and scattered his row of cigarettes. Then he got in and the two of them drove away.

Jack drove in silence for half a dozen blocks to Cleburne City Park. There was a swimming pool, some tennis courts, three baseball diamonds. Jack parked the patrol car next to a beautifully preserved antique locomotive painted jet black and surrounded by a chain-link fence. He turned off the engine and sat there for several seconds in silence.

Felix lit a cigarette and waited for Crow to speak. Now what? he thought.

At last Jack moved. He lit a smoke of his own, turned on the seat to face Felix, and with a smile said, "You know, Felix, you're going to die today."

Felix stared stone at the other man's smiling eyes. He didn't know whether to be scared or offended or . . .

"So am I," Crow continued. "That's the way it is. We took on this job and it's a never-ending goddamned deal and there are too many vampires and not enough of us and they're gonna get us . . . so we're gonna make 'em pay.

"Understand?"

Felix sure as shit did *not* understand. Any of it. Was this Crow's idea of some kinda joke or what?

But what it was was Jack Crow's notion of Style.

"That's the only thing that counts, Felix. We aren't gonna get rid of all the evil in the world. We're not gonna get all the assassins or crack dealers or child molesters.

"And you and I aren't gonna get all the fucking vampires. Sooner or later, they're gonna get us. We die, the earth keeps turning, and not trying just means we keep alive just a little longer and there's a lot more dead people saved from having all their blood ripped out but we still end up dying, Felix, you and me. There's no way out of that. And the earth will have plenty of turns left that we won't see no matter how long we live and so some stupid fools look at this and they don't see any point and that's because the dumbshits think it's a matter of keeping score.

"It isn't, Gunman. The secret isn't the score or the final result because there *ain't* no *final anything*!

"What there is . . . is Style."

There was more of the same. Jack talked some talk about samurai warriors and how they considered themselves dead when they first took up the mantle of service so that nothing could later intimidate them away from their duty.

And there were some other examples and Felix . . .

Felix said not a word the entire time. He simply sat there staring at Crow, not even smoking, until Jack wound down.

". . . just the Style, Felix. Nothing else. So they're gonna get us. So what? It's the Style that matters. Follow me?"

And when Felix spoke his voice was a harsh rasping crackle: "Crow, don't you *ever* spout that kind of crap at me again! Not ever. Do you hear me?"

And Jack thought, My God, I think the sonuvabitch is gonna shoot me if I don't agree!

And he said, "Okay, Felix."

Felix turned away and stared unseeing at the huge black locomotive.

"*Now* can we go back?"

Jack nodded, started the car, and drove away.

Thinking: Sheeeyit! What did I turn over here?

And then thinking: God, I blew that one. He wasn't anywhere *near* ready for that.

A few seconds later Jack sneaked a quick glance to his right. Felix still stared stone.

God! I hope I haven't frozen up my damned gunman again. We've *got* to have him on this one. We go in there and they come busting up and he *doesn't* shoot . . . ?

And then he thought: Fuck it! Nothing I can do about it now. If I blew it, I blew it. Forget it. Shouldn't have brought him along. Shoulda come out here alone like I always do, so, Okay, forget he's here, Jack, oh Great Stupid Leader. Forget it. Do your bit. Deep breaths. Deep breaths and forget Felix and go through those pictures, do 'em now, paint those pictures, because if you can't see it now, if you can't visualize success now, then you sure as shit won't know what to do at the split second . . .

And he began to do it. He steered the car with automatic pilot, seeing not the streets of Cleburne, Texas, through the windshield, but victory.

He set the aquarium filled with pig's blood in the elevator. Laced with speed and coke and rat poison and all the rest of it. Wouldn't kill 'em but, like the flare on that goon, it just *had* to be a little distracting to suddenly come on to twenty or so LSD trips at once. Sure, it would smell funny. The fiends would know there was something wrong with it but they could *see* it! That's why he'd had Cat get an aquarium, so they could not only smell the blood, they could see it through the glass. Just too damn tempting to resist. Plunging their rotten fangs into it like bobbing for apples and then all that poison and dope starts hitting 'em and then the elevator takes them up and by the time the doors open they're gonna be so stoned and sore and weirded out . . .

The crossbow cable pulls 'em out too fast for 'em to stop it, stoned as they are. The cable is attached to the Blazer because the winch is too slow to take a chance and I'll just whistle to Carl on the radio and he'll hit the gas and that fiend will be out of that elevator and through the doors and burning before it knows what hit it.

Sure as hell!

Shit! We might not even *need* a gunman!

But they did. And right then they didn't really have one.

Felix, sitting beside the oblivious Jack Crow, had begun to rock and tremble like a molten volcano.

Chapter 17

He sat there on the tailgate of the Blazer and watched them take care of last minute details and he hated everything he saw.

But he did not speak.

He hated the job, of course, and he hated the place and he hated the Plan and he hated the sight of his pair of Brownings lying there beside him waiting to be strapped on and he hated the . . . earnestness . . . with which the rest of the Team went about it all.

But mostly he hated the sight of Jack Crow stalking about giving orders and inspiration and knowing this guy in charge was clogged tight with that suicidal half-wit philosophy about . . . about what? "Everybody's-got-to-go-sometime-so-how's-about-right-now?" or some such obscenity.

But he did not speak.

He just hated and smoked and boiled.

He also feared, but he was too angry at Crow to realize that, too furious and disgusted with that crap Crow had spouted at him by the locomotive. Bad enough having to do this shit and probably die doing it, but to have the goddamn boss start jamming this juvenile Code of Half-Ass Karma at him . . .

As far as Felix could tell, Crow's philosophical foundations consisted of: "Oh, well, what the Hell!"

But still, the gunman did not speak.

What was the point . . . The job was on. The war was

moments away and they were all going to fight in it, himself included, and nothing Felix could say now was going to stop it or save a fucking soul.

And then he heard it: "Rock and roll!"

And they were going inside.

Past the great glass double doors taped black against the sunlight with even that tiny notch they'd cut for the cable covered with black cardboard flaps and the rest of the inside also dark and cool and dry from the air conditioning—he hadn't realized how hot it had been outside—but in here it was like a soft, dark tomb with every window taped up to be sure they came out of the elevator and Felix understood why Jack had decided to forget those damn gas masks and that gas because it was already tough enough to see in here even with the spotlights set up at every angle they could think of and all of them, Jack and Cat and Father Adam and Deputy Thompson and even Carl Joplin, gathered in front of the surveillance monitors Carl had set up at a little coffee table in the lobby so that Jack could see them while he worked the elevator and . . .

And it got very quiet and still with them just standing there for an instant, breathing in that air-conditioned air and watching those dark monitors.

"Hit the lights," said Jack calmly, "and let's see what we can see."

And the lights downstairs in the cells came on—Felix had no idea who flipped the switch, had no idea of the source of any other movements but his own and Jack's and whoever was standing dead inside of that tiny tunnel which had become his vision—and the cameras swept slowly back and forth showing the rows of bunked cells.

And no one was in them. They were empty.

For just an instant, Felix felt an exquisite thrill of relief until Carl Joplin lifted a chubby finger to one of the screens and pointed to an unmade bunk in the corner.

"There, I think," he whispered. He moved his finger to another bed beside it, also unmade. "And there."

Felix stared at the screens, unbelieving, and then back

at the others' faces, glowing in the lights from the screens, and then he looked back at the screens themselves, back at the two unmade bunks, and then he saw those outlines in the mattresses and knew the beds were unmade because some-one—or some*thing*, goddammit—was still lying in them.

And his fear rose and swirled up his spine.

"I don't get it," whispered Kirk. "I mean, I understand it's vampires and all that. Can't see 'em in mirrors and stuff. But what about their clothes? We oughta be able to see their clothes! I mean, it's a scientific fact that . . ."

"Deputy," said Father Adam, from just off his right shoulder, and Kirk turned around and looked at the priest.

"Deputy," Adam repeated softly, " 'science' can be helpful." He gestured to the screens. "And we use it all that we can. But," he whispered firmly, looking into the other man's face, "this isn't really about 'science.' "

And the deputy eyed him a beat or two before nodding and looking back to the screens and Felix felt another chill rise and twist within his guts because he *hated*, absolutely goddamn *hated* when the priest sounded so sure because he was always, *always*, right and about then Jack leaned over and around the screens for one last look at the aquarium, sitting blood-filled and ready inside the elevator.

Then he flipped a switch and the elevator doors closed and they all heard the groaning clunking as the elevator started down. It seemed so loud! It seemed loud enough to wake the—

"There!" cried Carl Joplin, and his stubby finger thumped the screen again and moved away and Felix saw.

Streaks, outlines, ephemeral . . . drifting . . . but with a purpose, with a pattern and direction and Felix could *see* them sometimes, really *see* them when they would move and then pause and for just a brief half second he could *see* them, see their outlines, see their *expressions*!

And they were smiling.

"I guess," offered Cat with a very dry throat, "they smell the blood.'

And just then all turned to the last monitor, the one that

showed the inside of the elevator cage, empty save for the bright-red aquarium and just then the elevator came to a stop and the doors opened and the streaks—there were three of them, clearly three, one man and two women—moved down the row of bunks toward the elevator and . . .

There! In the elevator screen they saw one of them appear and they could all tell, somehow—out of the corners of their eyes, sort of—that it was one of the women.

"Carl!" whispered Jack Crow harshly. "Get outside and get ready."

"Right," Carl whispered hard in return and he was gone.

Jack looked at the others.

"Get in position."

And they all moved back from the screens to somewhere—Felix was too numb to really tell or remember where—the others were somewhere over there to the right of the elevator door somewhere and he and Jack were supposed to stay here on the left . . .

He thought. He wasn't sure. He couldn't remember. He couldn't . . .

"How many do you want, bwana?" Cat asked.

Crow looked up at him and his face was hard. "Get to your spot, Cherry."

Cat hesitated, looked at the screens, looked back at Crow. "It's just that . . . you think we can handle more than one?"

Jack eyed him a moment. "Whoever comes up with it. Get moving."

Cat hesitated again, then nodded and left, the glare of the spotlights glinting brightly off the polished shaft of his pike.

And then, from a desk on the other side of the booking counter, just visible through the huge black grille that rose from the top of the counter to the ceiling, a phone began to ring.

At first they just jumped. Then they turned and looked at it. Then they realized just which phone it was and then . . .

One of the downstairs screens, the one showing the

guard's station just beyond the wide-open barred gate leading
to the elevator, showed a wall phone. The receiver was off
the hook and hanging in the air and sometimes Felix could
see the outlines and sometimes he could not but he knew
who it was, knew it was the man.

The vampire was calling them.

"Suspicious sonuvabitch," muttered Crow but Felix
didn't really hear him. Felix was staring at the other screen,
the one showing the open elevator and the aquarium full of
blood that appeared to be all but boiling.

"God!" he whispered almost silently.

But Crow heard it and looked and the two of them sat
there in silence as the outline-image of her came and went,
came and went, as she threw her open mouth at the blood,
sloshing it against the glass, and even as a ghost they could
see her frenzy, her hunger, her thirst.

Twice, Felix felt sure he could see the fangs.

Jack Crow leaned forward abruptly and closed the elevator door and started it up and growled, "Here we go,
troops! Rock and roll."

But everyone knew, everyone heard the elevator. Everyone knew what was coming up to see them.

And the phone stopped ringing and the screens showed
empty quiet cells and within seconds the shrieks of pain and
anger began to echo from inside the elevator cage. The poison, the drugs, were getting to her.

"Enjoy, bitch," muttered Crow and he stood up away
from the screens carrying his crossbow.

And that was it, then. That got Felix going at last, that
sight of Jack Crow's muscled hand gripping that crossbow
and moving into position and then Felix was moving also,
alongside Crow's left flank and as he did so he noticed Cat
up there, climbing atop the elevator cage holding his sack of
gasoline-filled balloons and Felix remembered standing there
earlier amidst the acetylene sparks when Carl had cut that
hole in the top of the elevator car itself so that Cat
could . . . could what?

And Felix's mind swirled with the remembered thought

that Cat was supposed to throw his little water-gas balloons down into that bloody elevator *along with a flare!* to drive the vampires out into their killing area and that was *insane*, that was *madness* and Felix's thoughts screamed, I've got to get *away* from these people!

But all he did then was draw one of the Brownings and that's when they began to hear the reverberations from the elevator shaft, the din of pounding and screeching and banging and Felix thought, My God! She's going to tear that elevator apart!

Then suddenly, quiet. No banging. No horrible echoing screams, just the rumble of the car as it rose the last few feet and stopped.

The elevator door did not open.

And it still didn't open.

And then it tried, old circuits buzzing audibly and the metal groaning and it wouldn't open . . .

And Felix and Jack found themselves over in front of the screens without thinking but there was nothing on them except shattered glass and blood everywhere, on the floors and the walls and they barely glanced at each other before moving back into position, weapons held high, and Crow called out, "Careful, people. Looks like she jammed it shut!"

And then he reached down for his little remote device Joplin had fashioned for him—it was on the floor about fifteen feet from the elevator—and that's where they were. Felix and Crow standing together, when the elevators doors just blew off their moorings and crashed into them.

The door got Crow first, hitting him flat and flush on his right side and then spinning over his head like a flipping card and smacking Felix a glancing blow on the side of his head and as he went down he saw her streaking out of the elevator through the darkness and the room suddenly filled with dust and then he was flat on his back staring blankly at the glare of an overturned spotlight on the ceiling tiles past the edge of the crumpled elevator doors on top of him.

Then movement in the lights and sounds of shuffling feet and someone called out something to someone else and he lifted himself up, shoving the door off to one side with his gun hand and—

—and she was looking at him.

She was there, standing just in front of the elevator heaving for breath and glaring at him, and he saw her eyes arc and her lips spread back and he heard the hiss and the fangs came out and he knew he was dead, knew it, knew it, but it was so distant, somehow, like happening on a movie screen to someone else.

Should shoot her . . . Knew he should shoot her and he had the gun in his hand still but he couldn't remember *how* to shoot but he raised the pistol anyway and she saw it and came at him, *at* him, *at him* . . .

And Father Adam's crossbow went off and the huge bolt crunched through her back from just under her left shoulder and punched out through her right breast and she *shrieked* and leapt high into the air, spinning and *shrieking* . . . *shrieking* . . .

And then she was gone.

Where? Somewhere. Somewhere to the left maybe? She had moved so *fast*.

And he felt himself being jerked to his feet and he almost screamed thinking it was her but it was only Jack, standing there with blood on his cheek and looking at him.

"Are you all right?" he asked.

And Felix nodded and looked past him to Father Adam, who stood frozen and pale beside the deputy, holding an empty crossbow and staring at the vampire as she thumped toward him—My God! she could hardly move, she was skewered by that thing and it flopped as she tripped toward him and that clear, thick bile was pumping out around the shaft and the deputy lifted the sharp pike he carried but *that* wasn't going to be enough and Felix shouldered Jack to the side and fired, a wild, frightened shot and hit her in the *foot* of all places, right in the instep of her left foot and she howled and leapt and turned back toward *him* and he fired again and the bullet seemed to take a chunk off the top of her left shoulder and more of that stuff bubbled out through the fabric of her . . .

Of her *blouse*? Of her Mexican peasant blouse, white with beautiful embroidery, and he looked at her at last, saw her as she really was with her deep rich eyes and plaintive whisper of pain . . .

Don't you want me? Don't you desire me and love me and want to take care of me?

And he did! He felt the molten pumping lust and wanted her alive and healthy and soft and tender in his arms . . .

And he dropped the gun to his side as she came toward him again and he was holding his arms out to receive her when the crossbow bolt jammed through her ribcage caught and she winced and he saw the fangs appear suddenly and he shot her three times through the chest.

And she *howled* and spat as the silver slugs slammed through her and she went straight down on her back, writhing and *howling* and *spitting* as the crossbow bolt twisted and torqued under her weight but then she was up immediately, up and moving, *streaking*, *blurring* white as she passed across in front of the elevator and the booking counter was in her way and she had to collide with it and when she did a chunk of formica topping the size of a chessboard all but exploded off of it but didn't slow her down at all. She bounced off and disappeared down the hallway into the back of the jail by the offices and they heard the slamming and wailing and crashing as she searched for a way out and then there came a tremendous thundering concussion and the lights began to flicker.

"All right," barked Jack when he saw the light. "Everybody out. Let's go."

The sound of his voice, habitually cool and authoritative, brought all of them around somewhat and they started for the door, except Felix who simply stood there and rocketed inside with that sweet exquisite memory of her soft eyes and yearning, tender . . .

"Felix," barked Crow, "move your ass!"

Felix looked at him, at his hard face and hated his choices but knew he must obey and . . .

"Jack!" screamed Father Adam and there she was again, coming at them with the crossbow flopping gruesomely and the fangs out and glittering and Felix shot her again.

And again and again and again, hitting her dead square each time and she slammed back onto the floor with the first concussion but he just kept shooting at her, the bitch, walking right up to her and firing and firing into her and her body warped and arched with each slug and he enjoyed the revenge he was having on the filthy rotten—

The automatic clicked empty in his hand and he automatically ejected the clip and reached for another and suddenly realized how goddamned *close* he'd walked up to her and again their eyes met and she was . . . hatred and horror and the *things* she was going to do to him!

And he started running back as she lurched up toward him and the second bolt, the one in Jack's crossbow, the one with the cable on it, slammed dead center through her chest and saved Felix's life and even over her wailing Felix could hear Jack barking at Joplin through the radio.

"Carl! Hit it!"

And Carl did, the cable went immediately taut and she was flung past them toward the door but the angle was wrong, she was being jerked around a pillar and as she went past it her suddenly taloned hands reached out and her fingers sunk two inches into the plaster and she *just stopped herself*!

Which meant she must have stopped the goddamn *Blazer*, too! And there was this high-pitched *ping* and distant grinding of metal and the cable went slack and she *smiled* this ghastly *smile* at them and then she let got of the pillar and ran past them toward the booking counter and she leapt into the air like a missile and went *right fucking through* the iron grille above it with an ear-splitting shriek of tearing metal and then there was this *hole* in the grille and it was all torn loose from its bolts to the counter and there was more dust in the flickering light from where the ceiling had given way too and . . .

And Felix grabbed Jack Crow by the upper arm and spun him around and screamed, "You didn't tell me they could do that!"

And Jack jerked angrily free and shouted back just as loud, "I didn't *know*!"

And Felix believed him. "Let's get *out* of here, then!"

Jack nodded. "Cat! Where are you?"

"Here, bwana," came the shaky reply from the top of the elevator.

"C'mon, dammit!" ordered Jack, moving toward him. "While she's out of range!"

Cat nodded, poised briefly at the top of the elevator, then dropped softly, like his namesake, to the floor.

"Everybody all right?" asked Crow to the others, who had gathered around Cat.

Each nodded, but Felix paid no attention. He was still moving toward the front door, toward the sunshine, toward *safety*, dammit! We'll count our wounds out*side*, how 'bout?

But the others still stood there. Not for long—just a few seconds, really. And then the cable that stretched between them, from the front door to the busted grille, began to twitch.

"How much slack," whispered the deputy, "does she really have?"

When she came bursting back through the grille toward them they all fell backward out of their huddle and Jack went in between Felix and the target and for just an instant the gunman almost fired anyway but he didn't.

And that gave her the time to lunge at Cat.

Cat fell back on the floor holding the pike out in front of him but it happened too fast—he couldn't get the sharpened end around toward her in time—and she got him.

Grabbed him around the waist and lifted him high in the air, one of the shafts that bisected her knocking loudly into his face—

And Cat was dead and they all knew it.

Dead in front of them . . .

Dead in *between* them.

And the cable warped and zinged along the jailhouse floor and went taut and jerked her off her feet through the wooden stake in her chest and she hissed as she flew toward the sunlight, hissed and spat and dropped Cat to reach out and grab the wall along the edge of the wide front door and she *did* it, she stopped herself *again*, but her feet flew out from their own momentum and smacked into the blackened glass and the door swung wide, wide open and the sunlight bathed them and exploded her body into deafening, howling, flames.

But she *would not let go*!

Felix did shoot her. He shot her again and again, but she wouldn't let go and except for the obvious concussion when a slug struck her body he wouldn't have believed he was hitting her and outside they could hear the strain of a motor and see her talons flexed into the wall and they knew she could do it again, wreck the cable or another Blazer or something, knew she could get free again.

Knew she was strong enough.

Cat clambered to his feet, planted his left foot, and drove his pike into her flaming back with every ounce of strength and fear he had left and the SCREAMING as it plunged into her, the SCREAMING . . . and for a half a second they all saw her claws lose their grip and by the time she had held fast again Deputy Thompson had stepped forward and thrown *his* pike and he was younger and stronger than Cat and when it hit it drove through the back of her flaming head and she SCREAMED that SCREAM again and her hands flew open and she was out the doorway and into the full sunlight and imploding with the flame, dead and gone at last, before the door had a chance to swing shut and cut off their view.

"One down," muttered Jack.

Felix eyed him a moment, then walked out the door and into the sunshine.

Chapter 18

By the time they were ready to go again, there were only ninety minutes left until sundown.

Not so good, thought Jack Crow. But he kept it to himself along with everything else and hurried them along.

The trouble was, they had had so much to do:

A portable generator for power to their spotlights.

Two extra spotlights to protect those that were smashed. A new cable.

They had removed what was left of both elevator doors. They had fixed the front door.

And of course they repaired the walking wounded. Cat's nose was broken. Jack had sutures on his cheek. Felix had a bandage on the edge of his forehead. And Carl Joplin had damn near lost all his teeth.

He hadn't lost a one yet. But he should have. Seems the first time he tried dragging the girl out, she had just torn the Blazer's rear bumper completely off. The second time he had used a police car, actually wrapping the cable around the engine block and getting a much faster start so that he was going almost twenty miles an hour when he ran out of slack.

But she had stopped the police car dead and Carl had gone right through the windshield and his face was cut in what looked like a hundred different places and his lips were split and all his front teeth were loose to the touch. Somehow he had managed to keep his lead foot on the throttle through the whole thing and, therefore, saved their lives.

Or at least kill her, which was what counted.

Cat still managed to bitch at him about being slow and Carl had angrily snarled back that he had changed cars and gotten moving again within thirty goddamn seconds and let's see Cat do it that fast and Cat had asked him if he knew how far a vampire could move in thirty seconds?

"How far?" he snorted.

"Nobody knows, Joplin," Cat shot back, "because there's so many *oceans* in the way!"

And it was meant to be funny but no one really laughed because they were all going to have to do it again two more times in an hour and a half and . . .

And nobody thought this was going to work.

Jack knew this, saw it in their faces, and didn't care, didn't *give* a shit because there was *no other choice*!

So, "Rock and roll," he barked and got his cast inside again, into the dusty glare of the spolights and the cool dryness of the air conditioning, which had stayed working all along somehow. While the others got into their positions, Jack walked over and looked at the elevator car. Pig's blood and broken glass were all over the walls and ceiling. There was a large pool of it on the floor.

Jack had nothing to replace their bait. No more blood. No other aquarium. But he thought, from the memory of her feeding frenzy, that just that pool on the floor would be enough to entice.

Or maybe not, he thought calmly and lit a cigarette. What does it matter?

"We're all going to die anyway," he muttered and then caught himself. Did he *say* that? Hell, did he say that *out loud*?

And he turned and looked at the others, at Cat clambering back atop the elevator, at the priest with his crossbow and the deputy with his puny pike and at the gunman with his dark thoughts and dark skills and he thought . . .

He thought: Why are we doing this? Why? This is *crazy*!

And that scared him most of all because he had never, in all the fears and kills and slaughtered friends, had such thoughts. And he wondered if he was going soft and then another part of his head stepped forward and quietly whispered that *anyone* can be pushed too far and there *is* such a thing as too much and for just an instant the desire to quit was so strong he thought he would weep.

But he did not.

Neither did he work it out. Not at all. He just stood there for a few seconds to be sure the tears had stopped welling and then mechanically shoved himself ahead, going through the motions instead of dealing with it and feeling like a cheat whenever he met another's eyes because he knew *they* would never try again unless they thought he believed and . . . Did he?

"Rock and roll!" he muttered angrily one more time, because none of this shit really *mattered*, because it still had to be *tried*, because . . .

Because . . . well, because "Rock & Roll," dammit!

And he looked around and made sure everyone was in place and set to go and then he just damn well got *on* with it.

The screens monitoring the cells were clear of streaks or ghostly movement, which only meant they weren't moving around down there, so Jack reached forward and flipped a switch to send the elevator down a second time and give 'em something to move for.

There was some creaking and groaning from the battered elevator car but it started down. Without doors on it, all could see it move, see its ceiling pass the floor, see the cables and wires sprouting from the top, see it stop with a truly horrible sound of grinding twisting metal.

And stay stopped, within six inches of the floor.

Jack muttered something under his breath and tried the switch again. The car acted like it wanted to move, sort of shivering in place, but it basically wouldn't budge. Jack sighed and flipped the switch off.

"You want me to call Carl?" asked Father Adam.

Jack stood up from the screens. "I don't know. Hold a second."

"I think," offered Cat from his perch atop the elevator shaft, "that it's just stuck on something."

"Okay," replied Crow. "Everybody else hold tight."

He walked around the TV screens, still carrying his crossbow, and went over to have a look. With his free hand he picked up one of the spotlights and took it with him, the cord hissing dryly behind him as he walked.

Cat hopped down to the floor as Crow got there and pointed down at a corner of the shaft.

"Looks like it's jamming up in there somehow."

Crow nodded, put his crossbow down, and lit a cigarette.

"It's never worked really great," offered the deputy from just behind him.

Crow turned to the voice and saw that everyone, even Felix, had crowded up behind him to see.

Are we undisciplined? wondered Crow to himself. Or just afraid to be alone?

But he said nothing, just puffed on his cigarette.

It was almost like, he thought idly, Somebody was trying to tell them not to do this.

Well, fuck *that*!

"Here," he said to Cat, holding out the spotlight, "hold this."

Cat took the light, frowning. "What are you gonna do?"

"I'm gonna get this sonuvabitch unstuck," growled Crow and stepped up to the edge.

What Crow was planning to do was just step on the roof there, on that corner Cat had pointed to, and just sorta hop up and down until he felt something give and then go back to Carl's little remote control box and try again.

And he'd begun doing that. Stepping out onto the top of the car, bracing himself first on the edge of the doorway and then on the walls of the shaft itself. And the whole assembly groaned and creaked when he stepped on it and he could feel it giving just a little right away and he thought about jumping back out before it fell or something but then it seemed to be more or less stable so he stayed put. But he looked quickly around for something to grab in case the whole damn thing went and as he did his eyes crossed across the hole they'd cut in the roof for Cat to drop his gas balloons and he saw, there on the floor of the elevator car, a brand new hole, a hole that had been torn in the floor, a hole that hadn't been there five minutes ago, had it?

And then something obscured his view and he saw and recognized the face, that *face* . . .

"Oh, my God . . ."

And the face smiled and said, "Crow" in that *voice*.

Crow was throwing himself backward out of the shaft to safety when the top of the car blew out and the air was filled with shrapnel and everybody else hit the deck and Jack, still on the floor, grabbed his crossbow out of Cat's hands and yelled, "Get back! It's him!"

But it was too late. He had already begun to rise from the hole he had just made and it was really the effortless way he did this that froze them so. The way he simply *raised* himself with the grip of a single beautiful hand, almost levitating toward them, his power and eyes and smile and terrible beauty so alien but so familiar, so pale but so solid, so horrible but so magnetic.

He wore black leather boots that laced to just below the knee and black ballet tights and a black silk sash and a huge white billowy shirt and he was magnificent and beautiful and scary and ungodly strong and the instant, almost spasmodic, desire to harm him was strong and deep and true but so, somehow, was something just as strong and deep—the itch to do something that would make him smile.

But he was smiling already as he strode casually toward them.

Jack took a step back and raised his crossbow.

He/It smiled more broadly and the white teeth against that pale skin surrounded by the fall of curly jet-black hair and . . . The headband, Jack thought. He's wearing a white headband. That means something.

Doesn't it?

And he raised the crossbow higher.

"Crow," it said and its voice filled them. "You and your

wooden stakes. When you are one of us, we'll have a big laugh together about them."

This was looking grim.

"Everybody back," ordered Crow. "Back away and out."

But before anyone could move, the voice came once more: "Too late. You've let me get too close."

And he/it took another casual step toward them.

"Get back!" ordered Crow again over his shoulder. "Move it!"

And they started to obey but the vampire took another step and Jack raised the crossbow all the way then, to firing position, and said, "Hold it there."

And the thing laughed and said, "Are you joking? Why? I'm not one of my women."

"Stop!" said Jack Crow.

And the thing smiled more and showed the big teeth and said, "Stop me."

And Jack Crow said, into his radio headset, "Hit it, Joplin!" and fired his massive crossbow at point-blank range.

The vampire caught it. In midair.

And then it took the baseball-bat-sized arrow bolt in both hands and, with a flick of his wrists, like a breadstick, broke it.

And the cable went taught and the piece still connected was zipped out of sight through the door and the vampire laughed again.

"You fools!" it said. "Did you really think you could slay *gods* and face no penalty?"

And it took the other half of the bolt, the pointed end, and hurled it straight down at its feet and the point disappeared completely out of sight into the floor.

Felix's gun was in his hand. He raised it.

The vampire turned sharply to him at the motion.

"You point that toy at me and I will, quite literally, rip your spine from your body."

Felix damn near dropped the pistol to the floor. Just from that voice.

Crow wasn't finished.

"Lights!" he yelled and keyed his on and there was a brief pause but then every one of them did the same and the halogen crosses burst forth and crisscrossed the wicked form and the thing frowned and winced and took a step back and raised a hand to shield his eyes.

"He doesn't like it!" announced Crow excitedly.

But the vampire just snorted in derision and said, "Why no, Crow. I don't like it. But *this* won't kill me either."

And it took a step forward once more.

"Anything else?" it asked and the voice was dry and sarcastic. "Garlic, maybe? Rabbit's foot?" And it looked straight at Crow. "Well, Pope's little altar boy. Very well."

And he started toward Crow and they all saw, in the glare from their lights, the clear liquid seeping from beneath the headband and suddenly Crow understood and, better, so did Felix. The silver-cross wound. The wound that would not heal.

Felix raised his pistol.

"I *told* you not to do that!" snapped the monster.

"So you did," replied Felix and fired three times and got him maybe two times? At least once, for sure, for sure, and then Team Crow scattered as one for the exit, for that big broad double door with sunshine beyond it and Felix skidded he took off so fast—had no *idea* where the monster was, he had practically disappeared he had moved so fast and then Felix felt this rush of air past his cheek and thought, My God, could it be? Could anything move so fast? It couldn't already be in *front* of me . . .

The monster loomed in front of him, glaring pale in the bobbing halogen cross. It reached forward and snatched the pistol from Felix's hand and, hissing slow and deep and wet, raised the gun in front of Felix's face and . . .

squeezed it . . .

and crushed it.

Crushed it like it was made of soft chocolate.

And Felix, unarmed and helpless, thought of this hissing thing which could rush thirty feet when he could only make two steps—with a *bullet* in it. This thing that could crush an automatic revolver.

And he looked into the blood-red eyes and saw the fangs go back and knew he was going to die . . .

. . . when the double doors came open fifteen feet behind the vampire, and from head to heels, he burst immediately into scarlet pulsing flame.

The monster turned instinctively toward the pain, and ice-cold spittle splashed Felix as the monster's face spun away from him and for just an instant the two of them, the monster and the gunman, saw Carl Joplin large and fat standing holding the doors open, huffing and puffing and then the monster was looking at Felix again and screeching and Felix knew it would kill him as it raced past him into the shadows and he drew and fired his second Browning and the silver bullet made a neat hole in the dead center of the headband and Felix dropped to the floor to avoid those claw/hands that flashed but the monster was already gone in a howling streak of scarlet popping flame, across the floor, all fifty feet of it and slamming into the elevator shaft and down through the hole it had made and out of sight . . .

And the *howling*. And the flicker of red flame still hanging in the air and reflected in the elevator shaft.

Then quiet. Quiet. The flame dissipating. Quiet. Still.

Felix looked up from his squat on the floor and saw all the others. They hadn't managed to move five feet the entire time and now they just stood there and stared at him and he thought: it was me, all me, just killing me, just flashing fangs at me.

Then he thought no more but to run, with all the others, toward the light. And then crouched over hands on knees and panting on the front steps in the sunshine, Jack Crow ordered Carl Joplin to keep those doors open, to prop 'em open if he had to.

Felix and the others, Deputy Thompson and Cat and Father Adam—all of them—nodded when Crow said this. Yes, yes, keep those doors open. Keep that sunlight streaming in. Keep it back, back downstairs. Down in the cells underground and out of reach.

Felix caught his breath and saw the others looking at him. He looked away, dammit, from those slow lucky ones, and back into the jail.

And the others, all of Team Crow, followed his gaze and looked and thought and knew they were thoroughly beaten.

Whipped.

We could *never* take that guy.

That god?

Chapter 19

Carl didn't say a word, just gathered them up and herded them over to the motorhome and sat them down in the shade. Iced tea. Cigarettes. More cigarettes.

Finally: "What happened, bwana?" asked Carl Joplin.

Crow looked at him. "Is the plastique ready?"

Carl frowned. "That bad?"

"Carl, I'm not sure *that's* going to work."

"Oh. Well, we may have a little . . ."

Carl stopped as the six policemen appeared.

"Kirk," said one of them, "we need to talk."

Kirk looked wearily in their direction, then stood up and joined them. They huddled up several steps away.

"They don't look happy," offered Cat.

"I don't blame them" replied Carl.

Crow sighed. "Okay. Let's have it."

"The Mayor & Co. are back and pissed."

"How pissed?"

"We're trapped."

Father Adam leaned forward. "Define 'trapped.' "

"Boxed in. Barricaded. Six square blocks of downtown. No in. No out. Just the team and those six cop buddies of the deputy's. And they're about to leave."

"They are?"

"Got to. The chief fired them by radio just about the time ya'll went in the second time."

"But they stuck by us?" asked Father Adam.

Carl shrugged. "They wouldn't leave without Kirk."

180

Cat, remembering the deputy's javelin-toss of the pike, said, "I don't blame them."

They looked up as Kirk came back.

"How does it look, deputy?" Crow asked him.

Kirk and the other policemen exchanged looks before he spoke.

"I think they're going to try to arrest us in the next few minutes."

Carl groaned. "Aw, shit!"

The deputy went on. "They've got riot gear and tear gas and assault weapons and the rest of it. They're plenty serious."

Jack eyed him a moment. "So are we."

The policeman standing alongside Kirk didn't like the sound of this.

"Mr. Crow," said their spokesman, "you see, they got the idea somehow that you're planning to burn down the jail or something."

Jack blew a smoke ring. "That's the plan."

The policeman snorted. "That tears it! Kirk, you've gotta get away from these loonies. They're gonna get you busted or killed or—"

"I've *seen* a vampire, Wyatt," snapped the deputy. "And I think he's right."

Wyatt snorted again. "Right to blow up the jail?"

"Remember, Wyatt. I've *seen* a vampire. *I* think they oughta use an atomic bomb on the sonuvabitch."

And for a few moments no one spoke.

Finally, Wyatt exchanged another look with his fellow officers and spoke. "Okay, Kirk. This is your deal. Do what you gotta do. But they're not gonna let you take out the jail— and *we* ain't gonna go along with you on the off chance that you're right."

Jack Crow nodded. "Understood, officer."

The cop glanced at Crow. "Mighty nice. But I was talking to the deputy." He turned back to Kirk. "Kirk, you gotta get away from here. Now. Take these guys with you if you feel you gotta. But get out.

"No," said Jack but the cop ignored him.

"Get away and regroup. Come back tomorrow, or maybe—"

"No!" barked Crow and stood up. "Look, officer, we can't leave and come back later. It'll be dark soon. They'll be out then. They'll be free. And these people here *will* be issuing warrants for our arrest . . .

"They already have."

"And outside of this zoo those warrants are going to look real and we'll go to jail and those beasts *will find out* where we're being held and if that place is a tin box like you have here or the Dallas County fucking Jail, they'll kick their way through the walls like you kick through a picket fence and they'll carve their way through anybody who tries to stop them and they *will kill us!*"

Crow stopped abruptly and stared at the other man and breathed hard and mad and for just an instant Cat was afraid the punches would start.

But they didn't.

Wyatt, the cop, just sighed and shook his head. Then he waved to Kirk, said, "Good luck, buddy," and then he and the rest of them were into their squad cars and gone.

"Alone at last," offered Cat.

"Not funny, Cherry," retorted Jack. "You and Felix and the deputy get off your asses and go see about this barricade business. See how tight the seal is. Maybe we can figure a way of buying some time." He paused, looked at the sun low in the sky. "What little there is of it."

"Don't bother," replied Kirk. "I know the emergency plans for this city. That seal is real tight." He eyed Crow defensively. "This really is a fine local department here."

Crow returned the look. "I believe you," he replied sincerely.

"So," said Father Adam, "we're stymied."

"Unless you're willing to start shooting peace officers," said the deputy.

Felix and Crow traded a glance.

"I don't shoot people anymore," said the gunman in a low, firm voice.

"It wasn't a serious statement," the deputy assured him quickly.

"Good," said Felix.

"Why," Kirk asked quickly, "don't you just set off the charges now? Before they can stop you?"

Jack shook his head. "It's more than one boom, deputy. We have to level the whole damn structure before they'll be driven out. We have to plant charges deep into the rubble usually, before they pop. It takes a while."

"Oh."

Carl Joplin leaned forward. "And how long you figure they'll wait, lawman, after they hear that first detonation?"

Kirk frowned. "They won't."

Carl nodded. "We got trouble."

"There must be some way to stop them," Adam insisted. The priest scanned the others' faces. "What stops the police?"

"You mean besides higher authority we can't get to in time?"

"Yes?"

Cigarettes were lit while everybody thought about it.

Suddenly Cat laughed.

"What is it?" growled Joplin.

"The media," Cat piped.

"Huh?"

"We'll become terrorists!"

The scheme, hatched to complete detail in less than five minutes flat, was pure Cherry Cat. ROTLA, the Republic of Texas Liberation Army, would get on the horn to the Dallas–Fort Worth "media cretins" and describe their situation as a hostage crisis. True, they had no hostages. And the mayor and the chief knew better, but with Telecopter Mini-cams less than fifteen minutes away, they just might hesitate a little, even after the first explosion, described to the media "as a symbolic act."

"We just tell 'em if they don't meet our demands we'll blow up a *second* building, like the courthouse there. *Plus* kill all the hostages."

"What demands?" Carl Joplin wanted to know.

"A complete list of our nonnegotiable ten-part program will be broadcast over the fascist police trenches at dawn tomorrow," replied Cat smoothly and he smiled.

The Team eyed him like he was from Venus.

"I like it!" twanged a deep voice from over Cat's shoulder.

The man they turned to see was about six feet tall, something under two hundred pounds . . . and relaxed. Totally and completely at ease, from the hands in his pants pockets to the half smile on his face to the ironic sparkle in his eyes. Felix tried to recall the last time he had seen a man so utterly sure of himself, so completely in control of his world.

And then he remembered—it was the *last* Texas sheriff he'd met.

"Boss!" cried Kirk happily. "When did you get in?"

"Coupla hours ago."

"Where have you been?"

"Been sniffing around."

"For what?"

The sheriff laughed and put a hand on his deputy's shoulder.

"To see which side of this mess is crazy."

Jack stepped forward. "What's the verdict, sheriff? Both?"

The sheriff laughed again. "Pretty much." He stuck out his hand. "How do you do, Mr. Crow. I'm Richard Hattoy."

The two shook hands.

"Glad to have you," said Jack. "You're just in time to be our first hostage."

Hattoy grinned. "They said you were a smartass."

" 'They?' Who?"

"Far as I can tell, everybody who's ever met you. Kirk, you're riding with the last of the cowboys here. Been promoted, decorated, and busted down more times than you've had safe sex. And not just the military. CIA, DEA, National Security Agency, Treasury . . . Crow, can't you find anybody to put up with you?"

"Not so far," offered Cat.

Hattoy eyed him. "You'd be—"

"That's right, sheriff."

"*You're* still following him."

Cat grinned. "Don't let his rank fool you. We all drew straws and he got Kimosabe."

"That make you Tonto?"

Cat shook his head. "Court jester."

Hattoy looked him up and down. "That figures. Tell me, did you really give up a corporate law practice in Oklahoma City to paint spaceships?"

"It was Edmond, Oklahoma, and I was a science-fiction book-cover illustrator."

"Okay. What's the difference?"

Cat shrugged. "A hobbit or two."

"Uh-huh," muttered Hattoy and turned to the others. "Enough small talk. Let's get to it."

"What's up?" asked Kirk nervously.

"Relax, deputy. For once you picked right. Mr. Crow checks out with his former associates. Nobody liked him much. And nobody but nobody wants to hire him again— but they do trust him. And he's got a lot of *very* important people behind the scenes believing in his vampires."

"Unofficially, of course," added Jack.

"Unofficial is being generous, I'd say. But it *is* a backup, of a sort."

The sheriff paused, took his hands out of his pockets, and stretched mightily and yawned and they saw the pistol on his back right hip the size of a Buick.

"Okay," Hattoy went on, "So. There are vampires and you're their hunter on this continent is the story I get. If that's so, what's your problem?"

"The problem is your mayor and your police chief," said Crow, "and who knows how many others, are doing what the vampires tell them to do."

"Oh, yeah? Why?"

"They have them under a sort of spell, sheriff," said Father Adam.

Hattoy eyed the priest unhappily. "A 'spell' . . ."

Kirk spoke up. "I don't know what else you'd call it, Richard. We took two jailers outta here that were about bled to death and crying 'cause it was over."

"Okay . . . But is that any reason to blow up my god-damned jail and maybe the whole block with it?"

Crow shook his head. "Not possible, sheriff. The charges are too small. You might lose a next-door window or two."

Hattoy's tone was one of withering disgust. " 'A window or two'?" he repeated. "What about fire? Shouldn't you have fire trucks all over the area?"

Jack Crow was starting to get hot. He didn't like the change in Hattoy's tone and he didn't like his antagonistic manner. Just when he thought he had *finally* found somebody, dammit, with brains enough to see!

"Yes, sheriff. You're right about fire trucks. But it wasn't my idea to seal them out of this area."

"No. You're just the one who's gonna risk a whole city block and maybe a whole downtown by going ahead anyway."

Jack met his eyes. "Yes."

"You take a lot on yourself, Crow. You think maybe that's why you got yourself kicked out of every fucking federal agency in the Congressional Registry?"

And that did it for Jack.

"Two things, sheriff," he all but barked. "One: you find me a president with enough *balls* to publicly recognize this nightmare and I'll be his janitor for life. Two: you *could* lose a couple of blocks. Or downtown. Or this entire one-horse town as far as I'm concerned and I'm not just real sure any-body this side of the interstate would *notice*, much less *care*! I'm not killing people, for crissakes! I'm killing old dead buildings. I'm trying to *save* the people in this dump. Or maybe you think the ones that died so far are AIDS victims?

"Look. We can kill *two* master vampires today. But only today. We know where they are. And they can't move for . . ." He looked up at the inexorable sun sinking lower and lower. Crow pointed at the horizon. "That's all the time we've got. It's a chance that won't come again.

"And it's a chance I'm fucking well gonna take if you send the *marines* in here! Risk? *Risk*? Lemme tell you something, Hattoy:

"Fuck your buildings and fuck your town and fuck your mayor and if you arent' going to help us—*knowing* we're right—just because you're afraid of a little risk . . . Well, then, fuck . . . you . . . too!"

Dead silence for three long beats.

Then the sheriff said, without taking his eyes off Crow, "I can see why you like him, Kirk. Let's go."

Kirk, dumfounded, managed, "Where to?"

"Well, I gotta save this here Jack Crow hero type and then get him outta town . . . before I have to kick his butt in half for talking to me that way. C'mon."

And then as they were walking away the sheriff looked at Felix, looked down at his hand, and Felix followed his gaze and only then realized he was carrying the squashed Browning.

"Having a little pistol trouble, boy?" whispered the sheriff and then he was gone.

Felix lifted his hand in front of his face and looked at what was left of the gun. In the sunlight the marks of the monster's fingers were clear. No machine could have vised like that.

Now when, he wondered, did I find time to pick this up?

And when, he wondered next, glancing down at his second pistol back in its holster, did I put this one back?

Hell, he didn't even remember drawing the second gun.

When, he asked then, is this luck going to run dry?

In the meantime, Carl was arguing with Crow over the sheriff.

". . . testing you, Jack. Picture this from his point of view for a second. It's one thing to call up some old favors and have you checked out. But this is his town. He had to read this face-to-face. And if you hadn't shown the balls to stand up to him for what you knew you had to do . . . Well, he probably wondered why you didn't detonate up front. Probably wondered why you tried to go inside in the first place."

"So do I," offered Cat quietly and Carl didn't like the look that passed briefly between Cat and Crow.

"He was trying to piss you off," Carl went on quickly. "I'm surprised you didn't see that one coming."

Jack lit a cigarette, looked tired. "You're right."

Carl's voice grew gentle. "Rough in there, huh?"

"If you hadn't opened that door," replied Jack Crow softly, "or if you had waited just five more minutes to open it, we'd all be dead."

"Felix," said Cat. "Show him the gun."

Felix tossed the lump to Carl and sat down on the curb. Carl caught it and drew in a sharp breath. "It did this?"

Felix lit a cigarette and nodded without looking up.

Carl shook his head. "Wow," he muttered softly. "Strong."

Jack's voice sounded odd: "Yeah. Strong. Unreal strong. Strong like we never imagined."

"Something," muttered Cat, "for you to look forward to."

"Huh?" asked Carl.

Cat lit a smoke of his own. "Haven't you heard? Jack's going to be a vampire."

"Not funny, Cherry," growled Jack.

"Not meant to be, buddy," was the response.

"What *is* all this?" Carl wanted to know.

"It's a fact," drawled Cat. "We just heard from his recruiter."

"You *talked* to her?"

"Well, for one thing we mostly just listened and for another thing, it wasn't her. It was *him*.

"The man?"

"The man. And I don't think he came up because he was thirstier than she was, Carl. I think he came up to kill us and take Jack here and make him a vampire."

Then they told Carl about the exploding elevator.

And about the crossbow.

Carl looked pale. "He actually *caught* it?"

Jack nodded.

"At what range?"

"Twelve feet."

Carl stared. "Lord!" he whispered.

" 'Gods' is the way he put it," said the previously silent Father Adam. The priest's voice was hard. "He said they were gods and he said we were fools with wooden stakes. He said Jack was the pope's altar boy."

Carl blinked. "Anything else?"

From Cat: "He doesn't like white crosses—but they can't kill him. He's not afraid of . . . what was it? Garlic? He said he'd break Felix's back or something if he even pointed a gun at him."

"What did Felix do?"

"Shot him anyway."

"Way to go, Felix!" gushed Carl.

And Felix, from his seat on the curb, turned and gave him a dead look.

And then nobody wanted to talk about it anymore.

"Enough of this," cried Cat suddenly. "What about the sheriff?"

"Yeah," said Jack, "we better get moving."

And everyone, save Cat, seemed to move at once.

Cat stared at them. "You seem pretty sure."

Carl grinned, shrugged. "He *said* he'd handle it, Cherry."

Cat frowned. "He's only one guy."

Carl grinned some more. "He's a Texas sheriff."

"And he has Kirk with him," added Jack, his own grin faint but still there.

"Great," drawled Cat dryly. "That makes two of 'em. What are they gonna do? Arrest them?"

Carl stopped what he was doing, said, "Probably."

"They mayor? The chief of police? All his cops?"

"If he has to. Cat. He's a Texas sher—"

"I know. I know. You keep saying that. So, he can handle it. Just like that?"

"Just like that."

* * *

And for the most part, that's just what happened. Team Crow never did get the details. All Kirk would say was some mumbling about the sheriff walking up to the barricades and telling 'em to break it up.

Twenty minutes later the Team had fire trucks and firemen and ambulances and police protection and demolition advisers the chief had brought in originally to stop them and all sorts of experts on local buildings like the jail. They even had structural plans and advice on how to blow it, and Carl and Cat did, in fact, move three of the charges a couple of yards.

Hattoy showed up in time to press the detonator personally, saying, "All my life I've wanted to kaboom one of these things." This was just smoke, of course, to hide his adding another layer of his personal authority on the event in case of future hassle.

They blew it once, twice, three times, in layers. Then they blew the rubble. Then they blew it some more before the female emerged, rocketing upward in a hail of bricks and screeching. She popped on Adam's side and the priest came through once more, taking only two quick steps on the uneven surface before delivering a clean bisecting shot.

He didn't appear until a half hour before dusk, a full-throated scarlet fountain of hatred and fury. His screams were ear-splitting. His flames were supernaturally bright.

But in daylight it didn't matter. Jack had seen it all before. He did get close enough to recognize the monster who knew his name before punching the crossbow through the burning chest. But there was nothing special about the shot. Or the end.

"When you're a vampire, Crow . . ." it had said.

Jack watched the ashes burn all the way down, then whispered, "Not today, little god."

He stood there awhile, lit and smoked a cigarette before moving. When he finally turned away, toward the Team now milling with the sheriff and his people, the realization struck deep.

My God, that was close

And then: Why did I try to go inside? I almost killed everyone! What was I trying to do?

Today was three years, three months, and some-odd days of this madness.

Shit.

"Thank God Felix can shoot . . ."

Chapter 20

Davette wore a khaki blouse and a khaki skirt and a light blue scarf Annabelle had found for her somewhere that highlighted her blond hair and rich golden skin. Felix was, quite simply, unable to look at her.

He was afraid of what he might say to her.

He was afraid of what he might do to her.

He was mostly afraid of the vampires, though, and it didn't matter if she had just lately come on board and it didn't matter that she was, technically, still a reporter doing a story—all that had long been forgotten. She was part of Team Crow now, sure as hell. Team Crow was home.

He was afraid of what he might do for her.

So now, nine hours into a most un-Team-like victory party, he sat in the lone chair in the far corner of what passed for a suite in the cheap motel the ladies had found and did his drinking and chain-smoking alone.

Because Jack Crow was wrong.

This deal would *not* play anymore. Not like this.

Not with me.

Fuck 'em.

Everyone noticed, of course. They could hardly help it.

When their gunman was planted so hard in that one chair. When he smoked so incessantly, drank so ferociously. When he would brood so hard he seemed to strobe . . .

Sometimes it seemed that chair of his, that whole corner of the room, really, seemed to corridor away into the distance.

Sooner or later, it was going to get ugly. It had been heading for it since the last pile of ashes.

Felix rode with Cat in the motorhome on the way to the rendezvous with the women. He rode in silence, ignoring what little Cat had to say, until Cat finally turned in the driver's seat and looked at him.

Is he relieved? Cat wondered. Stunned? Maybe he's in shock or . . .

No! he realized suddenly. That's anger! He's furious . . .

And just then Felix had turned and looked at him and those dead eyes had bored deeply for just a moment. Then the gunman climbed out of his seat and disappeared into the back until they reached the motel.

Even for Annabelle, who was used to the endless waiting, this had been a tough one. Her tears of joy were a little brighter this time, her hugs of welcome a little tighter, her voice a little more strident. Davette, on the other hand, seemed possessed by a surreal glow of happiness at their survival. She took turns with Annabelle hugging everyone and blushing furiously when Cat, with a wicked grin, hauled off and gave her a long, wet, sloppy one.

All save Felix. He stood at the edge of it all, nodding curtly to the women and asking for his room key and mumbling something about wanting to take a shower right away.

He got his key and a tense moment before Father Adam announced that he wanted to have special services immediately—while everyone was still sober enough to pray, ha ha.

And Felix took part in this but the way he knelt and rocked and prayed, so fiercely radiating anger and fear . . . By the time the priest could quickly break it up they all felt sprayed.

Then there was a knock on the door and Sheriff Hattoy and Kirk and a few other deputies appeared for a little celebrating and Jack brought out glasses and their special schnapps and instructed the newcomers on the toast: "Here's to the great ones . . ." began Jack.

"There's damn few of us left!" finished the others and they all downed the schnapps and all, but Felix, laughed and asked for more. The gunman went to his room, taking a bottle of his scotch with him.

They partied without him, while the women desperately tried to whip up enough food fast enough to absorb just enough of the alcohol to make Annabelle's hypnotic debriefing possible later on. It was going to be close. Even for Team Crow, the boozing was heavy. The sheriff excused himself early. There had been a good reason why he had been late to their troubles, and that reason still existed. He had more work to do. He exchanged a quick private smile with Kirk before leaving his best deputy behind, as everyone had known would happen.

They partied gamely along some more and no one said anything about Felix not being there. And when the food was ready and he called from behind his locked motel room door that he wasn't hungry, no one said anything about that, either.

But everyone noticed. Everyone, that is, except Jack Crow. Jack refused to notice, thought Cat. Or maybe he's just too high on Felix to care. Jack perched on the edge of the sink while they ate and, master storyteller that he was, relayed every detail of the miracles his gunman had wrought. Carl had been outside during the fighting and the women hadn't been there at all and the three of them listened raptly to every word.

About the woman with the stakes in her, streaking and screeching about in the darkness with Felix's split-second marksmanship on her all the way.

About him, the way he seemed to levitate out of the elevator and stroll so casually toward them, about his *catching* the fired crossbow bolt, about his looking right at Felix and warning him about the gun.

"And Felix shot him anyway?" Carl asked.

Jack sipped from his wine and nodded. "Three shots. Hit 'im twice that I saw. Then it was just a blur until he grabbed the gun."

"And crushed it?" Annabelle wanted to know. "Really?"

Jack nodded again. "With one hand. That's when Carl

here opened the door and it turned toward the light for a second. By the time he had turned back around Felix had drawn his other automatic, *left*-handed, and he shot him right through the center of his goddamned forehead."

Jack paused, lit a cigarette. "I think he would have killed at least a couple of us if it weren't for that. Hell, he could do that on his way past us out of the light. But not after that shot.

"Carl, our shooter is everything we could ever have wanted."

And everything Davette had wanted him to be. She sat there, in the silence that followed, with her eyes welling happy, happy tears. She could not explain her joy, her sense of hope, any more than she could explain, or even *fathom*, this viselike hold he had on her.

But somehow, because he was so . . . so wonderful at this, it made it all seem okay. Even the jagged vibrations of his presence.

"Yep," said Jack Crow, staring deep into his wineglass, "everything we could ever have wanted."

Then he looked at the smiling Davette and grinned.

"Then how come," popped Cat from amidst the others' concerned looks, "we're not all happy?"

Jack shook his head. "Aw, Cherry, give it a rest. Felix is just . . ."

"Where *is* he, Jack?" demanded Annabelle. "Why is he in his room? Even when he's here, he just . . . He looked at me like he hated me! Hated us all! He's not eating. He's there in his room drinking alone. He . . ."

"Relax, woman!" Jack snapped. He stood up and towered over them. "Let me tell you kids a thing or two. Felix is . . ."

Then the door came open and Felix was there, cigarette in the corner of his mouth, scotch bottle in hand. He stepped inside and stopped and looked at them, all of them, for a heavy silent moment, then turned curtly away toward the chair in the corner of the suite and planted himself there and drank some more.

Under Jack's silent directions, they tried to party any-way. Jack whispered to Annabelle to drop the debriefing for tonight, concentrate on the celebration and the booze.

"Party, babe! You know!" he muttered grinning in her ear.

And they gave it a try, starting with the music. ZZ Top, Stevie Ray Vaughn, Roy Orbison, everyone in their tape library. It helped. They danced and laughed and giggled and drank too much and it went on for hours and hours and early on somebody in the next room complained, a trucker type in a bad sleepy mood, so Jack had the women haul his ass in through the doorway and drink a little drinkie and "Don't worry about being dressed, stranger," he insisted, looking down at his bare chest and feet. "We'll find you a shirt and all the rest of us will take our shoes *off*! Race!"

And they all laughed and fell to the floor and Annabelle was the first to get her shoes off—in like one half a second. And Cat was the last—it took him three minutes of concen-trated effort before he gave up and put his drink down and tried with both hands.

Then it only took him another minute and a half.

The trucker loved it and wanted to know if he could call his buddies who were just down the hall and Jack said, "Hell, yes! Let's go *git* 'em!"

And they did go "git" 'em, all five of them. Plus Doris, the blond at the front desk, and her boyfriend Eddy Duane who, Cat felt sure, should have by God learned to play the guitar backward by now. They also gathered in a couple named Henderson, who had come into town for a funeral earlier in the day and said they could use a wake. About an hour later a skinny bald man in his seventies, who was easily six-foot-six, knocked on the door and asked to join the party. He produced a business card: "Mr. Kite, Layman Activist, The Church of the Sub-Genius."

"It's the world's first industrial Church," he explained to Father Adam.

"Industrial?" asked the priest.

"Right. We pay taxes and everything," replied Mr. Kite.

"I'm not sure I understand. What is it you believe in?"

"Everything," said Mr. Kite with a smile. "But mostly the free-market economy."

So they all had another drink on that, for the benefit of Mr. Kite.

Felix sat stone still and staring throughout. He didn't speak, didn't get up, didn't acknowledge anyone. There was something so threatening about his somber posture that none of the strangers even tried to approach him. And inquiries were put off by Team members.

Only Davette seemed unable to stay away. She got close enough to him to change his ashtray twice. And Annabelle thought she was going to speak to him a few times, almost on impulse. But she didn't and neither did anyone else.

But Jack seemed happy about it all. Weirdly content, in fact. Occasionally the Team would spot him standing off to one side, catching his party breath and grinning at Felix's back.

Does he know something we don't know? wondered Cat. Or is he just blind?

By three thirty the party was running out of steam for those with nothing to celebrate. The Hendersons, who had been trying to teach two of the truckers to dance and sing, had finally given up. Their only decent pupil had been a barrel-chested old man with "Pop" on his uniform who had actually learned a few steps of soft shoe in his heavy boots before collapsing from alcohol and years. Once that last person was off his feet, the sleepies began to creep in on all non-Team members. They *could* have reinvigorated for more fun—Team Crow had its ways. But no one wanted them to stay.

Felix had started talking to himself.

Angrily, forcefully, furiously . . . but in total silence. His lips moved, his face warped in rage, the words spitting bitterly out, but not one sound came with them.

Jack gave Annabelle a look. She used her deft touch and less than five minutes later the revelers had been poured out and the door locked behind them. Then they stood, Cat and

Carl, Annabelle and Davette, Adam and Kirk, and Jack
Crow, and watched. It was eerie. The music still played softly.
The cheap overhead lights of the motel room reached Felix's
corner only in shadows that played oddly on his working silent
face.

Annabelle stood next to Jack. She sounded more concerned than frightened. "Oh, Jack! How much *has* he had to
drink?"

Jack smiled softly down at her. "He's not drunk."

"Not drunk? I find that hard to believe."

Jack shrugged. "Oh, he is drunk. But not *drunk* drunk.
This isn't booze."

"What is it?"

Jack paused a moment, thinking.

He seems so confident, Annabelle thought, looking up
at him.

"What is it?" she repeated.

"Claustrophobia."

"What?" Cat whispered suspiciously.

Jack laughed quietly, looked at them all. "C'mon, people. Let's all have a seat."

And except for Davette, they did. She stayed fussing idly
in the kitchen while the rest of them found a seat on the floor
or sprawled on the couches. Jack took the only other easy
chair and drew it up to face Felix's, about six feet directly in
front of him.

Felix saw him, knew he was there. His lips went still.
But he didn't look directly at him or anyone else.

"Davette," Jack called out softly, "turn that off."

She eyed him nervously, then smiled and stepped over
and turned off the music. Very quiet, all of a sudden.

Then Jack leaned forward in his chair, propping his elbows on his knees and smiling pleasantly into his drink.

"Okay . . ." he said.

It took a couple of beats. Then the gunman's eyes riveted
onto Jack's. Still staring, Felix took a sip from his bottle, lit
a cigarette, leaned back in his chair, and spoke. Drunk as he
was, his words were clear. Very cold, like very sharp ice.

But clear.

"You're out of this, Crow. It's blown. They know who you are. They know what you do. They know your name."

"So?"

"So. Change your name, change what you do. Quit. Or every job from now on will be another trap."

"What about the Team?"

"Same as before. But as the hunters again. Not the hunted."

Jack grinned and leaned back in his chair. "You think I can do that now?"

Felix's smile was scary. "*One* of us can. Now."

"So that's it. *One* of us."

"That's it."

Jack glanced at the others. "If they don't follow you . . . Form your own Team?"

Felix looked surprised. He frowned. "I hadn't thought about that."

Jack's voice was hard. "I didn't think you had."

"What the hell is . . . " began Carl angrily.

"Quiet!" snapped Crow without looking at him. Then he relaxed, eyed Felix for a moment.

"Did it ever occur to you that we've finally got them on the run?"

Felix sneered. "Ever occur to you that you're not cutting it anymore?"

Jack held up a hand before any of the others could protest. He lit a cigarette, leaned forward in his chair once more.

"Yes," he said simply. "Yes it has. I can admit that. Can *you* admit running out on the job you were born to do?"

"I'm not running out on . . ."

"Like hell you aren't!" snapped Jack. He stood up angrily, began to pace back and forth in front of Felix's chair.

"This is the game, Felix. This is it. I *can't* quit because I'm the symbol. They know my name. You can't because you're the best there is and *that's* the part you don't like!"

"Bullshit, Crow!"

"Is it? *Is* it? Hadn't *thought* about your own team, had

you? Hell, no. If you *had* thought, which you by God didn't want to do, you'd have realized they wouldn't leave me and you would have to do it on your own. But you don't want to do that. You don't want to do it at all!"

Felix was out of his chair in a flash.

"You calling me a coward?"

And Davette couldn't take it anymore. Suddenly she was there, standing beside the two heaving chests, her voice that of a small child, a small doll.

"Don't . . ." she whispered, the tears already starting to pour, ". . . don't . . . please, don't."

"I don't know *what* I'm calling you, Felix!" yelled Crow. "Because I don't know what the fuck you are!"

Felix's voice was stone. "Then try something."

And they all thought the fight would start then and it should have, really. But a piece of Jack was also shouting at him. Leadership, goddammit!

And so he took a breath and backed off a bit and tried again.

"Felix, I *can't* quit just because they know my name. Is the *next* guy gonna do the same? That's all it takes. They know if they can find out who we are they can run us off? We can't. We're it. This *is* the game!

"Look. I'm *sorry* if this comes at a bad time in your life, Felix. But it *always does*, dammit!" And then Crow felt the anger spurt out and he lost it again.

"You're just gonna have to see if you're man enough to face it!"

And Felix barked, "Fuck off!" He turned to the others. "Fuck you all . . ."

And Davette's baby voice sighed, "No . . . no . . . no . . ."

And for a second they stopped and looked at her. But then Felix shook it off. He reached down and picked up his cigarettes and stuffed them in his pocket and stalked toward the door.

"Die, then!" he shouted at the room. "Die if you want to! Die for his ego or senility or whatever the hell it is!"

Davette was chasing him, her arms held out. "Please, *please* . . ."

"Forget it!" he stormed at her. "All of you, forget it!"

"You *can't* . . . " she pleaded and the sobs shook her tiny form.

But he could. He could do what everyone had known for hours he was going to do."

"I quit," said Felix.

And Davette's voice came out strong and full and she cried out, "You can't! You don't know what they can *do* to people! You don't know what it's like . . . You . . . "

And Felix and Jack Crow looked at her together and together they said: "Whaat . . ."

Davette looked at the two of them, back and forth quickly. She hung her head. Then she reached down to the hem of her khaki skirt and took it in her fist and raised it up, exposing the perfect silken lines of her golden legs and the sharp heartache contrast of yellow panties . . .

. . . and *there*, there high on her left inner thigh . . .

Like the bite of a monstrous spider.

It could be no other kind of wound.

"Help me," she whispered.

"Help me . . ."

Fourth Interlude: The Victim

The Team stood stunned and staring at her and she tried to get it all out at once, all of it that she had wanted to tell them from the beginning, about what had happened to her and how she had *really* come to see them that day in California—but it just came out as sputtering tears.

It was Felix, of all people, who rescued her, taking her gently in his arms and speaking soft, soothing nothings. He led her to his chair and sat her carefully down and dragged up a chair for himself, all the time still murmuring reassuringly to her.

The others unfroze at last, Annabelle hip enough to fetch Kleenex and a glass of water, the men moving slowly, still more or less in shock, into seats of their own to listen. And it *was* kind of like the Inquisition, with them all circling about her suspicious and staring but she didn't mind. She *deserved* this. She *deserved* it for what she had done to them—or *almost* had done to them.

Because she hadn't come to do a story on them.

She had come to bring their killer.

She had left him in the trunk of that car she had been driving.

He was the fiend they had just slain, the one with the headband.

The little god.

His name was Ross Stewart and she had known him for ten years, since she was eleven and had taken Miss Findley's Dance Class for Young Ladies and Gentlemen.

Ross had been in the class. But he hadn't been a gentleman even then.

She started sputtering again. Felix leaned forward and took her hands in his and told her to relax, to relax and take deep breaths and start from the beginning. And she knew he was right, knew he made sense, knew she should do it that way, but now, looking into his eyes, closer to him than she'd ever been, she wanted to skip all that and . . .

And get right to the meat.

Get right to the shame.

She felt compelled—obsessed, really—as she had from the very first time she had seen him, to tell him this. To have him know all about what she had done and what she had been made to do.

She wanted him to know everything. Every nasty detail.

But she did what he said. She tried again from the beginning. Not the very beginning, when she was young, but from when it had really started. Last spring. Easter vacation. Religious holiday.

Her Aunt Victoria had planned a wonderful party for her.

Aunt Vicky's house was the best-kept secret in north Dallas, a tiny, nondescript entrance on Inwood Road exploded, once inside the driveway, into a miraculous vision of a graystone mansion with multileveled terraces sprawling throughout the sculptured gardens and running brooks and towering trees that had tiny colored lights way up high in them, where the stars were. The party had spilled out over all the terraces and there was a band playing and people dancing and everyone was there, simply everyone she had grown up with, glittering and beautiful, the sons and daughters of wealth and private schools, and you just knew by looking at them that it wasn't just the fortunes of the past represented here but the fortunes of the future certain to be made.

And Davette was the princess.

Because she really *was* beautiful, she knew that, and tall

and blond and smart, too, editor of the university newspaper, and she laughed and talked and gloried in the attention, warm with friends when she wanted and unapproachable whenever she felt like it because Aunt Vicky had taught her that. You didn't really have to have that same conversation with *every* man.

But there were two details wrong and they nagged her. Her best friend, Kitty, had yet to show up. And Aunt Vicky was still abed.

Anyone else would still be "in" bed. But not Aunt Victoria, not in that huge three-hundred-year-old canopied bed in that immense bedroom full of all those beautiful chairs and settees and intricate knickknacks her brother, Uncle Harley, had brought home from around the world. The whole house was a treasure, but it was always this room, Davette had realized, that meant her aunt to her, meant romance and glory, which to Davette had always been one and the same.

She missed her mommy and daddy sometimes, so long dead now, but with Aunt Vicky and her brother, Uncle Harley, her rearing had been just as warm and loving—and a lot more fun. Uncle Harley, decorator to royalty, had shown her the world. And Aunt Victoria had shown her the ways of . . . the lady. Ways that made men sit up straight and turn their language soft and clean when she entered the room. A certain regal air—never haughty, exactly, but definitely, inevitably, superior. Reluctantly superior, as Aunt Victoria once confided to her.

Aunt Victoria had that look about her that made hard men wish for dragons to slay for her. Just for want of that twinkling smile.

But now she was ill and those beautiful lace bedclothes only made her seem more pale and less strong. She had received a few people, close friends who wished to look in on her, but she wouldn't leave her bed, wouldn't come to the party.

"Don't worry, dear," she had cooed to her niece. "Have a good time, be a lady," Then there was that twinkle. "Then come back and tell me every single detail."

And they had laughed and kissed and Davette had gone back to her rooms, where she found Kitty, who was staying with her, sitting naked on the side of her bathtub and crying.

Over Ross Stewart.

Davette couldn't *believe* it. Ross Stewart? No-Class Ross, as she *and* Kitty had dubbed him and the name had stuck with him from sixth grade to high school graduation because it fit! It really fit!

"I can't believe it!" she blurted, shaking her head before catching herself and realizing how she must sound.

When she heard Kitty's sobbing "I can't either!" she knew they had a problem

Davette sat down on the edge of the tub and put her arm around her best friend in the world and tried to . . . to what, to console her? Because Davette didn't really *understand* how this was even possible and all she could get out of Kitty was, yes, she *was* ashamed at being with Ross Stewart, but, no, she had no intention of leaving him.

"I can't help myself," she said, looking Davette straight in the eye.

And Davette had felt a cold, dark chill.

Now it was after ten P.M. and the party was in full swing and she still hadn't heard from Kitty and she was starting to fret. Maybe, she thought, Ross has changed. Maybe he really wasn't as bad as she had remembered. And she tried thinking back through her memories and images of him in a different light, in a more positive way.

But she wasn't having much luck. Ross Stewart had been just awful.

Good-looking, really, in a kind of decadent way. He had long black curly hair and he was tall and well built, she remembered. And smart, too, because he had made excellent grades and St. Mark's Prep, the brother school to her own Hockaday, was a very demanding place. No, Ross had no excuses for being the way he was, foul-mouthed and dirty-minded and totally without class. All the boys talked about sex all the time, of course. They were teenagers and that was practically their job. But Ross always talked about it a little too long, his jokes always a little more filthy, his leers always too damned piercing.

And the money, of course. Ross's family didn't have any, at least not the way most of the private school parents did. But that was no excuse, either. There were several students worse off than Ross and they were okay. At least they didn't go around so *greedy* all the time, talking about the prices of everything and dating the richest, most homely girls who had never before had such attention.

God, she remembered, he used to drive the *girls'* cars on dates! And once he even—

"There you are, baby!" sounded a familiar voice.

She sighed before turning around. She really wasn't up to this. But she was trapped. She turned around and smiled at her last high school boyfriend, football captain, senior class president, Taker of Her Virginity, Dale Boijock.

And also the most boring human being alive.

"How are you, Dale?" she said without enthusiasm. "I'm so glad you could come."

Dale stepped forward and flashed his perfect smile and said, in a voice rich with meaning, "I wouldn't have missed it."

And she thought she would die or run screaming from him or worse but she hung in there, talking small talk. She managed to get them walking toward the bar for some wine so she could keep running into other people and not be left alone to talk to Dale one-on-one.

Dale fought it, trying to get her off to one side to talk all alone. But he was getting quite a bit of attention, too, and enjoying it. Tall blond, beautiful blue eyes, a natural leader, a wonderful athlete—a Polish-American god was Dale Boijock. He had been the Catch of All Catches in high school but he was *so* boring and how could she ever have slept with him?

Curiosity, of course. She did not live in Aunt Vicky's era and almost all of her friends had "done it," many more than once, and here she was with the most eligible boyfriend around and she was just dying to know and it had been her suggestion.

He had been shocked. But he had come around.

At the motel he really was sweet and tender, treating her like a porcelain doll, and she had to face it, some parts of it were pretty interesting.

But somehow Dale had managed to make even those dull. And she knew, as he drove home, that she simply could not bear to be with him ever, ever again but she couldn't think of a graceful way to . . .

And then she had turned in the car seat and told him he was the best lover she had ever had.

He had laughed at that at first, of course. Then he had looked at her and saw she was serious and that tanned blond face had frowned and he had pulled the car over and the questioning had begun.

Looking back, she decided she had handled it just about · perfectly.

Did he know him?

Who?

The other guy.

Well, she knew Dale knew *some* of them.

Some of them? There was more than one?

Well, yes . . .

Who?

Dale, I don't really think I could—

How many, then?

How many? What difference could that possibly—

She had taken a positively wicked joy in bashing his pride. After she had strung it out a good half hour, she allowed him to force her to tell him the "truth," that there had been somewhere between fifteen and an even dozen. She couldn't remember exactly.

Then he had leaned across her and opened the passenger door and ordered her to get out.

Trying desperately to keep a straight face, she had climbed meekly out of his car, closed the door behind her, and stood there, head down, her hands together in front of her, until the car screeched off.

On the way back home she had giggled quite a lot.

It really was a perfect solution. His pride wouldn't let

him tell others about her and even if he did no one would believe it of Princess Davette anyway. And best of all, she would never be bothered by Dale Boijock again. And she hadn't been, for four long-years.

Until tonight. And this was looking grim. After four years of the Ivy League's worldly ways, she knew his attitudes had changed. She could tell by that look on his face. It could only mean one thing, his insistence at getting her alone to talk: He was going to, God help him, forgive her.

And she really didn't think she could handle *that* with a straight face.

She just had to get away beforehand.

"Dale? Would you excuse me just a minute?" she asked sweetly, then fled.

That's how she ended up hiding out on the terrace, in a metal chair behind an enormous plant.

And that's where she was when she heard the Voice.

It wasn't a deep voice. It wasn't rich and melodious. In fact, it was rather dry and thin. But it was so . . . *smooth*. Smooth and clear and it really carried, cutting through the other voices with it.

She had been aware, in the few minutes she'd spent in her little hideout—on the lookout for Dale—of a conversation going on on the terrace a few feet away. But she hadn't really been paying attention. Now, with that voice, she began to.

Sex. They were talking about sex. About the difference between men and women. About what each needed. What women needed. What women craved. What they had to have. Release. Abandon. Wantonness. Penetration.

*   *   *

Looking around at the faces in the motel room . . . Looking at Felix's face now so close to her, his eyes gentle but so acute . . .

She just didn't know.

Should she tell them? Should she tell them all—tell Felix—what *exactly* had been said? What words? What sweet, forbidden, pornographic . . .

She didn't know.

She didn't know if she could describe what it had been like, sitting there on the terrace and hearing those awful dirty words cutting through the night toward her. Surrounding her. Caressing her. Prodding her. The words he used were so filthy and his descriptions so graphic. No one else was talking but him, now, the entire terrace alive with electricity because it was *arousing*. She couldn't believe it. Never in her life had anyone spoken such things in her presence. Oh, she knew the words. She knew what they meant—every schoolgirl knew the words. But to hear them used, to feel them scything in her direction.

And to have them so erotic. To see what he described so clearly. To understand it so well.

Ladies and whores, he talked about. About the difference. About the need for ladies to be both. About what the right man knew to do with his lady behind the bedroom door, free her from her ladyship, from her courtly demeanor. Give her the chance to wallow and grovel and glow.

She could *not* understand how such talk could affect her so. But it had. It *had*. She had sat there—perched there, really—on the edge of her little chair, panting, chest heaving . . . Because she seemed to *understand* it. She seemed to understand just what release, just what euphoric abandon he meant. And when he went on and on spinning his pictures and images she saw her own skin glowing, her own fingers grasping, her own thighs wide and receptive and . . .

God help me! What is happening?

She didn't tell the details to the Team. She didn't. She glazed over it and hurried past it and she knew she wasn't meeting their eyes—his eyes—so she forced herself to look up and his gaze was steady and she believed he knew she had left something out.

And she believed he knew what it was.

It was when she decided she could simply hear no more that everything began to happen, that things began to whizz and spiral about her, that her life began to ricochet . . .

That her soul began its twist in the vise.

The Voice had stopped for the time being and she had risen, spontaneously, from her chair, jerked herself up and forward and away from this madness and the heavy air left by the silence and taken a step around the plant toward the sliding glass door to the library—she could do this! Just step around and through and no one would see her or even know she had been there . . .

And the other voice suddenly perked up and it was a voice she knew, knew well—had always known—and she couldn't help herself. She turned as she stepped and leaned wrong and her heel caught and she just *careened* into that awful plant, banging the branches with her shoulder and leaves went everywhere and by the time she had regained her balance—barely, with ankles out and knees together and wineglass spilling—she was among them. A semicircle of faces she couldn't meet were staring surprised looks in her direction and she heard that voice she had recognized again saying, "Davette!"

And she looked up and saw it was . . . Kitty!

Kitty and other girls she had grown up with. There was Patty and Debra and . . . Oh God! The embarrassment, because it wasn't just crashing through the shrubbery, it was the looks on their faces, the steaming-dreamy looks because *they* had been listening to that Voice, too, and their faces were flushed and their chest heaving and she knew they could see her own flush . . .

And, Oh my God, if *Kitty* was here, that meant . . .

"Davette," said Kitty again, "you remember Ross Stewart."

And he was there, looming over her, his black curly hair and ivory-white skin and black eyes so deep and forever and he took her free hand in his and said, with a wicked curling smile, "Davette! How often I've thought of you."

And that was that. Her lights went out. She fainted dead away.

It took her some time before she figured out exactly what had happened next. Ross must have caught her as she fell.

And though she was only out for a second she managed to have what seemed an endless dream—nightmare—of running through some awful wet-stoned maze of tunnels with someone she never saw but knew to be Ross Stewart, walking briskly after her and laughing.

But when she woke up she hadn't even reached the floor yet and Ross Stewart still held her in his arms with his eyes boring through her and she panicked and she flailed at his chest and arms and she screamed.

It was the sound of her own voice that shook her out of it, that and Kitty bending over her saying, "Davette! Honey!" And as Ross lifted her upright—so easily!—and she saw all the faces on the terrace turned to look at this crazy woman, she was so humiliated she wished she could just explode at will.

And then "Stewart! What do you think you're doing with her?" sounded out and she recognized the voice of Dale Boijock being macho and saw him shouldering his way toward her and she closed her eyes and wondered, Could this get *any* worse?

It could.

Ross, still supporting her—again, so easily!—transferred her to his left arm and turned and faced the oncoming Dale and said, "What I am doing with her, so far as it concerns you, is anything I damn well please."

It was meant to taunt him—all these people watching him—and it worked. Dale lurched forward, his right arm reaching out, and Davette whispered out, "Dale! No!" but she had no breath and her voice didn't carry and in any case it was too late.

Ross's right hand snapped out like a snake around Dale's wrist and held it fast and there was a pause as the two eyed one another and then she felt, rather than saw, Ross's smile as he began to squeeze and Davette had a chance to think how oddly beautiful were Ross's half-inch-long fingernails before Dale's wrist broke.

Ross released the wrist as Dale cried out with pain and jerked backward. Then came a beat or two as Dale stared, unbelieving, between Ross and his swelling wrist.

"It was easy, Dale," whispered Ross so that only the three of them could hear. "Want to see it again?"

Davette saw Dale's eyes go wide with surprise and growing fury and she saw it coming so clearly. Dale, who had probably never lost a fight in his life—and certainly not to that wimp-ass gigolo, Ross Stewart—simply could not help himself. And his roar *was* very leonine as he launched all six-foot-two-inches and two hundred thirty–odd pounds of muscle at his rival.

Ross's casual backhanded flick of his wrist swept, rather than knocked, Dale some three feet sideways through the air, through the terrace railing, and nine feet down into the gently rolling slope of the gardens below.

He wasn't really hurt. The slope was thick with rich ground cover and they could hear him moaning out in pain and shock. Within seconds others had reached him and pronounced him okay. But the fight was over. That was the point.

"I *wish* he hadn't made me do that," said Ross to the astonished onlookers and his sincerity seemed so real that Davette felt them collectively taking Ross's side of it.

"I'm terribly sorry about that," he then said to her, looking down.

Only then did she realize she was still in his arms and as she started to pull away he spoke again, but this time it was that Voice.

"I'm sure," he purred at her, "you've had enough excitement for one night. Let us take you upstairs before you fall asleep on your feet."

And she *hadn't* felt sleepy, had she? But now she had images of that soft bed and no voices or crowds or music, those cool sheets . . .

"Thank you," she whispered, nodding to both of them, for Kitty was back alongside her and the three of them left and took easy steady steps up the broad staircase and down the hallway to her rooms. Ross didn't seem to be there as Kitty helped the sleepwalker undress and climb into bed and lie down.

"He's really changed, hasn't he?" was the last thing Kitty

said to her and Davette saw her friend's pleasure, as though the evening had redeemed her association with him.

But Davette was too tired to answer. She thought she managed to nod before drifting off.

She had no dreams.

She wasn't sure it was true sleep at all. She felt only light and floating and still and intermittently aware. She knew when the band stopped. She had a sense of the party finally ending and the great house becoming empty. Kitty always stayed in the adjoining bedroom, ever since junior high, and later she was sure she heard her in there talking to Ross and then there were other muffled noises and she pressed herself back into sleep so as not to hear.

Much later, toward dawn, she felt the weight on the edge of the bed and opened her eyes to protest once and for all. But she could not speak at first. His eyes seemed to shine at her. His skin was so creamy white and softly carved around his smile. His black curls glowed in the light coming through her open balcony.

"Could you hear me well enough through that plant?" he asked.

She had been lying flat on her back, without moving, the entire night. Now she sat straight up.

"You mean . . . you knew?"

"Of course," he replied softly and the Voice was back. "Kitty has heard me before. The others didn't matter at all." His hand reached out and caressed her cheek and there was nothing, dammit, she seemed to be able to do about it. "No," he continued, "it was all for you."

And the blood roared through her and her breath raced as sharp hissing pants and when his hand pulled back she all but cried out, What is *happening* to me! when she felt disappointment at the loss of his touch. And his smile curled wide and full around his face, melding with her eyes, and his right hand came toward her again, with the fingernails of forefinger and thumb snapping together like a small animal . . . click . . . click . . . click

And she knew where, through her sheer nightgown, the

little creature would bite her. But she could not stop this,
either. She could not even stop the *wanting* of this. And when,
matching the heaving rhythm of her chest, the two fingernails
clamped with gentle pain on her left nipple, she fainted once
more—but not before an orgasm of more exquisite agony
than she could ever have imagined.

Sitting there in that cheap lime-green motel room and
telling the Team—telling *him*—about that first night . . .
it was the worst moment. It was not the worst part of her
story—there were many crimes to come. But, still, it was the
worst.

For now they knew what Ross could do to her, what he
was *always* able to do to her, anytime he wanted.
The . . . *humiliation*. The sense of being so simple and cheap.
Of being used goods. Easy used goods.

Because the sexiness was still *there*. Even now, thinking
back on it and thanking Sweet Jesus it was over, she felt the
trembling passion of it all. And the others around her felt it
also, it steamed from all the men save Father Adam, whose
pious visage seemed struck in granite. But even Annabelle
was affected.

And she tried to explain it to them. Tried, because
she wasn't sure she understood it herself. But it had to do
with the darker edge of a half-lie. Half-lie implying also a
half-truth, yes, she knew that. And that was the vampire's
secret.

What the vampire told you was true. He lied when he
told you it was everything.

The day after the party had been one of the great days
of Davette's life. Later, when she looked back on it, she knew
it was because she had spent the day hiding from an impending
sense of darkness. But at the time it was sweet, accustomed,
familiar silliness.

The first days of every school vacation for years and years
Davette had spent the same way: shopping with Kitty. Usually
they went with Aunt Victoria in the limo and that was always

fun because Aunt Victoria's entrance at the front door of some place like Neiman-Marcus prompted some truly *amazing* scurrying around on the part of the sales staff.

Aunt Vicky was too tired to come with them that day but that didn't prevent her from rousing the girls up early like her usual imperial self and getting them "dressed and pressed and made-up for the table, ladies!"

And Davette loved it, being rousted out of bed, rushing around trying to get ready, with Aunt Vicky's voice carrying over everything, laughing and giggling with Kitty as they used the adjoining bathroom.

Davette loved it because she didn't have to think.

Think about last night.

Or him.

Or herself.

Or . . .

Or whether or not she should tell Kitty. After all, Ross was *her* boyfriend. Lord, what would Kitty *think* of her if she told her that . . .

That what? What really happened?

Did anything really happen?

Maybe . . . Maybe it was just a weird dream. I mean, *nobody* can just reach out like that and make you . . . Can they?

And a tiny little voice answered back: Ross Stewart can. Anytime he wants to.

But she ignored it and giggled some more and then they were out there in the sunshine, checkbooks and credit cards with safeties off. And it was just as much fun as it always was. Shopping, SHOPPING, *SHOPPING*!

They laughed so *hard* and they laughed so *long* and they spent so much *money*!

It was great.

And they had lunch at the same place they always did, shopping bags piled up high all around the table, and Luigi waited on them like he always did, making those awful snide little remarks about rich girls and "Come the Revolution" and they were just as snitty back and all involved loved it like they always had.

Kitty loved it as much as she did, maybe more. She seemed to relish the air and the sun, and Davette thought she could use more of each—she looked just a trifle pale—but that didn't matter right now because the day was so perfect and then tonight, like every other vacation, the three of them would sit in the formal dining room, the girls wearing their new loot, and talk and talk with Aunt Vicky. And then Kitty, in some chance remark, mentioned casually that Ross would be joining them for dinner that night.

And the planet froze. And slowed down. And wanted to . . . grind . . . to . . . a . . . stop.

Because it had always just been the three of them on those nights, sitting and eating, and Davette had counted on that safe picture of at least one night, tonight, without having to see him again or hear that Voice.

Davette started to say something about maybe Aunt Vicky not wanting to share their traditional post-shopping dinner with an extra person and Kitty beat her to it, telling her how Ross and Aunt Vicky had become such fast friends, talking long into the night about philosophy and what-all, sometimes until almost dawn because Ross simply *hated* the daytime. He said it was only for primitive man, who had good reason to fear the dark.

And the planet slowed further and the faces in the mall seemed more distant and it seemed suddenly terribly important to Davette that she not make a big deal about this, not object at all.

Not let anyone know how she feared.

So she kept walking and she kept shopping and she managed a hollow echo to Kitty's laugh that she felt sure she had gotten away with and then, abruptly, when they passed a restaurant they had always passed by before, Davette suggested they drop in and have a cocktail.

"Because we are twenty-one now, aren't we?" was all she would reply to Kitty's startled look.

She ordered a bloody mary and when Kitty ordered just mineral water Davette kidded her until Kitty said, "Ross says he doesn't like women who drink."

And Davette thought: good.

And ordered another.

And then another.

She wasn't exactly drunk when they finally got home. But she was certainly feeling it, feeling pretty good, in fact, because the fear seemed more distant somehow and the alcohol seemed a kind of talisman, maybe, to ward off evil spirits.

And she giggled to herself thinking that. Kitty, sitting beside her in the bathroom toweling her hair, gave her an odd look.

"Are you drunk?" she asked her.

And Davette shook her head firmly and that made her *dizzy* and *that* was so funny she spat the bobby pins out of her mouth laughing and Kitty looked at her funny again but then she started laughing, too, and all was fine for a long time.

And then Kitty began talking about Ross. About how intelligent he was. How witty. How exciting. How *sexy*. And Davette stared, shocked, at her because they had never discussed such things before.

But Kitty, standing up to go into her own room, just gave her a sly, wicked smile and said, "You should find out for yourself."

And then she was gone and Davette sat there for several minutes before she could manage to move.

So, to dinner.

In point of fact, she never could remember the dinner much. It all seemed to go by so *fast*! She remembered the table being so beautiful and Aunt Vicky so lovely, but frowning that special frown because Davette was drinking so much but she *had* to, she had to do *something* . . .

Because he was there, looming at her from his dark eyes and perfect skin and immaculate tuxedo and knowing, knowing, smile. Not that he was intrusive or mean or anything; he wasn't. He was charming and witty and friendly and funny and he didn't seem to mind her getting soused. If anything, he encouraged her, refilling her wineglass again and again.

And with that thick cushion around her eyes the whole thing seemed less and less dangerous after a while.

And awhile after that, danger seemed kind of intriguing.

And just after that, she passed out.

She wasn't exactly unconscious. Not exactly. Her eyes were more or less open and she was able to recognize things. She just wasn't able to pick them up and hold them without dropping them.

They took her to bed with her weaving and slurring to Aunt Vicky that she was "so *sorry!* I'm just so *sorry!* I've spoiled *everything!*" And dear Aunt Vicky giving her that long cold look before finally, blessedly, relaxing and smiling and patting her on the cheek and saying that it was really all right, that anyone's entitled to a mistake in her own home and that just made Davette bawl some more because it was so *sweet*.

Ross excused himself while Kitty helped her struggle out of her clothes and into a nightgown and it felt great to just lie back and relax and she guessed the others went down to finish dinner because it was much later, after two A.M., when they came back and she woke up from that deep, deep sleep to see them sitting on the edge of the bed.

Why, she wondered, did I wake up?

But before she could think about that Ross leaned over her and asked, "Are you all right? Would you like to get sick?"

She had felt all right up until then. She hadn't felt nauseated, had she? Had she? But looking into his eyes she suddenly felt that alcohol vault and swirl within her and she lurched up tripping out of bed toward the bathroom and they both reached to help her.

But she didn't want their help, she thought. This was just *too* embarrassing. But ten seconds later she didn't care *who* saw her.

Ugggghhh!

She seemed to throw up for hours! She just couldn't stop, her bare knees hard on the tile on either side of the toilet, that awful wrenching in her tummy, those *dreadful* noises she kept making.

Once, hunched over with sweet Kitty murmuring gently and patting the back of her neck with that cool damp washcloth, she remembered thinking she was glad of at least one thing: she did *not* feel sexy.

In fact, she doubted she would ever feel sexy again.

But it happened.

She came to, more or less, curled up on the bathmat in front of the toilet seat, the nausea gone. She was dimly aware of being helped to her feet by someone gentle and very strong and she was almost to her bed before her beating heart allowed her to admit who it was. The top sheet and blanket had been rolled neatly to the foot of the bed and he lifted her up and carried her the last few steps, his hands cool and strong beneath her. She turned her head and swelled into his eyes as he put her down atop the broad empty bed.

He did not lay her down but, rather, sat her up against the headboard. And then he sat there beside her, boring his eyes and dreams of passion unknown to dull drab lives and fantasies of glorious ecstasy streamed into her when he smiled.

Her chest heaved. She panted and gasped and his face began to burn.

"Oops, I'm afraid you can't wear that anymore," he said.

He meant her nightgown, of course, and she did look down and she saw no stain . . .

But he wouldn't lie, would he?

"Better take it off," he said next.

And—God help me!—she did. She did, reaching up to the straps and pulling them slowly down off her shoulders and she knew *just what she was doing*.

And she did it anyway, slipped the nightgown down, exposed her breasts to the open air and to him and then . . .

Then his face was close to hers and tiny kisses all around her mouth as she slid backward, chest heaving, and then his hands were soft and cool and so strong on her shoulders and around her throat and the kisses slowly—too slowly—worked their way past her chin to her throbbing throat and across the top of her chest and to the breast the little creature had attacked the night before.

When he bit her the pleasure poured throughout her and her arms shot out into the air and her fingers spread trembling and she moaned and cried and undulated wantonly beneath him and . . .

There! There at the foot of the bed, perched like a grinning cat, was *Kitty*! She couldn't believe it! Kitty! And she wanted, for just an instant, to throw him off and run away. But she knew she couldn't do that. She knew she couldn't stop him. She knew she didn't want him stopped. Ever.

And Kitty's grin went wider and she leaned forward and her smile was bright in the moonlight as she said, "See? Didn't I tell you?"

And it was too strange, too bizarre. But she couldn't care now. She shrieked her whisper and wrapped her bare arms around the black curly head and pressed it deeper into her soul.

She slept all through the daylight hours. She dreamed deep and hard, long, exhausting dreams of intricate twisting erotica. When she awoke the tall french doors to her terrace were open, spilling in moonlight and soft breezes through her ghostly curtains, and they were there, sitting on the edge of her bed and smiling down at her.

For a brief moment she felt an icy jolt of . . . of what? Fear? And disgust?

But then it was gone, for they were so beautiful, Kitty sitting naked with her thighs tucked under her and that lustrous brown hair tumbling about her shoulders and he with that billowy black silk shirt open at the chest. So beautiful. And the smiles were so warm and genuine and happy.

"Swim," said Kitty with a mischievous tilt to her face. "Come on."

Davette shook her head that she didn't understand and Kitty grinned some more and said that Aunt Vicky was asleep and the servants were all out of the way and the pool was beautiful in the moonlight and it really was a warm night for the spring and let's go!

"I'll meet you down there," said Ross, rising to his feet.

But before he left he stepped around to Davette's bedside and leaned down and caressed her cheek with his hand,
boring gently now with his eyes. Then he bent and kissed her
softly on the cheek. And then he was gone and Davette was
once more full of tingles and catching her breath.

And when she remembered Kitty was still there and
looked at her she blushed. But Kitty just laughed and Davette
laughed, too, her cheeks red with embarrassment but also
humor because Kitty was in the same boat and the laughter
became schoolgirl giggles.

As she scrambled out of bed she felt a sharp pang from
her left breast. She gasped and looked down and when she
saw the swollen wound she gasped again.

"It won't last long," Kitty said, standing beside her.

Kitty was right. Davette worked the muscles of her chest
and gently massaged the area and the pain seemed to stretch
itself out. It still felt tender. But the sharp ache was gone.

It was then that she realized she was naked, that Kitty
was also naked standing beside her. The two of them: rich
girls, nice girls, ladies, standing naked in the moonlight of an
open door about to walk downstairs and swim, skinny-dip,
with a man who was down there waiting for them now and
who was quite sure they would come.

It seemed to incredible that she should be doing this,
that they both should be. But it seemed also so wickedly sexy,
so decadent and wanton, and with her best friend it seemed
a safe, dark secret and the two smiled and held hands and
walked naked out onto the terrace.

She had been out on this terrace barefoot before and the
possibility that anyone could climb over the walls and through
the gardens and see her was remote. But it was still there.
The wind caressed her bare thighs, rolling gently all around
her as they descended the broad stone steps to the pool and
Davette had never in her life felt so unclothed. So . . . available.

Ross reclined on one of the sun loungers like a prince
awaiting the court entertainment. He was turned over on one
side, a knee propped up with a forearm propped on that. He

had a half-smile on his face and the light seemed trapped between the moon and his eyes and the surface of the water and Davette thought: That's the color of his skin! Pale moonlight!

But she didn't think much. Instead, she blushed. For there was no way to avoid the pointed directness of his gaze or the fact that she continued to approach him. And she wondered once more which was more exciting—that she was behaving this way or that she knew what she was doing.

In any case, they continued to approach, still holding hands, until they came to a stop before him. He smiled at them. They smiled back at him. Then they looked at each other and giggled and turned and dove into the water and it was that, that flash of cold and clarity she felt in her icy spring swimming pool, that would come to haunt her later on.

It sobered her up. Immediately. What had been a gentle night of wicked secrets turned instantly into a cold, clammy, degrading sense of . . . cheapness. Of loss. What am I doing here? Was I drunk or drugged or what?

When she came to the surface she gasped in shame and turned and saw Kitty and she could tell from her shadowed gaze that she was feeling the same thing. The gritty stone on the side of the bank only added to the sense of shoddiness. She pushed her hair back away from her eyes and face, not looking at Ross, not even looking at Kitty.

I must look at him. I have to. She did.

And she cringed.

He looks like a pimp, she thought. Lounging there in those incredibly tacky tight—what are they? toreador?— pants, he looked not at all like what he had seemed. He looked more like . . .

How *odd*! He looks like an *imitation* of all of that!

How odd. But how degrading. She grasped the side of the pool and vaulted out of the water, shedding drops in all directions, and skipped toward the poolhouse toward warmth and composure. She wanted to try to cover herself with her hands and she started to. But then that seemed silly after all that had happened, and maybe even rude, so her hands stopped halfway and then she saw that Ross was in front of her, between her and the poolhouse and holding up a towel.

How, she wondered, did he get all the way around the pool in front of her so fast?

He was there, though, which was the point. She *didn't* want to see him or talk to him or—God no!—have him *touch* her. But she couldn't really avoid the towel because that really would be rude. She stopped just short of him, arms clasped in front of her chest for warmth, and turned her back to allow him to drape the towel about her shoulders and . . .

. . . and as he draped the towel the side of his hand touched her shoulder and there was that tingle once more and the chill flashed on her skin . . .

And the towel seemed to . . . coil . . . about her.

Like a knowing glove.

"Davette!" he whispered.

There was no alternative but to turn and face him and when she did she faced his glowing eyes and they held her and swelled down within her and the heat, the trembling frenzy, the . . . wicked ache . . . returned.

And soon it seemed they were back inside—Kitty with them, really *with* them—and they were laughing and hugging as they walked on either side of him, both women naked once more.

Into the kitchen, because they were starving. For steak. A big, thick super-rare steak, that was the craving. They sat Ross at the little counter that ran the length of the great house's great kitchen while the two of them, still naked, prepared the meal.

Still naked. Bright kitchen lights and cold floor and no reason for it at all except to be . . . nasty and wanton and . . .

And as she talked to the Team she didn't describe the way the two of them, she and Kitty, danced around in front of him making that meal. How could she tell them about it . . . how could she ever have *behaved* that way? Stretching up high to reach this, reaching way across him to get that. Bending over farther than she needed to for something else . . . She crimsoned at just the memory of it, of how she and Kitty, carnal tension sputtering in the air, had competed to see who could act like the cheaper tramp.

No. She couldn't tell about that.

But she could tell them about the food.

"Ross never eats," Kitty said chidingly when he said he didn't want a steak.

Ross's face had gone hard and he had used that Voice when he replied that he had his own diet and the smile he gave as he spoke softened it not at all. Davette had almost jumped at the tone, had felt a brief shiver of fear.

But learned nothing. She merely resolved not to question him about so sensitive a topic again.

The erotic atmosphere had been restored to its original tightness by the time the meal was prepared. Davette sat down but knew she was far too excited to eat.

"But you must be hungry," whispered Ross, gazing deep through her eyes. "You haven't eaten in twenty-four hours. And look at that thick juicy steak. Just what you need."

And even as he spoke she felt her hunger rush back so strongly that nothing in the world seemed more tempting than the smell of that food. She fell upon the steak like a starving beast.

"All better?" he asked pleasantly when she had finished.

Davette looked up, surprised. She had forgotten he was there, forgotten anyone was there, forgotten everything but eating. She looked down and saw her plate was totally clean.

How weird, she had thought at the time. Like I was in some sort of a spell or something.

Of course she was in a spell. His spell. A spell he could twist and curl as it suited him. With a knowing smile, he gazed their passions back into them.

Seconds later the three of them ascended the steps to her room and there, in the utter darkness he insisted upon, Davette sought within her some sense of shame as she lay listening to the couple embrace beside her on her cool sheets. But she could find no sense of shame or jealousy or anything other than pounding, aching need for her turn to come soon.

Soon, it did, and with it a bizarre hope that her cries would be as loud and thrilling as Kitty's.

When Davette paused a moment and Felix leaned forward to hand her the glass of water, she felt the heavy silence of the motel room. She realized she had looked at nothing besides the floor and Felix's face for the past two hours and she made herself look up and face their troubled expressions. They gazed uneasily back and she knew it was out of concern for her—she could read that. But she knew it was from embarrassment also. For the sexual charge was as heavy as the silence.

It's not your fault! she wanted to shout.

But she knew they wouldn't believe her. Not yet. They wouldn't understand that it was not them, it was a piece of them. A piece the magic had tainted her with and a piece she now passed on.

They wouldn't understand.

Still, she should try. And she did. She tried to tell them about the feeling of the bite, about the warping volcanic pleasure rolling through you, vibrating and caressing and powering you deep into your memory and far into your fantasies.

"Didn't it hurt?"

She stopped, looked around. It was Carl Joplin. His face softened and he smiled at her.

"I'm sorry, sugar. But we *are* talking about someone biting you."

"And sucking your blood out," added Cat.

Carl nodded, but his tone remained gentle. "*And* sucking your blood. It must—"

"But you don't *know* that!" insisted Davette. "You aren't *aware*. You don't know you're losing blood. There's so much else going on, you . . ."

"You mean he's also . . ." whispered Annabelle before catching herself and blushing.

Davette's voice was harsh and bitter. "No. No sex. Vampires can't have sex. Oh, the women can . . . pretend. And they do. But it isn't real. It isn't life. They're dead."

It was quiet for a while while they digested this.

And Felix thought, looking at her: There's still something left to you, isn't there, beauty?

But he didn't smile. She wouldn't know it was admiration.

Davette had another sip of water and tried to explain some more:

"There are really three stages to it. The first is . . . well, it just never occurs to you. Vampires? That's for movies, you know?"

They nodded. Yes, they knew.

She had another sip. "It's just sort of . . . kinky, I guess. And everyone has a part of them that likes and wants that. Vampires swell that desire inside of you and so . . . Well, you're enjoying it and it seems harmless.

"That's the first stage.

"In the second part you're so much of an addict for it, you don't *want* to examine what's going on. It holds you and controls you. You don't really ever think about anything else—you don't *want* to look at it. Because you . . . You don't want to think about it."

"And the third stage?" asked Felix. "You know then?"

Davette nodded wearily. "You know. The pretense is past. He *lets* you know. He lets you see it. And it's awful to see, the things they do to the living, the terrible smiles they get when they twist us. And . . ."

She drifted off, looking at something behind her eyes.

" 'And' . . ." Felix gently nudged.

She looked at him and her smile was grim and tight. "Maybe the worst part is not the knowing, the . . . admitting. The worst part is that you realize you *knew*, you *always* knew, deep down inside you, from the first. It's not the wickedness, the sex part. That's in everyone and that can be fine. It's deeper.

"It's basic.

"It's Evil.

"And you always feel it, some part of you does, when it grazes you.

"Always."

She was quiet for several seconds. Then she sighed, took a sip.

"The good news is that the last stage is rare."

Jack Crow spoke for the first time. "Why is it rare?"

"Because most people are dead by then," replied Davette, looking at him.

And Jack nodded back, as if he had been expecting the answer.

"So," began Felix once more, "were you an addict now?"

She looked at him. "Pretty much. But within the next week of that . . . The next ten days . . .

A week, she would think later. A week, ten days . . .

That's all it took for her former life to disappear.

Within a week she had learned what it was like to be teased. Within ten days she understood the end of the leash. Her life had shrunk to a single nighttime dot. She never went anywhere alone. She never saw the sunshine. She never talked with anyone besides Ross, Kitty, Aunt Victoria, and the servants. She did write one letter. To her college. Less than a month before graduation and she wrote them to say she wouldn't be coming back.

No life.

He teased her by being especially charming one night, giving her more than her share of attention. He was witty, he was tender, he burned her with that look. Then, abruptly, he left.

She lay awake until dawn. Steaming.

One night he didn't show at all. The two women sat around talking, wearing their most knock-out attire—for Ross preferred them to be either overdressed or naked—all night long waiting for him to show up.

But he never did.

It wasn't as if he had actually *promised* to be there that night. But he had been there every other night. Even if just to tease them. By the end of the night the two friends no longer spoke. They merely sat in front of the great fireplace in silence. Each of them knew then, Davette thought later. Each of them knew it was madness and darkness to continue. And if he *hadn't* shown up, if only for just a few nights, they would have been free. Or at least aware enough to instinctively flee.

He was back the next night, apologetic and charming and, later, as awesomely rapturous as ever.

They were his.

His property.

His toys.

And what good are toys if not to play with?

"You can make any man desire you," Ross said, smiling, from the center booth at Del Frisco's.

And they were all attention because it had been that kind of a night. For the very first time, he had taken them out!

Long black limousine. Long-stemmed roses. A gorgeous, tuxedo-clad Ross escorting them through the front door of the famous restaurant. Del, himself, there to greet them and lead them into that classic dining room with its carved deep mahogany and deeper rugs and immaculate diamond-bright crystal and the people! The way they stared at the three. Stared and (the ladies just *knew* it) envied. Davette was wearing her best and she had never felt so beautiful or attractive or, well, glamorous . . . in her whole life. Kitty was pretty show-stopping herself, though a trifle pale, and the service they received managed to be even better than Del Frisco's usual standard. The waiters positively swarmed around them.

"You can make any man desire you," Ross repeated. "Any man. Not just desire you. Crave you!" As he said the last he had leaned forward across the candlelight and beamed energy at them and they had shivered.

Because it *was* so exciting! To be out again and in the glitter. To feel so desirable—and Ross had seen to it they felt that way before they ever left Davette's house. They felt like movie stars, like . . . sirens!

"Let me tell you how," said Ross next. "First, you have to want *him*. Or, at least, imagine you do."

And so it began.

They were in his world now. And everything he wanted to be thrilling and acceptable was so. Every suggestion seemed fun or at least . . . harmless. A harmless secret between the three that somehow didn't really . . . count. ("This will not go on your permanent record.") It was easy to believe it didn't count. It was all so unreal anyway.

"Imagine," Ross purred, "that those two men in that booth over my left shoulder were so dynamic in bed that you *could not* resist them."

And so the women glanced over his shoulder at the two men in the booth. They were much older, in their fifties. Davette thought immediately of her friends' fathers, and though the older men's appearance was pleasant enough, the whole idea, the concept of it all, seemed incestuous. One of them was tall, even seated, with white hair at his temples and a lovely dark suit that seemed to glow in the candlelight. He was thin and erect and rather aloof. The second man was shorter, not much taller than she, Davette guessed. He was beginning to lose hair on top and gain weight in his middle but he had a warm ready smile and a friendly look. He wore a sportcoat instead of a suit but it was of the same high quality as his companion's attire.

Not for me, she thought.

But then Ross began to purr once more, purr with that Voice, and every single thought would seem to resonate their marrow.

"No, they're not as young as you would like. They are not what you would choose. Is that not what makes it so thrilling? Is it not decadent? These old men, old enough to be your fathers, can take you in their hands and make you sing. You cannot resist it. After a while you will not *want* to. And you know that. You know that. You will tremble and shake in their gaze. You will find yourselves doing things you cannot believe you are doing. But you will still do them. You will obey their every command. And, worse, you will enjoy it. You will see yourselves doing these wicked things—as if from afar—and you will be appalled and embarrassed . . . but also the carnal joys will jolt through you because you *really are doing them*! You! Ladies! Proper young ladies rolling wanton in their arms . . . My goodness, you think, if those people I grew up with should see me doing this! They wouldn't believe their eyes! The shame! The shame!

"And yet . . . Yes! Let them see me! I want them to see me, wallowing whore and free at last!"

Davette stopped speaking and her head went down and the motel room became quiet. Then, head still down, she tried to explain.

She tried to explain that vampires tell the truth. And she knew she had said all this before and all but she . . . just . . . wanted . . . everyone . . . to . . . understand. It wasn't the Truth. It was only a piece of it—a small piece, really, but . . . But people are like a spectrum, you know? They have *all* the colors and some have more of one shade than others but everybody has some of *any* shade and Ross, the vampire, could make that shade seem brighter and stronger than any of the others and . . . And, yes, it *was there*! He *did* have something to work with. But that didn't mean I'm really . . . Or *anybody* is really . . .

And she drifted off to silent tears until she felt a finger under her chin, gently raising her head up. She lifted her head and Felix was there, smiling at her.

"We know," he said softly. Tenderly. "We know. We understand."

And she knew he meant it. His eyes were so pleasant and sweet. She followed the gesture of his head, next, to the faces of the others in the room, to the rest of the Team, and the glow was still there. Smiling, understanding faces. Misty faces, small tears hidden in the corners of understanding eyes.

All of you act so hard and tough, she thought, gazing gratefully at them. Is that so no one will know about you?

"So," Felix continued gently, "you and your friend Kitty slept with those two men."

She could only nod, tears streaming down her cheeks.

"It wasn't fair! He made us helpless! And then he *told* them!"

Of course Ross had known the men. Of course he had told them to be there. Of course they stopped by the booth to say hello. And then they were following the limo to her Aunt Vicky's house and then they were all having a drink on the terrace and then, somehow, she was alone with one of them in the library, the short, fat, balding one who owned her, and abruptly he stopped being sweet. He put down his drink and leaned forward on the leather sofa and told her to take off her dress.

She wept and said, "*Please* don't make me do this!"

Even as she rose and exposed herself to him.

She did see it as if from afar. As if from the top of Uncle Harley's vast eighteen-foot bookshelves. And in this awful, obscene, filthy image of what she was doing, she reveled. She roiled and spun and gushed animal screams.

The only thing Ross spared them was seeing the money change hands.

It happened again, of course. And again. And again and again and one night there were two men just for her and then one night Kitty wasn't there and there were three. Three men she didn't know, back once again in her uncle's vast library, back on the vast leather sofa. And through her tears and shame she looked up and saw Ross there, standing and smiling at the uncurtained window. She called out to him from the couch, there on that couch on all fours wearing nothing but her jewelry that glinted and turned in the moonlight, she called out to him to make it all stop.

But he only laughed.

And then she felt added weight of the second man on the leather behind her and the animal cries soon returned to wash away the tears.

For a while.

Kitty was absent more than once. Soon she was hardly there at all and when she was she was as pale and wan as Aunt Vicky and Davette was starting to worry and fret but Ross would soothe her and comfort her and reassure her and fool her. She lived now in a constant dream state in which the oddest things were acceptable. She was exhausted from loss of rest and loss of blood and lack of . . . focus. She had nothing going on around her that she was used to, that she could count on or lean against. Aunt Vicky was always abed now, looking tight and worn and deathly pale. When they did talk, which was rare, they talked as strangers. For Davette's sense of shame and guilt encompassed her always these days, like the air around her. And when she sat in Victoria's great bedroom, the shame smothered her into silence. She was too engrossed with her own humiliation to notice her aunt's oddly distant behavior.

Then one night, with Kitty gone and Ross not yet arrived, she almost told her. Sitting there in that chair at her aunt's bedside, the pressure was almost too much. A sudden desire—passion, really—to throw herself to her knees and confess everything all but overcame her.

But then she thought of what the news would do to the lady, and she choked it back.

Weeping later in the corridor, she thought her tie with Aunt Vicky could never be worse.

But it could.

Two nights later, for reasons only Aunt Vicky would know, the frail elderly woman decided to get up from her bed in the middle of the night and go downstairs. She didn't even take the elevator, but rather the long curved front staircase. And that's where she was standing, on the bottom step, when she saw Davette, naked and rolling on the mansion's entryway carpet.

Davette did not cry out. She did not scream or try to explain or even move. Instead she closed her eyes and lay there waiting to expand and explode and be gone forever. But neither did this happen. When at last she opened her eyes everyone was gone.

When she woke the next night, so was her beloved Victoria. Forever.

Overdose.

Jack Crow spoke softly: "He had her, too, didn't he? Your aunt."

Davette looked at him and nodded. "All along."

"And she couldn't stand the shame . . ." finished Annabelle, her eyes welling tears.

Davette nodded once more. "Everyone was so nice. I guess I'd forgotten how many friends Aunt Vicky had. The medical examiner, Dr. Harshaw, came out to the house personally to take care of her—and, I guess, me—through it all. And the governor sent something. And the mayor came to the funeral; she's so nice. And senators and . . . everyone . . ."

Her voice drifted off and she simply stared for a few moments, at something only she could see.

The Team exchanged painful looks. All except Felix. His eyes never left Davette.

"Where was your Uncle Harley?" he asked. "He was Aunt Vicky's brother?"

"We couldn't reach him. He was in Samoa or somewhere."

"Samoa? In the South Pacific?"

"Uh-huh. Harley is a photographer. He's always going somewhere out of reach for *National Geographic* or somebody. I *think* he's in Samoa. Photographing diving pigs or . . ."

"Speaking of pigs," said Carl Joplin bitterly, "where was little Ross during all of this? The funeral was in the daytime, right?"

Davette smiled at him gratefully. "Yes. Yes, and I had to be up during the days, to do the . . . to handle all of the details. So I didn't see Ross at all for those three days except one night. Ju . . . Dr. Harshaw was with me all along and he didn't like Ross because I *was* all alone and Ross did have that horrible reputation. Anyway," she said breathily, looking to Carl Joplin once again, "anyway, it did change when he wasn't there. With the sunlight. And Dr. Harshaw gave me something so I *slept* at night, all night, and in the mornings I could *think* and I could *remember* and I *hated him*! *I hated Ross!*"

She was almost out of her chair. Her voice had become strident and wild and the tears flipped from her eyelids and

Felix leaned forward and took her in his arms to soothe her but she fought, not with Felix, but to speak:

"He would stand there and *laugh* when those awful men would have me. They would *all* have me. They'd pass me back and forth between them and Ross would be there laughing and calling me filthy names and saying what a lesson I was learning to treat him the way I used to and I wasn't such a lady now, was I? And—and I just *wallowed* there in front of him! I just *wallowed* for those men because I couldn't *help myself*! I couldn't *help* it! *I couldn't!*"

And she sobbed a painful sob and pitched forward out of her chair into Felix's arms and bawled and bawled.

In the heavy silence surrounding the child's weeping, Annabelle felt the full force of Team Crow's collective hatred pulsing about her. It was like a real and tangible force, so mighty was its purpose. The men looked not at each other or at her but rather straight ahead, each lost in his own thoughts of vengeance.

It's frightening, thought Annabelle. And I would be frightened, if I didn't feel the same way.

And then she thought: The vampires are very foolish to make men such as these *this* angry.

"When," asked Felix gently after Davette had been silent a long time, "did you see Ross again?"

Davette pulled her head off his shoulder and sat back in her chair, sniffling and wiping her eyes.

"The night after the funeral. He woke me to tell me he'd moved in."

"Into your house?"

"Yes. Yes. Into *my house*. And I sat up in bed and I didn't care what he looked like. I didn't care about his eyes in the moonlight. I told him 'No. No! I don't *want* you here! I don't want to ever *see* you again!' And I *meant* it!"

"And what did *he* say?" asked Father Adam.

Davette looked at him and she half laughed, half cried, and shook her head. "He just laughed and reached down and jerked me high into the air way over his head with *one hand* and . . ."

"And what?"

"And let me see his teeth . . ."

"And then, at last, you knew?" asked Jack.

"I don't know what I knew. Then. But I knew an hour later. You see, he carried me downstairs, in my nightgown, and threw me into my car and then he got in behind the wheel and started driving."

He drove to a part of Dallas Davette had never seen. She had heard about it, read about it, seen the police reports on the local news. But she had never been here in deep south Dallas, mostly black, mostly miserable, full of hookers and rival street gangs and crack dealers and fractious racial politics herded together by terrified and outgunned police. The faces through the whizzing car windows seemed alien and menacing and the streets seemed seedy and tense as a shaken fist.

Ross pulled the car into a crowded and littered parking lot alongside a place called "Cherry's" whose neon sign lacked an "r" and part of the "h" but still blinked spasmodically through the heavy gloom. The parking lot was full of people, mostly men and all black, standing around in little groups of twos or threes or sixes talking and smoking and passing bottles back and forth. A group of four were standing in the parking space Ross had selected. He pushed forward into it anyway, honking and lurching the great Cadillac bumper toward them. They leapt out of the way, one dropping his bottle, only just avoiding the car.

"What the fuck's wit you?" cried the largest, a huge black man with a great broad-brimmed hat and what Davette believed was a least two pounds of gold jewelry.

"Parking my car," snapped Ross as he stepped out. "This is a parking lot."

Then he stepped quickly around the car and opened Davette's door and lifted her, literally, out of her seat and onto the Cadillac's roof. She was still wearing her nightgown and she struggled to keep its dainty ends from fluttering in the heavy breeze. Ross sneered at her efforts, then turned back to the four blacks.

"Want to make something of it?" he asked them.

And when they hesitated, too amazed to speak, he added:

". . . niggers?"

As she spoke this next, the Team heard her voice change. As she had spoken of her own fall, Davette's tone had been rich with shame and fatigue and hatred. But now it became tinged with awe. Awe and fear and something else.

Resignation? wondered Felix. As if, now that she thinks back on it, they really are unstoppable?

Shit.

And she tried to explain, to describe what she'd seen. The might of him. The surrealistic animal force of the vampire among mortals.

When they heard the "nigger," they surged at him as one, as if choreographed. Ross had just laughed and then reached forward and snatched them up, just snatched them like they were dolls, like they had handles on them—on their stomachs, even. And they had *screamed* when he snatched them, crushing their bones with his fingers, collapsing their organs, they had *screamed*. And then he had laughed again and shaken them and at first they fought, stiffly blurring, but then they just flopped obscenely from side to side and he just—tossed them away. And the sounds when they hit, against the other cars, against the cinderblock wall of Cherry's were almost as bad as their screams.

The crowd formed immediately, some there to "teach this honky motherfucker." Two, three, six maybe, tried. Ross laughed and casually bashed them from side to side with the backs of his hands. Davette couldn't stand it and she turned away after the first two and Ross noticed and spat "WATCH!" at her in that Voice and for just an instant, everyone—fighting or watching—froze while she meekly obeyed. Then they came out of it and rushed him again and he slapped them as before.

Then a short man circled in darkly, looking serious and unintimidated and wielding a huge knife. Ross looked at her and smiled and then turned back to him and opened his arms wide for the charge and it came and Ross did nothing and the blade rose in a quick glinting thrust from below, splitting the chest to the hilt.

Ross grunted—Davette could tell it pained him—but did nothing else. Except smile. The black man went wide-eyed but hung tough. Instead of running, he just jerked the blade out and slammed it home once again. And again Ross grunted.

And smiled.

Then he leaned over the little man and opened his mouth wide and the fangs were there flashing in the neon and he . . . hissssed . . .

And the man with the knife fainted dead away.

The crowd melted off after that, save for a handful of men standing at the entrance of the club. One of them, Davette suspected, was the owner or at least the manager. She saw the pistol he had hidden behind his thigh, saw him trying to decide if he dared use even that.

Ross saw it, too, and laughed harsh and point-blank at him. The man stared numbly back.

Then Ross laughed again and his look took in all who were left to watch, at the front door, in the parking lot, hiding around the edges of the neon.

"So," he boomed harshly, "you want me to move the car? This car? Very well!"

He strode quickly around to the front of the Cadillac, reached down and grasped the huge chrome bumper. He tensed, strained, then lifted the car to his chest. Then he took four powerful strides forward and the rear wheels, still on the ground, whined and treaded thick black rubber on the asphalt and, just like that, the Cadillac was unparked. When he dropped the front of the car it bounced and Davette, still on the roof, was kicked sideways into the air. But Ross was there, as she slid to the ground, to catch her so easily.

And that's when she realized the knife was still in his chest.

He sneered down at her. "Well?" he Voiced at her.

She knew what he wanted. She took a breath, forced herself to grasp the handle, and tugged. The knife came immediately into her hand, as if being also pushed from inside. And there was no blood. Just a clear, sticky mucous something.

The knife clattered to the asphalt.

Ross snorted and shoved her inside the car. Then he went around to his door. There were still three people remaining, too stunned to move.

"Well, niggers?" cried Ross happily.

No one moved, spoke, died.

Then they drove away in silence.

And it stayed silent, almost all the way home. Davette was too overcome to speak, too astounded, too shattered by what she had seen. This wasn't just little Ross turned sexy. This was much, much more. Much, much worse. This was black magic Evil Oh God! Save me!

And she cowered over against her door waiting to die.

Only . . .

Only she knew that he wasn't going to kill her. Not here, anyway. Not right now. And . . .

And his stomach was hurting him, she thought. He rubbed it, hard, as he drove, constantly kneading it with his free hand. And the thought of this, the dream of his vulnerability, was like the tiniest slice of hope.

Hope for what, she didn't know. She only knew that he could be hurt and she couldn't take her eyes off his kneading and that's when he spotted her doing that and snorted with disdainful fury and jerked the Cadillac to a skidding stop on the side of the freeway, grabbing her with his right hand and dragging her across the seat to him and with his left hand ripping his shirt open and—

And the wound was closed.

"It itches, you stupid little mite!" he barked shaking her head with a handful of her hair. "It doesn't hurt! It *itches!*"

And then, when she just stared blankly at him, he reached up and grabbed the rearview mirror and tore it lose from the front windshield. He slammed her cheek up next to his and held the mirror in front of her eyes and . . .

And he wasn't there.

She could feel him, his hand in her hair against her skull, his cheek pressing into hers—she could *see* that, she could *see* the impression his cheek was making against hers in the mirror.

But he wasn't there!

And then . . . And then he sort of was. Sort of. Outlines, flashes, traces of his features when he moved. He wasn't completely invisible. But . . . But . . .

And then he dropped the mirror and turned and bored his eyes into hers and opened wide his mouth and the fangs were growing out.

"Vampire, mite!" he hissed that awful hiss. "VAMPIRE!"

And his mouth went wider and the fangs grew longer toward her and his features went red and demonic and unholy and she screamed a scream of hopeless irrefutable terror and all was black and dark.

The next night she signed everything over to him. The stocks, the bonds, the CDs, the cash, the houses . . . everything. Full power of attorney.

Ross, the vampire, owned her.

After that, things started happening pretty fast.

First, Ross decided to redecorate.

Soft things. Sickly-sweet, tender-to-the-touch things. Tasteless things. Expensive things. Gone were the great broad antique leather sofas from the library. He replaced them with silk-pillowed lounges. And he replaced the tapestries, some centuries old, with what looked to Davette like red satin bedsheets.

Ross actually did take the time to sit down and show her his new "motif." It looked like a cross between a sultan's harem and a Colorado Gold Rush Whorehouse. "No-Class" Ross's true colors were, quite literally, coming through.

He fired all the servants Aunt Vicky had retained for years. He replaced them with a handful of gray-faced, dull-witted, self-loathing slobs. It always amazed Davette how they simply could *not* seem to tidy up. No matter how rich and expensive their uniforms, no matter how much care and attention was paid to their appearances—their hair was always razor-cut, their faces always shaved, fingernails always clean—they still looked like unmade beds. Their jackets, however well pressed and tailored, never quite seemed to fit. And their starched white shirts never managed to stay tucked in for over a minute or two.

Davette had no idea where Ross had found these people who *knew* he was a vampire and still wanted to work for him. And she didn't want to know. Still, Ross managed to replace the entire staff in one single evening. He also managed to get a terrific amount of the redecoration done that first night— all the library, most of the main living room. An army of preened and primped men of all ages showed up to handle the work, all blatantly homosexual and each clearly enraptured by Ross's slightest notice of them.

In the midst of this, still in her bathrobe, Davette sat drinking vodka on the rocks and watching these dreadful people reshape her universe. It was all so distant somehow, as if this really weren't her house and Aunt Vicky weren't really dead and one morning she'd wake up . . .

No. Best not to get too detailed and lose the fantasy.

So she just sat and drank some more and waited for the scurrying trolls to leave. Which they did about midnight. Not because they were finished. But because Ross couldn't wait one more minute to try out his new playhouse. He dismissed the workers and went out to hunt.

Ross returned soon, just after two, with two couples driven in a limousine of their own. The four were well dressed and cultured and wildly, happily, drunk and friendly, the two men in their early forties, their wives a few years younger, and they laughed and laughed as they came tripping through the front door following Ross and they laughed as they got their drinks and they laughed some more when one of the ladies caught a heel on the edge of Ross's new red carpet and when Ross made some comment about Demon Rum they laughed some more and one of the men raised his glass and said, "I'll drink to that!" And they all laughed a lot at that and then Ross apologized for the unsecured rug, explaining that he was in the midst of redecorating and one of the women, who could *not* have known that the whorish red carpet was Ross's idea, picked up an edge of it and said, "Better hurry!"

And all four laughed longest and hardest at that until they realized Ross was not laughing at all. Davette was thirty feet away and above them, hidden in a shadowy recess, still wearing her bathrobe, still drinking her vodka, and she could not only see but feel the change in Ross. His coldness and anger, instantaneous, eruptive, seem to sphere out from him to the high walls of the living room and back, and the two couples, as the wave passed through them, caught their breaths and their faces went slack and pale.

And then Ross was all smiles and laughing one second later, his face animated and gracious and gregarious and endearing. And Davette watched the four stare and exchange uncertain, uneasy looks. But this passed because they had just been having *such* a good time and Ross was *so* charming, after all and . . .

And what was this? A game! How fun!

And Ross was everywhere among them, laughing, making them laugh and oh, yes! we're going to play a game, a drinking game, but we need one nondrinker, and somehow they were persuaded to fetch their chauffeur in while Ross and an ash-faced servant rolled out the plastic tarp left by the painters to cover the new red rug. The women had to take off their high heels, to keep from making holes in the plastic, and there Ross was, on his knees, to assist them and oh, the comments and the sly exchanged looks and the oh-ho's as he performed this sensual task.

But then all was ready for the game and Ross personally positioned everyone, including the chauffeur, at just the right place on the plastic tarp after first taking their glasses from their hands. And one of the men groaned and said, "I thought this was a drinking game!" and Ross smiled a sly smile and said, "It is! It is! You'll see!" and then he had one last person to position, the loveliest of the women, the only name Davette had caught from her perch, Evelyn, whose long black dress suited her so. Ross took her by the shoulders and stepped her over to the center of the tarp, the exact center, and then, with everyone smiling and laughing, turned her once more with her shoulders, turned her around so that her smiling faced his and slit a gaping gash in her throat with the edges of his long fingernails.

The blood fountained from her severed arteries and Ross had an impish moment to catch some of it in his mouth before turning and doing the same thing to her husband who simply stood there staring, with no chance to react. The second husband had enough time to open his mouth to protest, to raise an arm to object before Ross's vise-grip closed his throat and spinal cord forever. The second woman screamed a high-pitched scream before Ross grabbed her around the waist with his left hand and slammed his right fist into the center of her chest so hard she died, hemorrhaging, before her limp body had reached the plastic tarp.

Ross killed the chauffeur with another blow of the fist, straight down atop the man's skull. Davette heard it crack.

And then the feeding. The servants, panting the obvious repulsive sexual fervor, began scurrying about lifting the edges of the plastic to drain the blood into an enormous urn while Ross himself clamped a hand over Evelyn's still-spouting arteries. Then he lifted her body into his arms and positioned the throat within reach . . .

And then, before removing his palm from the wound, he turned and looked straight at Davette, straight *at* her, knowing all along she had been there, knowing her, knowing everything. Davette had time to gasp and put a drunken hand to her mouth before she heard the words, heard the Voice, slicing into her shadows.

"Entertained?" purred the vampire, before removing his hand and plunging his fangs into crimson.

Davette had been wondering what had happened to

Kitty. She hadn't seen her for weeks. Now she wondered no more.

She knew.

And she knew the rest.

I'm dead too, she thought.

Soon, I'm dead.

And then the doorbell rang.

"Get rid of them!" hissed Ross's bloody mouth.

It was not so easy. Pough, Ross's main slug, went dutifully to the front entrance, checked through the eyehole, and opened the door to dismiss whoever was there. Davette heard his voice briefly. Then, for several long seconds, heard nothing.

Then Pough reappeared. His face was, even for him, ashen. His eyes were wide and bright.

And fearful.

"Master . . ." he all but whined.

Ross put down Evelyn's body and stood up. He eyed Pough menacingly for an instant, then opened his mouth to speak.

But . . . "Ross!" sounded out from the front entrance and all present were silent.

"Ross Stewart!" then sounded out. And again, as before, it was from another Voice.

Davette watched Ross start toward the sound, then stop, find something to wipe his mouth, then continue. He paused at the step to the entryway and Davette felt sure he wanted to turn and look to her. For what? For reassurance?

Maybe.

Then he was out the front door and it closed behind him.

When she awoke, late the next afternoon, she found someone had put her in her bed. Her first thought was of the look on Ross's face as he had stepped toward the door. But her second was the look he'd had as he'd raised his fangs from the feast.

He had been drunk. On the blood.

* * *

Dinner on the terrace just after sunset. Candlelight, flowers, fine wine. Just the two of them. Just Davette eating. Ross wore a tuxedo and Davette, under orders, wore her glittering best.

And *that* part had made her feel better. Not dressing up. Ross often made her dress up. He liked to look at her, liked to show her off. Liked to make her strip. No, it wasn't the dressing up. It was that it didn't take two hours to do it like it usually had.

Because she would . . . just . . . sit . . . there . . . in front of her dressing table and she would reach for something, a comb or a brush or some perfume? Maybe? And . . . by the   time . . . her . . . her   hand   had . . . reached . . . out . . . for it . . . she had . . . forgotten what it was she was reaching for.

And then she would have to just sit there for a second until she remembered what she had been trying to do and to do that she would have to look in the mirror to see what was still undone and she hated looking at herself these days, hated it so much it would often make her cry and . . . And she was too tired to cry, too exhausted, too drained.

So she would just slump there and the dry sobs would rock her shoulders for a while. Sand-blasted by horror and fear and shame.

And then it would be time to continue getting dressed. And she would sit herself up, and reach for something, reach fast, before she forgot, and sometimes she missed and Pough spent a lot of time cleaning up broken bottles.

But tonight had been . . . okay. Not great, not the way she used to feel. But better.

Then she knew.

He hadn't bitten her in a week.

I'm recovering, she realized. I'm coming back.

And then she thought, looking directly at him, Whom do I kill first? Him or me?

He had started talking about high school. Not just about the school but about old friends from school and old events and old dances and parties and the way they used to dress and how everyone from those days was doing—well or poorly—and how much he thought of them and how much he missed them and . . .

And on and on and it came to her, suddenly, what he was trying to do.

And she also knew why:

Ross was scared.

The other Voice had scared him, made him realize he was not all-powerful to everyone, just to mortals. So he was retreating, now, back to the mortal he held most firmly in his palm. And pretending she really wanted to be there.

It was disgusting.

And worse, much, much worse, it was effective.

For Ross had turned up the heat again, the distant warmth of his Voice. His looks had become more pointed, his gestures more graceful and casually touching. And despite her best efforts to remember her hatred and fear, she was giving in to the vampire's magic.

When he reached out a perfect white hand to gently palm her chin she managed to mutter "damn you" before his skin touched hers and her breath caught and the awful wicked excitement stirred within her, fluttered from deep within, sprinkling up her arms and through her shoulders and . . .

And she did just what he said to do:

She stood up, in front of the servant-slugs, in front of Pough, and slipped her dress off, exposing her naked body underneath. And she did slide her manicured nails along her hips and thighs and she did tease her diamond-hard nipples and . . .

And *oh God*! but she enjoyed it as much as ever before, enjoyed the wanton, whorish nastiness of it all, the shameful, rutting depravity of it all.

She loved it, God help her.

But even more, she loved his laying her, with her eager consent, across the top of the quickly cleared dining table and opening her thighs to his exquisite, monstrous, bite. And she loved the sounds she streaked up through the leaves and clouds at the moon.

Perhaps she would not have hated herself so had she known it would be the last time he would do this to her.

By 7:30, he had lain her in her bed, saying something about an errand he simply had to run. Even as she dropped off, she could tell he was trying to be too flippant. That this was more than an errand.

In her dreams she heard that other Voice again and again and again.

"That was the night," said Jack Crow suddenly, "that he came up to Bradshaw and killed my men."

"Yes," said Davette quietly. "Only he missed you because he got there too late. Pough got lost. And the sun . . . Well, you know."

"Yeah."

"What did Ross do to Pough?" Kirk wanted to know.

"He had bruises all over his face when he came back. And he limped."

"Did Pough enjoy his pain?" asked Father Adam quietly.

Davette looked at him, surprised. "Yes. How did you know?"

The young priest shrugged his broad shoulders.

"Just a feeling" was all he said.

"What about," asked Felix leaning forward, "the wound?"

"Yes," added Cat eagerly. "In his forehead . . ."

"From the cross . . ." finished Carl Joplin.

"The Holy silver cross," amended Father Adam.

"Yeah."

"Oh!" sparked Davette, remembering, "It hurt him. It really *hurt* him . . ."

He thrashed about on the silken sheets of the huge bedroom suite he had furnished deep in the basement, wallowing in pain and frustration. And it was impossible to restrain him, with muscles hard as a bronze statue come alive and hurting and . . . *angry*!

"DO SOMETHING!" he raged and they tried, Davette

and Pough, they really tried, but the wound would not stop bleeding. The thick, heavy vampire mucus continued to ooze, rhythmically, with his panting dead man's pulse. And every time a new surge of matter pushed its way out, the monster howled and grabbed his head, or ripped the sheets with his long nails or tore one of his brand new tailored silk shirts from his chest or . . .

Or lashed out. At the walls, at Davette, or at Pough, who was either too stupid or too masochistic to step beyond his reach. The first time Davette went down was from being struck by just the *edge* of his hand. That blow had sent her rolling onto the floor and from then on, whenever she saw the glob begin to form at the wound's opening, she would step quickly back while the vampire raged in ˆagony.

But then she would jump quickly back onto the bed and sop up the stuff before it rolled heavily down his forehead and got into his eyes, because that seemed to hurt him more than anything else. When the mucus hit his eyes he would *shriek*!

Three hours at this and Davette was exhausted. More, she was angry. At Pough, the slug who liked being hit, at herself, for being here at all, for the vampire Ross, who, like the wicked infant he was, refused to accept the bill he'd run up.

She saw him differently now, in his pain, and her contempt was joyous. There was no seduction here, no hypnotic gaze, no Voice. His skin was no longer smooth cream, but mottled, crinkled, paste.

The Undead, she kept thinking.

All those movies and all those stories I've seen and read in my life were fantasies. But this is so true. He is not alive. He is Undead. He is Unhealthy.

He is scum.

Ross actually tried aspirin for the pain, a notion that Davette, in her newfound insight, found laughable, ludicrous, almost beneath contempt.

You're dead, pig. You can't take aspirin, she thought.

But she said nothing as Pough fetched the bottle and

Ross tore the top of it open with a flick of his fingers and
forced a half dozen of the dry white pills down his throat.
She stood *way* back then, eyeing the ornate quarters for a
receptacle. He had quite a few of those urns around against
the walls but they were too heavy. At last she spied some
awful, intricate, and expensive French washbowl—something
on one of the side tables—and sidled over casually to pick it
up while Ross lay frozen in his misery, staring straight up at
the ceiling, his hands outstretched and talon-taut in the ragged
sheets.

First he started to retch, his body warping on the bed as
if electrocuted. And when he finally vomited it was the most
vile, fetid, *loathsome* . . . Decay! That awful smell of Death,
rotting, sickly-sweet bile!

Davette dropped the washbowl to the carpet and staggered back from that smell.

"Ross, you fool! You're a vampire! You can only have
blood!"

And the monster's eyes rolled back in his head, the pupils
almost disappearing entirely, and his spine arched once more
against the bed. But then his head snapped forward and his
eyes were red and demonic and the fangs were there and he
looked at Davette and hissed:

"Yesss!"

And she thought she was going to die.

But Ross's arm streaked out and his taloned hands
clamped down on Pough's forearm and pulled it toward his
jaws and Pough screamed when the fangs sliced the arteries
and the blood began to spurt and Davette felt her scream
coming as Ross aimed the stream not at his mouth but at his
wound. And as the blood splashed and splattered across
Ross's forehead Davette looked at Pough and saw his eyes
go back, but not in pain. In ecstasy . . .

And her scream blew out from her soul and possessed
her and she collapsed, still screaming . . .

It worked. The wound didn't heal. Not completely. But
the opening shrank to little more than a large pinprick. It

still dripped that clear viscous fluid. But a headband was all it needed.

And the pain was less. Not gone, but less. It no longer incapacitated him. It just made him a bit more cruel.

Ross had looked into her eyes and told her she was tired, sleepy and exhausted, that she would go to sleep and not wake up until midnight tomorrow night, and it was so.

He awoke her with his mind or his Voice—she wasn't sure—at the appointed hour. He was standing in her doorway, the light from the hallway silhouetting him. She could hear voices downstairs, many voices laughing and talking.

She didn't want to go.

"Ross . . ." she began weakly.

"Get dressed," said the Voice. "Now. I'll be back for you."

And then he was gone.

She lay there a few seconds, then clambered slowly, dizzily, out of bed. She was exhausted, beaten, drained. She hadn't eaten. She had slept too long. She wanted to die.

She didn't know if she *could* get dressed.

"I'll help you," offered a soft, silky, familiar voice.

Kitty, even in the dim starlight from the terrace doorway, was incredibly beautiful. She was radiant, really, her features sharp yet soft, her walk lazy yet precise and sensuous. She was friendly and warm and obviously glad to see Davette and . . .

And a vampire.

"I'll help you," she said again, this time all but cooing as she strolled forward and took her friend's limp shoulders. "I'll make you beautiful."

And she did. She dressed Davette as one would a child. She fixed her hair and applied her makeup and never once turned on a light.

Davette simply sat there. Or stood up. Or raised her arms as told. She couldn't cry or disobey or think. She just let it be done.

And then she was ready and Kitty pronounced her beautiful and then Ross, who had reappeared at the doorway, agreed. Then the two of them took each of her arms and guided her downstairs.

On the long main staircase Davette managed to speak at last.

"Are you . . . going to make me a vampire?"

Ross's smile was satanic.

"No, my dear," he replied pleasantly. "I'm going to make you watch."

And when they reached the bottom of the stairway and turned in to the main living room filled with happy partying victims, Davette saw the plastic tarp had already been laid out.

She watched them feed from a far distance it seemed. The horror was too much, the screams of surprise and terror too piercing, the quantities of blood too enormous to accept. She didn't move, she didn't speak. She didn't respond, except to Voices. She wasn't there.

But she noticed them swelling as they drank.

Like ticks, she thought.

For their bodies did actually expand as they sopped the lives. And their eyes became dreamy and their voices, Voices, became slurred. There was too much blood for the two of them but they drank most of it anyway, gorging themselves and laughing about the presumed lives of the victims based on their clothing and personal effects and when they realized they simply could not drink it all, they laughed and rubbed it all over each other and Davette thought they really did look like serpents, entertwined and slimy with blood.

It was the same the next night. First, though, they had the orgy for the sheep, seducing them with Voice and Gaze, and the sexual tension was rich and thick.

But somehow carefully directed. One young couple in their twenties were somehow carnally separated. Ross had him bound and gagged while the young wife rolled and clasped with a series of men on the floor in front of him, knowing what she was doing, weeping throughout, but unable to help herself, unable to stop the rich, luxurious orgasms from rocking her again and again.

Davette watched the young man, his eyes red with tears, as he went through the torture of his wife the rutting slut. She didn't know how they had managed to keep the feeling of sex from him, only that they so much enjoyed seeing his agony without having any idea as to what was causing his wife to behave like this.

Then Ross just let them go, without explanation, before the slaughter began.

"Let's see them work *this* out," he said with a laugh as he watched their subcompact lurch away down the drive.

Davette wept silently. The two had been married less than three weeks.

And she thought, for a few brief moments, that it would have been less cruel to kill them. But that was before the night's slaughter began. Once she heard the new screams, she realized she was wrong. There was nothing worse than what she saw. Except, possibly, the vampires' pleasure in it all.

I cannot do this, she thought.

I cannot continue like this.

I cannot live like this.

And then she thought: So I won't. I know where Aunt Vicky kept her pills.

Davette lived because she overslept. She had no chance to sneak into Aunt Vicky's room to kill herself. Before she was half awake, Ross and Kitty and someone new, another woman, another vampire, a redhead named Veronica, were all in her room, rousing her out of bed to show her their new clothes. Vampire clothes.

They were all blacks and reds, the women's dresses trailing wisps of material to give the illusion of black widows, Ross's jacket and red ascot making him look just like a movie Dracula.

The three seemed to think this very witty. And they had a dress just like it for Davette. They also had victims on their way.

So Davette got dressed and went downstairs and listened to the three whisper among themselves and wondered what

adolescent horror would come about in her home that night.
The main living room had been just about transformed to
Ross's specifications. It reminded Davette of these absurd
outfits the four were wearing. If only the absurdity were not
so vicious and macabre.

I've got to get away, she thought. If I can just get to the
pills, and take them at dawn, it will be over before they can
do anything about it.

So just smile, stupid. And go along with these monsters.

And then leave this all. Leave everything.

And she took a deep breath and braced herself. She could
get through anything, couldn't she? This one last night?
Please? Only . . . what have they planned to show me tonight?

As it turned out, they had to change their plans.

The vast eighteen-foot-high french doors to the grand
terrace burst inward with a rush of air and electricity and a
White Giant walked into the room.

At least that's how Davette thought of this great huge
man, at least six-five and weighing close to three hundred
pounds with huge shoulders and a massive mane of snow-
white hair. He had the most piercing blue eyes Davette had
ever seen. He was supremely confident, blazingly intent . . .

And a vampire.

"Ross Stewart," he bellowed, "you have failed me. What
will it be?"

Davette recognized the Voice from the other night.

Ross had stumbled to his feet upon the man's appearance. Davette felt rather than saw him try to draw himself
up to his full height and power as the other vampire approached.

As she also felt him give in as the giant drew near.

"What is it," he asked, with no Voice at all, "that you
want me to do?"

The giant took one more step forward so that he literally
towered over Ross.

"Finish it!" he roared. "*Finish* it! *Kill* him!

"Kill Crow . . ."

*   *   *

"So!" hissed Cat, and his smile was not a friendly one, "*that's* the guy!"

"Yeah," rumbled Jack, sitting forward. "Who is it?"

"I don't know. They wouldn't let me know."

"Any ideas?"

She shook her head. "No. Even when they had me sign the papers, they had tape over his name."

"What papers?"

"I don't know. He brought them with him. And he made Ross have me sign them before we left."

Carl Joplin frowned. "You signed them without knowing what they were?"

Davette's eyes dropped as she nodded.

"Ease off, Carl," said Deputy Thompson gently.

Carl looked at him, nodded. "Sorry, sugar," he said to Davette, "I just keep forgetting . . ."

"Well, how?" sparked Davette suddenly, her eyes bright and flashing. "What did you *expect* me to do, with *four* vampires in the room?"

It got very still. The Team sat stunned at this bristling defiance from this meek little broken . . .

And then Felix started to smile and so did Davette and then everyone laughed and Cat thought, My God, girl! How do you keep shining?

And everyone felt a lot better. Cat got up and fixed more drinks. Even Davette had one. Only Felix declined.

Instead he lit a cigarette and looked at Davette.

"Still, it's important about the papers. More legal documents?"

"Yes. Like the ones I did for Ross. Power of attorney, I guess."

"How about a last will and testament?"

"It could be."

"A death sentence."

"What?" cried Annabelle. "What do you mean."

Felix frowned at her alarm. "Sorry, Annabelle. But she said she had to sign the papers before she left."

"Yes," replied Davette slowly.

"Where were you going?"

Davette paused, looked at Jack Crow.

Jack nodded and answered for her. ". . . to California."

"Yes," said Davette.

"Yes," repeated Jack. "That was the night you came to . . ."

"To kill you. Yes." She looked down, looked back up at him. "I'm sorry, Jack."

He shook his head. "Not your fault. How long did it take you?"

"Three days."

"You drove?"

"Yes. Almost straight through. We only stopped at all because I was so tired . . ."

She couldn't keep her eyes open but it was still too light for Ross to leave the trunk and tell her it was all right to stop. But she had to stop. She had to.

So she did, somewhere in Arizona, at a rest stop. In the shade. She pulled over and lay down for just a second to "rest her eyes."

When she awoke it was dark and Ross was shaking her awake to get moving and the couple in the Camaro convertible parked beside them at the rest stop were dead and drained, their lifeless eyes staring, a slack corpse's mouth hanging open over the driver's door.

She roared back onto the highway and, once more, Ross began to talk.

About being a vampire, about the trouble back in Dallas with the white giant. Something about invading another monster's territory without permission, something more about getting to stay as soon as he got this "Crow" person. Davette still didn't understand who this Crow person was and why they wanted to kill him. And she had seen so many murders, horrible slashing murders, already, that she found it hard to worry about anyone in particular. Every night someone else died. Names didn't matter.

Neither did any other details. Ross had always kept everything secret from her before, yet his wanting to let her in on this trip suddenly repulsed her. She didn't want to hear. She didn't want to know.

She didn't want . . . anything.

She didn't even want to die. She was too tired.

She had thought about it, thought about stopping the car at some little town and going to a drugstore and getting sleeping pills and maybe a little vodka (maybe a lot) to wash it down with. But even that seemed too much trouble.

Too numb. Too lost.

So tired.

And then, on the last moonlit leg of the journey, up U.S. 1 along the northern California coast, he finally got her attention. She finally realized why he was telling her so much.

This Crow person was not just a person. He wasn't just another victim or plaything. He was more. A lot more. Just a man, but a very powerful one.

He killed vampires.

And this thought, that someone existed who not only stood up to them, but fought them and *won* . . . ! It staggered her, it raced her blood and breath through her soul. She felt the stirrings of something deep within and long lost and she reached for it, reached deep down inside her until she could grasp it and identify it and . . . and it turned out to be her. The her that once, so long ago, had been.

And then she remembered that this man, this Crow, was going to die, too, and she tried to hide it all away.

Because he *would* die. You couldn't stop these monsters.

So she went along and listened to his plan and did just what she was told, dressed up and put on her Reporter Face and straightened her extra-clean clothes and went up to that great mansion on the ridge over Pebble Beach and knocked on the front door.

And she met them and she liked them and she refused to notice she liked them and she confirmed that this Crow person, Jack Crow, it turned out, wouldn't be there until the next day and she went back and told Ross and he was furious and thought about killing them all, all the others in the house, before Crow came back, but . . .

But he couldn't afford to frighten Crow off. He couldn't afford to fail again.

But neither would he leave. Just before dawn he closed himself in the trunk of the rental car and sealed the seal he had devised that no one could possibly break alone.

And she lay down in the front seat and went to sleep expecting to help him feed the next night.

But then . . . but nothing, not really. Crow's car driving past her had awakened her and when she awoke she awoke to the fourth day without being bitten and enslaved and maybe, just maybe, she had some extra strength and will and hidden crying hope.

So she just got out of the car and went up to meet this fool who thought he could stop evil with his drunken little band and . . .

And she met him and he was, yes, special, but not *that* special—no one was special enough for this job. And she played reporter and he walked her through those empty rooms of his dead comrades'—was it seven? Yes, seven who had been insane enough to follow him—and he told her their stories and they were wonderful stories . . .

And then he'd said they were going and asked if she wanted to go along and then she'd heard that music from downstairs and, well, she . . .

She just went. She just did it.

She didn't know how she managed such spectacular courage.

But she suspected the music.

"What *was* that music playing downstairs?" she asked Jack suddenly.

"Downstairs? Downstairs when?"

"When we were in California and you asked me to fly back with you?"

Jack frowned. "Oh. When we were in the zoo . . . That was Stevie Ray Vaughn. Texas rock and roll."

And she *smiled*. "Yes! Rock and roll. That's it!"

Cat, along with the others, found himself smiling at *her* smile. Because it was the first one in so long. But . . .

"But I don't get it. What's the music got to do with anything? Don't you like rock and roll?"

And she *laughed*. She really laughed.

"I love it. But Ross hated it. All vampires hate rock and roll."

"You're kidding."

"No," she giggled, sitting up straight. "He told me on that trip. All vampires hate it."

"What do they like?" Kirk wanted to know.

"Opera," replied Davette. "All kinds of opera."

"Figures," muttered Father Adam and they all turned and smiled at him.

"So," finished Jack. "That was it. You just . . . ran. When you heard that music, you just . . ."

"I just *did* it. I didn't think about it. I just went."

"And that's all?"

She sighed, looked at him. "That's all."

And it was quiet for a moment while they thought about this, this sweet golden human made slave and a swine, about all that she had been and all that she had lost and all that had been done to her and . . .

And Carl Joplin stood up and stepped over to her and looked down and smiled and held out his huge chubby hands to her. She hesitated, then put her two small hands in his and he pulled her up out of her chair and his smile went wider and he said, "You're a good, good girl."

Then he gave her a bear hug that almost hid her from view.

The other smiles glowed upon them from all around the room.

Chapter 21

Felix didn't know what he felt about all he had heard that night.

He was shocked? Yeah. Stunned and . . . repulsed? No. Not really. Not for her. Just stunned a bit. And dazed. Too much story. Too much data. Too much monster.

They really know how to rip up Life, don't they?

But how did he feel about her? How did he really . . . ?

Say it, you stalling buffoon! Do you still . . . love her?

Yes, he thought at last.

And he smiled.

Now what, he wondered, am I smiling about?

The only other door to the room—the one to the bedroom used by the ladies—opened. It was Annabelle.

"Is she okay?" he whispered.

Annabelle first closed the door carefully behind her.

"I think she'll sleep," she said. "You should try to do the same."

Felix looked around at the empty room filled with smoke and overflowing ashtrays and half-empty glasses. The others had gone to their rooms.

"I'll just give her a few minutes."

Annabelle smiling knowingly. Sometime during Davette's tale she had busied herself knitting some large multicolored whatever. She resumed her seat and picked it up again.

"You were wonderful for her tonight," she said.

Felix shrugged. "Not hard to do."

"Then what took you so long?"

"What do you mean?" he asked innocently. "I've only known her for—"

"Felix!" she intoned, sounding like everyone's mother.

He stopped short, grinned. "Yeah. Well, I'm not used to this falling-in-love-at-first-sight stuff."

Annabelle grinned at him. "That's better."

"And . . ."

"And what?" she asked.

He turned around and busied himself making a drink he didn't need.

"I was angry that she was with Crow."

"What?" Annabelle gasped. "You thought that she and Jack were . . . ?"

"Huh? Oh, no. Not at all. But . . ." He lit a cigarette and looked at her. "See, I've been waiting for my wife to come along all my life and, well, avoiding this kind of shit at the same time. Then I see her and there's Jack and . . ." He shook his head. "I shoulda figured I couldn't have one without the other."

She thought he looked almost embarrassed.

"She loves you, too, you know," she said.

He looked up. "You think?"

"I know so." She eyed him carefully. "Don't you?"

He looked at her quickly, looked down, smiled. "Yeah." This time he was definitely embarrassed.

"Figures," he added, "the way her luck's been running."

And then they both smiled.

How weird you are, Felix, she thought. What a weird, dark, scary young man you are.

They were quiet for a while.

"Felix, what have you been doing all this time? Since Mexico?"

He shrugged. "I run the saloon."

"All this time?"

He shrugged again. "The past couple of years."

"And before that?"

But this time he just looked into his glass.

Annabelle eyed him carefully, a smile curling up.

"Felix, just how rich are you?"

He looked at her, surprised. "What makes you think I'm . . ."

"How rich?" she insisted.

He looked at her, relaxed, grinned. "Very."

"Millions?"

He smiled. "Many."

She nodded, almost to herself. "Rich, single, young, obviously well educated . . . Young man, what have you been *doing* all this time?"

And he looked at her and had no answer.

But Jack Crow, at the doorway, did.

"He's been waiting for me."

"Sometimes, Jack," drawled Felix lazily, "you sound just like you."

And the three of them laughed.

Crow fetched himself a glass of ice water and sat down across from them and got right to the point: "What's it gonna be, Felix? You coming with us tomorrow, or not?"

Felix put his cigarette out and closed his eyes and rubbed them.

"I don't know, Jack. I guess so. You're going to Davette's house, right?"

"Got to. Got to try."

Felix nodded. "I know. And . . . well, it's not like anyone's going to be there waiting for us. It's not another trap."

"Not so far as I know."

Felix nodded again. "Then I guess I'm in."

"For tomorrow."

"Yeah."

"And after that?"

Felix lit a cigarette and blew the smoke out slowly.

"No, Jack. No. Jack, it's just . . . it's just that I don't think you're a good deal. Sorry."

Crow shook his head. "That's okay."

But it hurt. Saying this was hurting Felix. And he wanted the other man to understand.

"Jack, it's just that . . . Dammit, they know who you are and they're gunning for you. And they're going to keep gunning for you. And you keep on doing this alone—" Felix stopped abruptly, looked down. "You shouldn't be doing this alone."

Jack Crow's voice was so tired and his eyes were so bright as he replied, "I know. But I can't get anyone else to help me."

"Yeah," Felix muttered.

And no one spoke after that for awhile.

Then Felix stood up, said good night, and left.

Jack watched him go and after he was gone he sighed and dragged out a cigarette and a light and leaned back wearily without lighting it.

He looks so tired, Annabelle thought. I've never seen him so tired.

And then she thought: I've never seen him like this at all.

And she felt the resentment for Felix welling up. Because Jack needed him so—they all needed him. Davette needed him. And Jack had been counting on him so much and he *was* so good at it and Jack *was* alone . . .

So alone.

"Poor bastard," Jack muttered to himself.

"What?" she asked.

"Felix."

"Felix?" she asked, amazed. "Why do you feel so sorry for him?"

Jack's smile was thin and grim. "Because here's this poor jerk who's . . . Hell, he's young and bright and, in his own way, plenty, plenty strong. And he can't *do* a goddamned thing but shoot. But he doesn't want to shoot. Doesn't want to be a shooter.

"So he doesn't do anything at all."

Annabelle frowned. "Jack, you're not making me feel any better about him."

He grinned. "But don't you see? Don't you see how he's trapped? Hell, he's always been—"

"All I see is you in a spot and a young . . . young I-don't-know is too scared to help you."

"Whoa, there, lady. It's not just scared. Besides, scared is smart. He—"

"Jack! Would you stop defending him?" she cried. He stopped, looked at her. "The more you take up for him, the less I like him," she said with exasperation.

And he grinned again.

What *is* he smiling about?

She had a bad thought.

"Jack, is that what you're hoping for, that the vampires will stop scaring him?"

He shook his head. "Oh, no! They'll never stop scaring him."

"Then what?"

"Sooner or later," he whispered fiercely, "they're going to piss him off."

PART THREE

The Last Days

Chapter 22

Felix slept hard and woke up late.

He lay there a moment, staring at the ugly ceiling tiles that fit in just right with this ugly motel. Then he rolled his bare feet out onto the floor and sat up and thought: What if she won't come with me?

After all, the girl had no family—save for that wandering Uncle Harley, was it?—and the Team had clearly become everything to her. She and Annabelle were tight, very tight. She loved Jack and she loved big Carl Joplin and Cat and . . .

Shit.

He went through his morning ritual and then he took a shower and then he sat naked and dripping on the edge of the bed and had a cigarette and thought: What have I got to offer her?

"Staying alive, for one thing!" he muttered out loud.

But it didn't sound as firm as he would have liked.

So he stopped thinking about it. He stubbed out the cigarette and put on some clean clothes and gathered all his other stuff together and sat it on the little card table provided him.

Where his shoulder holster and gun were.

He looked at it a second, then abruptly reached down and dragged the Browning out of its holster and it slid—as had every decent goddamned gun he'd ever known—so *easily*, so *smoothly*, into his palm.

He knew, or at least had come to believe, that this feeling

265

was very rare. That most people never felt this natural with a firearm. Some people hated them and some who didn't couldn't see them and 'most always felt just a little awkward and . . .

But not him. Not ever. The Browning felt just like . . .

Just like the end of his hand.

My Lord! he thought wearily, with at least some trace of wry humor, what if it's all just as simple as that?

They were all being terribly cheerful when he got to the suite, but that was okay. Now that he had made the decision to go, nothing much bothered him anymore. He even liked it. Even liked them, sitting around that faded coffee table scarfing down take-out fried chicken, reeking of Team spirit and smartass remarks and just generally acting like the kind of people who got into this mess in the first place.

But . . . what the hell. They deserved a couple of grins. And Annabelle was there looking radiant as always. And *she* was there, dimpling and feeling safe. And, well, the chicken smelled good.

And then Father Adam's mass, after the meal—that felt okay, too. Felix had never even seen a mass before these people and now . . . now it felt perfectly natural. Logical, maybe.

Felix's good mood remained for another twenty minutes, until they started War Planning and Davette's sketch of the basement in her Aunt Victoria's house started to look too damn much like the Cleburne Jailhouse.

Seems vampire Ross had done quite a few renovations to keep sunlight and prying eyes away—looked like a bloody fort down there—and Davette hadn't even seen it all.

"You're going to have to blow it," said Felix, standing over them as she drew. "Just like the jail."

"Can't," replied Jack Crow calmly.

Felix stared at him. "What do you mean: 'can't'?"

Crow puffed on a cigarette and stared at him through the smoke.

"Blow up a mansion worth maybe four or five million dollars in the center of residential north Dallas? Shit, I'd have every Dallas police car, fire truck, and SWAT team and half the Texas Rangers on my ass in two minutes.''

Felix blinked. "Well, do what you always do—call 'em all up ahead of time. Have them there. Get authorization. I thought you knew people . . .''

"Not that many and not that well. They'd hang up on me if I told them I wanted to blow up a mansion in the middle of their city.''

"What did you do when you had one in a city before?''

"Never had one.''

"Huh?''

Crow grimaced, leaned back in his chair. "It's true. We've never had one inside a city, a major city, before.''

Felix looked at the others.

"It's true," confirmed Cat.

Carl nodded. "Had 'em everywhere from upper New York State to Montana. But never inside a big city. Always in the country. Some little town. Or outside some little town, really.''

"They don't like large cities," offered Father Adam, the historian. "Or at least they never have until now.''

Felix hated this. "Never been organized before, either.''

"We don't know how organized they are now," objected Carl.

"They're 'organized' enough to lay traps for you!" Felix sputtered. "How organized do they have to be?''

And it was quiet for a while while everyone thought about this.

"How 'bout," offered Carl slyly, "if we just take out one wall?''

"Huh?" said Crow.

"I could even muffle the sound some. Here.''

And he leaned forward and pointed to one of the outer walls of Davette's sketch. "It looks tough here. And it is, for a house. But you take out this one wall and all this structuring here, this support, these joists, will go. Hell, you could stand out in the garden and see the whole basement through sunlight . . .'' And he turned and eyed the window. "If we get some sunlight.''

Felix followed his gaze to the window. The pane was covered in running sheets of rain. He hadn't noticed it before. But it was really coming down.

"When you say 'muffle,' " Crow asked slowly, "just how quiet do you mean?"

"Well, it ain't gonna be what you'd call quiet, Jack. That can't be done with explosives. I mean, people outside will look up when they hear it, but . . ." He turned to Davette. "The place has got a wall around it, right? Pretty high?"

"Nine feet high," she told him.

"And lots of trees and stuff?"

She nodded. "You can't see the house from the street at all."

Carl looked at Jack and Felix and raised his eyebrows expectantly.

"Looks to me," offered Cat, with one arm around the deputy's shoulder, "like we have a Plan."

"So we do," pronounced Jack. "We go in there, set up the detectors and, if we get the readings, we let Carl blow the wall and we go in and get 'em. Questions?"

No one had any.

"All set?"

There were several nods.

But Felix was still staring at Davette's sketch.

"Felix," Crow growled, "am I gonna have to ask if you're in or out every damned hour?"

Felix looked at him, started to get angry . . .

But Jack was right. In or out. Decide, dammit!

"In," he said.

"All the way?" Jack wanted to know.

"On this one," Felix replied, tapping the sketch with a fingernail, "all the way."

"Well, *thank* you," Jack growled with heavy sarcasm.

"You're welcome, Jack," replied Felix calmly.

And for some damned reason that made everyone, Felix and Crow included, break up into laughter.

And then they kept laughing and kept laughing and they couldn't stop and Felix, tears running down his eyes and wondering what in the world was so goddamned funny, turned and caught Davette's eyes and her laughter was so pure and healthy and warm . . .

"I guess we have our moments," murmured Annabelle a few seconds later.

And Felix looked at her and thought: I guess you do.

An hour later they were on the road to Dallas, backed up in heavy interstate traffic snarled by a Texas thunderstorm leaning in from the north.

Chapter 23

The motorhome and Blazer were parked side by side at the cul-de-sac at the end of Davette's beautifully sculptured street by three that afternoon. But without headlights, they couldn't see one from the other.

"Look at it comin' down!" whispered the deputy in amazement.

Felix, sitting beside him at the far end of the motorhome, nodded and put out his newly lit cigarette. It was too damn smoky in there already. But every time they tried to open the door to get some fresh air, the bloody thunderstorm about drowned them.

Felix shook his head disgustedly. Midsummer, three o'clock in the afternoon, and it was probably no more than fifty degrees out there. And the damned sky was green!

Ker-plap! went another bolt of lightning, and everyone in the motorhome—which was everyone they had—jumped another foot.

"I do wish they'd stop doing that!" muttered Cat airily. Nobody laughed.

"Well, hell," said Jack at last. "I guess there goes today."

"Yeah," agreed Carl, staring out at the storm. "Funny thing is: we could've blown the whole damn mansion up in this stuff and I don't think even the next-door neighbors would have heard it." He looked at Davette and smiled. "As 'next-door' as this neighborhood gets, I mean," he added.

Davette didn't smile. She just looked at the floor between

her feet and continued hugging her elbows, her face drawn and tight.

She doesn't like being here, thought Felix.

And he wanted to go to her and do something or say something, but . . .

But he didn't. Too many people around and . . . and what was he going to say, anyway? They were going to do this one way or another, no matter how she felt. She was the reason they were here, if anything.

"Dammit!" sputtered Jack Crow. "I would like to know if they're here, at least. Joplin! Turn that thing on."

"It won't work," replied Carl.

"Why not? Are they busted?"

"You're trying to read the house, right?"

"Right."

"It won't reach."

"Because of the storm? It's only a couple of hundred feet."

Carl shook his head. "It's not the storm. It's the location. I could read the house from here *if* I had a sensor in the house. But you gotta have a sensor on-site."

"You mean already at the house."

Carl nodded. "Or in it."

"Now there's a happy thought," offered Cat.

Jack looked at him. "You up to it?"

Cat shrugged. "I wish I had a shower cap," he said and began stripping off his chain mail.

"What do you think you're doing?" Carl asked him.

"Don't worry. I'm not going in. An outside wall would be close enough, wouldn't it?"

Felix thought this was crazy. But he only said, "Are you sure this is a good idea?"

"Well, *I'm* sure," declared Joplin. "It's a shitty idea." He looked square at Cat. "It's also even stupider than your usual."

"Look, Carl," urged Jack. "It's just a matter of him taking it up there and stashing it in the bushes or somewhere."

"Yeah," agreed Cat. "Just Catting it in and Catting it out."

And he smiled.

And Carl Joplin all but erupted. "Bullshit!" he bellowed. "Bull*shit*! It's been dark for what? Two hours already."

"Yeah, but—" Cat tried.

" 'Yeah, but—' shit! You sit your butt back down or I'll dribble you from one end of this trailer to the other!"

And he stood over Cat, huffing and puffing, his arms out like a hungry linebacker, and it got very quiet until Cat spoke, in a small voice: "Okay, Carl," he said, shrugging.

Carl nodded firmly. "Okay," he confirmed, still heaving.

Then he noticed everyone watching him. He blinked, hesitated, then seemed to get more angry.

"We meeting at Felix's bar, that Antwar place?"

Jack nodded.

Carl turned to Felix. "You *sure* you got enough room?"

"I'm sure."

"Fine!" barked Carl. He looked around at the others. "Fine," he repeated. "I'll meet you there. I'm gonna get some more bullets for the Gunman and a suit for the kid." He nodded toward Deputy Thompson.

He looked around at the others another moment, trying to think of something to say. Then he grabbed up the Blazer keys and stomped out into the rain.

They could just hear the Blazer's engine start over the storm.

"I don't get it," wondered Kirk out loud. "What was he so mad about?"

Annabelle smiled. So did Jack and Cat.

"He wasn't really mad, dear," Annabelle assured him. "He was just worried about Cat."

Kirk nodded slowly. "So that threat . . ."

"Oh, that wasn't a threat," Annabelle said quickly. "That was a hug."

Kirk looked at her. Then the dawning showed in his eyes. He smiled.

"Oh, I get it. Carl's shy."

Cat and Jack nodded at each other.

"Well," muttered Cat," that's *one* way of putting it."

Felix didn't much care how they put it.

"Let's get going," he said.

"Okay," replied Jack. He looked at Davette. "Which way at the stop sign?"

She looked up vaguely, still clearly disturbed at where she was.

"Uh, why don't you turn right? No . . . Yes, right. And then . . ."

Felix shook his head. "Go straight. Then take the next . . . Never mind. I'll drive."

And he climbed over into the driver's seat.

Jack studied him. "You know this area?"

Felix shrugged. "I grew up about three blocks from here."

And Davette's head came up quickly. "You did?" she whispered.

He smiled at her and nodded.

"Where?" she asked.

"DeLoache Avenue."

Davette's head tilted toward him. She smiled.

"How nice," breathed Cat. "They're both aristocrats."

"Cat," snarled Felix, starting the engine.

But Cat held up both palms in the air. "I know. I know," he said. And then he added. "But it's still sweet."

Felix snarled as he made the motorhome move through the rain.

"We need to stop here," announced Annabelle as they passed a shopping center a few miles later. "There. At the pharmacy."

Jack frowned, looked at his watch. "What for?"

"That," purred Annabelle sweetly, "is none of your business. Felix, pull up close so we don't get wet and . . . Jack?"

She held her palm out to him and pointed to it with a long fingernail. Jack shrugged and dug out some money and started piling bills onto her palm. When she had about three times what they needed, Annabelle said, "Stop. We'll be right back."

Then she and Davette were out the door and tripping through the rain to the brightly lit automatic doors.

The men just sat there, not talking, just waiting for the women to spend the money. Jack watched the deputy find himself a comfortable spot on the motorhome's sofa. Even in civilian clothes, the kid still looked like he was wearing a uniform.

I ought to talk to him about paying him, Jack thought. But he doesn't seem worried about it. Just slipped right into us. We were lucky.

Felix sat drumming his fingers on the steering wheel, looking anxious but unworried.

Even you're coming along, Gunman, thought Jack next. That is, as far as you're willing to come.

"Think they'll remember cigarettes?" Cat asked suddenly.

Kirk waved at the smoky air. "Hope not."

They remembered. Felix cranked up the motorhome and they steamed through the rainy city to his bar. He was worried about the Antwar. He'd only had one chance to talk to them since he'd been with the Team, and he knew what happened to the staff of a cocktail lounge without someone standing over them. He had some pretty good people, but still . . .

Damn it was raining! And the thunder and the lightning—it took him thirty minutes to cross town, using his headlights the entire time.

It really does look like nighttime out there, he thought as he finally pulled onto his street.

Cat was sitting behind him playing with Carl's detector.

"Hey, Felix! Maybe I'll quit, too, and write a book."

"Smart move," said Felix.

"It'll be all about a gay vampire."

Felix frowned, Jack and Annabelle looked at one another and groaned.

"You want to hear the title?"

"Sure. What's the title?"

" 'The Tooth Fairy,' " replied Cat happily, just as Felix pulled the motorhome up to the Antwar's front door and . . .

. . . And the detector in Cat's hands went wild.

Beep-Beep-BEEP-BEEP-BEEP-BEEP-

. . . and Felix yanked the wheel away from the curb and tromped on the gas and the huge motorhome skidded, then righted itself, then vaulted down the street, fishtailing through the first turn.

But Felix didn't let off. He *knew* what that beeping meant! He *knew*! And he made that bloody motorhome jump!

"Felix!" Jack yelled to him a few blocks later. "Felix! They aren't coming!"

Felix's foot hesitated over the throttle.

"You sure?"

"Sure! Slow this thing down."

Felix reluctantly obeyed, slowing it all the way down until finally pulling over to a stop at the curb and turning off the key. Then he just sat there, in the silence and the pouring rain, breathing hard, before he spoke.

"They found me," he said quietly.

Then: "They know *me*, too. And they've found me."

It's worse than that, Gunman, thought Jack Crow. They know you. They've found you. And they're *after* you.

But he didn't say this. He didn't say anything. He felt like he knew what Felix was feeling. And he couldn't help but have sympathy.

But you're in it now, Felix, he thought. In to stay.

Jack Crow did not know how Felix felt.

Felix did not know how he felt.

He felt . . . nothing, really. Empty and numb and . . .

I knew this would happen, he thought again and again and again.

I knew it.

"Carl!" whispered Cat suddenly.

"Huh?" asked the Deputy.

"If they thought enough to have somebody waiting at Felix's bar—on the off chance he'd be there . . ."

"Then they're bound to have somebody at the new house," Jack finished for him. And he was already shoving Felix out of the driver's seat.

"Get dressed," he told them and started the engine once more. "We'll drop the ladies off."

"Carl!" whispered Cat again, almost to himself. He turned and looked at Annabelle's pale face.

She looks like I feel, he thought.

Carl! He's all alone out there . . .

Chapter 24

The detectors said: no vampires.

But they had been there.

Felix, wearing full chain mail, with halogen cross blazing on his chest, and with Browning drawn and cocked, stepped carefully through the shattered door of Carl's workshop and gazed about at the destruction.

Good Lord! Maybe they are gods!

Equipment was strewn everywhere, upside down, lying on its side, crushed. Workbenches were shattered. Heavy wooden packing crates lay tossed about like so many child's blocks. Parts of the ceiling hung almost to the floor, with wiring wrapped around it like a spider's web.

That clear sticky goo the monsters used for blood was everywhere, on the floors, on the walls, dripping from the ceiling and from pieces of splintered crossbow bolts. The puddles ran in a vague pattern, like a funnel. The wide end was by the doorway, where the concentration was the least. But as Felix, with the others moving quietly behind him, moved forward across what was left of the room, the vampire blood grew thicker and thicker, with huge splotches there and there and *there*, where a crossbow bolt had split an overturned chair. By the time they reached the far end of the room, by the time they reached that barricaded closet, the goo was so thick on the floor it was slippery to walk.

Carl Joplin had made them pay.

They found his body in the closet.

He was huddled, crumpled, beaten, slashed, in one small corner.

Too small, Felix thought, for that great body.

Jack's face in the halogen glare was unnerving. He was pale and drawn too tight and Cat, poor laughing Cat, looked a lot worse.

Surprised! realized Felix. They look so surprised!

I suppose, he thought next, that they thought Carl would always make it. Because they kept him in the rear. Because . . .

Because they loved him so much.

Damn.

Quiet in here, he thought next. No one talking. Everyone moving so slowly and carefully. Only the sounds of the storm whistling through, and even that had finally begun to abate.

There was a smear of that black bile the monsters spat when injured by his elbow on a broken countertop. Felix started to find something to wipe it off with, but stopped.

Let them come back. Let them come back and see this.

It was left to Felix and Father Adam and Kirk to take care of the body. Jack and Cat had left to stand outside by themselves in the rain. Adam brought the other two together and explained to them what had to be done to the body. That it must be staked and beheaded and that there really was an ancient Church ritual of interment that covered it all.

Felix was repulsed and sickened and . . . what? Scared? Certainly wired. His chest thumped and his thoughts went everywhere but to what he was doing as they loaded the tortured corpse into a canvas body bag on hand for just this purpose.

And the entire time some small sparking furious part of him was shouting up from his soul, Well, Felix! Is this enough? What does it take to set you off?

But mostly, he was numb.

He found himself watching young Father Adam, as they bound up and carried the body out into the rain. He knew the priest had been the one that kept the Top Secret Vatican records on Team Crow. And he wondered how he felt now.

One thing to read about it. Another to see it. Another to have them tearing at your own throat.

Cat and Jack stood still, side by side, the outlines of the great house they would now never live in rising starkly up behind them against the gray clouds and lightning. They looked . . . smaller than before.

They loaded Carl into the motorhome and Jack came over and told them that he and Cat would take the Blazer and go to the hotel and tell Annabelle and Davette.

And it was quiet again as they contemplated this grinding task.

"You want us to meet you there?" Felix asked him.

Jack shook his head wearily. "We're going to the bishop's. We're all going to the bishop's." Then he paused and took a deep breath and glanced, sideways, almost warily, toward the shattered workshop door. "See you there," he said at last and Felix thought his voice far too thin for so big a man.

Then Cat and Jack climbed into the Blazer and were gone.

Damn, thought Felix, watching their taillights disappear. Damn.

Because he knew what they were thinking, he knew about their guilt and those horrible goddamned pictures because he was having those same crushing visions.

Of poor Carl Joplin hearing his detector going off and knowing it was too late to get away and then desperately trying to barricade the door and then packing his weapons into the closet and then barricading that up, too, and none of it, absolutely *none* of it, doing any good.

And then alone in that closet it would be impossible, wouldn't it, not to hope? Not to think, not to dream, not to *pray* that the others would be coming to save him?

And what did he think when he knew it was too late? Did he hate everyone? Did he forgive them?

Did he forgive me?

Would he now? If he had the chance?

Damn.

Chapter 25

The bishop's residence was a heavy tudor mansion connected by wide sculptured gardens to the church of St. Lucius, the largest—and wealthiest—Catholic church in Dallas. It had balconies and a turret and several stained-glass windows sending multicolored hues into the rain.

Felix thought without the electric lights it could have been built two or three hundred years ago.

"Cat doesn't like this guy," offered Kirk as they pulled into the wide circular driveway. "Says he's too good for sinners."

Father Adam frowned. "I think you'll find he has a different attitude now."

Kirk smiled thinly. "Cat told us about that, too. After you pulled rank on him."

The priest shook his head. "After he's had a chance to think about it." He looked at Kirk. "There is a reason why people become priests, Kirk."

The deputy shrugged good-naturedly, his hair seeming even more red in the half-light from the bishop's front door.

"I'll go in ahead," said Father Adam as Felix pulled to a stop.

Felix nodded, lit a cigarette, and watched the priest skip through the puddles to the front door.

"Felix?" Kirk whispered from beside him.

Felix looked at him. "Yeah?"

"Do we really have to chop his head off?"

"Looks like."

Kirk shook his head and stared out the window. He shivered.

"Who's going to do it?"

Felix frowned. "Crow, I guess. If he's up to it."

"What if he isn't? He didn't look so good to me."

Felix shrugged. "Then somebody else, I suppose."

"You?"

Felix stared at him. "Why me?"

Now Kirk shrugged. "You're second in command."

Felix stared at him a second longer, then turned away.

Jesus Christ! Is *that* what they think? Hell! I'm the guy that's leaving!

Or was, he reminded himself, dimly, before they found me, too.

Shit! All the more reason to go.

So why do you feel so guilty?

I don't. I don't. I do not. I . . . I don't know what I feel . . .

And he stubbed his cigarette out too forcibly into the dashboard ashtray.

Lights hit them from behind as the Blazer pulled into the driveway alongside the motorhome. Felix exchanged a look with Kirk, then climbed outside to greet them.

Cat still looked terrible, ashen and pale. But Jack Crow looked . . . pretty damned good. His broad shoulders were straight and his bearing seemed to have . . . But no. Those eyes. Too deep. Sunken and dark and unseeing.

"Oh, Felix!" cried Annabelle as she came around the side of the Blazer, eyes pouring tears.

And then she did an odd thing. She threw her arms around him and pressed her head into his chest and sobbed.

Felix stared blankly at her. Then he did what she wanted: he put his arms around her and comforted her.

Not just what she wanted, he thought suddenly.

What she *expected*.

As he stood there holding the sobbing Annabelle, he saw Davette, tears also in her eyes. They exchanged wan smiles.

Who do these people think I am?

"Mr. Crow!" called out from the front door.

It was the bishop, with Adam and what looked like his entire staff trailing behind him from the house. The cleric came to a breathless stop before Jack.

"Mr. Crow!" the bishop repeated. "We are so grieved at your loss. We . . ." And then he stumbled, fishing for words. At last, he held his arms out, palms up. "I'm so very sorry, Mr. Crow. I didn't understand."

Felix watched Jack eye the cleric suspiciously for a moment. But what can you say, Jack? This guy clearly means it. Look at him.

Jack nodded abruptly, said, "Thank you, bishop. I appreciate it. We . . ." and he turned and made a gesture to include the others.

The bishop was way ahead of him.

"Father Adam has told me everything. Come inside. Please. Let us help you."

They did. And the bishop was, Felix decided later, quite wonderful. He was everywhere at once, it seemed, tending to them. And where he wasn't, his staff was, several young priests or priests-to-be—Felix was never sure which. They got them inside and dry and sitting down and got them something to drink and something to munch on while dinner was being prepared and were not offended when no one had an appetite and it was more the bishop's manner than anything else. That haughty, aristocratic, God's-house-is-too-good-for-the-likes-of-you attitude had been replaced by a focus of warmth and keen piercing insight.

Felix had never met the man before. But this guy was a priest.

But it was his help with Carl's body that meant the most to the Team. He listened quietly and patiently as the macabre necessities of a vampire killer's funeral were explained to him. He did this without evincing shock or repulsion or anything else they didn't need right then. After he listened he left briefly to change to his full bishop's robes and ordered his people to do the same and something that had always before been just one more dreadful chore would become, in the light of the many golden candles and the soothing symbols of the bishop's office, something else.

As soon as they found Jack.

Felix was in one of the many rest rooms trying to tidy himself up for the ritual to come. He'd managed to dry his hair and smooth out his work shirt some. Well, maybe the windbreaker would cover some of the wrinkles the way it covered the Browning. He had thought about taking it off, this being a funeral and all. But it really was a warrior's funeral, wasn't it?

There was a light tap on the door, followed by Davette's voice.

"Felix?"

He opened the door. She had made herself up, too. Her honey-blond hair was soft and clean and neatly combed and beautiful.

"Hello," was all he could think to say.

"Hello," she smiled back, her eyes downcast shyly. "Have you seen Jack?"

"Huh? No."

"We can't find him and . . . Well, they're ready to start."

Felix nodded at her and then stepped out of the rest room into the hall. Annabelle and Kirk and some of the bishop's people were there, looking concerned.

"Where's Cat?"

"He's in the chapel already," whispered Annabelle worriedly.

"What about Adam?"

"They're all in there, Felix," Davette said. "It's just Jack."

"Okay," he said, thinking. He started walking down the hallway but paused when he realized they were all following him. He turned and looked back, at their eager hopeful faces and . . .

And he wanted to scream at them: *What do you want from me?*

But instead he said, "We'll meet you in the chapel."

And then he just stood there waiting until they reluctantly dispersed.

When they were gone he thought a second, decided he knew where Crow would be. He continued down the hallway, walking on some thick paisley-looking rug that felt rich and expensive, with paintings on either side of him hung on the richly paneled walls that were probably more so. The hallway took him to the center of the house, a massive twenty-foot-ceiling, sixty-foot-long place called, for some reason, the Common Room.

Felix hadn't expected to find Jack there, but it was on his way. He paused for a moment, admiring this room that looked like the lobby of the world's most exclusive hotel. Nice work, if you can get it.

But he knew where Jack was and it wasn't in these magnificent rooms. Wasn't in the house.

Felix went through the formal dining room, through the grand oak-paneled entry hall, and opened the front door.

The night was still cool for summer, but the storm was over and the stars were coming out. Felix stepped through the door and closed it behind him and stood there a moment letting his eyes adjust to the dark. Ten feet away, a figure sat on the edge of the wide front porch, his great back a dim softness in the shadows.

"Jack?" he called softly, almost whispering.

"Here," was the tired reply.

Felix hesitated, then walked down the broad steps and sat down. The rain-drenched steps began immediately to soak through his pants and he stood right back up again.

He looked down at Jack, sitting forward—hunched forward—with his elbows on his knees.

"Kinda wet, isn't it?"

The dim figure shrugged, a slight motion in the dark.

Get up, you sonuvabitch! Felix wanted to scream, sudden anger and disgust welling from within him. He was furious with Jack cowering out here and he wanted to grab him and shake him and some part of him knew he was being unfair.

But dammit! Jack was supposed to be the leader of this deal and there were people in there waiting on him. Counting on him.

He tried to calm himself before he spoke, but he knew his tone came out hard. "Time to go, man. Time to do it."

At first Crow didn't move. Then he stood up slowly and put his hands on his hips and stared out into the night.

"Got a cigarette?" he whispered harshly.

Felix nodded. "Sure." He fished out a smoke and handed it over and thumbed his lighter.

Jesus, Jack! he thought when the flame illuminated the man's face.

For Crow looked tight and drawn and weak and . . . and beaten.

But he didn't say anything. And Crow didn't say anything. He just puffed two or three times on the smoke, still staring into the night. Then Felix felt him take a long deep breath and let it out. Then he tossed the cigarette away into sparks, pulled up his belt, and headed for the door.

"Come on," he said gruffly.

So off they went to do the deed and as they walked, Jack leading, Felix trailing behind, a transformation took place. At first Jack looked pitiful and sorry, with his wrinkled shirttail out and his baggy pants wet on the seat from the damp step. The walk wasn't much better, more like a reluctant lope. But steadily, the pace quickened and those great shoulders thrust up and those powerful hands reached back and thumbed the shirttail in and that big head went up high on his neck and . . .

And Felix felt himself smiling in amazement. Thirty seconds before he had been disgusted and now he thought: Look at this guy! *Look* at him, coming through.

By the time the reached the hallway outside the chapel Jack was strutting like a drillmaster. He stopped, abruptly, outside the chapel door and took another deep breath and turned and looked at Felix.

Felix looked back into those same sunken eyes and he saw the pain was still there and the weariness was still there and decided that was probably more impressive then any of it.

Jack nodded questioningly at Felix.

Felix nodded back.

And they went in and did it.

They had Carl's body wrapped up in some heavy white fabric and laid out on a table up in front by the a.. r. The bishop was there, surrounded by his robed attenc its and that smoking goblet-thing they used and dozens of candles. The women sat in a pew in the back row. The men, Kirk and Cat and a robed Adam, stood by the table.

The whole thing was, Felix had to admit, beautiful. You really needed Catholics for the big stuff.

Jack walked up to the table and Felix took the empty spot beside him. Felix had thought Carl's body looked awkward lying there. And that's when he noticed the saw.

The saw was not a saw at all, but a sharp stone fashioned to slip inside a grooved harness that supported the head and neck of the body. "Cutting" consisted of rapping the blunt end of the stone sharply with a heavy wooden mallet which lay there at Jack's right hand. Beside the mallet was the stake, an intricately carved piece of wood about half the size of a baseball bat and proportionately thinner. In the light from the candles Felix could just read, on the side facing him: "Carl Joplin." He could see further lettering on the other side of the rounded wood but couldn't read it.

First were the prayers, not too different from the mass Felix had become used to, but longer somehow.

Or maybe I'm just ready to get it over with, he thought.

And then he thought, Could I do this if I had to?

Can I stand here now while Jack does it?

Then the time was there and Jack Crow reached out and fitted the cutting stone in place and then he grabbed up the mallet and held it high and muttered something Felix couldn't hear and then the mallet came down and there was an awful "snick" noise and the fabric around the throat separated cleanly and then heavy fluid began to stain the edges.

Jack didn't pause to tamp the flow with the towel there

at his other hand. Instead he grasped the stake, placed it over the heart of one of his dearest comrades, and drove it mightily home with one solid rap.

There were more prayers but Felix didn't hear them. He didn't hear anything but the pounding of his own heart and wondered if that was fear or hatred of the beasts that made this necessary.

After a while, Felix realized he was the only one still standing there except for the bishop's men ready to take away the body. He nodded self-consciously and stepped back to give them room. But just before he did he craned his neck around to see the writing on the other side of the stake.

It read: "Not one damned regret."

Chapter 26

"Rome," said Felix and the entire table went silent.

"Rome," he repeated. "We've got to get to Rome."

And they looked at him like he was some rude interloper but he really didn't give a shit. He appreciated the meal and the bishop's hospitality and he knew damn well everyone had needed this restful few hours in this great house.

But dammit! It was time to face the facts. The vampires were still out there.

Still looking for them.

Still monsters.

Felix turned to Adam. "Can the Church get us there? Right away?"

Adam blinked, stared at him, looked to Crow, who was sitting across from him.

Crow sighed and looked down at his empty plate. He looked tired.

"Okay, Felix," he said softly, "let's talk."

He pushed his heavy chair back from the bishop's grand table and stood up. He looked at the others around the table.

"Let's all talk," he said with a wan smile and motioned them to follow.

Felix hesitated, suspicious, then stood up with the rest of them—including the bishop—and followed Crow into the Common Room. The bishop took his customary chair, a great embroidered something that looked like a throne. Jack sat in a big leather piece beside him. Felix remained standing next to the great hearth. The rest of them took seats around the huge pile of Team equipment piled up in the center of the room. They had brought it with them along with Carl's remains. Crossbows and crossbow bolts and pikes and spare pistols and several cases of silver bullets. The stack was a mess because that's the way they had loaded it into the motorhome and that's the way they had brought it into the house because there hadn't really been enough room in the motorhome to store it the way they had—far from Carl's body.

But somehow that had seemed important at the time.

When they were all settled and cigarettes were lit and attendants had found the necessary ashtrays . . .

"All right, Felix," began Jack Crow, "let's hear it."

Felix paused a moment, trying to read Jack's eyes. Was there a challenge in there somewhere? Anything?

Whatever.

And he got down to it:

They were being hunted. They *didn't* know who was hunting them or where they were. All they had was a clue that somebody had taken over Davette's house and even if that was correct . . . *If* that was correct, they still didn't have enough people to take the target.

"I would have no idea whatsoever how to blow that wall the way Carl planned. Does anybody else know explosives that well?"

There was a pause before they all shook their heads.

Felix nodded, satisfied.

"And it would be suicide to go down into those shadows away from the sunshine. Remember the 'god' in the Cleburne Jail?"

He didn't wait for an answer.

"This Team has had it. No place to run, not enough firepower to fight, no place to hide—but one. Rome. We have *got* to get to Rome. And I mean: now."

It was quiet after that. Uncomfortable and quiet and all eyes were on Jack Crow but it was the bishop who spoke next.

"If you will forgive me," he began with a kindly nod

toward Jack, "I think this young man is right." He moved quickly to soothe his own words. "I don't mean to intrude, Mr. Crow, I assure you. But I have tended people all my life and many of them were soldiers and . . . And you—all of you—must take rest."

And all eyes went back to Jack and then there was more silence, long heavy silence, before he suddenly nodded.

"Okay," he said quietly.

Too quietly for Felix. "What?" he asked leaning forward.

Jack looked up at him and his eyes were dead. "I said 'okay.' Rome."

Felix nodded. Nothing more.

"Fine," said the bishop, sounding relieved. "In the morning Father Adam and I will call . . ."

"What about tonight?" interrupted Felix. "And while I'm at it, don't you think we oughta get a move on? It's full dark and they know we know the bishop, don't they?"

The bishop smiled and rose up from his chair.

"I shouldn't worry, young man. I should think being within these walls would cause them great pain."

It did. It hurt.

Even here, from the far edges of the grounds, the wretched torment from that ghastly stained-glass glow blew racking agonies through the Young Master's temples.

And the beasts . . . The beasts did not form at his gesture, did not close about him at his shining will. No. They circled and keened and stepped their dead souls' weight from foot to foot with only the sweet smell of their decay and his own blissful memory of it to recommend them.

But they would obey him.

They would obey the Young Master on this, his premier solo task from the Great Master himself. They would obey.

Despite the pain.

Despite the searing misery of the Monster's temple.

Because they were hungry.

Hours and hours they are risen this day and the thirst was rich and clasping their brute selves and they would obey.

They would obey if he must fling their rotting forms through those agonized windows.

"Beasts!" he shrilled to them, filling his own mind with the volume of his determination.

"Children!" he sang out more and his thoughts penetrated them and they turned to him.

And he strode forward, ignoring the greater agony of this nearness, forward step after step, until he halted and raised a long beautiful pale hand and one shiny black nail and pointed at the shadows on the windows and spoke out loud *and* in his will:

"Food!

"Food!!

"Fooood!"

The collective hissing rose and broke happily upon his Young Master's ears.

"Foooood . . ."

Felix was feeling pretty good just before it all caved in.

He had gotten what he wanted from Crow. Given Jack's listlessness, that hadn't been so hard, and he had felt some pangs about ramrodding everything past the mourning leader, but Felix figured none of that made a bit of difference if he could keep *some*one alive long enough to bitch about it later.

He had them up and off their butts and getting ready to move. The bishop and Adam had called Rome, had gotten transportation, had arranged all the passport difficulties. Getting back *into* America was going to be interesting, but that's what voter-registration cards were for.

Frankly, Felix looked forward to seeing 'em try to keep Annabelle out.

All in all it was looking good. Better, even, than he had expected. For a change had come over the Team once it had dawned on them that it was over. A sense of grudging relief had come about, slowly at first, but after less than an hour, even Jack had given into it. Because, dammit, it *was* a relief to get down off your guard and know that rest was coming.

That vise-tight concentration, that desperate focus, was loosening up.

There were even some jokes as the men gathered together and organized their stack of weaponry and at one point Crow had looked around at the smiles on the faces and then turned to Felix and said, "Okay, Gunman. Okay."

He hadn't said any more than that. But everyone had known what he meant.

You're quite a dude, Jack, Felix thought admiringly.

But he had been too hep to say anything out loud.

Looking good, thought Felix. And he glanced over to where *She* sat, talking quietly with Annabelle and the bishop. Just that was enough for Felix.

She would live.

Yeah. Looking good.

And that's what they were doing, all fiddling and talking about the Common Room, with its wall of stained glass and beautiful furnishings and smiles, when Felix asked Cat about something that had intrigued him:

Carl's wooden stake.

"We've all got one," Cat told him. "We had this Belgian kid working with us a couple of years ago. Raised a carpenter. He carved them for everyone."

"Everyone? You've got one, too?"

Cat eyed him carefully. "I do."

Kirk, loading silver bullets beside him, grimaced.

Cat noticed and grinned. "You guys want one?"

"I think I'll pass," replied the deputy.

Felix was studying Cat. "Do they all say the same thing?"

"No. We all have something different. Mine's even shaped different. It's flat, like a paddle."

"What does it say?"

"My name."

"Is that all."

"No. It says something else on the other side."

"What?"

"I don't think you're ready for it."

"Try me."

Cat's grin widened. "Okay. It's the answer to the question: 'How do you like your stake?' "

"Huh?" said Kirk.

"What does it *say*?" Felix wanted to know.

Cat's eyes were devilish. "Medium Rare."

They had begun to laugh when the first of the stained-glass windows just *blew* into the room whizzing glass like shrapnel into the furniture and the far walls and then that *smell*—that smell of *decay*—and Felix thought, Oh, my God, my God! They're here!

And he got to his feet and spun toward the sound and dragged out the Browning and for just an instant all was calm and eerie and . . .

. . . and *impossible*, because they had just been sitting here, just sitting here laughing and talking and ready to go, to get out of this, out of all of it . . .

And they all were there, frozen with surprise and dawning fear, their mouths open and their eyes wide, frozen and unbelieving and so *tired*. And then the beast who had burst within them as if thrown through the window shook its shaggy head and reared up from its place on all fours in front of the window and those blood-red eyes shone on them and the black mouth opened those glistening fangs and it hissed . . .

Felix raised the gun to fire as the second window exploded and the glass flew again and there were screams and then another explosion and then another and the whole wall of stained glass collapsed into the room and the smell was there and the brutes were clambering through with their dead rotting skin through the broken glass and shattered window frames and the hissing, the hisssssing filled the house of God and their air and Felix felt spears of pain on the side of his neck and then the blood running down and he knew the glass, the fractured, flying glass, had got him and he fired at something through the crashes of debris just as the next screams began.

It was . . . who? One of the bishop's men . . . Bryan? Was that his name? One of the monsters had crashed through on *top* of him and now was on all fours above him, like

some slavering undead bear, and Bryan screamed and cried
and tried to pull himself out from under and the brute held
him there, fast, with one rotting hand on his chest and
Bryan screamed again and again and scrambled desperately
backward, flailing his hands and feet but he could get no
traction on that beautiful thick carpet and the beast above
him . . .

Did nothing.

None of them were moving! They seemed stunned and
stunted and almost paralyzed and two or three of them were
holding their heads with rancid hands. Hurting. Hurting.

But there were so many! So many of them!

"It's this place," cried the bishop. And he rose up and
strode forward, the robes of his office swaying out around
him, and he grasped the great cross about his neck and held
it aloft.

"This place!" he shouted triumphantly. "They cannot
bear the House of the Lord!"

"Get them back!" roared Jack Crow.

Felix turned to see what Jack was saying and saw *them*,
saw the *women*, saw *her*! The women were here—she was
here, My God My God!

"Get them back!" roared Crow again. "Cat! Adam!
Move 'em back!"

"Where! Outside?"

"No!" shouted Felix. "Put them . . . put them in the
entry hall and close it . . ."

"Yes!" echoed Crow. "And lock the doors and . . . Cat!
Get the Blazer! Move it!"

And that's when Bryan lunged backward and the black
nails at his throat tore the skin and the red blood welled out
and the dead bear awoke and his gray lips spread wide and
the fangs started down.

Felix and Kirk fired simultaneously and the monster
flipped backward from the impact, howling and screeching
those awful sounds and the others, the *others*! So many of
them! They woke up too! They lunged toward them—

And the bishop. The bishop roared back at them!

"Back! Back, you children of Satan! Back and be purged!"

And he walked toward them, holding the cross in front of him like a goddamned pistol or something and they shouted at him to stop, to come back with them, to fall back, but—

The one that got him was so huge. It had long black hair and grimy coveralls and it came from the bishop's side—he never saw it—and those huge dead arms fell like trees on the cleric and embraced him and squeezed him and . . .

And Felix couldn't get a shot! The bishop was blocking the shot!

The bishop didn't scream. He snarled with fury and twisted around in that death grip.

"In the name of Christ!" he roared into those dead, red eyes, into those greasy, slick fangs, and he shoved the cross into that peeling face . . .

And it *burned* it! It *burned* it! Steam spewed out and the stench of the burning flesh swam through the air and . . .

. . . And from where came that impossibly bright light arcing from where the cross smote the flesh?

The ghoul howled with pain and thrashed its burly head and tried to duck back from that acetylene cross.

But it would not let go of the bishop.

Instead, it squeezed. Spasmodically, monstrously, it clamped tighter its beast arms and the bishop wailed as his insides were vised together but he never let go of the cross, never stopped jamming it into the burning face, never stopped cleansing him.

Even as he died.

"No!" shouted Kirk, aghast, leaping forward. "Let him go, you filthy . . ."

"Kirk!" cried Felix. "No! It's too late to—"

But the deputy didn't listen. He took one more quick stride. Then two. And he was within a yard of the death grip when the ghoul, still in agony from the dead bishop's cross, had finally had enough. It jerked backward and threw the bishop's limp form away, his arms as thick as branches flying outward from his body and his right forearm bashed full on into the deputy's forehead . . .

And crushed his skull . . .

And snapped his neck . . .

And Kirk turned and looked with astonishment at Felix and then the gunman saw/felt the light go out behind the eyes.

And his strong young body slumped lifeless to the floor.

Felix was still staring, wide-mouthed and unbelieving, at his dead comrade when something crashed hissing and snapping into him from the blind side. They went careening over sideways into a side table and Felix heard the table legs splinter and crack and he ended up propped against the tilted tabletop but these were only minor distant details beside the spitting decay smell of the ghoul grabbing and hissing at him and Felix managed to twist about and jam his left hand into the throat under those snapping jaws and then he was eye to bloody eye with the monster and . . .

Those eyes burned red and primal and they wanted him. Those slick gooey fangs snapped for him. And he began to lose his grip as the gray skin at the zombie's throat slid away under his fingers and the hissing increased and the monster had him by both sides of the head and it leaned hard down to reach him, his throat or his cheek or his eyes and the pupils were almost sideways with some impossible glint.

Supernatural, Jack Crow had told him.

And the gunman wrenched his pistol under the monster's chin and emptied it.

BLAM-BLAM-BLAM-BLAM-BLAM-BLAM-BLAM-BLAM-BLAM

The monster warped and howled with each impact, spitting black decay and pain, but it still held him and those claws on either side of his head jerked with his pain and cracked the gunman's head like a thunderclap against the tabletop and Felix . . . lost it.

The concussion, the impact . . . Am I dead? he wondered, as all became fuzzy and indistinct and the shattering sounds and shrieks of battle faded down.

Or just dying? Or knocked out or . . .

The black man lay a few feet from him, twitching and shivering. Not dead, but not coming.

And the vaguely conscious part of Felix thought this was very good.

And then he thought he should maybe find his gun and: Here it is, in my hand.

And then he reached around and got a new clip—he knew how to do that. He knew how to change clips and he did and then he held the newly loaded gun in his lap and felt very proud and he felt the blood from his head injury flowing down his neck and he saw the other monsters had come to also, understood that they had been only temporarily stunned by the silver bullets . . .

And by God's House.

The bishop is dead, thought Felix.

Kirk Thompson is dead too, he thought next.

Soon I will die, too, won't I?

But I still have my gun and what I will do is: I will shoot them when they come near me and it will not stop them but it will hurt them and that is better than nothing and . . .

And so he lay there, stunned, against the overturned table, and watched them come for him.

And saw Jack Crow save what was left.

He saw it from a long way off, it seemed, as though Jack and the monsters and even the rest of the building, were far, far away. But he still saw it. And what he saw, even from the end of his conked tunnel, was amazing. Jack Crow did things Felix couldn't imagine being done. He did things no one else but Jack Crow, Crusader, by God, Jack Crow, could have done.

He was everywhere at once. And had to be. The other goons had arisen at the same time as the black man at Felix's feet, and though they were slow and ponderous and unthinking, there were too many of them. And they were so hungry, reaching for him, lunging at him, grisly fingers grasping and clawing and—

And Jack Crow bashed 'em back. He emptied his crossbow and emptied his pistol and grabbed up a handful of pikes and laid into them. He bashed them, he spitted them, he carved them with splintered ends. There was no one else: Adam guarded the women in the entry hall. Cat was out bringing up the Blazer. Felix lay almost comatose against the shattered table. For the next few crucial minutes there would be no one else to hold them off but Jack alone.

And Jack didn't seem to give a shit. He went after them with a ferocity that Felix, even stunned as he was, could hardly believe. It was like some sort of grotesque juggling act. Jack would slam two of them down somehow, but by that time two more would have arisen again, spitting and hissing and reaching for him. And he would slam them down again, spear them with the pikes or shoot them through their faces or once, just flat bust them in the mouth with his fist.

He's incredible, thought Felix. He's bigger than life.

And then he thought: I've got to get up! I've got to *do* something!

But then Jack was there, beside him, speaking softly but quickly: "C'mon, buddy. We've gotta move. C'mon!"

And then he turned and kicked the black man full in the face, the one with nine silver bullets in him, who had only now started to rise again.

"C'mon, Gunman," said Jack, lifting him with surprising gentleness, to his feet.

Pain seared through Felix's skull when his head came loose from the table and he saw Jack wince in sympathy but they didn't stop, they got Felix up and they got him moving and the pain began to clear his head and then they were in the entry hall and the women were there, Annabelle and Davette, huddled together against a wall and dammit if Annabelle didn't manage a smile for them.

And then Jack and Adam were closing the huge sliding oak doors to the living room and dragging some antique side table across the marble to barricade it. The other doors were already closed with other furniture stacked against them. Only the massive front door, standing open to the returning rain, was free.

"Your head," said a small voice.

Felix turned and saw Davette, her hand frozen in midair where she had started to reach for his wound.

"I'm all right," Felix managed to say.

And she nodded vaguely and stepped back to Annabelle and Felix thought: Move, Felix! Wake *up*!

And he shook his head for more pain and gritted his teeth and looked down at the Browning still in his hand and . . .

And it helped. Some.

"Where's Cat?" Jack wanted to know.

Father Adam shook his head. "Haven't seen him. Do you think . . . ?"

Jack was at the front door, looking warily out into the night.

"Do I think what?" he barked.

Adam swallowed. "We haven't seen any masters. Maybe they couldn't come in here. Maybe they're . . ."

And he gestured out the door.

"Oh, shit!" sighed Jack.

And the dead grasping hands began scratching at the sliding oak doors.

Jack looked at the doors, saw them start to lean inward with the weight and thirst of the dead.

"Well, we can't stay here. Maybe . . ."

Bright headlights framed the door and there was a loud crunching noise as Cat vaulted the Blazer up the front steps and came to a skidding stop on the wide front landing of the great home.

"Whenever ya'all are ready!" he shouted through the driver's window.

Jack herded everyone out and the Blazer doors were yanked open. Jack took the wheel. Annabelle sat in the passenger seat beside him. Felix sat in the back seat behind her, gun in hand.

And that's where he was when they bounced down the steps and over the curb and onto the street and were racing half a block away and a streak of movement appeared from the right and something slammed into the side of the Blazer and breaking glass slashed through the interior and the Blazer tilted up crazily on two wheels before bouncing back down on all four wheels, skidding wildly on the slick pavement, side-swiping a parked car and coming to a stop in the middle of the road.

The grasping talons through Annabelle's shattered passenger window finally woke Felix up. He lunged over the front seat and jammed the automatic into the Young Master's face and jerked the trigger three times.

The monster's face disappeared back out through the window and then reappeared, hissing and spitting and shivering, two holes in its moon-pale skin, the clear blood pulsing out with the black spitting mucus from the mouth and . . .

And Jack tried to move the Blazer but the engine had stalled and then it wouldn't start in Drive, so he had to work the gearshift and . . .

And the fiend lunged back at them, back at Felix, the source of his pain, and Felix fired again and again and the head snapped back once more but . . .

But one of the talons still grasped the edge of the doorway and the whole damned Blazer shook with the monster's pain and fury and Felix leaned way out over Annabelle's seat and out the window and twisted his body around and saw the monster, hunched against the side of the vehicle, and it looked up at him, hissed and spat at him, and Felix shot it through the right eye and it vaulted back and lost its grip on the Blazer.

The engine roared to life, Jack tromped on the gas pedal, and they were off.

They could see the creature through the back windows jerking itself to its feet in the middle of the road. Felix, still hanging halfway out the window, managed to shoot one more time.

The Blazer didn't slow for several blocks while Felix clambered past everyone to the rear of the truck bed to be ready to shoot again. But nothing came. No monster sprinted after them through the rain.

"Relax, Jack!" called Felix at last from the rear. "No one's coming."

But Jack kept his foot down hard.

"Where are you going?" yelled Felix, irritated by the careening car.

"Hospital," said Crow without turning around.

And Adam took Felix by the arm and pointed. He looked where he was told and saw her, saw Annabelle, slumped across the Blazer's console. Cat was frantically dabbing at her throat with a shirt. But the blood, from a dozen wounds of exploded safety glass, poured thick across her still features.

Chapter 27

"She *cannot* be moved."

Jack was getting angry. "Look, doctor, I'm not sure you know what's—"

But Cat grabbed his boss's arm.

"Jack! Goddammit! He's not just saying he's *against* it! He's saying she'll die! Annabelle will *die*!"

Crow looked darkly at the two of them, then shrugged the hand off his arm and stepped away down the hall. The three policemen eyed him suspiciously but made no move. Jack had called in every chit and favor he had with the Dallas Police to keep from being arrested, even for questioning. But nobody had actually told the patrolmen just exactly why these heavily armed and obviously fresh-from-violence people weren't to be touched. And they were wary.

"Dammit!" muttered Jack and looked at his watch. "Dammit!" he repeated when he saw the time.

Because they had already been here all night and most of the day. Because it was three o'clock in the afternoon. How many more hours until sunset?

Until night?

Until they came?

"Mr. Crow," the doctor tried again, "it's not just a matter of blood loss. It's the trauma to the system. Her signs are very low, her heart has fluttered, she has a concussion, she—"

"Hell, doctor, she's awake, for chrissakes!"

The doctor remained calm. He nodded. "Sometimes. Barely. She's a strong woman. But she's not strong enough to leave intensive care. Not for at least one more day. She *must* have constant monitoring. She *must* have the IVs. She *must* stay here."

He stepped forward and said, more gently, "Don't worry, Mr. Crow. We'll take good care of her. She'll be fine."

Jack Crow looked at the man and knew he meant it and knew he didn't know what he was dealing with and he knew something else: there was no way the Team could ever convince him otherwise in time.

Felix had been leaning against the corridor wall with his arms crossed in front of his chest, looking sinister with his bandaged head over the even dozen stitches they had had to give him. He uncrossed his arms and stepped away from the wall.

"Is there a place . . . a room, where we could talk?" he asked.

The doctor eyed him gratefully and led them around a corner to a small anteroom that, judging from the cigarette smoke, served as the break area for the Emergency Room staff. It had a couple of tables covered with soggy cardboard coffee cups and overflowing ashtrays, some plastic chairs, a vending machine, a pay phone.

The three men sat down and added to the smoke.

"Jack," Cat all but whispered, "we're going to have to risk it, you know."

Crow didn't look at him, didn't respond, just puffed hard on his cigarette.

Cat exchanged a look with Felix before trying again.

"We can't move her, Jack. And . . . well, we can put sensors outside, out in front, so we'll know they're coming. Hell, they might not even come."

Crow glared at him. "They know she's hurt, Cherry. Do you really believe they won't come?"

Cat just looked at him.

Crow turned to Felix. "Do you?"

Felix met his gaze. "No."

And it was quiet for a while.

"But we've got some options here," Cat continued. "We don't have to fight. They'll probably come in the front—why wouldn't they? And we'll hear them and we can move her *then*!"

"Give us that again," said Felix, interested.

"We move her out the back. Miles of hallways in this place. We'll just wheel her down the hall and into an elevator and just pick a route out the back. Look, I've checked it out. I know just where to park the Blazer . . ."

And he went on for a while in convincing style and much detail, like it was, really, a great opportunity instead of the disaster it was.

Felix sat in silence as he spoke, hating it. They all knew better. When would they come? From which direction? How *many*? How were they going to stop them at night? And did anyone really believe they could just trot through this hospital wheeling a critical patient? Fighting vampires along the way?

Felix sat there and listened to Cat and watched Jack Crow and saw him again, haggard and beaten but coming through to tend to Carl's body. And then relaxed and relieved and hopeful before ten minutes later having to save the whole show single-handed.

And now Cat trying to convince everybody this was all going to be all right.

The Gunman smiled.

Cat stopped talking abruptly when he saw the smile.

"What is it, Felix?" Jack asked. "What do you think of the Plan, here?"

"It stinks."

"I suppose you'd like to just get out of here."

"I sure would."

"Are you?"

Felix felt his own smile growing. Do you bastards really think I'd abandon Annabelle? Or you, Crow, after what you've done?

"Jack," he said at last, "you're a real prick."

Crow eyed him a moment. "True," he replied seriously.

And . . . "Okay, okay, okay," he continued wearily. "I guess we're stuck with Cat's little scheme. Unless the Gunman here has something new?"

" 'Fraid not."

" 'Fraid you'd say that. Okay. But I want two escape routes. Get back to the bishop's and fetch the motorhome. I want two ways out of this place. You and Cat figure out where we should stash the vehicles. And you'd better take Davette somewhere. Where were we supposed to stay last night? The one by the Galleria?"

"She won't go," said Father Adam from the doorway.

"Huh?" asked Jack.

Adam shook his head. "She won't leave Annabelle's side."

Felix snorted. "Like hell she won't. You just—"

Cat shook his head, too. "She won't, Felix."

Crow and Felix exchanged looks.

"This is crap," said one of them.

Cat leaned forward on the table.

"Hey, guys," he said gently. "We're getting down to it. And everybody's got his own style."

Felix stared at him like he was from Mars.

" 'His own style,' eh?" muttered Jack, almost to himself. "Well, that's nice."

Then he leaned over and put his cigarette out and started giving orders.

"We set the detectors and we fetch the motorhome and we scope out two escape routes and then, a couple of hours before dark, somebody—you, Gunman, it's your woman—pick up our pretty little martyr *and* her style and put her ass in a motel because that's *my* style and I run things here."

Felix grinned along with the rest of them and wondered why? *Why?* We haven't got a fucking prayer . . .

"Mr. Crow?" came from behind Adam. It was Annabelle's nurse. The men got to their feet.

"Is she . . . ?" Jack began.

The nurse smiled tightly. "She's awake again. She wants to talk to you."

"Right," said Jack, already moving. "The rest of you get moving. I want the motorhome here in an hour, with all the beds down. We've got to get some sleep before tonight."

Annabelle, near death, white as a sheet, surrounded by beeping electronics and pierced through with running tubes, still managed to be radiant.

Talk about style, thought Jack to himself as Davette got up and he took her seat.

"Annabelle," he whispered to her, "don't you *ever* sleep?"

She didn't even bother to smile. "Jack," she whispered huskily, "we've got to talk . . ."

But only she talked and Jack listened and he absolutely hated what he heard.

Annabelle had figured it out. She was half-dead, but she knew the score. She knew she couldn't move. She knew the night was coming. She knew the vampires, just like Jack, had their own connections. They knew who the Team was, knew all about them. Knew about her, had actually *seen* her and knew she was hurt.

And she knew they would come for her and the police would never know how to react or possibly even believe what they'd seen after it was all over.

No. She had decided. They must leave her here.

And Jack tried to reassure her, tried most of the junk Cat had just finished throwing at him, that it wasn't like they were trapped, they could always get out the back and, besides, there was no guarantee the vampires really would show up here and . . .

And she knew better, as always.

"Jack!" she pleaded, her eyes frantic, "you *must* go. You must save yourselves!"

And Crow looked right at her and said, "We'll see."

And she knew she had lost.

"At least get Davette . . ."

"I've already taken care of that," Jack whispered to her. "I put Felix on it."

And she almost smiled. "About time."

Then she sighed and looked away for a moment. When she looked back her eyes were filled with tears and she reached up her pale skinny arm to him and he leaned down so she could caress his dirty, unshaven face.

"Jack . . ." she sighed. "Sweet Jack. You were . . . You were always such a good boy . . ."

And he didn't cry because he couldn't let her carry that, too. But his eyes were hot and her tiny fingers on his face were the softest touch he had ever known.

Then she gave him a playful slap and pushed him a-way.

"Where's my purse?" she demanded. "I must look a fright."

"Huh? You look fine . . ." sputtered Crow.

"What do *you* know about it?" she replied in her lady voice. "Find my purse, please."

So he rummaged around and found it and opened it and handed it to her.

"Oh, good," she said after she had glanced inside. "I've got my mirror. Now, run along."

Jack frowned. "Don't you think you should be resting? Or—"

"I repeat: what do *you* know about it? Now go away."

He rose, uncertain. "I'll get Davette," he offered.

"Oh, please, Jack. I think I can put my own makeup on after so-and-so many years. All of you: leave me alone to myself for just one instant. Please!"

"Well, okay," he muttered back, defeated once more. And he stumbled out through the curtain drawn around her bed and informed Davette and left to find the others.

The glass of water on the hospital tray was close by, but it took her a long time to reach it and the effort exhausted her. She lay back against the pillow, careful not to spill the cup, and rested a moment. She closed her eyes and took a deep breath and tried to clear her mind but instead she saw the house in Pebble Beach and she saw the zoo and she saw the faces of all her boys who had died.

"Please, God!" she whispered. "No more of them. No more . . ."

And she leaned forward and fumbled one-handed through her purse and the pills were still there, where they had been for the last year.

My boys . . .

Chapter 28

Felix's disgust started kicking in when he had to shut down the Antwar Saloon.

He had to do it. It would delay his return to the hospital, but he couldn't have his customers and employees sitting innocently around the place while vampires wandered through looking for the owner.

No. He had to do it. And it only took half an hour.

But then, sitting there at his desk, with his closing note to his employees and their checks all written, it started getting to him. The waste. The whole, useless, worthless messy waste of it got to him. Dammit! It wasn't like he had much of a life, anyway, and he was going to have to lose even that?

Shit.

Jack Crow and the Crusaders. Noble and brave and tough and all the rest of it.

But losers. Losers because they were losing.

No way they were going to make it through tonight. No way they were going to stop the vampires at that hospital. Witnesses? Hell, the vampires wouldn't care and, anyway, who would believe it? And who would believe it after seeing it? A couple of days later—with everyone treating them like they were nuts—and even the eyewitnesses would think they had imagined it.

The ones that lived, anyway.

Shit.

Crow loses—what is it? Six, seven men? And he goes to

Rome and comes back with what? One priest. Father Adam was a good man. Well, better than good. In fact . . .

But he was still just one guy. Crow shoulda brought back twenty men, all priests, and a bishop of his own.

But he didn't. He didn't do a lot of things and because of that they were all gonna die.

He turned in his desk chair and looked out the picture window that overlooked the bar. Only it was dark in the bar now. The only thing he could see in the glass was his own face, in the reflection from his desk lamp.

All going to die.

I'm going to die.

"You're going to die," he said out loud. "Tonight."

Shit. It didn't even sound dramatic enough.

If it was anybody else but Annabelle . . . Well, if it was *her*, of course, Davette, he'd have to do it. And maybe . . .

But that wasn't the goddamned point.

The goddamned point was that they were going to lose.

And the vampires were going to win, those slimy, greasy, bloodsucking fuckers were going to keep at it. That really riled him. And that notion that they had been sitting here, in *his* bar, while *his* waitresses and bartenders served them because they didn't know. That was the deal. These miserable bastards would be treated as real live people by those who didn't know. Like they really weren't scum. Like they really belonged to the company of mankind, instead of . . . of what? What did they really deserve?

Sewage.

"I'm going to die," he said again.

And then he turned back to his desk and wrote what he hoped was a legal document and he hoped he spelled her name right. Then he put it in an envelope, labeled it "Last Will and Testament," and shoved it in the back of his checkbook. They'd find it.

Lousy Crow with his samurai bullshit. We're already dead so nothing matters but Style! Crap! Is that his excuse for losing? Because the only thing worse than letting the vampires run free was losing to them first.

Shit!

He stepped away from his desk and looked around his rooms one last time, at some photographs on the wall, some souvenirs, some knickknacks. Not enough to leave behind after thirty-odd years.

Well . . . then . . . fuck it.

Fuck it!

At least he'd make damn sure he hurt them first.

And he stopped and looked again into the glass and laughed.

Talk about your samurai bullshit.

Felix got lost in the vast complex of Parkland Hospital trying to find a new route from where he'd parked the motorhome. It took him ten minutes to finally come around a corner and see the sign for ICU/EMERGENCY. Below the sign, on a couch against the wall, were Cat and Davette. Adam stood against the wall beside them.

Davette was crying.

"What?" he called out, tripping toward them.

Davette lifted her face from her hands and it was all red and bright and tears streaked her cheeks.

"Oh, Felix!" she cried. "Annabelle *died*!"

And she leapt up and threw her arms around him and sobbed like a child, her fragile ribs heaving under his rough hands. He held her and patted her dumbly. Past her, Adam still leaned against the wall, his face grave and pale. And on the couch, Cat looked a whole lot worse, staring straight ahead, boring his eyes at nothing.

"I don't get it," Felix managed. "The doctor said—"

"She killed herself, Gunman," rasped Cat in a voice from the grave.

"What?"

"Sleeping pills," added Adam in a quiet voice.

"But . . . why?"

Cat turned his head at last and looked at Felix and his eyes were scary.

"Because she knew we'd stay to protect her. And she . . . couldn't . . . stand . . ."

And then Cat lost it, broke down completely. He collapsed, folding into his own miserable dry sobs, and Felix didn't think he could stand it, Cherry Cat bawling, and even Davette, hearing that awful wrenching sound, pulled herself loose from Felix and returned to the couch and embraced him and the two of them shook and rocked together.

Felix sat down hard on the magazine-littered coffee table in front of the couch and fumbled around and found a cigarette and put it in his mouth and managed to light it and . . .

And he was too stunned, too shocked to do much else. Too blown to think. Numb and stupid and . . . Annabelle dead? Dead? *Killed* herself? He couldn't bear their tears but there was no place to go and Adam didn't look much better so he just sat there and stared at the hospital tiles under his feet.

I should feel relief, shouldn't I? I mean, I'm not going to die tonight, after all. I should feel relief.

Why don't I?

He started to take another puff and realized the cigarette had burned, unsmoked, down to the filter while he sat there numb and stupid and—

Waitaminute!

He caught Adam's eye and mouthed: Where's Jack?

But Adam only shook his head grimly.

What the hell . . . ?

Felix got up and went over to him and moved him down the wall away from the others.

"Give," he said tersely.

Adam shrugged, looked miserable.

"Jack's gone."

"Where?"

"We don't know. He . . . He just walked out when they told us."

Felix glared at him. "Did he say anything?"

Now the young priest looked about to cry.

"He said, 'I even managed to get her killed.' Then he just walked out."

Felix looked around. "Is he outside, then?"

Adam shook his head. "He took a cab. Felix?"

"Yeah?"

"He didn't look good."

"Like how?"

"Like . . . like crazy."

Great. Felix looked at the other two. They were still crying.

Great.

Davette had finally gotten Cat to go to sleep in the main bedroom of the hotel suite. His sullen silence on the way from the hospital had been almost as unnerving as his weeping. She had fallen asleep watching him, curled up on the edge of the bed. Adam lay dozing on the lounge beside the bed. Felix sat in a chair by the great picture window that overlooked the Galleria Shopping Mall. The ashtray beside him was full.

And the sunset was lovely.

Shit.

He looked at his watch. Five hours now. No sign of Jack. No call. No word. No clue.

He looked over at the sleeping trio. He didn't blame them. If anything, he envied them. He was tired, too. But he was more worried than anything else. He had brought them to this hotel because it had been the place they were planning to go and because . . .

Because he didn't know what else to do.

No one had heard from Crow. He had called the hospital half a dozen times. He had called the bishop's—the late bishop's—office and home and church. He had called the Team's new house three times without answer. Each time he had imagined the phone ringing in Carl's destroyed workshop.

He stood up slowly, thought about sneaking into the other room to try calling everyone again. But he knew better. Crow wasn't at any of those places. Not now and not later.

I even managed to get her killed.

And the sleeping three looked mighty small without him there.

They look like I feel, he thought, and sat back down and added to the ashtray and stared at the blasted sunset.

"Where's Jack?" came from behind him a moment later.

Felix turned and looked. It was Cat. He looked better. Still pale and drawn and . . . hurting. But better. The sleep had done its deed.

"Where's Jack?" he repeated, sitting in the chair beside Felix's.

"I don't know," Felix replied.

"What do you mean?"

"I mean he's gone. He left from the hospital. No one's seen him since."

"But it's almost nighttime!"

"Yeah."

"I don't understand!"

Felix looked at him. *I don't understand either,* he felt like saying.

At least I hope I don't.

But he didn't say that. Instead, he gave Cat what little he knew from the beginning. When he told him what Adam had said Jack had said, he checked the other man's face closely for a reaction.

But there was none. Just the same confusion. And concern.

Davette and the priest, he noticed, were up and about once more. Listening.

"I was hoping," Felix said next, "that you might know something."

Cat frowned. "No. I've been sorta . . ."

Felix nodded. "Yeah. But you know Jack better than anyone. In fact, you're the only one here," he added without thinking, "who's known Jack for any . . ."

And then he stopped, shut up, as the realization hit him. As it hit Cat. As it hit the rest of them.

Two months ago, a full Team Crow. With soldiers and money and Carl and Annabelle and Cat and the monsters on the run.

And now . . . just Cat left. In this room anyway.

Felix held his breath watching Cat, but the smaller man came through the moment. It took a few deep breaths, a little concentration, but he stayed on top.

Good for you, Cherry, Felix thought.

But they had things to do.

"Where do you think he might go?" Felix continued. "After Annabelle. Would he go get drunk or . . . ?"

Cat was silent a moment. But when he spoke his voice was clear enough.

"He might. He . . . we all . . . loved her. He might just get drunk."

"Where?"

"Huh?"

"You know his favorite joints. Where would he go?"

Cat nodded, thought a bit. Then he stood up and went over to the bed and sat down next to the phone and rummaged under the end table until he found a phone book. He opened it and started thumbing through it, his other hand resting on the phone. Then he stopped.

"The thing is, the only places I know where he'd go . . . Well, *they* might know about them, too. And he wouldn't go there in case they came looking for him. The only places he'd go would be the places no one knows he goes. And that could be anywhere."

He put down the phone book.

"I guess we'll just have to wait for him to find us. He knew we were supposed to wait here until the plane leaves."

The plane? Oh, yeah, Felix remembered. The plane for Rome.

But Jack Crow wasn't thinking about that plane.

"Where," Felix asked casually, "is his favorite spot?"

"Huh? Well, the Adolphus. He loves the place, the rooms, the service. He loves the bar. But he couldn't go there. That's the one place they'd be sure to look for him."

"Give 'em a call," suggested Felix, his voice still casual.

Cat frowned. "C'mon, Felix. He wouldn't go there! They know about the Adolphus."

Felix shrugged. "It's worth a try."

Cat shook his head. "That would be *asking* for it and Jack—"

"You want *me* to call?" This time his voice was as strong as his mood.

Cat eyed him a moment. Then he picked up the phone

and started dialing. Cat seemed to know this number. And he seemed to know the voice that answered.

"Terry? This is Cat. Mr. Catlin. Hi. I'm looking for Mr. Crow. I just thought . . . What? You're kidding. Ring him for me, would you? But Terry. You know me. This is an emergency. I . . . Okay. Okay. Never mind."

Cat hung up and stared at the others in amazement.

"He's there. In the Governor's Suite. He's turned off his phone."

Felix just sighed and turned away and puffed on his cigarette.

"I don't get it!" Cat cried next. "Does he *want* to die?"

"I think," said the Gunman quietly, "that's the idea."

Chapter 29

By the time they got to the Adolphus, Felix's only remaining emotion was disgust.

Disgust with the whole damned deal. Disgust with the loss, with the waste. Carl Joplin and the bishop and the bishop's people and poor, brave redheaded Kirk and Annabelle and . . .

And disgust with Jack Crow and, come to think of it, disgust with himself for being a part of it all.

But mostly disgust for the two cowboys in the back of the Blazer wearing their full chain mail and toting their crossbows and in such a hurry to be killed rescuing a man who wanted to die.

Felix wore no chain mail because he had no intention whatsoever of going up there.

And he said so. Often.

"This is bullshit, Cat! And you know it. And Adam, you oughta know better than this. It's suicide."

Cat stubbornly shook his head. "Not if we can get him out of there before they show up."

"What if they're already there?"

Cat was silent.

"And what if he doesn't want to come, Cat? Ever think of that?"

"He'll come when he sees us."

"Will he? Cherry, he *wants* this."

"You don't know that," retorted Cat desperately.

317

"Then why is he there?"

Cat was silent.

But Adam said, "We can't let this happen to him."

And Cat added, "How can you?"

Felix turned around in his seat and glared at him.

"Because it's none of *my* business, either. Can't you see that?"

"Felix is right," said Davette suddenly. And firmly.

And that stopped the conversation.

For Davette had been silent throughout the argument and the drive, sitting quietly behind the wheel of the Blazer. Now, in her voice was the tone of someone who knew exactly what she was talking about.

"Felix is right," she said again. "Jack is a victim, just as much as anyone. Just as much—as I was. And . . . it wears you down."

She pulled to a stop at a red light and turned and faced the others.

"Sometimes you get so tired. Then all you want is for it to be over. Jack has had it differently from what happened to me. But he's had it for three years."

"It's not the same," insisted Cat.

Davette's voice was warm but her eyes were very direct. "You don't know that, Cat. Jack is tired."

It was quiet for the next few moments. The light changed, the Blazer began moving again, and soon the Adolphus was in sight. Davette pulled to the curb across the street from the famous entrance and turned off the engine.

For a few seconds, no one moved. Then Cat took a deep breath and reached for the door.

"Don't do it, Cat," Felix told him.

Cat hesitated, then ignored him. Both he and the priest climbed out. Felix got out, too, and stood on the sidewalk glaring at the both of them.

This was *bullshit*!

"Have you ever thought how Jack's gonna feel if you go down, too?"

Cat's grin was thin. "At least he'll be alive to hate me."

"No, he won't," snapped Felix cruelly. "None of you will."

"Felix," said Adam slowly, "we just can't let a Jack Crow die like this."

"Oh! *You* can't. Thanks, God."

Adam just shook his head and the two of them started across the street.

Then Cat stopped and looked back.

"Tell me this, Felix. You're so sure Jack wants to die. If he lives through tonight, you think he'd be happy? Or would he just do it again tomorrow?"

When Felix didn't answer, Cat smiled again.

"He's down, now. Annabelle . . . But he'll come back if he can get the chance."

Cat smiled again and waved.

"Don't worry, Gunman. We'll get a taxi."

And then he and Adam tripped across the street to the hotel entrance.

Ouch.

Felix stood there a long while, watching them enter the lobby. Then he lit a cigarette. Then he looked at the Blazer, at Davette sitting behind the wheel. Then he got inside and closed the door and stared straight ahead.

Ouch.

Davette started the engine and they pulled away from the curb a few yards to the light and stopped again.

Ouch.

"Felix . . . ?" she began.

But he shook his head.

Ouch. Ouch!

Because hadn't there been a moment, lying there on the bishop's rug, when he'd just wanted it over with? When he wished Jack would just give it up and let them get him? Stop prolonging the inevitable?

Wasn't there?

Wasn't there a moment like that? And wasn't he glad Jack had kept it up?

Shit.

Shit!

"Pull over."

"Felix! You can't—"

"Pull over," he repeated and his voice was hard.

"Felix! Please . . ." she urged. But she began pulling the Blazer to the curb.

"I know," he said harshly. "I know, I know I *know*!"

And this time his disgust was all for himself.

He got out of the truck. An elderly couple, both black, were staring at a window display of garish, cheaply made leather shoes.

Is this the last store I'll ever see?

He looked at Davette. He shrugged his shoulders.

"Did you know I love you?"

She smiled grimly, nodded.

He nodded back, shook his head, and sprinted across the street to the hotel.

The polished bronze doors opened smoothly, almost silently, onto the twenty-first floor and . . .

Ha! There in the thick, rich carpet—the impressions of chain-mailed boots! The Two Stooges were here!

If he had laughed—and he almost did—it would have been a wild, broken cackle.

Felix had never known such fear.

Such anger.

Such . . . disgust.

He knew his face would frighten a passing stranger.

He knew he was going to die.

He knew he was never going to see Her again and he knew he couldn't have Her unless he went ahead.

He knew it was madness.

It was out of control.

Two ways into this prestigious hallway. The fire stairs at one end, the half-open oaken double door to the Governor's Suite at the other. He glanced briefly toward the fire stairs, then strode boldly along the footprints in the carpet and pushed the suite's door open all the way and then just stood there and waited for something to happen.

But nothing did.

Not going to be that easy, eh? Fine.

He stepped into the room.

Magnificent room. Antiques and imported carpets over polished hardwood floors and fifteen-foot ceilings and flowing diaphanous curtains pushed in from the steaming terrace breezes. The terrace ran the length of the L-shaped living room and there, at the far end of the huge room, in the dim light from the downtown high rises, were Cat and Adam, crossbows in their fists, crouched down next to the open french doors.

Felix almost laughed. He almost shouted out to them.

But he didn't. Instead he looked to see what they were seeing.

It was easy. There was another set of french doors by the front entrance, right next to him, also blowing hot the diaphonous curtains, also pale against the lights from the towering downtown buildings, also open to the terrace where, less than thirty feet away, closer to Felix than Cat and Adam or the safety of the fire stairs, sat Jack Crow.

On a stone bench.

Talking to a vampire.

Felix stepped closer and felt the disgust welling up, swelling up and through his eyes and out the top of his head. By *God*! but it was beautiful.

He had forgotten how beautiful they were.

It was young and thin and blond and tall, lazing confidently and casually against the four-foot walled railing, the lights from some glass tower delicately illuminating his stark yet smooth and precious features. White shirt and black pants and black leather boots. Not the same outfit as the little god in Cleburne. But close enough. The same grimy elegance.

The same shoddy, sexy, decadent, beautiful . . .

Fuck you, little god. Fuck you and all the rest of you.

And fuck you, too, Jack Crow, for talking to it.

Talking to it. Like it was human. Like it was only half-bad. Like it was misunderstood or "two-sides-to-everything" and not a crushed, smeared, cockroached soul.

And then he saw the crossbow Jack had hidden.

It was down behind the bench on which he sat, propped up against some huge potted terrace tree, and Felix really did almost laugh this time, at the puny, pitiful, all-destructive self-deception of it all.

Felix read it all, now. Saw it all. The whole sad script.

What was Crow going to do? Just wait up here with arms flung open, yelling "Bite me!" into the night? Oh, no. Gotta at least pretend you're going down nobly, don't you, Warrior Jack? Gotta make believe this is a Something, right? A Something, a last bold thrust, instead of the seamy suicide it really is.

And he almost left right then. He almost left Jack Crow to his paltry, sickening, disgusting little Passion Play.

Ha!

But what about the Two Stooges? All crouched down and ready to rush up and save him and ensure that three, rather than just one, get swept to ugly, ugly hell. Can't leave the Two Stooges, can I? ·

Especially since I'm the goddamn third one?

Out of control.

He heard his heart and he could see his pulse, throbbing through the thumb wrapped death-grip tight around the Browning.

Madness.

But a lovely night, he thought. If a trifle warm.

Then he crossed his hands, with the Browning, behind his back and kicked the french doors open all the way and stepped out onto the terrace just as loudly as he knew how.

"Hey, you! Little god! Is it true your dick doesn't work anymore?"

Silence. Then surprise from those piercing eyes, then understanding of what was said.

Anger flashing his way.

"Felix!" shouted Jack. "Felix, no! What are you doing?"

"It's not just him!" popped Cat, stepping out onto the other end of the terrace.

"Cat!" yelled Jack, stricken.

"It's all of us," added Father Adam, joining Cat.

"No!" whispered Jack weakly. "No . . . no . . ."

"What is this?" flashed the monster. "Am I to be trapped here?"

And then he smiled that cocky, beautiful smile.

"Hey!" snapped Felix with his own smile. "Tell me about your dick." And then, in a conspiratorial tone: "Can't get it up, right?"

And the smile vanished and the evil sneer spread out to him.

"Puny little man . . . How I will enjoy your crushing, bleeding, death cries and your—"

"Sure, sure, sure," replied Felix calmly. "But let's face it. You can turn 'em on pretty good. But when it gets down to it . . ." And he held the fingers of his left hand out in front of his loins and dangled them limply. "When it gets down to it, it's floppity-floppity. Right?"

Its burst of loathing, even from fifteen feet away, all but staggered Felix backward. The eyes went black, then red. The mouth slit itself wide as it stepped toward him.

"Welcome, puny mutt-man, to the . . . yolk . . ."

. . . and the fangs sprung out wide . . .

". . . of the egg . . ."

And the laughter was a spear.

But Felix just laughed back and shot it right between those fucking fangs.

"Heeachaaaahhh!"

And it hissed and shook and the black gob spat out with the pain and surprise and . . . the hatred—

And Felix shot it again, through the chest.

And it staggered back, off-balance and reeling, and the backs of its legs bounced against the walled railing and . .

It almost went over the edge!

And that gleaming thought, that wish, that insane hope . . . It stalled Felix for just an instant, just long enough for the monster to right itself and warp open its full monster's face to the Gunman and Felix heard a crossbow go off . . .

. . . but so did the beast . . .

And it caught it. It did catch it in the air, goddammit!

Felix shot it again, in the shoulder of the hand that snatched the bolt.

The shoulder warped and shivered and there was more hissing and more black bile spat and Felix shot it again as it jerked toward him and the second crossbow—Adam's? Jack's?—tore through the air and crunched loudly through the center of its chest and out against the city lights.

Ungodly, unholy screams filled the night and the city and their heads and the monster's frenzy was a blur of pain and horror and fury as it bounced and twitched and grabbed at the spit and there was another *thong* and another bolt pierced its chest from the side, splitting it neatly in the center, and the monster splattered black bile and rocked backward and hit the wall again and reeled, losing its balance and . . .

Yes! Yes! Go over, you prick! Fall! *Fall!*

And Felix fired again and again but the shots had so little effect next to the wooden stakes piercing it and there! From the side, motion rushing forward! Jack coming on!

And Felix wanted to shout "No!" but he could not, he could not. It was their only chance and he fired again and again, fired the Browning empty to keep it off balance and then Jack was there running full speed into it but at the last second . . .

At the last second it saw Jack.

And held up its hand.

And stopped him, all two hundred plus pounds at breakneck speed.

Stopped him. Caught him. Held him, ignoring its own pain and hissing:

"You foolish little . . ."

Before Father Adam appeared and slammed point-blank into the two of them . . .

The three went over the edge.

Just like that.

And quiet. So quiet, suddenly. Only the breeze and a far distant car horn and his own breath heaving and . . .

And Cat beside him, staring wide-mouthed at the wall.

Felix did manage to approach and look down and just glimpse, twenty-one stories down, three forms on the pavement, before . . .

"NoooooooOOOOOO . . ." burst slowly from Cat beside him and Felix felt his forward movement and he dropped his pistol as his right hand shot out and snatched a chain-mailed shoulder and he spun the smaller man toward him and away from the wall and sank his fist deep into his middle.

"Ooomph . . ." went Cat and sagged.

Felix didn't wait. He followed with a right uppercut that caught Cherry full under the chin and decked him flat onto the terrace tiles.

Then he pounced on either side of his chest and jabbed a finger into Cat's face and spat, though he knew the other man was too groggy to hear him: "No! You are not following anybody down!"

Then he rolled him up into a fireman's carry and somehow bent down and picked up his empty gun and spun around for the door.

We've got to get out of here! We've got to get out of here *now*!

Because no fall, even twenty-one stories, was going to kill a vampire.

Back through the french doors and that huge room and those oaken double doors into the hall and mashing the elevator button. Should I wait? Should I take the stairs?

Or will *it* take the stairs? Just streak up them, floor after floor, to come get me?

But then the bell and the doors opened and the elevator was still there! Had it happened too fast for them to start down? Or some luck for a change?

Does it matter, stupid? Get moving!

The long ride down, floor after floor after fear of what might be waiting when they opened at the bottom.

But nothing. Just the lobby and startled people. Felix trotted down the steps toward the front door before pausing, suddenly, at the sights out on the street, people milling and cars pulled over and—

Oh, shit! This is the side they fell on! It's on this side!

He turned so abruptly toward the back entrance he almost dropped Cat.

The back entrance was at the end of a long tunnel-like corridor with nothing on either side of it but display windows and his own reflection and he thought about stopping before bursting out. Stopping and sneaking a peak. But he was too scared and too shaken and he might not have the nerve to move again, so when he came to the glass doors he simply bounced them open with his hip and he was out onto the sidewalk and there, parked across the street, was the Blazer.

"You stupid broad!" he cried delightedly and sprinted toward her.

Davette had the engine running and the side door open by the time he got there. The smile on her face was sweet and warm and simply everything.

Then she noticed it was just the two of them.

"What? But where . . . ?" she began before he cut her off.

"This is it, dammit! Hit it! Let's go!"

And she hesitated, but only for a second. Then she slammed the Blazer into gear and screeched away from the curb and ran the first light, turning right with the one-way street and then right again for the next one before Felix realized they were going back around to the front of the goddamned hotel!

"Uh . . . uh . . ." he tried to say. But it was too late. She had already made the turn and the front of the hotel was there with its growing crowd out in the street.

"Hit it!" he yelled. "Faster! Faster! Don't slow down!"

She barely glanced at him before obeying, slamming her foot down even harder on the gas and bursting past the pale, opened-mouthed faces and around the cars that had haphazardly stopped short, and then they were past them all.

But not before Felix had a chance to see it.

One body. One bloody crumpled form.

Adam.

But there had been three! He had seen three! What could it want with Jack's dead body?

What?

Chapter 30

It would have been so simple if the plane for Rome had left the next day.

But there were papers and official documents and things to hassle over and the only thing that saved them was the Vatican being a separate nation, capable of issuing its own passports. Even with that, it was going to be three days of waiting.

Three days waiting and thinking and mourning.

And more thinking.

Cat thought fast. The first day, while they were sitting around the suite playing with their room service food, he suddenly looked up, shyly, at Felix and said, "Thanks, Felix."

Which meant thanks for saving me? Thanks for coming up to help with Jack? Thanks for not letting me throw myself off the ledge? All of them?

Felix had looked at him and not really known. So he had just shrugged. Nothing more. Because he wasn't sure, thinking back, if he had managed to do *anything* right.

So weird.

Every time he thought about what he'd done—going up to that bloody terrace—he got the willies. The hair and the goose pimples went up on his arms and he . . . got scared!

But then, every time he thought of that little god's smug smile . . .

Then he got angry. And the desire to kick some ass was so strong!

But mostly, he was afraid. Deathly afraid.

Because they were still out there. Still wanting them. Still knowing who they were and still hunting them down. He knew this. He could feel this.

And so could the other two. He could see it in their eyes and in their posture and in the way they jumped whenever the elevator bell rang outside the suite's door.

Felix finally had them moved to the end of the hall after that first night. That helped some. But that didn't really solve it. They could still be found. Felix could still get to die. Or he could still get to kick ass.

You're a mess, he thought to himself.

And then there was the matter of Davette. And the showers.

Cat hadn't said a word all the way from the Adolphus to their hotel. When he had gotten to their suite he had gone straight to the little minibar there in the corner and tried to drink it dry and damn near succeeded. He was all but co-matose within the hour and Davette had helped Felix pour him into one of the suite's two bedrooms.

And after Felix had stood over him a few dark moments, watching him fit and start and twitch in his horrors.

"Sorry about your family, buddy," Felix whispered at last.

Davette was waiting for him on the couch in the living room. She patted the seat beside her and said, "Tell me."

Only then did he realize she didn't actually know what had happened.

Good girl, he thought.

Then he thought, I could never have been that patient.

He sat down beside her on the couch, next to the fresh drink she had made for him, and told her.

It seemed to take such a long time, somehow. Because it was so sad and awful and because he didn't know how much to tell her about his madness and he didn't much want to think about it himself.

And because he was suddenly so goddamned tired. He never looked at her once as he spoke.

She moved closer to him as he told it. Not clinging. Just the warmth. He heard her weep toward the end. Felt it. He got up to get another drink for himself. Maybe he sat down a little closer when he returned.

When he had finished, it was so very quiet. Just the three of them left and just the two of them awake and alone and the night out there haunting. There was a large television in the room with its cabinet doors open and a remote control beside his hand and it was so very quiet—he reached down and flipped it on.

Some movie channel. Some silly comedy. Slapstick and pratfalls and nothing even remotely serious and ten minutes into it the main character did something inane like jamming his hand in a drawer or something . . .

And they laughed.

Not loud. Not hard. But enough.

He turned and looked at her for the first time and she was lovely and smiling back.

Then he hid again in the screen.

They laughed some more. Not because it was funny. Maybe because it *wasn't* funny. It was stupid and mindless and so . . . easy. So silly and safe. And they laughed. And they drew closer and closer and when the film finally ended Felix had his arm around her shoulder and he turned to her and realized he stank and needed a bath.

She was already getting up.

"I've got to have a shower," she told him, rather shyly.

He grinned. "Me, too."

"Oh!" she replied. "Do you want to go first?"

"No. I can use the other."

"But Cat's asleep."

"Yeah. Well, I'll wait."

"You sure?"

"Yeah. Go ahead."

"Really?"

And he looked at her and they laughed again.

"Okay," she said. "I'll just be a minute."

"Take your time," he called after her.

And meant it. Because he was scared again.

He stayed scared the whole time he listened to the water running and his heart beating because he knew . . .

He knew . . .

He knew he wasn't going to be able to do this.

He didn't know why. Not yet. Not clearly yet. He only knew it was so. And unfair.

"Okay!" she called out cheerily. "Your turn!"

He sipped the rest of his drink dry in one sip and stood up and puffed on his smoke and put that out. Then he walked into the bedroom.

Utterly, impossibly beautiful. Toweling her hair in the dim bedroom, the light from the bathroom soft from behind her and across her bare shoulders wrapped up snug and clean in a huge white towel and he didn't blame her for this. From first sight it had been the two of them, rich and strong and needing each other. What she was doing was not wrong. Simply more painful.

He got past her somehow and into the bright bathroom lights. He even managed to close the door behind him without slamming it shut. He got his clothes off and into the huge sunken shower that smelled like her and drenched himself but none of it would go away.

Why can't I have her? Why do I feel like I can't?

Why do I feel like I can't *yet*?

What the hell more do I have to do?

Sure, they're still out there and, yeah, they're still biting people. But that's not my fault! Christ! I've fought and fought and everybody else is dead. They killed everybody else. Am I supposed to feel unworthy because they haven't gotten to me yet? What kinda samurai bullshit is going on here? Is it a disease or something? The Jack Crow Samurai Bullshit Syndrome?

It's not fair!

I don't want to kick any more ass. I'm scared, dammit! It's unfair to feel like I'm supposed to.

To feel like I must.

I don't want to have that goddamned torch passed on to me. That torch kills people. It kills everyone.

"I don't *believe* this shit!" he shouted out loud into the cascading water.

But it was true.

But maybe it was only true . . . now. Maybe it was just part of the grief and the like. Yeah! That was it! I'm just run-down and tired and my comrades are gone and I feel like I'm taking advantage of them now but . . .

But that will pass.

Right?

Right?

He waited over an hour to come out. To sneak out, on tiptoe, bathroom lights already out before he opened the door.

She was asleep. At least she was lying still on the shadowy bed and that was good enough for him. He sneaked past her into the living room and found an extra cover in a closet there and wrapped up in it on the couch and turned off the light—all without making a peep.

Tomorrow this will pass.

Right.

Sometime in the night the sound of someone sobbing woke him up. He rose up on the couch and started to go to her but it stopped. Was that Davette?

Was that me?

Is this ever going to end?

The next morning she was sweet and friendly and gracious as if nothing had happened and he knew damn well he had hurt her feelings but . . .

But he didn't want to think about that now.

Cat came to a little later and he was shaken and ashen gray once more but he was back.

They talked about nothing while they ordered and waited for breakfast and then it came and they sat down together and ate it and it was somewhere in the middle of that meal that Cat had looked up at Felix and thanked him.

And Felix shrugged.

A few minutes later Cat spoke again: "So. What's the next move?" he asked Felix.

And Davette had looked to him as well, as if it was the most natural thing in the world—for him to decide.

He almost punched Cat again.

He wanted to say, Don't start looking to *me*, now, god-dammit! I ain't carrying anything on.

But he did not say this. He was calm. He played the game and gave them what they wanted. He told them they would stay here, in the suite, until tomorrow afternoon, when they would go to the bishop's office, as planned, and pick up the documents and tickets for the nonstop to Rome that left the next day.

Calm. Reasonable. Leader-sounding, if that's what they really, really, fucking wanted.

But, he added silently, don't think this changes anything. This doesn't change shit.

We are out of the vampire business.

So they stayed in the suite. All that day and all that night. Room service food and movie channels and alcohol. When it got late, Cat went to crash in his bedroom. A few minutes later Davette went to the other.

Felix took his drink and went to the window and looked out over north Dallas.

Odd to be able to do that. When he had been growing up, there was nothing this far north. No shopping malls, no freeways, no high-rise luxury hotels. But now he could almost see his house. He could almost see hers.

That started him remembering, for some reason. He had loved that time. The money, the lovely homes and people. The country club parties. The debutante balls. He had always wanted to be a part of that because he saw it as more than just upper-class frivolity. It was a celebration of men and women, generation after generation of them, who were raised to shape the world. Maybe they were a little smarter? Because their parents had been smart enough to build so much and they had kids as smart as them?

Or maybe not. Felix had known a lot of dumb rich kids.

But still, the expectation had been there. You were expected to accomplish something. Invent something or at least manufacture it and make payroll and support your employees and expand something. Expand everything.

But I didn't. I didn't do shit. And here I am, waving goodbye.

Shit.

Is that why Davette's story had sunk so deep into him? Because it was about people ripping up the best of his past? The best of his memories?

Should I try to go in to see her now?

He had another drink. And another. He was drunk after the third and, well, the couch was right there.

And he didn't want to think about it.

The bishop's office staff at St. Lucius got very quiet when Felix walked in the next afternoon. There was another bishop there, filling in, who escorted Felix into the inner office and gave him the documents and tickets.

Then he asked what to do about the bodies.

Of Carl. Of the bishop. Of two of his aides. Everyone else on the bishop's staff, it turned out, had run to the church during the attack, where they had been safe.

But what to do about the bodies?

Felix didn't know enough to tell them. And he damn sure wasn't going to go out to the Blazer and bring Cat in to explain.

"Call Rome," he said.

"But what about your friend?" the bishop asked him. "I understand that his remains have already—"

"Call Rome," Felix repeated, then left.

It was still only late afternoon when he drove them back to the hotel. And the sunshine was bright on the great glass building and maybe that's what made it seem so like a prison.

Felix stopped the Blazer in front of the hotel entrance. The entrance to the connecting Galleria was less than one hundred yards away, with its shops and its people and . . . He realized he had cabin fever. Had it bad.

"Anybody want anything?" Felix asked them, suddenly.

Cat and Davette exchanged a smile.

"Sure," he said.

"Let's look," she said.

And they all grinned and Felix let the hotel park the car and they went inside and through the lobby to the mall doors and by the time they got there they were almost trotting. The mall was full of people strolling up and down, children skipping and pointing, old couples sitting on benches with their sacks between their legs. The place was four stories high and four blocks long, with the stores stacked on either side of the Great Atrium, which ran the length of it all. Topping everything was a great curved multipaneled skylight.

Retail heaven.

They almost did some actual shopping. After a few moments Davette saw something in a window that she liked: a pair of brown shoes. She asked the men what they thought of them and Cat and Felix said they were pretty, why didn't she buy them and she said she would.

But they just stood there, instead, looking into the window. After a few moments, they moved along down the mall toward the smell of food. Most of the restaurants were gathered in the center of the Great Atrium, on three stories overlooking a skating rink. There were steak houses and little bistros and Tex-Mex joints and Chinese food and two or three little bars.

They compromised on a bar that served food, finding a table that overlooked the skating rink.

And they sat down and had a drink and another drink and something to eat and watched the skaters and made comments about them. But they never talked about anything serious. Never. And they didn't leave. And the sun slipped slowly away.

What are we trying to prove, Felix wondered, when he realized they were going to stay.

What are we trying to deny?

An hour and a half later, with the skylight black above them, they saw the vampire.

Or noticed him, rather, which was the part that got to Felix.

That and the goddamned unfairness of it all.

Because they had been looking at him for some time before they realized what it was, before Davette's breath suddenly caught in her throat and the men looked at her, looked to where she was staring, at that same guy standing down there at that other bar . . .

And saw him. Really saw him for what he was.

It was a long, polished, curved wooden bar that skirted along the edge of the rink. Weary shoppers could pause, hop up on a stool, and grab a quick one without breaking stride. And then they might sit there a little longer, watching the skaters. And maybe have just one more drink before trying to find Uncle Stan's birthday present. Maybe they would just stay until closing.

The vampire was at the far end of the bar to their left, standing there alone pretending to drink something clear on the rocks. A few feet to his right, sitting alone, was a young woman in her mid-twenties with long legs and auburn hair and a stack of shopping bags piled around her stool and no one to save her.

Because we're the only ones who know, Felix thought bitterly. And we can't do anything because it's dark and . . .

And what? *What?*

The deception is what got to him. Just walking up and ordering something and spotting his prey and getting away with it. He could have sat down next to anyone—but us. Anyone could have sat down next to him.

Hell, I could go sit down next to him now!

And do what? Nothing. Die, maybe.

But I could do it. And he wouldn't recognize me, either.

Felix didn't know why that notion so intrigued him.

But then the hunt started and no one thought. They just watched.

It happened so fast. It happened so smoothly. Suddenly he was just there, closer to her. And they were talking. And then she was laughing and then she couldn't take her eyes off him and Felix turned to see if Davette could watch this, knowing what she knew. But she stared just like the men.

And it went on and on until Felix just couldn't stand it any longer.

"Get the car," he told them.

Cat looked at him. "What are you planning—"

"Just get the car. Bring it around to . . ." He looked around. "Bring it around to that entrance over there. What is that? The west side? And wait for me."

"Felix," Cat began again. "Tell us what you're—"

"It won't hurt to find out where he takes her," was all he would say.

They left. Felix stayed. And watched.

When the new couple, master and slave, stood up from the bar, Felix checked his watch. Nine minutes. Nine lousy minutes between life and death. It was like watching a slow-motion traffic accident.

Felix paid the tab and trailed along behind them. It carried all half dozen of her shopping bags in one easy grip. The girl was on its other arm, smiling and looking hypnotized up to its face as they made their way to the exit.

They walked out the glass doors and to the edge of the sidewalk and waited there, talking, as if for a taxi. Felix meandered on around to one side toward the Blazer, parked several yards away.

He got in and told Cat, sitting behind the wheel, to pull away and around a line of parked cars before they got noticed. Cat obeyed. By the time he had steered them back around to where they could again see the couple, the limousine was there.

It was a long black Cadillac and it pulled to a smooth stop at the curb in front of the couple. From the driver's door stepped a tall pale man wearing a chauffeur's uniform. He stepped to the door closest to the couple and opened.

Davette gasped when the tall, handsome, silver-haired man stepped out.

"My God!" she whispered. "It's him!"

"Who?" the men demanded.

"It's him!" she repeated and turned to Felix. "The man who sent Ross to kill Jack!"

Felix hadn't taken his eyes from the man. "Are you certain?" he asked her in a strange voice.

"I'm positive. It's him. He's the one. I saw him twice. I . . ."

"What?" Cat asked.

She tilted her head, staring. "I don't know exactly. It's just that . . . Well, he looks so familiar. I mean, he looked familiar then. And he still does."

Felix was still watching the silver-haired vampire as he got out of the limo, was graciously introduced to his procured victim, even more graciously—with many bows and flourishes—ushered everyone into the rear of the black car.

"Follow them," Felix said.

"Felix!" said Cat excitedly, "if this is the guy, then he's the one who's been after us."

"Yeah."

"Well, Felix? *Say* something!"

"Just follow them, Cat," the Gunman replied and his voice was too hard and too dry for further conversation.

They all went to far north Dallas, past the yuppie suburbs and into the sprawling countryside, with its sprawling golf course and estates, to a fortress.

It didn't look like a fortress, not to an untrained eye. It simply looked like a glamorous, incredibly expensive country home. It just happened to have a seven-foot-tall rock wall around it and a black iron automatic gate and a gatekeeper's booth. Hidden along the wall, where you could only see them if you looked for them, were electric wires, electric lights, and, Felix could only assume, penetration sensors.

A fortress.

The limo had already turned into the gate and Cat was slowing down as he passed the entrance when Felix barked at him: "Speed up! Speed up! Go past! Don't let them notice this car!"

"I just wanted to see the name on the—"

Felix roared at him. "Move, goddamn you, Cat! Move the fucking car!"

Cat blinked, obeyed, hit the gas. They sped quickly past the entrance.

"Now," said Felix a mile later, "take us to the hotel."

And his voice was calmer but his tone—his tone was still sharp ice. Cat and Davette exchanged a look but didn't speak throughout the trip. Felix sat alone in the back seat. He stared out the side window. He didn't move. But the pulse on the side of his neck throbbed rhythmically with the lights from passing traffic.

By the time they got back to the suite, Cat couldn't stand it anymore.

"Felix, dammit! If you had just let me see who it was!"

Felix eyed him with a scary calm. "Really?"

"Yes! Really. Just let me slow down enough to read the mailbox. Just let me get the bastard's name!"

Felix looked at him a moment, then carried his drink to a table next to the picture window that overlooked the lights of the city. He put the drink down without sipping it. And spoke.

"The bastard's name is Simon Kennedy."

"Of course!" Davette cried. "I know that name. I've heard that name."

But Cat couldn't take his eyes off the Gunman's back.

"But you, Felix. You . . . you *know* him. Don't you?"

Felix turned slowly toward them and his eyes were hard to look at and his grin was a death-mask's grin.

"For fifteen years," he hissed.

Chapter 31

Gunman Felix never did actually start raving as he spoke of Simon Kennedy.

What he did was worse.

It was low and slow and chilling, a bitter, vicious, grinding, dull roar of a voice, rich and fat with venom.

It was terrifying.

Because they could see the mounting rage, the virulent agonized fury, bubbling up and up.

But never out.

He paced as he spoke, back and forth, back and forth, his face a tight gray skull, his eyes always distant and inward. Always dark.

Gunman Felix remembered the very first time he had been introduced to Simon Kennedy, remembered his face and his smile and his handshake. Remembered seeing him *dance*, for chrissakes, at debutante parties and charity balls.

Gunman Felix remembered his laugh.

"Very big social figure. Very prestigious to have him at a party. Very big deal. Because he was so smooth, you know. Smooth and polished and cultured. Very big into culture is our monster. Patron of the arts, they called him—probably still do.

"And all those people and all those kids are looking up to this pig, told to look and act and think like him and be gracious and smooth when you meet him. Young guys told to stand up tall and the girls straightening their gowns and touching up their hair as he comes down the bloody receiving line because everybody loves him, you see. Everybody thinks he's such a grand person!"

Gunman Felix turned and looked at them, at Cat and Davette, and his face was hard to meet.

"He just walks right up to them. Because they don't know. Right up to them and smiles and shakes their hands and talks to them and they talk back—just like he was real. Because they don't know!"

He walked away from them and spoke again, so low they could barely hear him.

"No one knows. But us."

Gunman Felix was quiet for a while, pacing again back and forth, smoking furiously and inwardly boiling.

Cat and Davette exchanged a glance when they heard his teeth grind.

"Ha!" he shouted without any humor, and stopped abruptly.

He looked at them and his tone was reasonable and deeply wicked.

"Honey, when your aunt died and the medical examiner came over to take care of things for you—you ever met the guy before?"

Davette thought a moment. "I think so."

Felix nodded. "Sure. At your level you meet everybody eventually. But did you know him? Did your aunt hang out with him?"

"Well . . . no. I don't think so."

"So he suddenly drops everything and comes to your aid. I mean, she had lots of old friends, didn't she?"

"Yes. Of course. But—"

"But don't you see! Your Aunt Victoria committed suicide. An autopsy is automatic, by law. That M.E.—what's his name?"

"Dr. Harshaw."

"Yeah. Harshaw. He gives her an autopsy—he's got to. It's the law with all suicides. And he sees the marks. He sees the bites. And he knows what's what and . . . that's how they

found Ross! Don't you see? Harshaw sees it's a vampire and
he tells Kennedy. That's the only way a vampire can survive
in the middle of the city. He owns the medical examiner.
Owns him or one of his bitches does. Maybe he owns the
poor guy's wife . . . It doesn't matter.

"The point is: he's strong. Strong and powerful and he
knows people, and the people he doesn't know socially, he
owns.

"That fucking house of his. That fort. No way to get to
him there. Daytime, high noon—it doesn't matter. Think you
can get through that wall? Through that Fort Knox front gate?
And, even if you did, are you prepared to kill half a dozen
security guards who almost certainly haven't got a clue as to
what's what? Then the staff, of course. They'll try to stop
you. Some of them know, too. And they'll really put up a
fight.

"And by then, just how many SWAT teams and police
choppers and Texas Rangers do you think will be surrounding
you—shooting at you on sight—for trying to pull some ter-
rorist act on the home of so prominent a man?

"A pillar of the fucking community?

"Patron of the fucking arts."

Gunman Felix sat down, abruptly, and turned to his
watery drink and drank it dry and held out the glass for
another. Cat took it from him and went to refill.

"Ha!" laughed Felix again . . .

. . . and that awful laugh made them jump . . .

"Ha! I still get solicitations from him. Or some charity
board he's on. You know?"

Davette jumped again at his look, nodded. "I remember
him now."

Gunman Felix nodded and smiled. "Yeah."

Davette didn't like his smile.

"He had some favorite charity goodie, didn't he? Got
something at the office in the mail along with a bunch of
clippings."

"Opera," said Davette.

And he looked at her and his eyes went wide and his
smile was too bright and tortured.

"Yes! Of course! Opera. Isn't it all just so wonderful?"

Davette didn't know what to say. Cat, standing there pale and staring, remembered the drink in his hand and handed it to the Gunman. Felix drank it dry in a single gulp.

"Yeah. Opera. Some big project about . . ."

And he stopped and looked at Davette and it hit her, too, and she looked back at him.

"The Opera House!" she whispered.

"Yes," he replied. "The Opera House."

And he looked over at the newspaper Cat had left crumpled on the floor, open to the Entertainment Section because they had been thinking about going to an afternoon movie.

Gunman Felix stood up and strode over to it and picked it up and rifled quickly through it.

"Ha!" he cackled when he found what he wanted.

And he came back and he leaned down to where Davette was sitting on the floor and *planted* the open newspaper on the rug beside her and punched his index finger into it so hard it went through the newsprint.

They looked. It was an ad. For the much delayed, greatly heralded, grand opening of the Dallas Opera House. One week from today.

"He'll be there," whispered Gunman Felix and his voice was old dead wood. "He'll be there. And they will rush up to him and shake his hand and congratulate him and love him.

"And in return, he'll slash their throats and swell fat and thick on their blood."

No one spoke for a few moments after that. Cat and Davette couldn't speak, could only stare at the maniacal grin sitting before them, relishing and cherishing and worming the pain deeper into his own soul. He seemed to take such dreadful delight in the crushing irony of it all.

"Yes," he said after a while and he was much, much calmer.

Impossibly so.

"Yes," he repeated. "He could just walk up to people and talk to them. But they could just walk up to him, too. Even somebody who knew what he was. He would not sus-

pect. He would simply smile at them, like a big . . .
fat . . . tick.

"He would be completely off his guard, wouldn't he?"

"Felix!" gasped Cat. "You can't mean . . ."

"Rock and roll, Cherry Cat. Isn't that what you always
say?"

"You can't be serious!"

Gunman Felix just smiled and stared at the newspaper
ad.

"Got to, Cat. Got to."

Chapter 32

Oh! What a gala night! Oh, what an event! Everyone, simply Everyone, was there. What a pity it had to be in the summer, in this dreadful hot weather. But those workers had just taken their time and those awful unions—everyone *knew* how they could be.

Yet it was done now. Finished and complete and shining and wasn't it simply marvelous! All those slopes and weird shapes? What *was* that architect's name? Doesn't matter, doesn't matter. The important thing is it's all done now and what an event we are having tonight. Everyone was there.

Even the streets were dressed for the event. With banners and streamers and a band playing both before *and* after the show, as all those people would be strolling out. And, oh, the cameras and the street all blocked off and the chairperson of the Opera Committee arriving in that two-horse carriage with the mayor and his wife and . . .

Oh, the street entertainers! Look at them! Aren't they *cute*? All those mimes and those jesters dressed in those cute, tight stripes with those hats with the bells on them. And even more fun were the period people, with those costumes like the opera itself, selling—what was that? Mead? Or some such thing? And meat pies. And turkey on a stick. And those two artisans, wearing that cute chain mail and selling those old weapons that were positively guaranteed to be authentic but shouldn't they have at least painted over the plastic parts, ha ha?

Pity about the opera part of it all. It was pretty, of
course—beautiful, some of those costumes. But it was rather
dreadfully long, wasn't it? Of course, operas are *supposed* to
be long and one knows it's Great Art and all the rest, but
still one wonders—perhaps if it was just a teensy bit shorter?
And if we could understand what they were singing? Perhaps
they should just speak some of it? But then it wouldn't be
opera, would it?

Of course, it wouldn't have to be subsidized then, either,
but not to think of that now, because it was *over* and everyone, Everyone, had woken up from their little naps
and . . . Oh! The afterparties! All those delicious afterparties! Because this was such an Important Occasion, such a
Cultural Milestone! Like New Year's Eve, wasn't it? With all
the limousines and there goes the mayor in his little buggy
and wasn't it so much nicer now that it was cooler and that
hot sun had gone down? People didn't look quite so . . .
wilted, somehow. One should never look wilted in a formal
gown—how tacky! And the men, how handsome in their
tuxedos. Oh, they always complain and gripe, but secretly,
everyone knows, they love to dress up. And they really are
so handsome. Nothing like black tie to make a man look
distinguished, even those men who have—how shall we say
it?—aged both in years and size? Both up and out? Ha ha!

Like that handsome silver-haired fellow just now coming
down the steps, the one alone going between the new brass
pillars that hold up the awning, going toward that limousine
with that tall chauffeur holding the door.

What *was* his name?

"Kennedy!" barked Gunman Felix, coming around from
behind his "authentic crossbow" stand.

The vampire turned and smiled and the crossbow bolt
as big as a baseball bat shot right through the gleaming ex-
panse of his starched white tuxedo shirt and splattered clear
drops out the back and the umbrella barbs popped open and
held it fast . . .

And for just a moment, only Felix, binding the cable to
the thick brass pillar, was moving. Everyone else was frozen,

too startled to gasp. Unbelieving. This wasn't possible was it? Or part of the show? A trick? An assassination? Too surreal . . .

Even the monster stood as he had, staggered back a step, his arms flung wide by the impact, his redding eyes focused on the wooden stake piercing his blackened soul.

For just an instant . . .

Then the eyes went up and the mouth spread wide the fangs and the howl began . . .

And Cat stepped in from the left and fired and his bolt plunged deep, crisscrossing the first, and as he scrambled to tie his cable to the other brass pillar, the monster . . .

. . . detonated . . .

The howling, the ungodly, unreal howling shot through the crowd and echoed off the street and the maniacal frenzy was impossibly violent and crazed. Oh, God! The howling, screeching, *tearing* sound . . .

And the people watching who had first thought: murder. Murder! Murder!! . . . now thought, What is *this*? What is *that*! It cannot be a man! It cannot be! Not that sound! An animal? What kind of an animal could . . .

Thrash and rip and screech and the hissing burst forth upon them and the first desperate evil wrenching-away shook the thick brass pillar and the second made it rock and creak and the awning above it sway and then the second cable was tied fast and the monster frenzied even wilder with the terror of being trapped and . . .

. . . and the *anger* . . .

. . . the blazing *fury* . . .

. . . at this young man who presumed to *attack* a god! . . .

And instead of pulling away, the monster burst forward toward Felix.

And into his balloons.

They weren't water balloons that broke and splashed on his face and chest, that awful smell in its gleaming mouth.

They were gasoline. And they broke, one-two-three, across his front and soaked him and Cat already had the flare lit and he tossed it and it hit the rushing chest and bounced off, but not before . . .

The flames rushed up and out and around him, his clothes and hair and skin bursting with it, a flame that *could not* be that color, *could not* be that bright and crackling loud and when the black glob finally spat forth, it was burning.

And *nothing* could have that evil, hell-wretched smell.

No thought of anger. No thought of vengeance. Not anymore. No more. The pain . . . the *pain*! And it howled and warped into madness and wrenched back and the pillars swayed and gave some and it wrenched some more, the *screaming*, the *screaming*, and the pillars started to buckle where they were bolted against the sidewalk . . .

NO! No! It can't get free!

The Gunman squatted and aimed and fired at the right knee and missed and fired again and hit it. And then the left knee and the *howling*! The *howling* as it crumpled, crippled and imploding with the agony, still wrenching itself back and forth, back and forth, faster and faster, *screaming* and *screaming* and the pillars . . .

The pillars broke free and it fell backward, rolling, and lay there for a second as two more silver bullets rammed into its chest. But then it was up, a ball of scrambling flame backing away, thudding into the side of the limousine and then crawling like a crab across the top into the street and . . .

And Gunman Felix fired again and again and again and, yes, there was an effect. It jerked and swayed with each impact . . .

But there was no stopping it. It was into the middle of the street now, scrambling, scrabbling away, the ends of the crossbow bolts sparking on the asphalt and . . .

We can't stop it! It'll get away and the flames will go out and it'll pull those stakes out.

Now! We've got to stop it now! Just for a few *seconds*! It couldn't take much longer.

The Blazer, the one Davette had *sworn* to stay hidden in two blocks away, was doing twenty-five when it vaulted across the sidewalk, thirty when it bounced across the curb into the street, and an even thirty-six when its front bumper slammed dead-center into the warping flames.

The noise! The streak of fire as the vampire flew past them, the awful crash as it splintered against the front bumper of its own black limousine, the terrible keening wail as it lay, a frenzied flaming blur, against the curb.

Gunman Felix was standing over it when the burning hands tried to raise up, was staring down when the blazing tortured eyes focused on him, was smiling when they collapsed backward into the fire.

The swell of flame was twelve feet wide and hot and bright and impossibly loud.

Then the loud hissing, as though gas were escaping.

Then sparks. So many sparks.

Then that loud POP, thunderous and deep.

Then nothing. A tiny circle of blue-and-white flame flickering out around a small pile of ashes.

The people watching had no idea what they had just seen. But something inside was glad. Something inside was relieved. Something inside was grateful to the pair in the chain mail. Later they would forget. Or try. But now . . .

Supernatural.

"We did it!" shouted Cat, unbelieving himself. "We did it! Felix! We killed it! We killed a master! At *night*!"

Felix nodded, said, "Yeah."

Then he turned to the tall, pasty-faced chauffeur and thumped two fingers hard into his chest.

"Spread the word."

Last Interlude

It was only Will. Will and Hatred and Revenge.

Over Pain.

Will and Hatred and Revenge were stronger, were they not?

I am stronger, am I not?

Did I not bear the cramped capsule across the seas, with the sputtering, plaything mortals seeking to caress me and join with me?

Could any other have done that?

Would any other dare?

Would any other know what I know about this Disease-Felix?

Will and Hatred and Revenge must be satisfied.

So up and over the ancient walls that could never be too high or too strong for his powerful claws, nor could the drop over the side be too high or any creature or mortal fool be able to sprint across these famous gardens with such breathtaking speed and grace.

Yes, the pain. The awful pain. The greater pressure of the pain, across his temples and into the bones of his face and skull as he drew nearer and nearer to this, the Lair of the Monster's Beast on Earth.

Oh, the agony. Oh, the pressure as it grew. It stumbled once, with this pain, with this agony.

But Hatred and Revenge and Will!

For the Disease-Felix would not leave! It would not come

out! It stayed and stayed, happy and breathing and warm in the center of the pain and . . .

And it thought it was safe! It can*not* think it is safe! It cannot *believe*!

The walls of the building were as slick as the outer barricades but its claws, even with the pain, were no less sharp or strong. It could spring up these walls, up or down or sideways, until it *found* the terrace and *found* the window into its room.

Its room. Did he not know this room? Was this not *his* room when once he, too, was Pawn of the Monster's Beast on Earth? Did he not . . .

Ohhh! The pain. Stronger here is the pain. So close to the center. So certain of its wretched might.

But there is still Will. There is still Hatred.

He would still swallow deep his Revenge.

Somewhere on the grounds below the alarms began to sound and the lights began to glow through the trees and there were the sounds of mortals running like fools and calling to one another.

But too late.

The ancient terrace door and all its locks and bolts and sneaky wires were too late. The door gave easily in his claws and, Yes! The pain was greater inside, much, much, greater. But he summoned his Will. He summoned his Hatred. And he stalked across the centuries-old room. Stumbling, yes. With pain, yes. The great pressure seared through him.

But then he was at the bedside and there! Before him! The form of the Disease-Felix so smug and safe in its sheets.

And he ripped at the sheets, agony though this movement was, and exposed the form underneath and cried, "Felix! Feeeelixxxx! I have come for you!"

But the face that turned to his own was an elderly one . . .

"No! Noooo!" it shrieked.

And the Old One said, its voice gentle and sad, "Jack . . . My son! My poor son . . ."

And the wrinkled hand, so softly caressing its cheek . . .

The flame exploded across his face and skull and down his spine before spreading across the rest of his body. His howl of pain was impossible to bear. The flame swirled around him and raised him up and consumed him, Consumed him, sent him rocketing about the walls and the ceilings and all those places his soul did touch could never ever be wiped completely clean . . .

And then the scream ceased. And the flame condensed and boiled in the center of the room.

Then it shot upward out of sight.

The man stared a long time at the spot on the ceiling where the flame had gone. It was only when he moved at last that he realized he was crying.

And noticed the young Gunman standing in the doorway, the forbidden pistol in his hand.

"How did you know?" he asked.

Felix's face was grim as he reholstered the Browning.

"It's what I would have done."

Epilogue: Team Felix

The young man sitting beside him enjoying the gardens had not spoken in some time.

"Are you well?" the man asked him.

Felix looked at the man and smiled thinly before looking away.

"I was just thinking . . . It's never going to end, is it?"

The man was silent. What could he answer?

For, of course, it would not end. Not for this planet. It would end for this brave young soul seated beside him. But not well. This is one of the great tragedies.

For the man had come to love this Felix. He loved "dealing" with him. The Supreme Pontiff was unaccustomed to having to "deal" with anyone, save heads of state. He had enjoyed it immensely.

Felix had gotten everything he wanted. One dozen priests, recruited from all over the world, all strong, all brave, all devoted. He had gotten the bishop he had demanded, an American-born bishop, who even now waited for them in Brazil, where the Team would first train for a month.

There was a happy peal of laughter and both turned to the source.

Several of the sisters had come to see the young bride's ring. It was hardly in keeping with the poverty vows, of course, but the Man believed every single sister in Rome had managed to come and view it at least once.

How lovely she is, thought the Man, seeing her proud display.

There was another peal of laughter, and then a wicked squeal, as the other young American, the one called Cat, made a comment the two men seated could not hear.

No doubt something off-color once again, thought the Man.

But even in this he was glad, for this one had been such a thin and shallow scarecrow of a soul when first he had arrived, uncertain, unbelieving—suspicious of all save his leader.

But now look at him! How he smiles and jokes and how devoted are he and Davette! Hard to believe they were not brother and sister.

The Man glanced again at Felix, who was still watching the show.

He was right not to tell his friend about Jack.

He was right about much. Though foolish.

"Thanks for the ring," said Felix suddenly, almost shyly.

The Man nodded. It was an ancient stone, three hundred years in the Vatican treasury being dusted. Now it shone on a bride's finger, as it should.

"And thanks," added Felix, with more than a little embarrassment, "for marrying us."

The Man smiled. "It was our pleasure," he said sincerely.

And it truly had been. His aides had not understood his enjoyment, for Felix had, at the last second, refused to be converted to the Church. To everyone's amazement, the Man had waived the requirement and had performed the ceremony personally.

He had, he must admit, found it terribly amusing, this young American's stubborn "point of honor." And he would smile whenever he thought of it.

What was that American phrase? Like being "a little bit pregnant"?

For the young warrior was converted. He simply refused to admit it.

An aide appeared at the edge of a terrace door, eyeing him expectantly. The Man knew what he wanted, to remind him of his scheduled duties for that day. But the Man did not wish to go until the others did. This was their last day, their last hours, in his personal care. And . . .

And do I fear I will never see them again? Or do I fear my own sense of guilt when they go?

But no. He could *not* help them more. He could not shout from the rooftops their plight. He could not tell the world what he—and they, and the victims—knew to be so.

Neither could he explain it to the young warrior. He had tried, telling him of the long, hard journey of the Mother Church, of the awful tragedy if they should return, or even be perceived to be returning, to those dark, Dark Ages.

For there were *not* many vampires. There were not. And soon, with the power of world knowledge, there would be none. And that would, as the young warrior had insisted, be a great goodness.

But what then? When every priest felt emboldened and empowered to see evil everywhere? To think nothing of the witch hunts of other authorities, once the boundaries of law had been "temporarily" lifted.

The Man prayed and grieved every night for the victims of the Beast.

He did not wish to pray and grieve for the excesses of man unwittingly doing the Beast's business for him.

He had tried to convey some of this. But the young warrior's ears had been deaf. "Scapegoat" and "guinea pig" had been his bitter terms.

And, of course, he was right.

But I am right, too, am I not, Lord?

Please, then, help me bear the loss of this brave one!

"When do you leave, my son?" the Man asked.

Felix shrugged and stood up. "As soon as your man comes. What is his name?"

"Father Francisco."

"Yeah. Right."

As if in answer, Father Francisco suddenly appeared, rushing out onto the terrace, bowing to kiss the Man's ring, then breathlessly explaining his tardiness.

The Man assured him all was well. Felix did the same, shaking his hand. The young priest seemed relieved.

He also seemed a titan on earth.

He was over six-foot-five and weighed almost three hundred pounds, with enormous shoulders and thighs and a great bulging muscular neck.

Felix nodded pleasantly to him, then called the others together to go. Then he whispered to Francisco to go on ahead and turned back to the Man. His voice was almost a whisper.

"Father, Jack loved you, didn't he?"

The Man hesitated, said, "Yes, he did."

"He also hated you, didn't he?"

"Yes."

There was a pause. The young man looked pained, looked reluctant, miserable. At last he sighed.

"I suppose I'll start to hate you, too."

The Man did not answer. What could he answer? Of course the young warrior would soon hate him.

And, of course, he would be correct.

Do not go! he wanted to say. But he could not say this. Stay and enjoy my gardens and the sunshine and your lives!

But he did not say this either.

Father, forgive me!

The crowd had gathered at the door to the terrace. More goodbyes were said. There were final smiles. A final embrace for the bride. Then it was time to go.

Cat, who had not yet met the towering Francisco, was impressed. He stared openly at the massive build, the great tree-trunk legs, and particularly at the bulging neck as wide as his own waist.

"What," he asked suddenly, "*is* the Church's position on steroids?"

"Never mind," he added quickly to the cleric's surprised face. "Come with me Francisco," he said next, guiding the larger man through the door.

Then he stopped, looked up at him.

"Tell me, Father, can you drive a car?"

"Of course."

"Good," replied Cat and he started them through the door again and down the hall out of sight. "You can drive. Then, if it breaks down, you can carry it . . ."

Then they were all gone. Only the Man stood alone in his garden, smiling. Proud. Sad.

Oh, Sweet Savior, how you must love them . . .